PRAISE FOR INNISFALLEN ACCURSED

"*Innisfallen Accursed* is an intriguing and intoxicating fantasy story with a feisty young fae and two of the most charismatic and cheekiest damn fae alive. And lordy, Shay and Nova, what can I say? I am obsessed with those two, possibly more so than I am with the shadow daddy himself, Rhysand. What I really loved about the writing style of this author . . . is that, despite the world-building and background information she provided, she didn't let that slow down the pace of the story. Overall, this story was . . . intriguing, intoxicating, and very hard to put down. I am excited to see what comes next for Reagan, Shay, and Nova."

— CARMEN MITCHELL, RED INK BOOK
REVIEWS

"*Innisfallen Accursed* is a debut fantasy novel that weaves loyalty, loss, and magic into every snow-laced page. Set in a cursed land gripped by an unnatural winter, the atmosphere is thick with mystery and quiet dread . . . If you love dark fairytales and heroines with a heart, *Innisfallen Accursed* could be your next obsession. The cold might freeze the land, but Reagan's fire burns through every chapter."

— BETSEY KULAKOWSKI, BEST-SELLING
AUTHOR OF THE VERITAS CODEX SERIES

INNISFALLEN ACCURSED

INNISFALLEN ACCURSED

JENNY SIMARD LABRANCHE

BABYLON
BOOKS

Copyright © 2025 by Jenny Simard LaBranche

eBook ISBN: 978-1-964832-31-9

Paperback ISBN: 978-1-964832-32-6

Hardcover ISBN: 978-1-964832-33-3

First edition by Babylon Books

To my husband and best friend, Paul LaBranche. Thank you for believing in me, even when I doubted myself, and for giving me the courage to chase this dream. You are—and always will be—the sun that chases away my shadows, reminding me of who I am and what I'm capable of. This book is as much yours as it is mine.

INNISFALLEN ACCURSED

JENNY SIMARD LABRANCHE

BABYLON BOOKS

CHAPTER 1

Sometimes I want to burn this place down and watch the fire consume it all—including everyone inside—with a purifying vengeance. Other days, it feels like the only real home I've ever known. I've never thought of myself as violent, though I'm also not the same fae I once was, not after all that's happened to me. And the people here, gods, how I hate them. They call me Reagan the Whore, or Whore, because of my mother. If only they knew, if only they had the slightest clue, they'd call me much, much worse.

Here at Outpost Three is where the new Queen's Guards are trained. These skills-training programs are a joke. The group's royal-born will return to the capital and have a comfy position. The only things they will be protecting the city from are thieves and the desperate and starving. The high-born are the ones who guard the outposts and instruct the recruits. They all had the luxury of choice that I was not given.

My room is in an older stone section of the outpost. The other trainees are in the new barracks—wooden-style dormitories where they are divided up by age and status. It suits me fine to be separated and alone. I'm the only female trainee. My room used to belong to one of the guards, so I also have a private bathroom.

It's quite nice compared to where I was raised. I have a twin bed, a wardrobe, and a desk and chair. As a low-born, I'm denied education and access to libraries. Fortunately, I have sticky fingers and an anonymous ally.

Blowing out my candle, I close my eyes and, as always, hope to see my little sister, Willa, in my dreams. What does she think about my sudden disappearance? Does she think I abandoned her? That one thought has broken my heart over and over these last four years. Watching the last tendrils of smoke dance away into the darkness, for a heartbeat, I'd swear they took the shape of Willa.

The sharp scent of the candle still lingers when a pounding on my door wakes me.

"Rea, there's an emergency meeting. Get to the courtyard now," Fin shouts.

Reluctantly I crawl out of my warm bed and dress quickly, shivering in the frigid air. The winter chill of the north is supposed to make us stronger. The guards are always feeding us that kind of shit.

Standing in the courtyard, freezing with the others, I ask Fin what he thinks this is about.

"Something big is going on. Our liberties are going to be restricted now, like yours."

"Don't look at me like that, Fin." How many times do I have to remind him? Pity is the last thing I need.

Lieutenant Murphy hushes the crowd of trainees. The frozen courtyard falls silent, clouds of breath filling the air. Murphy, like the other guards, is a high-born. He chose to be a guard and worked his way up through the ranks, becoming a Lieutenant about seventy years ago. Even though he is over one hundred years old, like most mature males he resembles a human at age thirty. He has a strong jawline that often goes unshaven for days at a time, olive green eyes as all summer fae have, and brown hair that he keeps cropped short.

He's an imposing figure at six feet tall, and I'm certain he is well built under his red-and-black leathers. He has the characteristic pointy ears that define all of us fae, although they aren't as elongated or pronounced as those of elves. Our ears, in fact, closely resemble those of humans, except for their elegantly pointed tips, which give us an air of otherworldly charm.

"We leave in two days for Outpost Four. We will remain there for a couple of weeks before making the trek back to the capital for the graduation ceremony. Reagan, you're to remain at Outpost Four for your official appointment and assignment as a member of the Phoenix Queen's Guard. Welcome. It was well earned, and it will be an honor to serve with you."

"Don't I get to return home to see my family?" I ask before I can stop myself.

"Family of bastards," someone snickers from the crowd, causing others to laugh along.

Were it not for the guards, I'd turn around and lay Kyle out. For four long years, I've been dealing with his bullying. He hates that he has never been able to beat me in hand-to-hand combat or with any weapons, poor baby. I would like to punch him in the face for every hour of my life wasted crying alone in my room because of his endless torment, questioning myself and wondering where in this world I will finally fit in.

"That behavior will not be tolerated in any position within the court," Murphy states. "I will hold back anyone I find too immature. From this moment on, no one will be permitted to leave the confines of this outpost."

He pauses, taking a deep, measured breath, eyes darting around through the ranks, searching for I don't know what.

"Two dozen guards await our arrival at Outpost Four. They will accompany our group back to the capital. Over the past four years, the number of our missing loved ones has exploded.

Understand that this is for your protection, and there will be no exceptions. You are all dismissed."

I know Murphy enough to know that the pause he took means he's hiding something. Are more of us disappearing or was he frightened? If so, of what? And more importantly . . . "Why can't I go home, Fin? This makes no sense. I shouldn't even be here."

"It's probably because your mother's not a member of the court. You've never had privileges here. I don't know why you're surprised."

Clearly, he does not grasp what's happening to me. "I need to talk to Murphy."

When I turn and walk away, shouts at the gate draw my attention. Fin's right back at my side. For quite some time I've known he's had a crush on me. I thought he'd outgrow it, but no such luck. He's my only friend here, but that does not stop him from going to the village with the other trainees on his days off, knowing I'm stuck here alone.

That does not bother me, at least not as much as his trips to the library. You would think he would bring me something to read but he never has. While Fin is tall, he is very skinny, wiry even. Like all summer fae, he has olive green eyes, though they seem out of place on his thin, shallow face. When the gates open, a lone guard on horseback enters, clad in the red and black leather uniform that represents the Phoenix Queen's Guard.

"That's my father," Fin exclaims, taking off to greet him.

His father, Captain Hamon if I remember correctly, embraces him. I'm happy for him, but it makes me feel even more alone in this world. I'm not one for pity parties. Fists clenching, I shove my hands deep into my pockets. Heat blooms on my face as I watch their exchange. Fin looks nothing like his father. The captain has a strong, solid build, bigger than Murphy even. He has a hard jawline, framed by his shoulder-length brown hair, and though I have no idea how old he is, he would be considered attractive.

Fin waves me over, so I pick up my pace. He's introducing his father to me as I get closer and, my gods, the captain suddenly looks as white as a ghost. His gaze meets mine and holds me captive, his eyes, twin green orbs, wide and unmoving. Fear and confusion wash over me in an uncomfortable wave, and I stop in my tracks. I'm not even sure I'm breathing.

"Father," Fin says, clutching his shoulder.

The captain seems to snap out of whatever in the depth of the shadows that was, then speaks to his son in a hushed tone. "Listen to me. You must stay within the safety of the outpost here and Outpost Four when you reach it. I will meet you there in two weeks before you depart for the capital."

"What's going on, Father?"

"Bodies have been found mutilated, and two hundred have gone missing this past month." The captain's eyes bounce back and forth from Fin's to mine before settling back on Fin. "I fear dark and sinister things are afoot. We believe it's shadow beasts."

Shadow beasts? They haven't been seen for centuries. This must be what Murphy was hiding. Although it does not explain the captain's reaction to me. I need to get out of here. Whatever this is, it's not my fight.

"Father, I'll come with you."

"No, I must leave." He grabs Fin's arm, pulling him in closer, whispering. My hearing is one of the things no one here appreciates. "Protect the girl at any cost. Do you understand what I'm ordering you to do, son?"

"What?" Fin looks as confused as me.

Fin still tries to plead with his father to tell him what's going on, but he's already on his horse. The captain takes one last long, disturbing look at me that sets my teeth on edge, then he's gone. We stand there dumbstruck, in the now nearly empty courtyard, watching as his father gallops away. The horse's hooves kick up the trampled snow in thick clumps.

Not my problem. Not right now. With Murphy my target, I

storm off. His eyes lock on mine, the other guards clearing out at my approach. Good. He begins speaking before I reach him.

"Reagan, listen to me. I know this must be upsetting you—"

I cut him off, not in the mood to be placated. "That makes no sense, and you know it. I should be able to see my family."

"I understand and agree. I informed the commander I would take full responsibility for you. He shut down my requests."

"Why would he do that, Murph?"

"I honestly don't know."

"Murph, you are the only one here who understands me. What if my little sister Willa thinks my sudden disappearance means I abandoned her, and she hates me for it?" That's the second-most haunting thought that consumes me. The one that wracks my body with guilt. Because our hateful mother and sister most likely told her I fled.

"I can bring a letter to Willa for you. I will speak to her directly. And when I return, you'll be working as my lead instructor, teaching the recruits to fight. You're the most skilled trainee to ever come through this program, Rea. It truly is an honor."

Before I say something I'll regret, I pivot. Even worse, I can't let anyone see tears forming. My room is my only escape now.

Once again, Fin shows up at my side. "What'd Murphy tell you?"

"Exactly what you said, which is why I won't be going to Outpost Four. When we depart, I'm making my break for home."

"Let me talk to my father. He can sort this out."

"Your father has enough going on." Icy chills run down my spine, recalling Captain Hamon's face. I shake it off as best I can. Priorities and all.

"I'll ask him as soon as we see him again. I have questions of my own."

"Willa is almost fourteen, what if my mother makes her a—"

"Don't think like that. I'm sure my father can help."

"I won't risk him saying no. I need to go home."

"I'll come with you."

"No, you have too much to lose. You have a future planned."

"That's the first time I've seen my father in four years. He could've shared more information. I'll be eighteen in six weeks and I'm graduating—"

Fin continues to complain about being treated like a child by a father who embraced him lovingly, so I cut him off too.

"Willa's all I have."

"I'll help you, and my father will see who I've become."

Inwardly rolling my eyes at what an ass Fin sounds like, I head for my room for the third time. It wasn't that long ago my life changed completely. One moment I was doing my chores, then the next my mother dragged me to the stables and insisted I was to leave immediately for the four-year, skills-training program. Fantastic opportunity for a worthless bastard, she'd said. Then she was gone. Not even a goodbye. My hateful older sister Kira didn't get this opportunity. The question that had gone unanswered for four years: Why did I?

AVOIDING THE OTHERS, I spent the last two days in my cold, musty room. Fin and I have been sneaking all the extra dried food we can for the journey, and he's acquired a map because we need to avoid the main roads.

We are about to become deserters.

It doesn't take me long to pack. I came here with only the clothes on my back. Thrice since then, someone has left a bag of clothing in my room filled with undergarments, leggings, socks, and tops. My gray leather pants, jacket, and boots (which are all too big) are the only clothing provided for trainees. We don't get the red and black leathers until we graduate.

But of all the things left in my room, my favorites are the books. I often find them under my pillow and have long suspected it was Murphy leaving them. They are what kept me going. I've never taken it personally that during my second year here, an educational book meant for younglings (very young as I half expected to find coloring pencils with it) was left in my room. It provided me with a basic understanding of our three gods who created our world of Innisfallen, the human world of Earth, and the Elven world of Delunavir. If only I had been allowed in the libraries or to attend temple, I could have learned more about them. The rest of the books were all works of fiction, and those are my favorites.

Even though I hate my big sister, Kira, I'm grateful my mother had her teach me how to read and write. In between the lessons and the beatings my mother would give me when she heard of my mistakes, she told me it would make me more useful. Some of the pain I suffered was worth it.

Not once have I even been allowed to go to the village like everyone else. I've been confined to this outpost for almost four years. I'm done. I won't miss this place, though I will miss Murphy. And maybe I'll miss the three solid meals a day. Hopefully, Willa's had enough to eat since my mother no longer needed to feed me.

Fin's giving me second thoughts. He obviously wants to prove something to his father, and he could be using this as an opportunity to be alone with me. Yet if I were to leave without him, would he inform the guards of my plans? Too late now, I suppose, since we leave at dawn. When our chance comes, I won't miss it. If I were to follow orders and proceed to Outpost Four, and they tried to hold me captive there as they have here, I would raze that place to the ground.

A BLINDING storm hits three hours into our journey. The fresh snow crunches beneath my feet and sticks to my boots, making it harder to navigate the uneven terrain. Murphy insists we need to make our way to the base of the mountain to look for shelter, but I can't see a mountain. I can't see anything except the snow whipping around in front of me. Despite having my scarf wrapped tightly, the pelting snow stings my entire face.

Our once green and flourishing valleys and mountains have become as frozen as the northern Kingdom of the Wolf Moon. Our Kingdom used to be mostly summer, contained by the power of the fae of old. But no longer. After four years of constant cold and snow, you'd think I'd become accustomed to it, but I haven't. Nor have I adjusted to no longer seeing the sun and moon. During the day, the sun casts a tainted yellowish glow behind the permanent cloud cover, and the nights have never been darker.

Sometimes I can almost smell grass. I remember the way it tickled my feet, and I miss spending time there with Willa. We would often sneak away after our work was done. We would swim in the lakes and streams and sometimes lay in the soft meadows, aware of nothing more than the wonderful sunshine on our faces.

Alone in the outdoors was the only time it was safe for us to talk about running away together. Finding our place in this world. A place to belong. Away from our abusive mother and older sister. Willa and I would sit under the stars for hours while she cleaned my wounds and comforted me.

Is it too much to hope that the weather is better where we're headed? Too much to hope that Willa is safe?

The gusting wind and snow cover our tracks and obstruct our view, making it hard to see more than a few feet ahead on our current journey. But that means the rest of the regime will find it difficult to see us through the storm. This is our chance. Reaching out, I grab Fin's arm, slowing our pace and allowing the others to pass.

"It's now or never. Let's turn back on the path we made," I whisper near his ear.

Fin nods, and we make a break for it.

It only takes about a hundred feet before we can no longer

see our old footprints. It only takes about a hundred more to realize we've made a huge mistake. But once again, we have no choice. We must push on.

After an exhausting two-hour search, I find a small cave to shelter us. We make our way inside, lying down as far from the opening as we can, curling up together for warmth. "That did not go as planned. At all. But the storm made it exceptionally easy to slip away."

"But we have no idea where we are now, Rea. Maybe we didn't think this through enough. Was this a mistake?"

"No, we can do this. After a night's rest." Figuring out everything else, that will come later. Like informing him I don't have feelings for him. I've never given him one indication that I'm interested in more than friendship. It's quite the opposite. Judging by the way he's holding me, I know there's more to this embrace than the need to warm our frozen limbs. A jolt from his body startles me, and his arms squeeze me tighter. I shift in his arms. "What are you doing?"

"Just a bit cold."

The frigid temperature seeps into my bones. I'm scared, exhausted, and unnerved by Fin's embrace, but now isn't the time for that conversation. There are more pressing matters at hand. We need to get through this together, no matter how uncomfortable or afraid we may be. Fin shifts, startling me again.

"Rea, I saw something move by the mouth of the cave."

Twisting to get a look, I see two large shadowy figures appear. That can't be good. "Get up, Fin." Jumping up, I assume my fighter stance, four years of training kicking in on instinct. I'm terrified, and it takes me a minute to realize why: I know how to face off against an opponent. I've just never faced a real opponent, a real threat.

The hooded strangers come closer with their hands raised, palms out, showing us they have no weapons. Thank the Forgotten Gods. They are clad in all black, with no colors visible.

Their plain attire reveals they're not of the Queen's Guard. Could we be this lucky and not need to fight?

One of them starts to speak when out of nowhere Fin charges them. I reach for him, but it's too late. I'm unable to stop him or stop my eyes from rolling.

Idiot.

The pair quickly step into defensive positions. Having no choice, I charge the one on my left to defend my moronic friend. Weightlessness hits me, my feet no longer propelling me forward. I'm in the air. A gust, as cold and more powerful than the blizzard we escaped, slams my body as I'm blasted backward. Bright white light is the last thing I see as my head cracks against the cave wall.

An intense pounding in my head wakes me. A surge of nausea washes over me, saliva drips from my mouth, and sweat coats my body. As my vision begins to clear, I spot Fin. If I sit up too quickly, I'll vomit for sure. The cloud of confusion surrounding my brain slowly starts to dissipate. I can't see the hooded strangers. "Where are they? Did they have powers?"

"They put cuffs on over my gloves. If I can remove my gloves, I can slip the cuffs. Get up, Rea. They're not here right now." Fin glances around nervously. "This could be our only chance to escape. Otherwise, we could wind up dead, like the victims in the reports my father was talking about. I think they were using forbidden magic."

"What is forbidden magic? Are you injured? Because I don't feel like I can stand on my own."

"You're uneducated, you wouldn't get it."

"What?" He's lucky I need help, or I would knock him out. He doesn't answer; however, he manages to remove his gloves and slip off his cuffs. He helps me sit up and then starts to work on my restraints. A new surge of nausea hits me. Consciousness feels like it's slipping from my grasp. Darkness waits on the edge of a shadowy precipice, arms open, ready to catch me if I fall.

"Your cuffs are too tight. I can't remove them." His words are muffled by thick fog.

Inhaling deeply, I try to clear my head. "Try something else then. Or help me up, slowly."

"I'll be back soon. I'll get help."

"You're not seriously talking about leaving me here! How long have I been out? Help me up."

"We're not far from Outpost Three. My father is in the village."

In an attempt to stand, I plant my hands on the frozen, rocky, cave floor. Unfortunately, being cuffed, dizzy, and nauseous is not a good combination, and I fall on my face. Sharp rocks rip away bits of skin from my chin. Lifting my head feels like a weight too great to bear. Fin's backing away from me, toward the mouth of the cave. "You have no idea where we are. Don't you dare leave me here."

"I'll be back with help, I promise."

"Help me, Fin. Please don't leave me here."

"I'll be back."

This can't be happening. If the hooded strangers return, I'm vulnerable right now. *Breathe, think, then act.* "You're a coward, Fintan." He flinches at my words. Good.

But he turns away, and without so much as a backward glance, walks out of the cave, leaving me alone, a captive of these two strangers. Fin's abandoned me to death—or worse. Then what he said hits me. What is forbidden magic? The pounding in my head intensifies until it reverberates off my eardrums, creating an almost deafening silence. Red bursts flash behind my eyes, and then I explode.

"I hate you! I hate you!" I scream, over and over.

THE HEAT from a fire wakes me. Its warmth fills my nose and lungs with every breath. The soft padding I'm lying on and the blanket draped over me are surprising. Did these two strangers show me more kindness and compassion than my friend or anyone else in my life, right after knocking me on my ass? A flood of depression envelops me. *Deep breaths in, long slow releases out.* Control . . . I know I must stay in control, but I no longer have the will. Darkness wants to reclaim me, so I allow the heat from the fire to seduce me back into its warm embrace.

A tapping on my arm wakes me. Hands grip my arms firmly, pulling me to my feet. As my eyes focus, I'm looking into the most beautiful, bright blue eyes that I have ever seen.

"Wolf Court eyes," I speak aloud, not meaning to.

The gorgeous winter fae male before me quirks up a cocky smile. "Listen, Love, I wish there was time to explain about the three hostiles coming after us, but, unfortunately, I don't have the time. I need you to run with my brother and me. Right now." He leads me toward the entrance of the cave. "We are being tracked and not by your Queen's Guard. I assure you, my brother and I are not your enemies. Can you accept that? At least until I have time to explain who we are and why we're here?"

The icy air hits my face with sharp relief. Stopping in my tracks, I stop him too. My eyes lock on his as my head finally clears. They kept me warm all night while I cried and let's face it, what other options do I have right now? None. Zero. Nodding my agreement, I lift my cuffed hands, still holding his gaze. "I am not your prisoner."

His blue eyes remain fixed on mine, taking the full force of my conviction. He nods slightly, somewhat respectfully, before he removes my cuffs. Then I follow the pair out into the unknown.

CHAPTER 2

We walk in silence nearly all day, the two males swift but silent, clearly on alert. As the last of the day's light gives way to night, the brothers begin looking for shelter.

"I'll be right back. I need to pee." When I return, only the cocky one is there.

"I'm Shay."

He has a swagger and a smile that I'm sure the females swoon over. I couldn't care less right now. He's beautiful, there's no denying it. Dark, shoulder-length hair. Those bright blue winter fae eyes. A powerful jawline. Perfectly straight, white teeth. And he's easily six and a half feet tall. And peppermint—he smells like a cool peppermint breeze. Interesting.

"Where's your brother?" I ask without offering up my name.

"Nova. He's not far. Follow me."

We enter through a large opening at the base of yet another snow-covered mountain. The acrid scent of fire reaches me, and I become aware of how exhausted and hungry I am. Fin had the food. He left me, I still can't believe it. I swear to the Forgotten Gods, if I ever see him again, I'll punch him in the face so hard, he'll land flat on his ass.

"Watch your step," Shay cautions me.

I do. It's dark and our path begins to twist and turn through a large crevasse. We weave back and forth like the flow of a perilous river. Frozen stalactites, sharp as spears, hang down at awkward angles above us, sometimes too close for comfort. The pungent scent of mold now mixes with the burning wood. We enter a large cave, and there in the back corner is Nova, standing at the fire.

He has the same hair, bright blue eyes, and build as Shay. Their faces, however, are so different. Shay's is open and playful. Nova looks menacing. His is a face that promises certain death if crossed. He seems to fill the entire space just standing there, doing nothing.

"Come sit by the fire," Shay offers, startling me from my thoughts. He sits next to his brother, leaving a padded seat across from them for me.

The heat from the flames seeps through my clothes and into my bones, relaxing me. Using this quiet moment, I try to collect my thoughts. They need to give me more information about the three hostiles they warned me about. And did I imagine the brothers have powers or is it my concussed head making me remember incorrectly?

The pops and cracks from the flames are the only sound until my stomach growls. They turn and look at me in unison, heads tipping to the same side as they observe me. It's fascinating how similarly they move. A brother thing, I suppose. What do they feed the wolves in the north? They're huge.

Shay tosses me something, and I catch it. It's a chunk of dried meat the size of my hand. "It's venison."

"Thank you." I stuff it in my mouth and rip off a bite.

"As I said, I'm Shay. This is my brother Nova. And you are?"

Sinking my teeth back into the dried venison, I rip off another bite and start chewing, staring at him. The pair exchange a quick look.

"My brother and I are the Wolf Court's third attempt to reach The Court of the Phoenix Moon for help."

"Help?" I inquire while still chewing on a mouthful of deer. "What do the wolves need help with?"

"Our fae are disappearing at an alarming rate and now some of our trade ships and their crews have gone missing."

They're obviously dealing with similar issues to those we'd been warned about at the outpost. Our ships and their crews have also begun disappearing. We have no wars between our kingdoms. Our guard posts have been a longstanding spot of peace since some epic battle long ago with The Darkness and his Shadow Demons.

"So, you two are making your way to the capital city of Glendalough?" Hopefully, they'll say yes. It would be great to have real traveling companions. They nod in unison, and it's kind of adorable. They intrigue me, and I need to get to the capital as quickly as possible. If they're headed there as well, why not have protection, food, warmth, and company? It's a long journey back. Four weeks at best. I don't even want to think about the worst. Fin and I were completely unprepared. However, with these two, I stand a stronger chance of seeing Willa sooner than I would alone. I can confirm that she is safe and finally get a chance to explain everything that happened to me.

"We are," Shay replies.

"My name is Reagan. You can call me Rea. I'm making my way back home to Glendalough, to visit my family."

The pair exchange another look, and now I wonder if they can communicate mind-to-mind, but it doesn't feel like the right time to ask.

"Forgive me for asking," Shay starts. "Are you a summer fae?"

He's probably wondering because, while I have green eyes like all summer fae, mine are unusual. They aren't the typical olive green but the color of emeralds, bright and brilliant. "I am."

"Who's the boy that was with you?" Nova inquires.

"He's nobody. He's none of your concern. Or mine anymore,"

I answer, unable to mask my disdain. I'm so mad at Fin that I don't even notice myself shaking, heating up, and maybe even getting a bit nauseous. "I need to get to the capital. Maybe we can travel together. Think about it." Standing, I head outside for one more quick bathroom trip before trying to get some sleep.

The cold night air hits my face and relief soon follows. Like the weight of a pack slipping from my back, the heat and shaking subside. Good. I still can't believe Fin left me, knowing all the horrors that could've befallen me. He should've dragged my ass out of that cave. I meant what I said to him. He's a coward. A boy, as Nova called him.

They're good males. They only wanted to talk to us in the cave last night. If they had wanted to hurt me, they had plenty of opportunities. Bet they'd have my back, unlike Fin. At least I hope they will. I don't want to overthink this, because if there are, in fact, three dangerous males out there, I need as much help as I can get. When I get back to the entrance of the cave, the brothers are standing outside, waiting.

"I was perfectly willing to share my bed, Love. However, Nova thought you would be more comfortable sharing with both of us."

I nod even though I have no idea what he's talking about.

Back in the cave, I see what he means—two large bedrolls are pushed together, blankets on top. So much for not over-thinking things. This is not a big deal, we are traveling companions sharing supplies. I go to my pack, grab my blanket, and lay down in the middle as if I make a habit of regularly bedding down between two hot males. Two really hot males. Sharing warmth makes sense from a survival sense. That's all this is.

It's nice not having someone telling me what to do. No one is insulting me. I have control over my life and my choices. I'm going to make the most of this, enjoy the trip, and maybe even have some fun. I've been miserable my entire life, and I've had enough. I've made some friends. Yes, friends. Nothing else.

The sound of my new friends' footfalls echoes through the

tunnel. And my gods, they are breathtakingly beautiful. I have never seen males that look like them. I slam my eyes closed. Friends do not think that way about one another.

They climb onto the outer sides of the bedrolls, their backs to me. A flash of heat washes over me, leaving me nauseous in its wake. I throw the blanket off, hoping the cool air will help. We need to stay warm through the night, but this is a bit much.

Nova begins fidgeting, then there's a thump on the ground, not far away. Whatever that was, it sounded heavy. I stay quiet rather than ask about it. Inhaling deeply, the heat within me subsides until thoughts of the two males and their nearness cause a different type of heat to stir. I'll never get any sleep like this, so I cast my thoughts about for something to distract me.

Closing my eyes, a familiar smile stretches across my memory. Picturing Willa always makes me happy. I can only hope and pray to the Forgotten Gods that her quick wit has kept her safe these past four years. In the thoughts of Willa, my troubled mind finds peace.

The sound of crackles hissing and popping from the fire wakes me. The heat of the flames still envelops me in its warmth. Rolling onto my back, I notice Shay and Nova aren't here. I sit up too quickly, and dizziness washes over me. My injured head throbs. The fire's still going. Their bedrolls and blankets are still here. Then I spot Nova, leaning against the wall by the mouth of the cave, standing with his back to me, staring out into the winding stalactite path.

Thank the Forgotten Gods. It's not that I can't do this alone. I just don't know how I would've handled being abandoned again.

"Morning," I get out, somehow managing to sound calm.

"Good morning, Reagan. Shay will be back in a moment."

"Great. I'll wait to see to my needs then." My tone is a bit sourer than I intend for it to be. It's not their fault I woke up thinking they'd left me. "Look, I'm sorry. I woke up and thought you guys had left me here."

"Reagan, I understand you're being cautious with your trust, which is smart. However, I assure you my brother and I are not your enemies. We will respect you."

"I'm not used to kindness from others, I guess. It's no excuse. I meant no disrespect."

He pushes off the wall and storms toward me, each step more menacing than the last. He stops a couple of feet in front of me, and my gods, he's tall. His flowing black hair cascades to his shoulders. The intensity in his eyes is unnerving, so different from his brother's cocky, playful demeanor. The bright blue eyes suit him, too. He gazes down at me below hooded eyes, lashes so long any female would envy them, myself included.

"I give you my word: Shay and I won't harm you or disrespect you in any way."

The sound of his deep, midnight voice reverberates throughout my entire body. He smells like wintergreen leaves. It appears that the wolves have individual scents.

"Thank you, Nova. I do trust that."

The sound of Shay approaching reaches us. Nova's gaze is still locked on mine. His beautiful blue eyes hold me captive, like staring into a sea of tranquility. He finally breaks eye contact and steps away as Shay enters the cave. A breath escapes me that I was unaware I was holding. That was intense.

"Good morning, Love. Don't you look just as beautiful this morning as you did last night?"

"Good morning, Shay. And don't you sound just as cocky this morning as you did last night," I reply, pivoting and walking out.

The sound of Nova's laughter follows me, making me laugh a bit to myself. I like them. Shay makes me feel like I'm already one of his friends. It's easy with him. Oddly, this is the first time I've ever fit in. And it's only been one day. I have good instincts and intuition, and I've always known when to listen to what my gut tells me. The one exception is that I was wrong about Fin. I'm grateful to have met these two.

When I return to the cave, the fire is out and they're packed up. My blanket's been rolled and placed neatly on my pack. Shay walks by, handing me some dried venison, an adorable pout on his face. I've never been treated as a regular female before. And I've never had someone flirt with me.

"Thank you, Shay. You're so very generous. Unlike your brother."

Stopping in his tracks, he looks back at me over his shoulder, that cocky smile of his on full display. Males have never looked at me the way these two do. I know I'm physically attractive at five foot seven. My emerald green eyes complement my light brown hair. I'm a little thicker than the average female because I like to eat—it's a matter of survival and as part of our training, we work out almost every day. I'm full-figured, as one of the guards once called me while trying to fit me with a breastplate. Shay's blue eyes, bright and now hooded, gaze into mine. A sudden chill runs down my back followed by a wave of heat on my face. "I'm more generous than my brother in many ways, Love." He turns and walks out.

Heat floods my entire body as I realize I'm completely out of my depth when it comes to flirting. Nova rolls his eyes at Shay, but a smile appears on his face before he, too, walks out. What in the depths of the shadows have I gotten myself into?

As we begin the long trek to the capital, Shay explains more about their court's plight.

"About four years ago, winter started in the Wolf Court's territory and hasn't stopped."

"That sounds similar to what has been happening in ours," I tell him.

"We would like to share something with you," Shay reveals. "My brother and I found an ancient artifact, the Staff of Storms. We located it in the mountains above the Wolf Court's castle, inside an old, abandoned temple, and . . ."

"And?" He can't start telling me something and not commit to finishing. I don't need the unnecessary suspense. What I need to know is if they have powers.

"It reveals things, Love."

"What kind of things?"

They exchange another look, longer this time. I bet they can communicate with each other. Nova walks to us. Another wave of heat and nausea overtakes my body as he pulls a silver rod from his weapons belt and expands it to its full height, taller than he is. The solid white tip looks like it could pierce the hide of a shadow beast. Its center is covered in what appears to be ancient runes, though I've never had a proper education so I can't be sure. All I can make out are dots or dashes, maybe stars. Then he collapses it back to the smaller length.

"Reagan," Nova explains, "we believe there is a spell or a curse, a two-part spell that has been cast over Innisfallen. The first is a glamour that's made us believe our powers have been weakening every generation. The spell makes us forget to gather twice a year for the Summer and Winter Solstice on the Isle of the Crescent Moon to replenish our powers."

"Because of the glamour," Shay informs me, "we have not gathered for twenty years."

"The second part of the spell or curse is repressing our powers, and make no mistake, Reagan, we do have powers."

I knew it. I have noticed I'm stronger in the summer around the solstice, which would make sense if what they're telling me is true. I've also heard of the Isle of the Crescent Moon. That's the home of The Courtless. They are governed by those they elect and the laws and rules they've written. They want nothing to do with court politics. They don't believe only the royal and high-born should have all the privileges while the low-born don't. Willa and I often dreamed of running away there. Starting a new life. "What does it do?"

"Can you feel the Staff?" Nova asks.

"What do you mean? I can't feel that thing."

"You seem to be shaking."

"I'm nervous," I admit. Maybe more for myself than for him.

"Do you feel hot or cold, inside your body? Maybe even a little sick to your stomach?"

"Kind of, yes. How do you know that?"

"It's similar for me," he says with a knowing smile.

"That's what you threw last night in the cave."

Nova smiles. "It was."

"That's why I started to feel hot and shaky when you two laid down."

"That might not be all from the Staff, Love." Shay grins mischievously.

"If you hold it, it will reveal the last solstice gathering and eventually it will help you discover your powers."

Why don't I reach out and grab it? Have I not always dreamed of having powers? Have I not always believed I do have them hidden somewhere deep inside of me?

"Afraid?" Shay taunts.

"No," I sneer, reaching for the Staff. Vibrations course through my hand even before I've made contact. Tingling resistance meets my fingers as I move them through the thrumming currents.

The moment I wrap my fingers around the metal rod, everything changes.

CHAPTER 3

I mmediately and almost violently, I feel as if I am on fire, burning from the inside out. As heat blooms over my entire body, my stomach lurches. Images assault my mind: Fae of all kinds, dressed so beautifully, though I can't make out their faces. They appear veiled.

The images suddenly change.

Their beautiful visages morph into twisted, mutilated faces, distorted in all kinds of grotesque ways. Sweat drips down my forehead as the burning in my chest intensifies. I need to help them, but I don't know how. I shake, helpless to stop the horror unfolding around me. What's the point of seeing it all if I can't even help?

The sour taste of bile fills my mouth, and I've had enough. I open my hands, letting the Staff fall into the snow below. Trembling, I look accusingly at Nova. "What was that?"

Nova picks the Staff up and returns it to his belt before stepping about five feet away. The distance between us eases the heat in my chest. I force myself to calm down with deep breaths in, long slow releases out. "What was that?" I repeat.

"Tell us what you saw, Love, what you felt," Shay prods.

Still a bit shaky, I relay what I saw in my vision. This is not what I expected when they offered for me to touch the Staff. I feel as though I might throw up.

"Reagan, how old are you?"

"Eighteen, this past summer. How long was I holding that thing?"

"Maybe ten seconds," Shay chuckles.

"Seriously? That's all?"

They nod in unison.

"As we've said, Love, we believe the Staff of Storms is directly linked to our powers being repressed and to the glamour."

Deep breath in, slow release. "How? And why do I feel like I'm going to be sick?"

"We don't yet understand the sickness," Shay admits, "though I assure you it will pass."

"Thanks for the heads up."

"We need to break the glamour over the Phoenix King and Queen, help them see the truth, remember who they are," Shay implores.

"Reagan, you were born under the glamour, so you don't have prior memories of truth to be revealed. However, your contact with the Staff will help you discover what your powers are, and it does get easier each time. If you were to try holding it a little longer, you will see less and start to feel more."

"I'm not touching that thing again. That one time was long enough." I don't add that it would have been incredibly embarrassing to have vomited in front of them.

"You barely held it for ten seconds, Love," Shay insists, much to my annoyance.

"Incredible. I felt like I was holding it longer. Maybe I could try for fifteen and throw up on your feet."

"Nova, we believe, can access his full powers with the Staff."

"Really? What kind of powers?" Despite my ire, I'm intrigued and at least I now have confirmation that they did use powers that night. The pair share another one of their looks.

"I'm able to manipulate the snow within a certain radius of myself."

"What do you mean by 'manipulate'?"

"I can clear pathways in front of me to move quickly and can fill them in behind me, covering my tracks."

"Seriously? That's it? That's a pretty specific ability."

They observe me for a moment before sharing another one of their secretive looks, and so help me, gods, I want to smack them both in their faces. They are talking behind my back right in front of my face.

"If I found out after all this time that I have powers but could only blow the leaves around, I'd be a bit embarrassed. I'm just saying, I was expecting something bigger." My annoyance at their private communication feeds my petty insult.

"I can also create and control winter storms. Like hurricanes of ice, for example."

"Hurricanes?" I wish I had kept my mouth shut. Probably better not to insult someone who could sweep me up in a frozen whirlwind.

Nova extends the Staff to me. "Would you like to try again?"

"No," I insist, even though I can't take my eyes off it.

"Tell us, Reagan, what position do you hold in the Phoenix Court to bring you this far north?"

Figuring it can't hurt to tell them a little bit about myself, I answer carefully. "I just finished a four-year training program. There are many different skills to be learned. Our coastal outposts are where the sailors are trained. Outpost Two is for officers in training, and Outpost Three, where I was, is where the Queen's guards are trained, in whatever suited us best."

"What suited you best?"

"Weapons." My mouth stretches into a smile. I'm proud of my skills.

"Impressive. I've never heard of females being in the Queen's Guard."

"I'm the first. When I arrived at Outpost One, my new lieutenant asked the transport guard what skill station I was to be put in, as everyone came knowing what theirs were ahead of time. He replied, 'Queen's guard.' Now that my training has ended, I'm going home to visit my family. I would've been instructing the new recruits in different fighting skills, like swords, daggers, and hand-to—"

"Would've been?" Nova questions, raising an elegant eyebrow.

"Why did you not have a training assignment before your arrival? Had you not decided what you wanted to learn?"

What a fool. How could I have been so careless? I let my guard down. Do I share my personal life and tell them who I really am? I don't want their pity.

"Reagan, we saw you and your boy companion break away from the Queen's Guard and flee. We won't turn you in; don't fear that at all. We need to know if they will come for you."

"Why?" I hope I don't sound as nervous as I suddenly feel.

"Because Shay and I are in the Wolf King's Army, and we need their help."

"Don't worry, Love, we want no part of the Queen's Guard," Shay assures me. "We have no quarrel with them. We need only to reach the King and Queen, as we've told you. We don't care one way or another if you're a deserter."

"We need to know so we can keep the three of us safe," Nova insists.

He said the three of us. They're not talking down to me, and there's no pity in their voices or on their faces. They've known this entire time that my presence could endanger them, and they are helping me anyway. I've never known anyone like them.

"My mother's not a member of the court, so technically, I shouldn't have been a part of the training programs as a low-born. She is a maid, and for a brief time, was the queen's wet nurse while pregnant with me and my little sister. I didn't choose to go to training . . . One day, my mother just informed me that I was leaving that afternoon. I never had the chance to say goodbye to my little sister Willa, and I'm afraid she thinks I abandoned her. So, when I found out that my commander wouldn't allow me to return home, I panicked and ran. I need Willa to know the truth."

They exchange another look. I don't care this time. My heart aches with a lifetime of weariness.

"Who is your mother, Reagan?"

"Her name is Ciara, and . . . she's a whore, okay? Now you know I'm a worthless, bastard daughter of a whore."

"Reagan." Nova's voice is a gentle storm. Tears are forming in my eyes already. I never should have said that. "Reagan." He speaks softer this time. As I look up at him, one of those traitorous tears decides to slip from my eye. "Never be ashamed of who you are or where you come from. It does not define who you are. We will always see you as the fierce, brave female who jumped up in that cave ready to take on the pair of us."

"We also saw your intelligence, Love. In the cave, you considered the possibility that we weren't a threat, at least until your friend went on the offensive. You didn't jump to conclusions, you thought. That's how we see you."

I hear echoes of the things I try to tell myself in Nova's and Shay's words. I'm not my mother. Nova's right, my history doesn't define me.

"You used the Staff on Fin and me that night in the cave. My head still hurts, thank you very much." I rub the back of my head for emphasis.

"Sorry, Love, that was me. I don't have access to my full powers like Nova, yet. My powers are similar to Nova's, but when I wield the Staff and try to use my powers at the same time, mine can be unpredictable. I'm still learning."

I realize that's a lot for him to admit. Maybe I should start training with them, trying to figure out what my powers are. With Shay admitting that it's difficult for him, I won't feel as uncomfortable. Who knows? It might be fun. A little scary, but fun. I'm so grateful for him sharing that with me, I tell him the first thing that comes to mind.

"Aw, Shay, feeling a little impotent, are we?" I blurt out, trying to deflect from the seriousness of the moment.

Nova's roar of laughter bounces off the surrounding mountains, echoing back at us. The sound of my laughter quickly joins his.

"I'm just kidding," I whisper. "I'm sure you're an alpha among wolves." Shay's fighting hard to not laugh, though I can tell he liked that one. He gives up and joins us. This right here is why I made the decision to enjoy the trip.

As night and the temperature begin to fall, we look for shelter. I could fall asleep right now, standing where I am.

Once they find a cave, Shay heads out to see if he can find some fresh meat, and Nova starts building a fire. Feeling a little awkward after revealing some of my past, I feel the need to be useful, so I ask if there is anything I can help with. He tells me I can start setting out the bed rolls if I want.

"You both seem to have a much easier time seeing at night than I do." I'm hoping for a little small talk.

"It runs in the male wolf line only, much to the annoyance of the females."

"What are the females known for?"

"Their bite."

I turn to see if he is serious, and the look on his face reveals that he knows from personal experience. Interesting. Wonder how many females have bitten him? This is the perfect time to ask the question that's been on my mind. "Why do you call me Reagan and not Rea?"

"I have always found the name Reagan beautiful. I've even thought a time or two when I find someone to marry, if we had a female child, I'd like to name her Reagan."

Turning to look at him, I'm greeted by a crooked half-smile laced with uncertainty, as though he's afraid he's shared too much. I decide that this is my favorite Nova smile. He looks younger somehow, with those harsh edges softened.

He obviously trusts and feels comfortable enough with me to allow me to see this side of him, maybe because I took the first leap of faith. I shared some of the nightmares of my past, and he shared some of the dreams of his future. A dream of a wife and child, of a family. "Thank you for sharing that with me. It's a beautiful dream."

ALL NIGHT I dreamed about having powers and awoke thinking of holding the Staff again. "Good morning. Be right back."

They nod and grumble good mornings, then go back to studying their map for today's route. Maybe it will be difficult today. When Fin and I started discussing our trip, we knew we'd have to avoid the main roads into Glendalough. Nova and Shay have been doing the same by keeping the Iron Fang mountain peaks to our west for the last few days, which put some very craggy landscape before us. Once we break free of the mountains, the journey will be much faster.

From the mouth of the cave, I peer out at the frozen world of Innisfallen. Surprisingly, it's not snowing today. That cheers me up. I like when we're able to talk along the way. It makes the journey pass much faster. Bark has been stripped from the bottom six feet of the skeletal tree trunks by starving deer. This far north, bushes no longer bear fruits and berries. The treacherous snow-covered mountains still dominate our western view, but fortunately, we are headed south, then east.

Without the falling snow or as many trees, I can get a better view of the route ahead, so I venture out a bit farther from the cave. Way out, there's a wide-open space we might have to cross, possibly a lake or meadow. It's a huge expanse that will leave us exposed, and I bet that's what has made them grumpy this morning.

When I've taken my fill of the surroundings, I turn to head back to the cave. Standing in front of me is a dark figure. He's so close that I nearly run into his chest. I jump back and find myself staring into the most terrifying face I've ever seen. His eyes are a molten mixture of muted blacks, greens, and grays. He has no pupils, just those multi-hued irises swirling endlessly, like smoke. My body locks up with fear as his twin hollows of death bore into me. His putrid breath makes me gag, but it snaps me back to reality. What in the depth of the shadows is this thing? He's missing both ears like they were ripped from his head. I react to movement on my left, turning just as someone's fist connects with my face.

CHAPTER 4

A painful throbbing in my jaw wakes me. When I come to, it's near dark, my hands are bound, and I'm being carried over someone's shoulder. How long have I been out? The lack of rotted breath lets me know it's not the gruesome male carrying me. It must be the one who cold-cocked me. Coward.

The side of my face hurts and I'm pissed. Unlike the night in the cave with Fin, my head clears quickly. Good, that means no concussion this time. I try to think of a course of action before they figure out I'm awake. Where are Nova and Shay? What if they were injured? Or worse? No, I can't think like that right now. Get free first, then I can find them. My breath catches in my throat when I recall the face and eyes I last saw.

"I already know you're awake, sweetheart. No need to pretend," Creepy Eyes spews at me, and the stench from his mouth carries over and makes my nostrils burn.

"Put me down on my feet then," I order sounding much braver than someone in my position should.

"Very well. Rekker, assist the lady to her feet."

Rekker, who I assume is the male to whom I owe a solid throat punch, throws me from his shoulder and I land with my face in the snow. It takes me a moment to stand with bound hands and numb legs. Have I been unconscious all day? Taking a minute to get to my feet, I use the time to start covertly working at freeing my hands. When I finally stand, the two males are facing me. I will not show them one bit of fear.

"Who are you and where are you taking me?" Behind them is a large snow-covered ravine and judging by the direction of our tracks, we're headed up. It strikes me as unusual that it's still not snowing.

The one with the creepy eyes and death breath terrifies me. Something is not right with him. Something foul, something dark and sinister like the Captain of the Guard told Fin. This creature has to be what he was talking about. This male, this thing, is not natural. I don't even think he's fae.

"We are but members of the Queen's Guard. You went missing, we were sent to retrieve you. "

"Liar. You're not members of the Queen's Guard."

He gets in my face so fast, it takes everything I have to face him and not shake or gag. Yet my body's starting to betray me. That breath is noxious.

"I can smell your fear, girl. It's wise to be afraid. It's also wise to keep that mouth of yours shut, or I'll shut it for you. You're powerless against what's coming for you. The life you knew is over," he spits, then turns and walks away with a preternatural grace that I have never seen someone possess. It seems out of place in one so hideous.

"Yeah, I don't think so." I kick out as fast and hard as I can into Rekker's crotch, and he goes down like a ton of bricks. I smash my fists down on the back of his head for good measure.

"Stay down," I tell him. Turning, I face off with Creepy Eyes, though he doesn't move at all. He starts laughing at me, an empty soulless laugh. I want to ask what he finds so funny, but before I get the chance, I'm grabbed into a chokehold from behind. Ugh! I forgot Shay told me there were three of these bastards.

"What would you like me to do to her, Cormac?" Mystery male number three asks, sniffing my hair. Throwing my head backward, I smash into his face hard. No one wins in a head butt, but it was worth the pain. I hope I broke his pervy nose.

"Get your hands off of me." Swinging my left leg out, I kick him in the knee. His scream of pain ignites my rage, and I drive my fist into the side of his head with all my weight. Sensing movement behind me, I pivot on my feet and spin around as quickly as I can.

Creepy Eyes, Cormac, is in my face so fast that I have no time to react before he backhands me, and I land flat on my back. It's as if he turned into smoke and reappeared in front of me. What in the depths of the shadows is he?

"Both of you, hold her down," he orders. "I'm going to show this bitch how powerless she is." Cormac takes his sword off his belt, sticks it into the frozen ground, and then removes a small black dagger from his waist. "I don't care if I deliver you to my father injured or not. He didn't specify that you had to be undamaged. I'm going to bleed you out almost to death, then drag you there."

"No! Let me go!" I buck, thrash, and kick as hard as I can, but I'm outnumbered. Cormac punches me in the chest so hard that every bit of air whooshes from my lungs. This can't be happening. I won't allow him to bleed me out like an animal. I gasp in desperation, and finally, my lungs free up. Inhaling every bit of air I can, I scream louder than I ever have. "HELP!" I knee him in the crotch, then in one continuous motion, I tuck my knees up to my chest, plant my feet on his chest, and explode my legs out, launching him off me.

Cormac's arms shoot out as he tries to catch himself, when the four of us are suddenly blown forward by a massive blast of winter snow.

Landing face down in the snow again, I look up to see Cormac flying over a hill some two hundred feet away. The other two that were holding me are still here. Nova approaches the two males while Shay runs off after Cormac.

Nova impales Rekker's skull with the Staff, then walks over to Cormac's remaining companion.

My angels of death. They came for me.

"Who are you?" Nova demands.

"Osman." Male number three looks terrified.

I get to my feet gasping for air and half-walk, half-stumble the few steps to Nova's side.

"Who are your companions?" Nova demands the simpering male.

"Rekker and Cormac."

"Which one did I just put down?"

"Rekker."

I manage to ask a question. "Where were you taking me?"

"Cormac's father wants you."

"Yeah, I got that part. Who is Cormac's father and why does he want me?"

"Something about the day you were born. I don't know more than that."

Nova puts his booted foot on his chest. "Who is Cormac's father?"

"I don't know! I'm only a hired hand." Nova presses the tip of the Staff to Osman's forehead. "I don't know! Please, you have to believe me."

"I don't believe you." Nova pushes the Staff down harder. Blood starts to drip from Osman's head, staining the snow crimson. The thug squeals in pain and fear.

"The Shadow King! Cormac's father is the Shadow King!"

"The Shadow King? There is no Shadow King." Nova looks toward me for a moment, and that split second of distraction is all it takes. Out of nowhere, Osman stabs him in the thigh.

Nova's howl of pain has me reaching for the Staff. I rip it from his hand and lift it high over my head as heat flashes throughout my body, filling me with rage.

"Enjoy an eternity of darkness," I howl. Putting all my weight behind me, I drive the Staff through his useless face and right into the frozen ground below. Energy from the Staff flows through me, as if it's meant for me, comfortable and powerful in my hands.

"Reagan, release the Staff, please." Nova startles me from my thoughts.

Without a word, I remove my hands, stepping back.

When Shay returns, he pulls a needle and thread from his pack along with a flat piece of wood. Nova is already seated on the frozen ground, his pants down to his knees, exposing his muscular and bloody thigh. Shay hands Nova the wood, and he puts it in his mouth, biting down hard. Shay stitches him up quickly like he's done this a thousand times. Then Nova pulls his pants back up and straps his pack to his back while Shay grabs Cormac's sword. And then we begin our way back south, a little slower due to Nova's injury.

"We have to keep moving," Shay informs us. "We must put distance between us. Cormac appears to be incredibly powerful. This Obsidian Sword is an artifact like the Staff. I can sense a little power coming from it."

"I wasn't certain he was fae until I drove my knee into his crotch. He felt it."

"You fought hard, Reagan. Well done." Nova nods in praise.

When the adrenaline rush ebbs away, my body begins to feel cold, numb almost. If Cormac would bleed me out to get me to his father, what would his father have done to me?

After a good ten hours trudging through the snow, we enter the foothills of the mountains and look for shelter. Once we find a decent cave, albeit tiny, the boys set up our bedrolls against the wall, starting a fire directly in front. We sit in silence, soaking up the warmth. The usual concerns about Willa weigh heavily on my mind, but tonight, my mind is spinning with other mysteries.

"We're almost clear of the mountain," Shay tells us. "It won't be much farther to Glendalough from there. Once we reach the

Queen's Road, we'll take it straight to the capital. No more avoiding main travel routes, it's too dangerous out here."

What was wrong with Cormac? I'm shivering visibly, and Nova hands me my blanket from my pack. Even though I smile, I'm certain it doesn't reach my eyes. I came so close to becoming one of the missing. Is that what happened to them? Were they dragged away to the Shadow King? Leaning back, I inhale a deep breath in an attempt to keep myself from falling apart.

"I'm sorry," I sigh. "I know I shouldn't be so unnerved."

"Don't be sorry," they assure me in unison.

"We all experience fear, Love. Nova and I have been unwinding since we saw you alive on the mountainside. We were afraid when we couldn't find you."

They scoot to either side of me, pressing up against me, shoulder to shoulder. I'm safe with them. What happened today makes me realize that a bond is growing.

Nova takes my hand in his and holds it on his lap. It brings me so much comfort. No one has ever comforted me, not even my mother. Shay wraps his arm around mine, while at the same time holding my other hand.

"Fear is part of life, Reagan. As Shay said, we all experience it. What you must decide is how to control that fear so it doesn't control you. We will always come for you. We will never abandon you."

Deep breaths in, long slow releases out. Release the fear, control it so it does not control me. For the first time in my life, I no longer feel alone. Somehow in this short time, in our way, we are connected now. Sitting in this cold cave with them at my side, it's like I'm home for the first time in my life. Closing my eyes, I let that thought sink in, relaxing even more, and this time when sleep comes for me, I don't fear the darkness.

CHAPTER 5

Every day, Shay shares more and more about the history of our land, and today he has been telling me about the gatherings on the Isle of the Crescent Moon which would take place during the Summer and Winter Solstices. The gatherings were for everyone, regardless of status.

There's a sacred temple on the isle, which was only used for these occasions. Located in the center of the temple is a large moonstone that allows the celebrants to combine their energies to draw in the power of the solstice moons. The power of the moon is then dispersed evenly throughout the gathering.

"The gatherings were masquerade balls," Shay smiles, perhaps bringing to mind a fond memory. "Everyone would dress in their finest attire, donning matching masks that conceal part of your face."

"That explains why I couldn't see anyone's faces in my vision the first time I held the Staff."

"Shay and I were three years old the last time we attended one." He hands me the Staff, and the vision of the gathering returns, only this time, I'm prepared for what I'm seeing.

"It all looks enchanting." I've never worn a dress, but I can't help wondering how I'd look in one as the figures in this captured memory twirl and dance in celebration.

The Staff starts to vibrate in my grip. The images become clouded in the same muted grays, greens, and blacks as Cormac's eyes. Opening my hand, I release the Staff. I don't want to see those twisted images again.

"It's a lot to take in, Reagan," Nova advises. "You must do it in small steps because there's something dark and sinister at work here. Those darker images are out of place, and you're right not to trust them. We must be careful not to be corrupted. You'll have to learn how to ignore the images, focusing only on that spark of power that's in your core."

Nova's deep intensity stirs something in me, and the contrast between this serious persona and the playful side of him I've seen when he and Shay tease each other and roughhouse gives me a sense of closeness I've lacked in my life.

Sometimes, when the terrain is difficult, even when I don't need help climbing over things, if Nova offers me his hand, I take it. Proximity to the charge I feel from the Staff is irresistible, and when I'm near Nova, I always feel the pull toward it. It's like it wants me to reach out and take it. But I keep that to myself.

The runes on the staff are interesting. The boys don't know what they mean. One looks like a tiny dagger, another a star, a circle, and one somewhat resembles a fork. When I hold the Staff, it's warm in my grip, almost like an extension of my arm. I'm no longer affected by nausea, thank the gods. I wonder if I can make that warm sensation spread farther than just my hand. I'd love to have the ability to warm myself. I hate being cold.

"It's strange, all of this that you've been telling me about us forgetting the solstice rituals. It's like we've all been robbed of who we truly are. To be honest, though, I've always felt different during the Summer Solstice, even without the gatherings. I felt more powerful. Do you know what I mean?"

"There are some in the Wolf Court that feel more powerful during the Winter Solstice," Shay replies.

"That makes sense, I suppose."

"Reagan, when exactly during the summer were you born?"

"On the Summer Solstice. Do you think that's significant?"

The boys exchange a quick look the way they so often do. I'm certain they can communicate and it's like being left out of the conversation. They both shrug in answer to my question.

The boys tell me about their encounter with Cormac, Rekker, and Osman the night Fin and I fled. They had received a report about them and other news.

They'd been tracking them for quite some time and the trail led them to our group of trainees. Once Fin and I separated from our group, Cormac followed us. Had they been targeting me all along?

"Before I left Outpost Three, Fin's father, Hamon—he's Captain of the Queen's Guard—told us of reports of disappearances and deaths. I wonder if it has something to do with them?"

"Did the Captain inform you of anything else, Rea?"

"He told Fin we must stick to the confines of the outposts, that he would meet us at Outpost Four before we departed."

"Did he give you a reason or warn of anything else? Think for a moment, Rea. Any detail might be helpful to shed some light, even if you think it's not important."

"He said bodies have been found mutilated and that they believe it's the work of shadow beasts. Have you heard similar reports?"

"We have." Nova's jaw sets, and I can almost hear him grinding his teeth. "That was the other information we received when we were advised of Cormac and his crew."

"Anything else you can think of, Rea?"

"No, at least nothing at the moment. I'm curious, why did you both volunteer to try to bring the Staff to the Phoenix Court?"

"Once Nova and I discovered the Staff and it broke the

glamour on us, we took it to the king and queen immediately. We knew we couldn't just sit around the Court, knowing the truth of what was happening."

"Reagan, our lands always had cold climates, particularly in the northern mountains. But whatever kind of darkness this is has made our kingdom a frozen wasteland. Your lands are not as harsh as ours, at least not yet. We fear it's only a matter of time if we can't figure out what's causing this and stop it."

"This is why it's so important we reach Glendalough," Shay affirms. "Because now, with our kingdom's glamour broken, we decided it had to be us to make the third attempt. We need to figure out who and what is causing this and more importantly, we need to gather during the upcoming solstice. We need our powers back."

THE FOLLOWING DAY, we push through another blizzard, stopping only periodically to rest. This is the worst storm we've seen. Even with Nova using his powers with the Staff, it's still extremely difficult to see and navigate the terrain. I'm freezing and grumpy. Summer fae have no tolerance for being cold, and this storm seems to be coming at us from every angle. Finally, we find an abandoned hunting shack, and Shay asks me to help him get a fire started while Nova finds dinner, but Nova's nowhere to be seen. "He's going out there alone?"

"Worried about him now, are we?"

"It's a blizzard out there. He could get lost."

"That sounds an awful lot like worry to me, Love."

"Don't be such an ass, Shay. Aren't you worried about your brother? Can't I be concerned for someone without it meaning something?"

"Except it's not just someone, is it?"

"I'd be concerned if it was you out there, too."

"Would you?"

"Yes." That seems to placate him for the moment, and I should probably leave it there, but before I can stop myself, another question tumbles out of my mouth. "What was it like growing up with Nova as a brother?"

He stops what he's doing and looks at me, though it's not his normal cocky smile; he's all serious again in the intense way Nova normally is. The same heat stirs within me, like when Nova looks at me that way. Oh, my gods, what am I thinking? Clearly, there's something wrong with me. Frozen delirium? Lack of sleep? The last thing I need to do is develop feelings for them both.

"I would not be where I am today, were it not for my brother. I was the troublemaker when we were kids, whereas Nova was always the top pupil in class, quiet and attentive to everything and everyone."

His words are filled with admiration and respect for Nova. It's written all over his face. There's a deep history and bond between them. Unbreakable, I bet.

"When we turned fourteen and entered our skills training programs, Nova started following me down the path of rebellion, which is a story for another time. Fortunately, he had more sense than me and pulled us both back to our respective paths. Without him, I would not be The Commander of the Wolf King's Army."

"You're the commander of the Wolf King's Army?" I'm a bit shocked, not to mention impressed.

"Indeed I am, Love."

"I was not expecting that, Commander."

"It's just Shay. Even members of the army and my cadre call me Shay. I'm a normal male, no different than anyone else. Who I am is in here." He points to his heart and his head. "Some only see the title and not the male that I am inside."

"I'm glad I met you as Shay, and not as the Commander of the Wolf King's army."

"I was born into this position, destined from birth."

The tone of sadness in his voice is hard to mistake. "It sounds like you had no choice."

"I did not. And I do appreciate that you recognize that. The members of my cadre are like family to me. To Nova and me both. They understand the burden I've carried since birth, as they have each carried similar burdens that have linked us all. Only one among us wasn't born to fill these positions."

"And how did that one become a member of your cadre, if he was not born into it?"

"He was found, near dead, on the shore of Port Kennedy, beaten within an inch of his life. I happened to be there when he was found. The rest is his story to share."

"And he is like your family too?"

"Absolutely. Family does not always have to be blood. I would give my life for him. For all of them."

He runs a hand through his hair, then rests his forearms on his knees. The firelight reflects off his bright blue eyes, and I know most will never see this side of him. My heart nearly stops when a smile spreads across his face, relaxed with no pretenses, no cockiness. Blue eyes, open, warm, and endless now gaze into mine.

Why can't I look away?

Why do I want to? There's a darkness in them calling to me. Like a thunderstorm off in the distant depths of his pupils waiting to take what it wants. Is that why I can't break free of his stare? Do I enjoy gazing into the darkness? Tension thrums inside me, and I feel like I need to break this moment before I find out how deep those eyes go.

"You said Nova was always quiet, watching, paying attention to everything, everyone."

"I did."

"He's still that way now. From what I've seen, anyway."

"How so, Love?"

"He's always monitoring me, watching me."

"How do you know he's always watching you? Are you always

watching him, monitoring him, to know that?" There is a taste of disappointment in his words.

"Why can't it be that I'm just observant?"

"So am I, Rea." He pauses, as if he has more to add, but thinks the better of it. "Have you not always had others make choices for you? Haven't you been forced to be where you're told to be?"

"Yes, and that's behind me now. Never again will someone else choose for me."

"If you're sure about that, then what about making quick decisions?"

"What's that supposed to mean?"

"Remember, Rea, we have choices. You have choices. Don't rush into things." I can't help feeling that he's referring to something very specific.

He turns his back to me and starts building a fire. For someone who is always joking, Shay, thank the Forgotten Gods, seems to know when not to push. Does he think I'm interested in Nova? Is Shay interested in me?

Why do I feel so unnerved? Closing my eyes, I picture Nova's calming sureness and inhale deeply, trying to settle myself. When I open my eyes, it's as if my thoughts conjured him from the air, as Nova's massive form appears at the mouth of the cave. My heart stops. He stands there, three rabbits in hand, looking over the small cave and fire.

Am I even breathing? Nova turns and looks at me. No, he looks *into* me. It's unlike anything I've seen or felt. His eyes pierce straight into me, seeming to ignite me from within. Heat blooms on my face, slowly warming and tingling its way down my throat and chest, and gods help me, straight to the apex of my thighs.

After we've eaten, we lie down to sleep, and just when I was starting to think Shay was unusually quiet, his laughter breaks the silence.

"What are you laughing at?"

"Just having a conversation in my head, Love."

"Care to share with the class?" I ask, foolishly taking what I can only assume is bait.

"I was thinking about your care and concern for us."

"I knew I should've kept my mouth shut."

"You asked."

"Why do you and Nova smell like peppermint and wintergreen?" I find it interesting, and I've never smelled scents on other males.

Silence. Absolute silence and it's out of character for him.

"It's . . . it's a winter fae thing," he mumbles and rolls over.

This is the coldest night yet. My bones feel frozen as shivers overrun my body almost to the point of pain. Rolling onto my side, I curl up in my blanket. Without a word, Shay and Nova move at the same time. Nova is spooning me from behind while Shay is in front, cocooning me in warmth. How, in the depths of the shadows, did they do that in unison? They move together in such a fluid rhythm. It's fascinating and annoying.

Lying this close to Nova, I can feel the power vibrating from the Staff. "Nova, why are you sleeping with that thing?"

"That's not his Staff you're feeling, Love."

Nova delivers a punch to him, right over my body, effectively silencing him. Good. After that, Nova throws the Staff in a direction away from us. Blushing deeply, I close my eyes and try to sleep, with Nova still on my mind.

CHAPTER 6

Upon waking, it takes me a moment to remember where I am, as I am comfortably warm. Much to my delight, I'm half-sprawled over Nova's massive body. Inhaling deeply, I prepare to stand. Oh no.

Peppermint.

It's Shay. I've even managed to throw one of my legs over him and something hard, maybe a dagger, is pressing into my leg. I should get up quickly, before he wakes.

"I assure you, Love, that's not Nova's Staff you're feeling this morning," Shay mumbles in my ear, breaking my frantic internal monologue.

"I curse you to The Darkness." Tightening my fist, I punch him in the gut before getting up, grabbing my coat, and walking out of the cave, humiliated. As I step outside, the brightness momentarily blinds me. This is so embarrassing. Those two idiots were probably lying awake the whole time, having one of their special conversations knowing I had woken up, panicking. Why couldn't I have woken up snuggling Nova? It was him I was thinking about when I fell asleep. Shay will never let me forget this.

When I return, they're not there, which is a relief. Feeling mortified, I decide to occupy myself by packing. As I gaze at Nova's pack, I notice the Staff lying underneath it. Almost instinctively, I reach out to pick it up, my mind racing with curiosity. A warmth spreads through my core, and my body trembles.

The welcoming warmth intensifies, and I'm relieved the disturbing images are gone. The Staff hums comfortably, stirring the power in my core. Having power within me and being unable to unleash it is an unusual sensation, one that leaves me feeling both frustrated and euphoric at the same time. It's like trying to breathe with a heavy weight on my chest.

"Easy, Reagan." His voice startles me, and the Staff falls from my hands as I stumble back with the loss of its power. No, the loss of *my* power, I realize. Nova catches my arm, steadying me. "Your eyes had flickers of flames in them," he adds.

"Does that mean I have some kind of fire power?"

"I'm not sure. But it would explain why your core heats up."

"How so?"

"Because I experience a freezing effect with my winter-storm-like powers, and Shay feels a static charge."

"How does fire power work? What can I do with it?"

He shrugs with a smile. "I'm not sure. Fire seems like more of a Summer fae thing. But something tells me that this will come to you quickly. Just remember, you must pace yourself. Like Shay, your powers will be sporadic at first. I can help you understand your powers beyond our journey to Glendalough. Imagine breaking the spell that's been holding us back, unleashing your true powers and abilities. Once we break the spell and release the glamour, you'll be ready."

A little breathless and not knowing what to say, I nod. Nova smiles my favorite smile before turning to pack. I watch him for a moment, inhaling his wintergreen scent.

"You all right, Love?" Shay chuckles, startling me, appearing literally out of nowhere. He has a wicked, annoying knack for doing that.

"You should wear a bell," I grumble. "I'm curious, what's so special about you that the Wolf King himself would let you leave the kingdom with the Staff of Storms? The one artifact that can break the glamour and reveal the truth?"

"I already told you, Love, I'm the Commander of the Wolf King's Army."

"Okay, so if you're the Commander, why did you bring Nova with you?"

"Nova is one of the few I trust in this frozen wasteland to have my back." He grins, and I find myself grinning back. "It's also pretty damn convenient to be able to communicate without speaking."

"You and Nova read each other's minds?"

They share, yet again, one of their special looks. "Yes, we can communicate telepathically."

"I knew it!" I exclaim. Now he's smiling like a fiend, and suddenly, a new fear grips me. "Can either of you read my mind?"

"I know what you're thinking just by looking at you, Love."

"No, you don't. Please tell me you can't." For the love of the Forgotten Gods, please let him say no.

"As much as I'd love to know what's going on inside that beautiful head of yours, we are not able to read anyone else's mind." He sighs melodramatically, finishing it off with a pout. Adorable jerk.

"It's been that way as long as we can remember," Nova states. "Despite the spell, we have always been able to communicate telepathically."

"What do you feel beyond the heat when you hold the Staff?" Shay probes, changing the subject.

"It's like a pull. As if I'm drawn to it. Is it the same for you?"

"It is," Nova confirms. "We can do this together, the three of us. We can speak to the King and Queen, find your sister, then we can try to figure out what's repressing our powers and causing the glamour."

"We work well together, Love." I can't tell if Shay is trying to reassure me or flirt with me.

"Whoever this Shadow King and Cormac are, it has to be related to them," Nova surmises.

"What do you say, Rea? Interested in taking a position with the Wolf King's Army?"

They look excited and eager to combine our quests, stay together, and help each other. Shay's right—we do work well together. After another moment of thought, I nod.

"Together," I announce.

"Together," they agree.

Their smiles turn devious, and something tells me I'm going to be in deep trouble with these two. "So why do I suddenly feel like I made a deal with The Darkness?"

"No darkness here, Love, just the handsome Commander of the Wolf King's Army and his less attractive twin brother Donovan, the Crown Prince of The Kingdom of the Wolf Moon."

"Twin brother? Crown Prince Donovan . . . Nova?"

"Yes," they respond in unison, their devious smiles still on full display.

"Well, shit."

"Don-o-van." On the walk outside the cave I sound it out because the way Shay said it sounded like *Don-a-vin*. That's where they got the nickname Nova. Unbelievable. "That's why you were able to leave with the Staff. Because he's the Crown Prince, and you're the commander."

"We had already decided no more would be lost," Shay tells me.

"Why did you not tell me?"

"Did you not hide who you were at first?"

"That's different."

"How so, Rea? We had just as much to be cautious about,"

Shay points out. "You only told us because you slipped up," he adds, knowing he has me there.

"Fair enough, but you can't blame me for being surprised." Surprised is an understatement—shocked is more like it. This entire time I have been traveling with the princes of the Wolf Moon. Unbelievable. Shay is looking at me like he can read my mind, and I know he sees my wheels spinning. Then the insufferable jerk winks at me.

"You're an ass," I tell him.

"You love me, and you know it. You're just too stubborn to admit it."

"Oh, my gods. The sheer level of arrogance you possess is astonishing. Although it makes sense now, Prince Shay." I add a mocking bow.

"You'd find something else I possess quite astonishing, too." He laughs.

My face must be beet red. I can't come up with a comeback.

"I've heard from the females in his army that he's a jackrabbit in the sack and often leaves them unsatisfied," Nova chips in from over his shoulder.

"Ha! I knew your mouth was compensating for something. Hilarious. I bet you have a mirror on you that you practice that sexy pouty face of yours in."

"So, you do find me sexy. Intriguing. Tell me, Love, did it start the night you held me tightly in my sleep?"

I knew he would throw that in my face eventually. Shame flares and turns to anger. I charge him as fast as I can, slamming my body into his. The impact almost depletes my lungs of air as I tackle him to the ground, shoveling snow in his mouth.

"Not so sexy with a mouth full of snow, are you, Prince Shay."

The jerk is laughing so hard that he's not putting up a fight. It takes the fun right out of it. We sit up, him still laughing, when out of nowhere, a snowball hits him smack in the face. Laughter bursts from me, and it takes me a moment to catch my breath.

"What was that for, brother?" Shay wipes the snow from Nova's surprise attack out of his hair.

I turn toward Nova and take a direct hit to my face. "A traitor in our midst! Shay, you're about to become the crown prince. Let's get him!"

Shay and I jump to our feet, but Nova's already drawn up his powers and has created a highly localized shield of storms. It's incredible how he's learning to create and manipulate winter storms. I stop, mesmerized by what looks like a spinning vortex of snow. I can't see anything behind it. It's amazing and beautiful.

"That is not fair, you do—" Another snowball to my face. "Are you kidding me?"

I run as hard as I can because there's no way Nova will let me slam into that shield and hurt myself. Four feet away I launch into the air, smiling because I know he's going down hard.

My neck crumples painfully into my chest as I bounce off his shield and land flat on my hindquarters.

"You are both insufferable jerks." Grabbing my pack, I flip them off and walk away.

I'm beginning to suspect there might be a little jealousy between them. Does that mean they're both interested in me? How have I gone my whole life with no one showing the slightest interest in me to two males at once—and they're brothers? I know I should avoid them romantically, no matter what their vulnerable moments, intense stares, and rumbly voices do to me. They have a bond I refuse to come between. I won't be the cause of infighting among brothers, especially ones with destinies as important as theirs.

"Shay meant what he offered you."

I spin around with my hands on my hips, infuriated.

"He has the power to make you a part of the Wolf King's Army and become a part of his cadre."

I swallow my anger and try to see the bigger picture. This

could be the first step toward freedom for me and Willa. "You've mentioned your cadre before. What is it?"

"It's my elite military unit," Shay reveals. "It's made up of what I like to call unique fae."

I'd be interested to know what he considers unique. "Why are you the commander of the King's Army if Nova's the Crown Prince?"

"Nova's job will be to run the kingdom, my job is to protect it. And until the day of his coronation, he is a member of the Wolf King's Army and my cadre."

"Shay has complete power and authority over the King's Army, over and above our father, and one day, over me. When we were born, our father decided that we would have equally important roles. As the firstborn and heir apparent, I was named Crown Prince, and Shay was raised as our kingdom's protector."

"If I agree to join your cadre, and I'm not saying I will, would I be able to take Willa with me?"

"Of course. Arrangements can be made for you both," Nova answers. "Lodging and education for you both if you would like. She wouldn't be in the army unit, of course, but she could be named as your ward."

"So, it's the same in the Wolf Court that only the royal and high-born get an education?" I hear the accusation in my voice but cannot control it.

"Don't be so quick to judge, Reagan. Our parents have long disliked that education was not offered to all. It's something our Kingdom is actively working on despite the glamour."

"I'm sorry, sometimes I don't know when to keep my mouth shut." Sometimes? More like all the time. What is it with me and my fiery temper? "This is all a bit overwhelming. Thank you. It means a lot and it does sound wonderful." This would be my choice. "I want to think about it a little more, please."

"Of course, Reagan, we would expect nothing less."

CHAPTER 7

Since our encounter with Cormac, we have increased our pace considerably. Our main objective is to reach Glendalough as quickly as possible. Who is this Shadow King? What does he want with me? And are the disappearances related?

Thankfully, the snow is shallower and easier to navigate now that we're out of the mountains. The forest floor is only covered with around an inch of snow, which makes the barren forest floor a relief. Nova doesn't have to magically clear a path for us.

"Do you feel that?" The ground rumbles beneath my feet.

"It's horses," Nova says.

We dart behind snowy bushes near the edge of the tree line. A rush of fear and anticipation washes over me. From this vantage point, we'll have a clear view of whoever is coming. The ground beneath me trembles as the thundering of hooves fills the air. My heart races with excitement as I prepare for what's to come.

"There." Nova points west.

"It's the Queen's Guard. It's Fin and the Captain," I say, my jaw dropping in surprise. Over and over I scream their names, yet they can't hear me from this distance. Breaking from the woods and into an expanse of flatlands, I run forward, the boys hot on my heels as I throw caution to the wind. They're almost across the flatlands. Once they enter the forest, they'll never see or hear us.

My feet dig into the snow-covered ground as I skid to a stop, causing the boys to almost collide with me. "Nova, the Staff! Use your powers."

He takes a deep breath, his piercing blue eyes seem to intensify, and suddenly a flurry of snow swirls around us. The temperature drops rapidly, sending shivers down my spine. I exhale, and my breath transforms into a dense, frosty mist that envelops my face and obscures my vision, adding to the already palpable sense of anxiety I'm feeling at the thought of Fin disappearing into the trees. Nova unleashes a fierce winter storm that engulfs Fin and the guards, leaving them struggling to keep their footing amidst the howling winds and blinding snow. I start running forward again, closing the distance between us.

Once it clears, I scream Fintan's name again. This time I have their attention.

Hamon, Fin, and about a dozen Queen's Guards circle back around to us.

The moment Fin sees me, he jumps off his horse and runs toward me with a big smile on his face, like a happy puppy in an almost euphoric state, shouting my name over and over.

Before he's even come to a complete stop, my right arm is already cocked back, ready to deliver a well-deserved punch into his cowardly face. He crumples to the ground, landing hard on his ass, just as I've been envisioning for weeks since he abandoned me.

Rage fuels me as I remember what it was like when he left me alone, bound and cold. If it had been Cormac who found me instead of Nova and Shay, I could be dead right now—or worse. He was my only friend. Jumping on top of him, I pummel his face. I get a couple of solid shots in before someone's arms suddenly wrap around me, and I smell peppermint. It's Shay.

He lifts me off Fin's body, backing us away before putting me back on my feet. Placing his hands on my shoulders, he looks me straight in the eyes. "Easy, Love. I understand you were betrayed, but I assure you, you will regret this if you kill him. Trust me, that was enough."

"I will regret nothing."

"What's going on here? Who are you, and why are you touching her?" Hamon questions.

Sidestepping Shay, I close in on Hamon. "Who do you think *you* are to presume you can ask why someone's hands are on me?" His guards tense around him, and he raises a hand. It stops them instantly. Impressive.

"Please let us get back to the capital, then I can explain everything more clearly. I'm still looking for answers myself. We can figure this out together." He's trying to reason with me. Why? He's got a full complement of guards, and I just attacked his son. My suspicious mind spins.

"'Together' is what your son told Reagan before he abandoned her in a cave." Nova steps up behind me. I feel the wall of his strength at my back. "We had just come back and heard the exchange."

"You were both there when he left me?"

"We were standing right outside the cave, Love. It was just after we led Cormac and his crew away."

"Why did you let him leave?"

"You seemed to be the sensible one," Shay replies. "The last thing we wanted to deal with was a panicking boy. We let him make the choice."

"Choice between what?" Fin pouts. Blood coats his nose and mouth and much to my delight his left eye is beginning to swell. He grabs a handful of snow and holds it against the dent my knuckles left.

"Standing like a male and protecting Rea or running away like a scared rabbit to save your own skin." Shay spits on the ground, making his opinion clear.

"You tucked tail and ran, like the coward you are," Nova adds. Storms begin building in his eyes. The air chills around us.

Hamon looks both embarrassed and angered. "Is this true, son?"

"I was going to get you to help us, Father," Fin alleges, now trying to stand taller. It's not working at all.

"Captain, she was only handcuffed," Nova informs him.

"Don't forget he took the food, too. And if he was going for help, why is it a surprise to you, Captain, to find out that he left her?" Shay eyes Fin like he would like to add a broken nose to his injuries.

"Fintan!" Hamon shouts so loudly it almost scares me. "You said you lost her in the snowstorm."

"Father, I was going—"

"I ordered you to protect her!" Hamon bellows.

"He's not too good at following orders." I turn my rage back to Fin. "You should've dragged me out of that cave, not left me to fate. This is not over." I wonder again why Hamon gave a specific order for my protection, but Fin interrupts before I get the chance.

"I was trying to help her. It's their fault, Father, they attacked us. I'm not a coward. I went for help."

"Do not blame us, boy," Shay growls, fighting to maintain his control. "It was you who attacked us, and we had no choice but to defend ourselves. When you deserted her in that cave, she was begging you to help her. And yet, you still left her behind."

The realization hits me that they heard all of it.

Fin looks away from Shay and has the nerve to glare at me with hatred in his eyes.

"Why is he calling you 'Love'? Are you sleeping with him? With them? Figures you turn out to be a whore like your moth—"

A blizzard explodes around us, and Fin is blasted back about a hundred feet, landing face down in the snow. When he rolls over, he is looking into the face of death, because incredibly

Nova is already there. Did he just transport himself within a storm?

"If you ever disrespect Reagan again, you sniveling coward, I don't care who your father is, I'll impale your skull with this Staff. Do you understand?"

I hope Fin pisses his pants. I can't believe he called me a whore.

"Reagan," Hamon intones, his calm demeanor presumably intended to defuse the rapidly escalating situation, and probably to save his treacherous son. "I'm sorry for my son's inexcusable behavior. Please, let us all speak for a moment. It's about time introductions are made."

"Indeed it is, Captain," Shay states, pulling himself up to his full height. Suddenly he seems . . . regal. Hard to believe this is the same male that flirts and makes sexual innuendos.

I gather my wits and step forward, one eye on my former friend. "This is Shay, the Commander of the Wolf King's Army, and that"—I point toward Nova—"is Donovan, the Crown Prince of The Wolf Moon Court." Hamon's guards drop to one knee, bowing. "And I am now a member of Commander Shay's army."

Hamon is shocked by this revelation. "Reagan, you must return to Glendalough with me. I will not abandon you—"

"Nova and Shay will not abandon me."

"I understand that you are angry, but you are a summer fae, and we have much to discuss. Can I please have an explanation as to what in the depth of the shadows that weapon is that Prince Donovan carries?"

Thunder booms in the sky above, and we all turn toward Nova.

He takes a step away from Fin, disappearing into the snow, and reappears directly in front of the captain. Nova towers over him. Hamon, much to his credit, shows no sign of fear or discomfort. Again, impressive.

"Reagan goes where she likes. Your son's betrayal absolved

her of any fealty to the Phoenix Court. Is it your intention to honor her choice?"

Hamon considers for a moment, then answers carefully. "It is not my place to make decisions for her."

"Then we may greet you in friendship." Nova offers his hand. Hamon shakes it without hesitation. "Captain, you may call me Nova. Only my parents call me Donovan."

"It's a pleasure to meet you, Nova." Hamon bows respectfully and then walks the few steps to Shay. They share the same exchange.

The boys fill him and his guards in on all the details about the glamour and potential curse repressing our powers. Once this is over, it will be my turn to ask questions.

Hamon looks as skeptical as I was as he takes hold of the Staff. I wonder if he'll last as long as I did. After fifteen minutes, Hamon collapses to the ground, sobbing.

"Father, are you okay? What did you do to him?" Fin shoots a nasty look at Nova.

I'd really like to punch Fin in the face again, repeatedly. Shay places his hand on my shoulder, mouthing *no* to me. I guess he's gotten to know me pretty well throughout our journey.

"Fintan, for once in your life, read the crowd. Does anyone else look worried?" Hamon grumbles as he struggles to stand. Nova offers him a hand, and Hamon accepts with a nod.

"But, Father—"

"Fintan, for the love of the Forgotten Gods, stop talking."

"It's a lot to take in," Nova tells him. "It's been months for Shay and me, and we still struggle, both physically and mentally."

I love how Nova and Shay are unashamed to admit weakness. I've never heard males do that so openly.

"It's like I have been living in a fog, confused," Hamon expresses. "It makes sense now. Some of it anyway. Can you unglamour my guards?"

"Hamon, why did you order Fin to protect me? Are you . . . are you, my father?"

"No."

"Do you know who my father is?"

"It's more complicated than that. I will explain once we return."

"Why do you get answers, but then won't answer my questions? I deserve to know the truth, which you are so obviously hiding."

"If I could show you what I just saw through the magic of this Staff, it would answer your question," Hamon tells me.

"Hamon," Nova starts. "Your memories are now infused into the Staff. We don't understand what magic allows the transfer, but if you hold it with Reagan, you can direct, somewhat, what you want her to see by thinking about that time."

"However, as you have now seen, it's always the last solstice gathering," Shay adds.

"That's what I saw, the last solstice gathering where my sister was married. Reagan, we are related, I'm certain of it."

The answer to who my father is could be right there. Why am I hesitating? I only need to reach out and take the Staff. I'm no coward. Would that mean Willa is not my sister? Is this why I hesitate?

Reaching out, I take the Staff from Nova. A raging fire builds in my core with every beat of my heart.

"Reagan, your eyes are flames. Like twin suns burning bright," Nova's voice is filled with wonder.

Power courses through my veins like a thundering river of lava. "Take the Staff, Hamon," I demand. I'm certain I could breathe fire right now if I wanted to. He hesitates for a few seconds before finally reaching out and taking hold of the Staff.

Instantly, I'm back at the Summer Solstice ball. This time, though, I'm closer to the center of the dais, near the moonstone. I see the kings and queens of both kingdoms. A wedding. The Phoenix King and Queen remove fiery orange-and-black-feathered masks.

The queen's face is my own.

Is this past or future? Why am I marrying a king? Not just any king: the Phoenix King. Hamon's here too, standing at my side. Somehow I recognize him, even despite the mask he wears. What is this? Something doesn't feel right. Bile rises in the back of my throat and sweat coats my body, but I refuse to let go of the vision.

A winter fae female with bright blue eyes stands at Hamon's side, holding his hand. As they remove their masks, I notice the matching wedding bands. Hamon's married to a winter fae, and she's strikingly beautiful.

I open my eyes and see that Nova is also holding the Staff.

"Why did I see myself getting married?"

Hamon's eyes pop open at the sound of my voice. He seems to hesitate again.

"Hamon!"

"That was my memory of my sister Ava getting married, not you, Reagan."

"Why do I look identical to your sister?"

"Reagan, you have to believe me. I don't understand how any of this is possible. Whoever is pretending to be your parents are not. My sister Ava is your mother. You're my niece."

"But your sister is the . . . She was marrying the . . ."

I'm a princess. Well shit.

CHAPTER 8

After what Hamon experienced, he recommends that we secure the area while the boys unglamour the Queen's Guard, figuring it could take a couple of hours. There are gasps of shock, and some of them get sick afterward. You would think I'd be happy to hear that Ciara's not my mother, that I'm a princess instead.

But that would mean Willa's not my sister. What should be joyful knowledge feels like despair. The only good thing in my life was a lie. My mind swirls with questions instead of being excited at what might lie ahead of me. Why have I spent my life knee-deep in abuse and poverty? Have my parents ever tried to find me? Why has no one noticed my resemblance to the queen? What in the depths of the shadows am I to do now?

The boys glance at me often, making sure I'm okay. I smile and nod, but the smile is hollow, and they know it. Some time later, I'm standing alone by a small fire when Nova and Shay approach.

"Mind if we join you, Reagan?"

"Not at all."

"What's going on in your head?" Shay's words are playful, but his tone is tender.

"Willa," I mumble. "She's . . . she's not . . ." I can't get the words out. It's almost as if saying it out loud makes it more real.

"It doesn't matter if Willa is not blood. She's still your sister, Reagan."

I understand what he's saying, and in my heart, I know he's right, but somehow, I'm not comforted. "Then what of my claim to her?"

"Reagan, you're the Princess of the Kingdom of the Phoenix Moon. Your parents are the King and Queen. You have the authority to remove her from an abusive home if that's what you want to do. You will still have your sister."

"I wish I could make you understand why I feel so desperate about this. Ciara abused me right up until she put me on that wagon of trainees. She said the beatings would make me stronger. Willa has been alone for four years with them. She doesn't know I did not abandon her. And because she doesn't know that, I feel like I did." Tears prickle the corners of my eyes, and I squeeze my eyes to try to keep them from falling.

"Reagan, I had no idea how bad things were for you—"

"Of course not. How could you? I need to take Willa away with me, with you both, like we talked about."

"You can still come with us, Love, but things need to be discussed with the King and Queen of the Phoenix Court. They are your parents."

"Then why have they never looked for me? How could they let me be raised like that? I want no part of them. You have no idea what it's like to be a low-born, to be poverty-stricken."

"Don't forget they have been glamoured your entire life," Nova reminds me. "There's no telling what effect it may have had on their minds and memories. Give us a chance to reach them, to free their minds. This might have been out of their control."

"We are here for you, for anything, and I understand why you'd be angry with them. But Nova's right. You have to find out the answers to your questions." Shay lays a comforting hand on my shoulder. "It will be your choice to go with us or stay in Glendalough. Just don't go off half-cocked and angry."

"I'm not going to change my mind."

"We need to go. Hamon's guards are ready," Shay advises. "He has horses for us. I hope when you see Fintan, it will cheer you up a bit."

The boys and I assume the rear position alongside Hamon. It affords us a bit of privacy to fill Hamon in on Cormac kidnapping me and the information we got from Osman.

Hamon agrees it's something we should look into once we reach the capital. After meeting the king and queen. I look at Fin to see what Shay was chuckling about. When I finally spot him, I see that Fin's riding doubled up with one of the Queen's Guards. It's hard to tell which one looks more uncomfortable. I queue up an appropriate insult to hurl at him, but I choke on it before I can let it loose because I realize that Fin and I are cousins. Figures.

"So, tell us, how did you become Captain of the Queen's Guard?" Even though he's so much younger, Shay is all business as he talks military with Hamon.

"King Fitz and I have been friends since the age of fourteen. We met during the skills training program. Everyone else was afraid to spar with the crown prince. I, however, had no problem knocking him on his ass, over and over. And yes, we all know my sister is the queen. However, I have earned my position after decades of hard work. It was not just given to me. "

"We may become friends yet," Shay guffaws. "My cadre is made up of similar members. The ones not afraid to knock Nova and me around. I respect that, Captain."

"Please, call me Hamon. If I'm to address the Wolf Moon Princes so informally, I insist you do the same, Commander."

At this rate, there won't be much left to surprise me by the time we get to Glendalough. Life seems to be this ever-evolving deluge of events one right after another. If the last few weeks have taught me anything, it's to always expect the unexpected.

WE ENTER through the city gates, and the familiar sounds and smells wash over me. Street performers juggle or put on puppet shows for the children while their parents chatter about inconsequential things. Vendors with carts sell everything from clothing to freshly baked bread. The smell makes my stomach growl and my mouth water. This market is in one of the wealthier areas of the city, and the goods are far more expensive than anything I've ever been able to buy. I find myself grinding my teeth when I think about the social segregation in my home city. Just one more thing my parents need to answer for.

The low-born make their livings down the darkened alleys, so close to these bustling streets, but always away, apart, conveniently out of sight so the privileged might enjoy their pampered lives without having reality stare them in the face. Gods forbid they see we're underfed, poorly clothed, and clad in black and blue hues like the jewelry adorning their bodies. A single piece could feed a family of four for an entire year. Out of sight, out of mind. This is exactly why The Courtless exist. This is exactly why hatred spreads like wildfire, infecting every poor, hungry, cold person out here.

When the castle comes into view, I am shocked by its appearance. The normally bright bronze spires, turrets, and keeps are muted by the snow. Inside, the walkways are coated in murky slush. It should be a thing of beauty, but the permanent winter has taken its toll.

Walking into the throne room, though, is unlike anything I've ever seen. The massive open space is filled with bustling servants. Guards line the walls. The king and queen peer down at our approaching party from their thrones on a raised dais. The king and queen. My parents. This still doesn't feel real. I have no connection to or love for the aloof couple in front of me, but I came here for answers. And for Willa. I'll do anything for Willa. This will all be over soon, and we can leave. Together.

While I did spend fourteen years of my life in this city, I've never been anywhere like this. Our court crest hangs in every other window from the floor to the fifty-foot ceiling. It's painted white, trimmed in gold, with a large golden sun and a Phoenix in mid-flight.

There's so much wasted space between us and the thrones. Who needs this much space? It's ridiculous, or maybe it's me. This feels like the longest walk of my life. I understand what Nova said—Willa will always be my sister. Can I take her away with me, like Shay said? Or could we possibly live in this castle, like sister princesses? If I had a position of power, maybe I could use it to help the poor. This might have possibilities.

And what of Emily, the current princess? Who is she to me? An impostor or a blood sister? Fear overtakes my anger. Nova must sense my faltering and offers his arm. I gladly take it, which steadies me and starts to calm my nerves almost immediately.

"Willa is still your sister," he whispers.

The queen's face comes into focus as we approach. She *is* my mother. I can not only see it in our similar features, but I can *feel* it. It hits me right then, the connection, our bond. It's a pull, like a tugging sensation on my heartstrings, drawing us together. She stands at the same time. The sharp intake of her breath fills the silent room. Something in her eyes clears, and I hear her say, "My daughter." And then she comes toward me, as if pulled by the same bond I feel. She moves like flowing water, so graceful is she as she descends from the dais.

Guards move in to surround her, but Hamon stops them with a simple gesture. She runs the last few steps and wraps her arms around me. I overhear Hamon explaining who the boys are and what's been happening. This is awkward. I have no love for this female, only contempt for a distant and uncaring Queen. Yet tears escape my eyes.

"Look at me, Reagan. I always knew that sweet child Emily was not mine, but I loved her and raised her as my own. But I see you, I feel you. We will always be together now. Come. We have so much to talk about."

She wipes my tears away. The gesture causes more and we laugh, identically. Unbelievable. This is overwhelming. I spent years in the gutters of this city while the queen ignored us low-born. It's unsettling. I need to take this one step at a time. After this, I'll ask about Willa.

The king walks over and looks at me with tears in his eyes. My father. It's the same connection. "You sound like your mother when you laugh," he whispers, his voice cracking with emotion.

"Unfortunately, she has your mouth," Hamon quips.

"Truly?" The king laughs, and it's a warm and comforting sound. He puts his arm around my shoulders. "Let us go to a more private room to discuss this joyous development."

Once we enter an opulent private dining room, I find the voice for the most important thought in my head. "What about my sister, Willa?"

"Is she the sibling you grew up with?" the queen inquires.

"We also have an older sister, Kira, but she's as hateful as the monster who raised me. I don't care about her."

Hamon sends guards to locate Willa and Ciara and finally introduces Nova and Shay to my parents. My parents? I still can't get used to it. The boys explain what's been happening with the glamour and repression spell or curse as they call it, then my parents take hold of the Staff together.

"I'm a falconer." The queen's eyes are glazed with the memory. "How could I forget that?"

"A what?" I have no idea what she's talking about.

"A falconer. I'm able to link my mind with any of my falcons, see what they see, and have them go where I wish. Our minds become one."

"I'm still not sure what my powers are. I'm not even entirely sure what powers exist in our world."

"I will help you, my child. There is so much you have to learn."

As the guards enter with Ciara, my body recoils at the sight of her. She is alone.

"Where's Willa?" I demand.

"We were unable to locate the child, m'lady," the guard responds.

"I'm not asking you, I'm asking *her*." If I could stare a hole right through Ciara, I would. She sneers at my question.

"Is this the female who raised you?" The queen's voice has an edge to it.

"Listen to me, girl. You don't belong here," Ciara snarls. "You're destined for much more. The King and Queen have never cared about the suffering of the low-born. They live in this lavish palace while we scrape and beg for food. I opened your eyes to them. I saved you from being like this." She waves her hand dismissively at the royals before her.

I hate this female with every fiber of my being, but I need to play along, for Willa.

"You and I both know I'm no princess. I don't know what you mean by my destiny, and I don't really care either. But I must know, is Willa my sister?" I can't help sounding desperate as my hubris vanishes.

Ciara's eyes narrow. "I suppose you'll know the truth soon anyway. Willa is not your sister, but Princess Emily is. You share the same father." She licks her lips while looking at my father, and I get the sudden urge to vomit. "Kira isn't your sister either. She's my sister. Much younger, of course."

"This is preposterous. I've never laid with this female," my father splutters.

"How is all this possible?" My mother looks like she can't decide if she's angry at Ciara or my father.

"I glamoured myself to look like you." She laughs. "It was simple. The night you gave birth was horrible for you. Under the influence of all the tonics administered to you, you had no idea what you birthed that night. I glamoured you to believe Emily was yours. A missing princess would have created problems I did not want to deal with. A blood-heir swap was easier and quite easy for a wet nurse. And that's exactly what I did a few days after I gave birth."

"How can you be so crass when you're speaking of infants as if they're clothing? I will have your head for this!" The queen's fists clench in rage.

"Ciara," I begin again, trying to keep the focus on Willa, and not on Ciara being beheaded, "please, tell me where Willa is."

"All I can say for now is that there is a prophecy about a female born the third generation in a row of female Summer Solstice births. That's you." Ciara points a grubby finger at me.

"I was born on the Summer Solstice," my mother mutters, trying to understand. "As was my mother before me."

Shay and Nova are exchanging a look, having one of their silent conversations. I don't have time to wonder what's going on between them right now.

"I don't care about your supposed prophecy, Ciara. Stop with your games. Please let me have Willa."

"Come with me, or you will never see her or Princess Emily again." She turns her wicked gaze to the king.

"What's the meaning of this?" my father thunders. "Where are Emily and Willa?"

I hold up my hand, silencing the king. I must keep her talking, find out what I can before she stops. "Why did you put me into the training program? And where are Willa and Emily?"

"Come with me, girl, and I'll tell you everything. They'll use you for the power of three."

"The power of three? What are you talking about? I asked where Willa and Emily are? Enough of these riddles, Ciara."

"Not unless—"

"Enough!" my father shouts. "Guards, seize her."

The guards start moving. In the blink of an eye, Ciara pulls a dagger from the inside of her cloak, and before I realize what's happened, it becomes shadow and smoke. I scream as the shadowy blade sails through the air, piercing my father straight through his heart. Grabbing his chest, he turns to my mother. "I'm sorry, Ava." The dagger resolidifies, then he collapses to the floor, dead.

My mother is screaming. Am I screaming? Everyone is screaming, although I don't hear what they're saying. This hateful female who has tortured me my whole life took my father from me before I even got to know him.

Blood pounds in my ears as despair and rage consume me. Running, I grab the Staff from Nova's side before he has time to react. I let my hatred of Ciara fill me with a need for revenge.

Cocking my arm back, I swing the Staff right at Ciara's head. A satisfying crack sounds when it connects with her skull. She hits the floor hard, landing on her hands and knees. Hopping forward on my left foot, I swing my right leg as hard as I can and kick her in the face. The force propels her over, and she lands flat on her back.

Blood pours from her mouth and nose. The look of fear in her eyes shouldn't make me feel this good; nonetheless, I embrace it. I welcome it. I stand over her, breathing heavily. "Last chance. Where are my sisters?"

"Not unless you leave with me."

"Reagan!" the queen shouts, but I don't look away from Ciara, my heart full of fire and my mind numb with molten rage. "We need her alive," she pleads with me.

Guards move in around me. Before they reach us, I lay the Staff at my side and bring my fist down across her nose, breaking it. I can't think of a single good reason to keep her alive, so I wrap my hands around her throat, ready to choke out her last breath.

Someone grabs me from behind, pulling me off Ciara. I quickly grab the Staff. The guards roll her onto her stomach and secure her hands with cuffs. My heart pounds with rage with every beat.

"Reagan, let me have the Staff, please," Nova begs me, and his voice cuts through my vengeful haze when nothing else has. "Your mother speaks the truth. We need her alive. Your sisters are now among the missing. Refocus, breathe." He leans against me, filling my senses with the cool, relaxing wintergreen scent he exudes.

He's right. I need to calm myself. After a few deep breaths in and out, I finally release my death grip and give the Staff to him without a word. Tears stream down my mother's cheeks. Ciara screams and babbles like a lunatic as she is led away, fury written all over her face.

Chaos erupts around us. The queen, my mother, is ushered away for her safety as the palace is put on lockdown. Hamon leads us to the guest rooms we will be sharing. He insists on extra security, and the boys and I do not object.

CHAPTER 9

The days following my father's death and funeral are a
fog. My mother gained her true daughter only to lose
her husband the same day. It's amazing watching her
handle her grief with such grace, and I wonder if that's where I
inherited my determination. She's pushing through pain and
heartache while still managing some of the daily tasks of running
her kingdom. Although I'm angry and filled with rage because
she is responsible for keeping the low-born repressed, now is not
the time to voice that. My two sisters are among the missing,
and I can't help but feel like it's somehow my fault.

Hamon brought me a book on fae powers last night, and I
stayed up far too late pouring over it. It's the first thing on my
mind this morning. As I glanced through it, what stood out right
away is that there are different kinds of mind readers—some
have powers of telepathic conversation like Nova and Shay, but
some can read your thoughts without you knowing. That
frightens me.

Some fae have the power of telekinesis, the ability to use
their mind to move things. Nova's storm magic is sort of like
that, except he uses the snow and wind to do it. I flip through,
hoping to find a section on fire wielders. The boys saw flames in

my eyes, so maybe I can wield fire the way Nova can wield snow. The book is thick, though, and it will take me a while to learn all of this. I only got started last night.

"Morning." I force a smile as I enter my mother's private dining room. I have not adjusted to palace life and still feel guilty eating in such opulence. Thank the Forgotten Gods only Nova and Shay are present, since contempt is surely written all over my face.

"Good morning, Reagan," Nova replies. "Hamon stopped by earlier while you were sleeping. He is ready for us to go see Ciara."

"Has anyone questioned her?" I ask.

"Hamon has, and she keeps babbling about the power of three and saying that the Shadow King cannot be stopped."

"You need to eat before we go," Shay advises.

"Agreed," I affirm, then start piling food on a plate. Nothing seems to kill my appetite. Energy and strength are important to my survival.

"How are you feeling?" Nova lays a hand on my shoulder. "Yesterday was . . . a lot."

"Well, Ciara is not my mother. Willa is not my sister. My real father was murdered in front of me right after I met him. Princess Emily is my half-sister and now she and Willa are missing. I'm also part of this mysterious power of three that the so-called Shadow King wants me for. And let's not forget, my mother, who I also just met, is suffering the loss of her husband. Confused and angry sums it up."

"We will get answers from Ciara," Nova assures me. "One way or another. Let's go find Hamon, and we can start there. The guard outside will take us to him."

The walk to the dungeons adds fuel to my growing rage. I want to beat the answers out of Ciara, but I'm certain I won't be allowed to. Guards line the hall of the cell block where she is being kept. We follow in silence. The guard leading us stops outside a cell and motions for me to look in.

"We can't enter, m'lady. But you can see that the prisoner is secure."

Ciara is chained to the wall. The putrid smell of urine and feces smacks me in the face. I'm disgusted until I realize she is stuck festering in her waste. This makes me happy.

"We can't risk her using whatever power she possesses," Hamon announces, approaching us from the opposite direction. "I've sent some of my guards to seek the aid of a sorcerer or sorceress to cast a binding spell on her before anyone can enter."

"You should also have them cast a spell of protection," Shay muses.

"Has my daughter come to see me?" Ciara seethes, acid in her voice.

"I am no daughter of yours," I answer back. "What does the Shadow King want me for?"

"I already told you, your powers are special."

"Yes, yes. My mother, grandmother, and I were all born on the same day. The power of three. What does that mean? My mother said my grandmother isn't even alive. So would that not make us the power of two?"

"No, you foolish girl. You are the third born of Summer Solstice births. The power is in you and you alone."

"What kind of power?"

"Godlike. Like Nanaka."

Who is Nanaka? I've never heard of whoever that is, and I'm not going to ask and let her see how ignorant I am. Godlike powers? Me? Right. This woman hasn't said a true word in my life. She cannot be trusted. "Enough of your lies. Are you working for the Shadow King, like Cormac?"

"What are you talking about?" Ciara seems genuinely surprised.

A surge of anger flows through me and my heart pounds as I attempt to keep my breathing and voice calm. "We met Cormac, Rekker, and Osman on the road. Only one of the three lives. The other two? Nova stuck a Staff through one of their skulls, and I did the same to the other."

A hand touches my arm. It's Shay. He raises his hand up and down, motioning for me to calm down. His hand goes to his chest and he mouths, *Breathe.*

"Who did you kill? Who lives?" she begs. "Please."

Manners now? Is she serious? "Where are my sisters?"

"Willa is not your sister."

"Yes, she is. She will always be my sister. Love will always hold us together."

"Who did you kill?" Ciara repeats.

Why is she so upset about this?

Nova leans in and whispers, "I just remembered we have an abandoned outpost in the Northwest. About a week's journey, maybe two, north of Port Kelsey." He takes hold of my arm and begins to lead me away. I don't object.

"No, wait! Come back!" Ciara shouts. "Who did you kill?"

"She's not coming back," Hamon asserts, "unless you tell us where Emily and Willa are."

"There is no need!" Shay shouts down the hall. "We know where we need to go."

"See you in a few months, Ciara, if you don't die of rot first," I yell down the hall.

She shouts to come back, but we don't. I feel intense satisfaction at the sound of her pleading. She will never tell us where they are.

"Osman is Willa's father!" Ciara yells at the top of her lungs.

Those words stop me in my tracks for a moment. I killed Willa's father? Pivoting on my feet I head back to her cell door not caring what I say now because we have a place to start.

"Osman is Willa's father and your lover?"

"Yes," she whines.

"I stuck Nova's Staff through his disgusting face as he begged and cried like a baby for mercy." Her blood-curdling scream of agony only makes me smile. "You can take comfort in the fact that your cruelty made me so very strong. I'm a survivor thanks to your lack of maternal care."

Her scream cuts off abruptly as she leans and stretches her head toward her chained left hand. Opening her mouth, she strains to get a finger in her mouth. Shocking us all, she clamps down, drawing blood.

"What is she doing?" I grimace. "Should we stop her?"

"She is trying to lure us in," Hamon warns. "I'm not allowing anyone to enter. She will not die from losing a finger."

The sound of bone snapping sickens me as bile coats the back of my throat. I worry I might actually vomit.

"We should intervene." Shay sounds frantic. "Something is not right."

Though reluctant, Hamon agrees, reaching for the key to the cell. Before he can use it, Ciara spits the severed bloody fingertip into the nearby burning brazier and then begins chanting.

"Run!" Hamon screams all but pushing me down the hall. We saw how she killed the king, so I run as fast as I can. The stone floor beneath our feet begins to rumble. Is this the forbidden magic Fin spoke about? "Up the stairs!" Hamon shouts, urging us past him one by one.

Daylight momentarily blinds me as I exit into the stables. The smell of manure is ironically a relief compared to Ciara's cell. One by one, Hamon's guards, the boys, and finally Hamon emerge. Screaming erupts somewhere around the corner, and we run toward it.

"Captain!" one of Hamon's guards shouts, pointing toward the sky.

As one we turn and look in the direction he's indicating—a dark wisp of cloud moves swiftly away from the castle, getting smaller with every second that passes. No one says a word. We don't have to. Ciara has escaped.

∾

QUEEN AVA, Hamon, the boys, and I are finishing dinner in her private study when word comes that Fin has finally made himself useful. He has discovered a possible lead on the identity of the Shadow King. He doesn't bring us the information himself; rather, he sends a message to his father. What a jerk. He has not once sought me out to apologize or give me condolences for the loss of my father.

"What news?" my mother asks Hamon.

"We'd been researching the missing to see if there was a pattern to the disappearances. As far as we've been able to ascertain, there are no connections with the dates of birth of those who have been taken. However, Fin discovered through our records a male named Gibbs was exiled for wanting to create an army. He had an unnatural thirst for power, and The Courtless are a peaceful group. They believe he murdered fae in his quest for power."

"Curious. Tell me more," she urges, the candlelight highlighting the darkness and puffiness around her eyes. I have to admit to being impressed that she's even able to speak, much less maintain an interest in polite conversation.

"He's one of the founding members of The Courtless, one of their first elected leaders. He was banished over twenty-five years ago."

"You need to find out why he was banished," the queen comments.

"Agreed," Hamon nods.

"Queen Avalyn," Nova beings, "because my brother and I discovered the Staff of Storms in one of our abandoned temples, I suggested for Hamon to have yours searched. Are you familiar with any particular temple, maybe from childhood, that was more symbolic than the others?"

"I don't recall. My memory is still a bit foggy."

"Nothing was found in the city temples. Fin is searching the records for any abandoned locations farther out in the countryside," Hamon adds. "But we think the Isle of the Crescent Moon would make the most sense to search for an artifact or weapon, given that the moonstone is there. After that, we'll visit The Courtless."

"Hamon, I want guards stationed at all the open temples to protect the priests and priestesses," my mother announces. "And I assume you have someone researching the meaning of the runes on the artifacts?"

"Of course. Fin is on that. I'll also have guards sent to the temples immediately."

"Reagan,"—my mother pats the empty seat beside her—"you have fire in you, and based on what you and the princes have told me, I believe I've figured out what kind."

"There are different kinds?" I rise from my seat at the table and sit in the one she's indicated.

"Yes, your uncle is a fire wielder. Care to show off for your niece?"

Hamon stands, holding his hand palm up. All of a sudden, a small ball of fire appears in his hand. Fascinating.

"I used to be able to amplify any weapon I held and to set fires." He smiles. "So odd that the glamour made me forget this."

"Ham, grab the large family history book, please."

"Ham?" I try hard not to laugh.

"For the love of the Forgotten Gods, Avalyn!" Hamon shouts.

She frowns, raising her shoulders in mock innocence. Hamon rolls his eyes. Yeah, they are definitely my blood.

He retrieves a large book with a Phoenix beautifully carved into its soft brown, leather cover from a glass case in the corner. My mother explains that this court has always been in her family's bloodline. Most females have affinities for falcons, hawks, and, a rare two, phoenixes. That's what our kingdom was named for.

She flips through the pages, stopping on an image of a female holding one of the flaming birds in her upraised hand.

"That, my child, is a phoenix, held by the demigoddess Nanaka. Our banners do not do her justice."

"She's beautiful," I exclaim, glancing over the drawing.

"I believe you have the fire of a phoenix, like Nanaka did."

"Ciara mentioned Nanaka," I point out. I need to find out more about her. "Will I have a phoenix, like her?"

"I do not know. Although my mother, your grandmother, had the fire of a phoenix, she never had one. It is said that the last one never rose from the ashes."

"That's kind of sad, but either way, I need to learn more about phoenix fire." Looking back at the book I notice— "Wolves. There are wolves mentioned here!"

The boys approach, leaning over my mother's shoulders to get a closer look.

"Our families have a long history of wargs," Nova says, "where our male line can slip in and out of a wolf's mind, the same way you can with falcons. Our father is a warg."

"And a rare few in our line," Shay adds, "can shape-shift into wolves."

"Can your father shape-shift?" my mother inquires.

"No," Nova answers, "but our grandfather can. Or could."

"Nanaka was also a shape-shifter," my mother tells us, pointing at a picture. "She could transform into a lioness with wings of fire."

"Queen Avalyn," Shay says, "do you have shape-shifters in your family?"

"Please, both of you call me Ava. I can't recall, although I have remembered something while looking at this. Long ago there was only one kingdom. The wolves of the North used to be our kingdom's most fiercely loyal protectors. There are many stories told of how the wolves single-handedly fought back against the Darkness and his Shadow Demons, ending his reign of terror. However, once the war was over and so many lives were lost, the fae of the Wolf Moon grew tired of being the kingdom's enforcers and wanted a chance to live prosperous, peaceful lives. So, long ago it was decided to split into two kingdoms. The wolves wanted the North, so they took it."

"Nova, how did you discover the Staff?" Hamon asks.

"Shay and I were in the far North hunting when we spotted an old temple, The Pyramid of the Moon. I felt a pull toward the building that I felt compelled to follow. We found the Staff behind the altar. When I grabbed it, it made me incredibly sick to my stomach."

"Did anything else happen when you touched it?"

The boys exchange a look. "Shay and I were knocked out. Shay was injured, but I was not. I've had access to my powers ever since."

"This happened in the temple? Unprotected?" Hamon inquires.

"Yes," Nova replies. "Shay and I have been discussing it, and concluded it now seems suspicious, though it didn't occur to us at the time. We thought we were just really lucky, but so much has happened since then. We went to that region to hunt because one of my father's guards reported that someone told him a large herd of deer had been spotted heading toward the temple. Who told him that is something we need to find out."

"When the Staff broke the glamour and revealed the truth," Shay continues, "we knew we still needed it for whatever purpose it serves."

"How do you know it's called the Staff of Storms?" my mother asks.

"One of my father's advisors, he's . . . how should I put this to not be disrespectful . . ." Nova begins.

"Ancient, Nova. Use the word ancient." Shay chuckles.

Nova rolls his eyes and then starts again. "His advisor was quite familiar with the Staff of Storms. Our history tells us it belonged to Alarick, the first guardian of the Wolf Moon who was also the very first Wolf Moon fae. His father was the demigod, Nivia. The story says Alarick went with his father to visit his grandfather, The Moon God Aytaç, to beg for help fighting the Darkness and that Alarick stole a piece of the moon to create the Staff. As punishment for his theft, he was banished from the after realm forever."

"So, it should have the power of the moon, if the stories are true." My mother nods.

"Indeed it should," Nova replies. "Our father's advisor confirmed it breaks the glamour and that another weapon could possibly be here in your kingdom helping to control the glamour."

This is new information to me, and the folklore is fascinating. Nova withdraws the Staff and holds it up. I imagine everyone is looking at it from a new perspective.

"We have a similar story. I can't quite remember, I'm still in a bit of a fog," my mother remarks.

"Take your time, Ava," Hamon urges.

"I'm fine. I will do some research myself. I need to stay busy, or else I will be overwhelmed by my grief. I will consult my ancient advisors." She musters a small smile.

"That is the second reason we have come here," Shay reveals. "We are hoping to locate another Staff or weapon to help break the glamour over all of Innisfallen and potentially also the curse repressing our powers."

"How come I've never heard of Alarick and his demigod father or Nanaka?" I ask.

"My child, they're the forgotten ones. The ones you all curse to."

"It's probably your lack of education," Shay supplies indelicately. His eyes quickly shift to Nova. "Sorry, that came out rude. I didn't mean it to be insulting."

"I didn't take it as an insult, it's true. Who are the demigods, Mother?"

"According to the old stories, our world began when three gods of creation came together. The Moon God, Aytaç, The Sun Goddess, Suvi, and Orpheus, The Darkness himself. They created the demigods whose names I cannot recall at this moment."

"The Darkness is a god?"

"Yes, my child, all three gods have the power of both creation and destruction. Orpheus is the god of volcanic creation."

I can't help thinking that these things should be taught in school for everyone, not just the royal and high-born. But now does not feel like the right time to bring it up.

"It appears that you two are telepathic." My mother doesn't miss anything. "What were you boys communicating about when Ciara mentioned the power of three?"

"We were wondering if the power of three might be me, Reagan, and Shay," Nova answers.

"We have two unique weapons," Shay states, withdrawing the Obsidian Sword we nicked from Cormac. "If it's truly the power of three, there must be a third weapon."

Turning, I look at Nova. "What makes you think the power of three is the three of us?"

"Shay and I were born on the Winter Solstice, as were our father and grandfather."

Well, shit. I didn't see *that* coming.

CHAPTER 10

I t was not hard to say goodbye to my mother. I felt for her
pain, because she, too, was a victim of Ciara's cruelty and
madness, but we are family in blood only.

When the time comes for us to leave, our hug is an awkward
one, but when I take her hand in mine, my whole heart comes
through my words.

"I am sorry for your loss," I mumble.

"I will be fine, my child. I need this time to grieve the loss of
my husband and make sense of all that has happened to me and
my kingdom."

The thought of what Willa and Emily could be going through
breaks my heart. Which is what makes it so easy to leave. Emily
was only a child, like me, she has no fault in what happened. Nor
did my father, another victim.

"Nova, the day we met, how were you able to move yourself
and Fin within the snowstorm? I know there are telekinetic
powers, but yours seems to be unique."

"Honestly, that was the first time I've done that. I didn't even
know I could. I was four during the last solstice, so this is new to
me. If there is a name for this ability, I can't recall it."

Hamon tells him, "I was fully grown and in control of my

powers when this gods forsaken curse took effect, but it might as well be new to me. I can't make more than a small flame in my hand. It's like I'm a youth again."

"I wanted to be standing over him. I was enraged thinking about how he abandoned Reagan when she was begging him to help her, and when he called her a whore, I wasn't going to stand for it. I was so angry, Hamon. I was thinking that I wished I could become the storm. Then, when I took a step, the world around me slowed down, and I became the storm. In the time it took to finish my first step, I was there. Then I simply repeated the process to get to you."

"Have you been able to do it since?"

"Not at all, and I've been trying."

"Shay, how about you? Can you shift into a non-arrogant ass?" I joke.

"You would not like me very much, Love. Alas, I still can't get control of my powers."

"Hamon, have you ever tried to become fire, as Nova did with the winter storms?"

"Never thought of it once, Rea."

I like the way my nickname sounded from him, warm and familiar. "It seems Nova was able to do it because he was angry."

"I'm not sure where you're going with this. Planning on pissing me off?"

"Hamon, would you like me to call you uncle?"

He puffs up a little in the chest with something that looks like pride and a small smile plays around his lips. I like him. "If you would like to call me uncle, that would be fine with me."

Clever man, he put it back on me. I know he wants this, too, but he wants me to know that I have the choice. I won't deny either of us. "Uncle Hamon," I speak aloud, testing it out. "Or just Uncle."

"I like Uncle a lot."

"Me too."

"Or Uncle Ham," Shay quips, and we all laugh except Ham.

"Hamon, you know I wouldn't have stuck the Staff through your son's skull, right?" Nova interjects.

"I'm not going to lie, Nova, my heart stopped for a moment."

"I was only trying to scare him after everything he put Reagan through."

"It worked," Hamon replies. "To be honest with you, he needed that. He was a softer child. He is unaware of the harsh realities of the world. He loved to read and write and was simply not cut from military cloth. I urged him to take a different path, one that better suited his temperament. He insisted he wanted to be a guard like me. He has this need to prove something to me, but he's my son and I don't need him to be something he's not. I wish he would understand that. I want him to be himself and do what he truly wants."

I refrain from making a snide comment about the fact that at least Fin had a choice.

"Our father raised us that way, too," Shay says. "Insisted we never try to prove ourselves. He believed it showed weakness to bow to the expectations of others."

"Your father sounds intelligent. That never seemed to stick with Fin. Not only does he feel the weight of expectations no one has ever put on his head, he has a sense of entitlement, and I just don't know where he gets it. We live a humble life away from the palace. I raised Fin in the Village of Loflen, on the edge of Glendalough. My wife didn't want anything to do with court life. She threatened to leave me if I didn't agree to live in the countryside, away from Court politics."

"She sounds like someone I would like, Uncle," I chime in.

"You would've loved her, Rea. She was so warm, so bright. It only took me one time to learn not to piss her off. My gods, you wolves bite hard."

"It's a female wolf trait." Shay laughs. "We males think we run things but are reminded often that we don't."

"Rea," Hamon begins, measuring his words carefully, "I would like to share something with you, with you all. When I held the

Staff, the reason I was overwhelmed and brought to my knees was because the female standing next to me at the solstice ball was my wife, Fin's mother, and your Aunt Jaelyn." Tears begin building in his eyes, and he squints to keep them from falling. I keep my mouth shut for once, allowing him time to collect himself. "She went missing, about a month after Fin's birth. She was heading for Port Kennedy, to meet up with her family. They were coming down from the Wolf Court to meet Fin. She never arrived, nor did anyone else she was traveling with, guards included."

"I'm sorry, Uncle."

"Please, Rea, don't be. The events are long past, but ever-present in my heart. So much so that I've never sought to remarry. I just thought you should know."

"Tell me about her," I urge him.

The conversation makes the time pass quickly. We arrive at Port Kennedy the following day. The last time I was here was four years ago on my way to start the training program. However, this time I board a ferry to make the crossing. I've never been on a boat, so rather than going inside the cabin, I remain on deck. The sky is as gray and bleak as ever. The waves rock the ferry from side to side, the wooden planks groaning beneath my feet while the cold briny sea sprays my face and clings to my cloak and scarf. Shay tells me that once we make landfall, it will be a two-day ride to the Temple of the Rising Moon.

WE APPROACH the temple from a hill above, and I'm speechless. It's an enormous circular stone structure of orange, black, and white stones, and I'm amazed when I see it from this angle rather than through the Staff's visions. Its massive stone columns and pillars support what looks like a wagon-wheel-type ceiling of interconnected pieces, leaving the top almost completely open.

It's beautiful. When I was holding the Staff, the images showed the entire surrounding grounds was a massive city of tents, with bright, colorful fae lights and garlands strung everywhere, filled with many different varieties of flowers and food, which makes me realize just how hungry I am.

My stomach growls loudly, and the boys turn and look at me. Shrugging my shoulders, I jump off my horse and walk into the temple. The floor is smooth, polished, and completely flat.

"It's about a five-minute walk to reach the center of the temple," Nova informs me.

The outer three rings are made of smooth, white, marble columns. The next three rings are solid obsidian, polished so smooth that it's like looking into a void of darkness. The interior rings are also marble although these look like they're on fire. Bright oranges and reds blend beautifully with the dark lines of the marble. It's breathtaking, truly.

As I'm approaching the center of the temple, the dais stands utterly empty. The base is fiery marble the shape of a triangle, with a perfectly smooth obsidian basin on top where the moonstone is supposed to sit. The images I remember from the Staff showed the stone as a perfectly carved replica of a full moon, not smooth the way moonstones usually are.

Shay startles me again, appearing out of nowhere.

"The moonstone is missing!" he announces. "I honestly didn't expect it to be here."

"You really need to wear a bell. You feel okay?"

Shay shrugs his shoulders. "I started feeling a little nauseous when we reached the center, but it's passed now."

"Me too. Why did you not expect to find the moonstone?"

"Creating a glamor and a curse to repress our powers would need the power from the solstice moons. Let's split up, search the temple, see if we can't find ourselves a third artifact," he says.

We work systematically from the center outward, but we find nothing. No weapon, no moonstone. We search for hours before finally setting up camp for the night. It is much too dark to continue tonight. The following morning, we begin the process again, this time looking for secret levers or switches that might reveal a hiding place. Again, nothing. It's frustrating.

Each of the three sides of the dais has what appears to be a drawer. There's a slit, about six inches long in the center where a handle might be missing. There are also three holes in the bottom of the basin itself. Slipping my fingers inside, I pull. It doesn't open.

Nova tries to pry the compartment open with a dagger. That doesn't work either. We're not desperate enough yet to smash and destroy the dais in our most sacred temple built by the gods. We decide to move on to The Courtless. The temple is useless without the moonstone anyway.

THE FOLLOWING EVENING, we arrive at the Village of the Crescent Moon, where the bulk of The Courtless are quartered. The trip here felt endless after the failure at the temple. We drag ourselves into the first inn we can find, get a room big enough for the four of us to share, and have dinner sent up.

We eat in silence. The mood is somber. A sudden banging on the door has the four of us on our feet in seconds. Hamon reaches for the handle and looks to make sure we're ready for whatever might be waiting on the other side, then he opens the door.

An imposing male summer fae with black hair and olive green eyes stands at the door, looking angry. "We have scouts that saw you entering the village. We are a peaceful community. We want no trouble."

"I'm Hamon, Captain of the Phoenix Queen's Guard. We only need information on an exiled member of your court, then we will be on our way."

"Gibbs, no doubt," he states, surprising us all. "I thought the day might come when The Queen's Guard would come asking about him. I'm Sloane, one of the community leaders. It's a pleasure to see you again, Captain. We met once long ago."

They exchange handshakes, and then Sloane asks us to meet him downstairs in about thirty minutes while he retrieves the other community leaders. We finish dinner and then make our way downstairs. Sloane and eleven others are already present. After quick introductions are made, Nova withdraws the Staff and explains about the glamor and the spell representing our powers. Then the unglamouring process begins again.

This could take hours, so I whisper to Shay that I'm going to try and take a quick power nap because I can barely keep my eyes open. He promises to come get me if anything big is revealed. After using the en-suite bathing room, I climb into one of the beds. The last thing I remember is my head hitting the pillow.

The sound of a door closing wakes me in our darkened room.

"Sorry, Reagan, we did not mean to wake you."

"It's okay. How long have I been asleep?"

"Only a couple of hours. Sloane decided that it would only be the community leaders unglamoured tonight. Tomorrow, before we leave, he will meet with a small select group he would like unglamoured."

Closing my eyes, I hope to fall back asleep quickly. Then what he said hits me. "Why only a select group and not everyone?"

"We were wondering the same thing. We told him we would stay until everyone was set free of the glamour, but he refused. We have more urgent matters and did not want to press the issue."

"The Courtless live by their own rules," Shay adds. "Outside of both our courts' politics. And even though we strongly disagree, this is not the time. Too many moving parts with this unstable group for just the four of us to confront."

The meeting the following day with the community leaders is strange, to say the least. Sloane decided only the members of the community, twenty years of age and older, would be unglamoured. "For now," they added, as if that helps. They have no idea how long things could take. It's a stupid idea. I thought The Courtless was different. Apparently, not.

Hamon's giving me a look I recognize all too well, begging me to keep my mouth shut, and conveying with his eyes that this is not the time or place for me to go on a rant. He needn't worry; I won't say anything, even though I want to. Sloane claims he does not want to create panic, but I don't believe him. It's unfair, controlling, and worse, selective and privileged. I don't like him at all.

With Sloane unglamoured and memories somewhat restored, he confirms Gibbs was indeed one of the founding members of The Courtless and one of their first elected leaders, but that he was never reelected.

"Why?" I ask, not masking my sour tone at all. I catch Hamon rolling his eyes.

"He always wanted more. It was never enough that we were free of the Royal and high-born, and their court politics and privileges. He wanted to build an army, train them and prepare for war."

"What war?" we all ask.

"That's what we were trying to figure out. He began developing unusual abilities, not our familiar powers, something foul-smelling. Little by little we found he had several accidents, and lost five fingers, then two separate accidents resulting in . . ." He cringes at some distant memory.

"Were his ears missing?" I interrupt. I don't care how he feels anymore. Everyone here should have been unglamoured. This time I catch Shay smiling. I don't bother looking at Hamon's look of disapproval.

"Yes, how did you know?"

"We met one of his followers, Cormac, and his ears were missing. It looked like they'd been ripped from his head. What else?" I can see he is fighting to remain calm, like he wants this over with quickly. He doesn't like my tone of voice, and I couldn't care less. I can't believe I dreamed of living here.

"His son Cormac was a just boy when I last saw him. His daughter, Ciara, a year or two younger, and Kira, the baby." He looks back at Hamon like he does not want to answer my questions.

My eyes go wide in shock. "The Shadow King is their father?" I was not expecting *that*. Nova, Shay, Hamon, and I all exchange glances. Sloane seems pleased by my reaction. Thankfully, Shay speaks before I can and it allows me a moment to collect my thoughts.

"What about his wife?"

"Ivy? She was a beautiful, kind female who loved her children fiercely."

"Loved?" Shay prods.

"She died in what Gibbs described as a terrible hunting accident. He said he burned her body, that it was too mangled to bring back. It was then that the community began having serious doubts about him. His story didn't wash, but we had no evidence to accuse him otherwise."

Nova rubs his temples. "How do you think Gibbs gained these unusual abilities?"

"Forbidden magic," he answers hesitantly. "There were some amongst us who suspected the death of his wife was somehow connected to it all."

Chills shoot down my spine, and an unsettling feeling washes over me.

"What is forbidden magic?" Nova inquires.

"It's not truly magic at all. The forbidden magic of immolation, as we understand it, requires the sacrifice of part of one's body to The Darkness himself, to gain temporary abilities or powers."

"How do you know that's what he was using?" Nova asks.

"Not long after Ivy's death, one of the community leaders saw him with a copy of *The Book of Shadows* and confronted him about it. He claimed he'd found it and was planning to bring it to the community leaders. Not long after, he was exiled and the book vanished."

"That's how Ciara was able to kill the king and escape." Nova's eyes grow wide as he puts the pieces together "Immolate means to sacrifice by fire."

"I agree." Hamon turns back to Sloane. "Is there anything else you can tell us about him? Where might he have gone?"

"The Isle of Darkness. He talked for years about setting up a base, a second location. If he's anywhere, it will be there."

"I've never heard of it," I grumble, still not quite believing what I have heard.

"It's near our abandoned outpost that I told you about," Nova reminds me. "In the northwest of our kingdom, there's a small island where an old monastery once stood."

"Remember your mother telling you about the wolves beating back The Darkness?" Shay says. "It was the Darkness's last stronghold before being forced back into the volcano from where he came. Mount Orpheus. The monastery was built shortly after, but the priests there tended to go mad, so it was abandoned."

"Understand that if Gibbs is there," Sloane warns, "he's trying to raise The Darkness. He will bring that malevolent god back to our world and destroy us all if someone doesn't stop him. Gibbs never understood that forbidden magic comes with a price. He will not be able to see that he is only a puppet being used for The Darkness's needs. The use of it is forbidden because the result, no matter who wields it for any purpose, is the Darkness being raised."

"That has to be where Emily and Willa have been taken. We need to leave," I beg. "We have to save them, save them all."

∾

When we arrive at Port Kennedy, Nova and Shay are warmly approached by members of The Wolf King's Army. Both our courts have coastal outposts here. I can't hear their quick conversations, but a guard hands something to Shay. Then they salute and go on their way.

We make the short walk to Outpost One and are greeted by none other than Lieutenant Murphy himself. My mood changes instantly, and I feel a tight squeeze in my chest that surprises me.

He almost crushes me in a hug. We quickly fill him in on everything that happened since I fled, and then Murphy suggests we head inside.

"Reagan, what in the depths of the shadows were you thinking, young lady?"

"I'm sorry—"

"I don't want to hear your apologies, Reagan. What were you thinking?"

"I wasn't, Murph. I panicked. I needed to get to Willa."

"I expected more from you." His words convey disappointment, but his face is all relief.

How did I not realize how much he cares for me, how much I truly care for him? I don't like his disappointment. I know what I should say, but it's hard to admit it out loud.

"It was selfish and stupid. I let my emotions guide me rather than my reason, as you taught me."

Murphy walks us to a table, pulls out a chair for me, and we sit. Everything that he's learned about the potential fate of the world, a glamor, a cure or spell and his only focus is my safety. How did I overlook this? He wipes away my tears and has to take a moment to contain his feelings before he speaks again.

"I've never been so terrified in my life. I thought you were dead. I lost my wife years ago, she's . . . she's among the missing. We never had a child, Reagan, and you . . ." He hugs me again, tightly.

"You're like a father to me, Murph. I didn't realize it until now. I'm truly sorry for what I put you through."

"And you are like a daughter to me. I do love and care for you, even if you are a pain in my ass." The training camp was never my home, but Murphy was. Is. "It was not right, the way you were forced here, Reagan. I know you felt like you never belonged and how everyone treated you. I tried to do what I could."

"I know you did. It's what got me through."

"The bags of clothing were from me. They belonged to my wife."

This revelation causes my heart to contract again, even tighter.

Murphy provides rooms for us for the night. We freshen up before meeting him back in his private dining room for dinner. It's nice to have hot food, and I greedily shovel it in my mouth. Hearing laughter, I look up and see the four of them smirking at me.

"What? I'm hungry." My mouth is full of potatoes, and it makes them laugh harder.

"Leave it to you," Murphy sighs, "to make a foolish decision that could have taken your life and wind up running into the Wolf Moon Princes."

"I wish we could stay with you longer, Murph."

"I know you will be in good hands this time." Murphy turns to my uncle. "Captain Hamon, you'll be leaving with the fastest horses we have."

"Thank you," Hamon nods.

"We appreciate that, Lieutenant." Shay claps him on the shoulder. "We'll unglamour everyone here and at Outposts Two and Three on our way through. Unfortunately, Outpost Four will have to wait until our return."

"I understand, Commander, and appreciate you taking the time," Murphy tells him. "We've lived in ignorance long enough."

Saying goodbye to Murphy is hard. He wants to come with us, but he has his duties. He is awaiting the next wagon full of trainees before taking his group to Outpost Three. The boys unglamour everyone, without a single conversation about how long it will take or who should and shouldn't be freed. Unlike Sloane and the "free" fae of Innisfallen.

A WEEK and a half later we finally arrived at Outpost Three. Everything went smoothly at Outpost Two, but here, where I fled from my position, I'm not expecting to have a warm welcome like we did with Murphy and at Outpost Two. Hamon sends a guard to retrieve Commander Velius, the very one who denied my request to return home.

"Velius is the one who refused to let me return home when training ended," I inform Hamon and the boys. Hamon looks angry. The boys, I'm not sure what's going through their heads. But one thing is certain, it's nothing the commander's going to like.

When Commander Velius walks in, he zeroes in on me. He begins shouting about the mess I caused and that I will be heading to Outpost Four first thing in the morning if he has to drag me there himself. This, I expect.

What I do not expect is what the boys do next.

As a blinding blizzard engulfs the room, dark shadows flit around us, making it impossible to see anything. When the snow eventually settles, and the visibility returns, a chilling realization dawns upon us—the boys and Commander Velius have vanished into thin air, leaving Hamon and me alone, bewildered and stunned.

CHAPTER 11

"Where did they go?" I look around but it's just me and Hamon.

He shrugs, looking as bewildered as I feel. Hearing shouts outside, we start running. When we reach the courtyard, the sound of fighting fills the air. Nova and Velius exchange violent blows, kicking up clumps of snow in their wake. Though Nova moves fast and easily, Velius counters and lands hit after hit.

Looking around I notice Shay, on his back in the dirty snow, his body motionless except for the shallow rise and fall of his chest. Blood pools around him, staining the ground a dark crimson. His face is battered, his nose grotesquely twisted and broken, blood pouring from his nostrils, a brutal sign of the damage he's taken. His body is limp, the fight drained from him, but I can see the faintest twitch of his fingers.

"Shay!" I shout, my heart hammering in my chest. Without thinking, I bolt toward him, the chaos of the fight fading into the background. My feet pound on the ground as I reach him. Blood smears his face, and his breath is ragged, but his eyes flutter open, flickering with recognition. Despite my protest he's back on his feet in seconds.

Turning my attention back to Nova, it's clear he is on the defensive and unable to free the staff at his side.

"Enough!" Hamon screams, so loud it startles both Shay and me. Velius pauses and looks at Hamon, unintentionally allowing Nova the moment he needs to unstrap his staff and blast Velius with a powerful winter storm, pinning him to a post. He did not see that coming. Shay, now on his feet, quickly ties the commander's hand behind it securing him to the post.

Shay, spitting out blood, walks back to Hamon and me and whispers so only we can hear. "It did not make sense the first time you told us you were not allowed to return home. Now it does."

What have they figured out? Nova is glaring at Velius, with violent, angry storms in his eyes that carry a promise of death.

"Hamon, now would be a good time for introductions," Shay requests, still uneasy on his feet.

Hamon walks forward. "Commander Velius, forgive my manners," he begins as if we are not in the middle of an intense situation. "That is Donovan, the Crown Prince of The Kingdom of Wolf Moon, and his brother Shay, the Commander of the Wolf King's Army." Velius's eyes go wide in shock. "And, Commander, allow me to formally introduce my niece, Princess Reagan." Velius doesn't seem surprised at my title at all, and we all notice. Nova steps up to him, only an inch from his face. "You have one chance, Commander, to tell us who you're working with. I won't ask a second time."

I would hate to be in Velius's place right now. Nova looks like he wants to rip his throat out with his teeth.

"This is outrageous. I am a member of the Phoenix Court!" Velius screams.

Thunder begins to build in the sky above us as Nova grips the Staff in his hands, expanding it to its full length.

"You can't kill me," Velius protests. Nova takes a step back, getting in position to run him through. "Stop this, Hamon, you're betraying your kingdom by letting him do this to me!"

"He is not the one betraying his kingdom," Shay states. "I suggest you answer the question the Crown Prince asked."

Velius is panicking. He knows he's been caught. Although caught with what? What do the boys know? The commander looks around helplessly for an ally.

"Stop looking around. No one's going to help you," I tell him. "You better answer not only who, but why?"

"I'm aware of who you are, Princess." He seems to sag in defeat. Or is it a relief?

"How? Have you known this whole time?" I wonder if it would be considered wrong for me to stab him just a little. Maybe in a place that wouldn't kill him.

"My sister and her two boys went missing five years ago. They were only ten and eight. I would've done almost anything to get them back. He said you would not be harmed, that they needed your powers."

"He who?" Hamon asks, clearly losing patience.

"Who are you working with?" Shay looks a little murderous himself.

"His name is Cormac. He said he could get my nephews back if I agreed to allow Reagan into the training program."

This I was not expecting. He sold me out to Cormac. Inhaling deeply, I try to calm my nerves and not let my emotions take over again.

"Cormac said his father has been kidnapping our kin, keeping them alive, using their powers for twenty years now."

"What makes you think they are still alive?" Hamon demands.

"He said he needed them alive. Although, I get the feeling he has a separate agenda from his father's." Now that his part in this conspiracy is revealed, Velius seems almost relieved.

"What makes you think that?" Shay's temper is flaring up. Velius does not respond other than to shake his head. "Answer me." Shay's voice is filled with such ferocity, and I swear his eyes flash black for a moment.

"He had a shadow beast on board his ship. I overheard him tell his crew not to mention it to his father. You have to understand that they're the only family I have. I didn't know some of the captives would be killed. He said eventually they'd be set free."

I can almost understand his predicament. I'd sell my soul to the shadows to have Willa back right now. Yet to sell me out rather than get help? That makes it personal—and harder for me to sympathize.

I'm not inclined to forgive his betrayal, but we need his information. Trying to do what's best for all, I walk over to Velius and begin untying him. He collapses to his knees, gasping for breath.

Hamon touches his shoulder to get his attention. "Come, Commander Velius, it seems we have a lot to discuss. The missing are still out there."

The possibility of the missing still being alive is weighing heavily on all of us. It makes perfect sense that the Shadow King has stolen the moonstone and is keeping the missing alive to use their powers to somehow repress ours. According to Velius, Cormac also made some snide comments about the younger ones lasting longer.

Nova points out that we can't just remove Velius or have him arrested because his removal from his post will tip Cormac off that we're getting closer to unraveling his plot. Velius's punishment will come in time. But for now, Hamon pulls rank and orders some of the guards at the Outpost to keep an eye on him and not let him leave.

IT TAKES us days to cut through the mountains before finally hitting the road to Port Kelsey. It was smooth going until three hooded figures appeared, blocking the road ahead.

"Mojo!" Shay's voice takes on an odd and excited affectation, the way someone would talk to a baby. Turning to see who in the depths of the shadows he's talking to, I spot a small, black, four-legged creature running at us from our left, heading straight for Shay. The Commander of the Wolf King's Army bends slightly at his waist, and the creature jumps into his arms, licking his face with kisses. Is it a dog? Or is it a cat? I can't tell; however, one thing's certain when I look at the grinning group of strangers on the road.

"Your cadre, I presume." I smile in spite of myself and go over to see the adorable creature in Shay's arms.

"This is Mojo." Shay grins.

"Your pet?" I look into the tiny face. It has the head of a small canine with ears too large for its small body, making it appear almost feline. It's black all over except for a white chest and white-tipped paws.

"No, although allow me to introduce a few members of my cadre." He passes me Mojo, and I eagerly take the little beast. It starts kissing my face, and I giggle. I don't think I have ever giggled in my life. "Who's a good boy, Mojo?" I scratch the animal's ears, and it nearly wiggles out of my arms in delight.

"Yes, you are a good boy," I gush, petting him, and that's when I realize they've put clothes on the creature. He's wearing a tiny brown jacket with pockets. "What is he?"

Nova comes over, placing a hand on my shoulder, leaning in for Mojo kisses.

"We believe he's a cat-sith," Nova tells me. "It's a rare, ancient creature that we believe is from the elven world of Delu-navir. However, this one found Quinn."

Nova nods toward a tall, extremely slender male. He must have heard his name because he turns to us and approaches. Starbursts of bright orange flare from the pupils of his brown eyes as he runs his fingers through short-cropped orange hair. His coloring tells me he's an Autumn fae.

"I'm Quinn, though I go by Q. It's a pleasure."

As I shake his extended hand, I notice it's covered in scars from tiny bite marks. I count at least seven small, suspiciously Mojo-sized bite wounds. He may be a good boy, but maybe I should be careful. Looking back at Mojo, intelligent eyes gaze into mine.

"This is Riel, my ship's captain." Shay inclines his head in greeting to the most beautiful female I've ever seen. She struts toward us, hips swishing back and forth. Her dark hair is braided over the center of her head, and she has the boys' bright blue winter fae eyes. She's powerfully built beneath her skintight leathers.

"That walk, Riel. That, you need to teach me," I say by way of greeting.

"I can teach you a lot of things, girl, given the time," she purrs with the same sensual tone Shay often uses.

"Riel, I don't mean this as an insult, but you have got to be related to Shay." I smile to let her know I mean that as a compliment.

"Unfortunately, we are cousins, although publicly I only claim Nova." She turns to the boys, her face shifting from sensual to absolute relief when she looks them over. "Don't you ever put me through that again, cousins. You've been gone a lot longer than you told us you would be. You have a lot of explaining to do."

The cadre appears to have a tight bond. They aren't just colleagues, not just a team . . . they are family. I'm so focused on their exchange that I don't notice the gigantic male at my side.

"Ahh!" I huff, stumbling back a little.

"I didn't mean to startle you, little lady. I'm Gabriel, but my friends call me Gabe." His voice is so deep that I swear I feel tremors in the ground when he speaks.

"You don't have any friends," Shay teases.

Gabriel has to be seven and a half feet tall. Same winter fae blue eyes and dark braided hair, except Gabe is built like a mountain. His arms are the size of tree trunks.

"I'm Reagan—Rea—and it's nice to meet you all."

"And this is Captain Hamon," Shay advises.

I put Mojo down and Hamon and I shake their hands. Shay fills them in on the last few weeks' activities, and we decide to camp for the night. We'll start making our way to Port Kelsey in the morning.

Hamon and I collect wood while Nova hunts and Shay and his cadre set up camp. As we are heading back, we hear Shay giving orders. Reaching out, I stop Hamon, and he looks at me in confusion.

"Hold up a minute. I want to listen. He sounds so different when he speaks as their commander." I strain a little so I can hear Shay talking.

"Get a crew together, dressed in plain clothes, and start stocking the ship for the voyage. Also, send out riders to my parents with this," Shay orders, handing Riel a folded piece of parchment. "In the morning, take Gabe and load the special cargo as soon as it's light."

"Understood." Riel nods, then walks away without questioning his orders or asking for any explanation at all. Gabriel follows her, even without orders. I wonder if I could ever be this . . . obedient. And what is this special cargo?

Shay walks away with Q, and he's telling the tall one that he needs him to procure some unique items and that they must remain concealed. I can't wait to find out what he means by unique. It's different watching him interact with his friends as their commander. There's no formality, just absolute respect. It's years of working side by side, and I wonder again if I could ever take his orders the way they do. Would there even be a place for me in a tight-knit crew like this? I've never been good with blind obedience.

After dinner, I retire to the small, private tent that's been set up for me. I'd like to sit by the fire and socialize, but I'm too anxious with Willa on my mind. She is the Shadow King's granddaughter, and I killed her father. I've accepted the fact that she's my sister regardless of what blood flows through our veins, but I can't help wondering if she knows the truth and if she feels the same way.

Is she angry with me, thinking I abandoned her? I wish I had thought to ask Ciara what she told Willa about my sudden disappearance. What is the Shadow King telling her now? If the missing are still alive, how is he using their power through The Forbidden Magic of Immolation? Is that what created this curse? Is he using their body parts as sacrifices to his evil god? Chills shoot down my spine at that thought.

Digging out a book I brought from my parents' library, I read more about the Gods and demigods to educate myself. I flip to a page about Orpheus. His name means "the darkness of night" yet there are no images of him.

It says his children, the Shadow Demons, created thousands of shadow beasts. There are images of them, and they look terrifying with hides of dark, leathery armor. The four claws on their front paws look like curled daggers. In one image, the mouth of one of the beasts is gaping wide open, its maw packed with two rows of razor-sharp teeth. Crimson eyes stare back at me from the page. This is what nightmares are made of. I put the book away, having seen more than enough for tonight.

The following morning, we make our way to Port Kelsey, where we'll be boarding Riel's ship, the *Riptide*. Shay informs us that we are going to drop anchor out of sight before we reach the island, and then take a skiff to shore. I'm trying to stay positive, praying to any god that will hear me that my sisters are there.

CHAPTER 12

S hay and his cadre have been standing at the helm almost day and night the last five days, hardly taking time to rest at all. They're a powerful presence, standing together, unified. As I watch them work, it's like they are actors in a well-rehearsed play, knowing their parts so well that the action has become second nature. I can't imagine what role Shay thinks I can fill.

Hamon, Nova, and I have been stationed together today, thank the Forgotten Gods, at the front, which Nova tells me is called the bow. I've never been on a ship before, and I don't have any idea what language the crew is speaking. The cadre has been shouting orders to aft, to port, to stern. Whatever. It's probably why they moved me.

My face is wrapped from my nose down with a scarf like everyone else. With the constant spray of the briny sea, I'm frozen and wet. Icy mist hangs over us, and my sodden cloak no longer blows in the breeze. It's stiff and heavy. This is no place for Summer fae.

Nova says that when we finally make it to the island, there's a winding road to reach the top of the volcano, which takes hours to climb. However, off the coast, there is a faster, albeit more dangerous, path that cuts straight up the side of the mountain. And he assures me that it's been centuries since the volcano last erupted, spilling The Darkness and his demons from within.

Endless mountainous islands capped in thick fog are our constant companions on the journey. We drop anchor, and then I hear a voice that squeezes my heart like a vise.

"If a single one of you moves a muscle, she's dead," Cormac shouts.

My heart stops, then kickstarts so fast I almost choke on it. "Willa!" I shout, but my voice is muffled by my scarf. Cormac has a sword on her back. The dark-haired girl next to her must be Emily.

Ripping the scarf from my face I scream. "No one moves. No one." I fix my gaze back on Cormac.

"Looks like you've smartened up since we were last together." They're standing on a smaller island, hidden from our approach. We never stood a chance.

Inside I'm dying. This is the first time I've seen Willa in four years, and she's with that monster Cormac. "I'll exchange myself for my sisters," I yell across the water. It's me he wants, not them.

"No," Nova insists, low enough that Cormac can't hear him.

"Nova," I answer back through gritted teeth, "I have no choice. This psycho would have nearly bled me out on that mountainside. There's no telling what he'll do to Willa and Emily. It's not your call to make." Nova growls but doesn't argue, so I turn my attention back to Cormac. "How do you want to do this?"

"Jump in and swim over," he orders.

"Only the Forgotten Gods know what's in these waters, and they're freezing. Can't I take a skiff?" I need a plan.

"That's a risk you'll have to take. You have five seconds to jump, or I run her through, and maybe have fun with her after. I don't need her."

My hand hits the icy rail, and I propel myself overboard

without a second thought. Hitting the water, I lock up instantly as the icy waters slice through my body like knives. My sodden cloak drags me down so I struggle to unclasp it and then rip the scarf from its vice-like grip around my neck. Though my muscles have seized painfully, I kick as hard as I can and break the surface, gasping for air. It's so cold I can barely breathe, and my lungs feel incredibly tight. I begin swimming for shore, but I stop halfway there.

"Let them go, Cormac," I shout over the waves, despite my chattering teeth.

"I have scouts in these trees and surrounding islands. If anyone moves, they're dead. You two." He points at Nova and Shay. "Show me your swords."

Nova pulls his short sword from its sheath, holding it up, the folded steel reflecting the light.

"And now you." He points to Shay at the helm who has been carrying Cormac's Obsidian Sword. He pulls a long sword from his side; however, it's not the obsidian one. Nova is not carrying the Staff either, and I hadn't noticed. Cormac looks between them, seeming to consider if it's worth it.

"Please, let them go," I shout. My frozen body needs movement, and I need the girls off the shore and aboard the *Riptide*.

"Don't swim to them," Cormac orders me, then pushes Willa forward.

She lands on her hands and knees in the sand. Standing, she brushes her hands off, then turns back for Emily. Emily takes her hand without hesitation, and they wade into the icy waters. My brave little sister. I begin to cry, recognizing that she has my compassion and strength, and I will probably never see her again.

"Swim hard, ladies," I yell over the breaking waves, almost choking as one slams into my face.

Willa shouts something back, but I can't hear her. Once they begin climbing the ladder, I swim to the shore, stopping a few feet from Cormac.

He's yelling for the *Riptide* to leave, that they will be followed, and if anyone is seen getting off before Port Kelsey, the entire crew will be killed.

I must be strong. Willa and Emily are safe onboard. Still, my heart starts to break watching my family and friends sail away until I can no longer see them, then turn to face my fate.

"Hello, sister," comes a venomous voice.

I almost forgot about my fake sister, Kira. That was the last thought running through my head as her fist connects with my face.

COLD AND PAIN WAKE ME. I take in my surroundings and realize I'm in a cell. Crumbled stones lay all around me. Cobwebs dangle from the ceiling, filling the corners of the room. There's a drain in the center of the floor and a pipe coming out of the wall where it connects to the floor. The taste and smell of mildew coats my every breath.

I push myself up into a wobbly standing position. Walking to the door, I grab hold of the bars, pushing and pulling to no avail. What did I expect? The door is solid, unyielding, locked, and appears to be new. There is no handle, only a keyhole.

"Come and face me, Kira," I shout out the door. "Or are you a coward?"

Waves crashing not far off catch my attention. Where in the depth of the shadows am I? There are no windows, but the not-so-distant sound of crashing waves tells me I'm near the coast. What are the odds of a monastery having a dungeon? What if I'm somewhere else completely? I know they will come for me, but I hope they will take the girls to safety first.

WITHOUT ACCESS to the changes in daylight, I'm uncertain how much time has passed. It could be two full days, judging by how hungry and thirsty I am. Someone has been keeping a torch burning in the hall, but I never hear anyone. I assumed it would be warm by Mount Orpheus—it's a volcano, after all.

Today, I keep hearing things crawling in the pipes. I have no idea what. Imagining what gods-forsaken slimy things could be skittering around in there sends a shiver down my spine.

As I sit in this cold, damp cell, the irony is not lost on me that I believed I was a prisoner at the training outpost for four years. I had no idea what prison was. Yes, my freedoms were restricted, though where would I be if I had never entered the program?

There's no point dwelling on the past, so I refocus on my present predicament. How will this Shadow King use my powers? What is his end game? And how does the power of three figure into all of it?

My thoughts are interrupted by footsteps in the hall, so I mentally prepare myself for what's to come. I expect to see Kira's gloating face, but the visage peering at me through the bars is Ciara's. She looks more terrifying than I have ever seen her. I killed her lover, and she appears ready to exact her revenge.

"I'm going to kill you." Her voice is taunting as always, but there is a certain satisfaction in her tone that only adds to my anxiety.

I step back as she unlocks and enters the cell, ready for a fight. Rather than fists or blades, dark magic slams into me, hard, sending me stumbling backward. My back hits the wall, and I know she's preparing another blast. Gathering my wits, I quickly pivot and dodge, and I hear the stone crack in the space I vacated. I grind my teeth. She won't get the best of me that easily.

I take two steps to the right, and then I lunge, landing a shot to the side of her head. She staggers yet straightens up quickly.

My fist connects with her face again before she can feint to the side, sending her buckling over. She may have dark magic, but she's no fighter. Then I strike with my left leg and deliver a kick so powerful to her chest that air escapes her lungs. She collapses to the floor wheezing, and just for good measure, I stomp the heel of my boot down on her severed finger. Her screams fuel my resolve. She quickly gets to her feet, but I'm already behind her.

I wrap my arm around her neck, then twist hard and fast to the left, slamming us both to the ground. This is it, I'm going to kill her. She tries to pull and claw my arm away, but she will never break my grasp because I'm fueled by a lifetime of rage, and I won't let go until I'm certain she is dead.

"This is for Willa and Emily!" I scream, tightening my forearm against her throat. "This is for my father, the King you killed." Squeezing tighter, I lean back, pulling with everything I have as she flails about helplessly. "And more importantly, this is for me! I hate you! Where is your forbidden magic now?"

Someone screams to let her go, but in my blind rage, I continue to choke the life from her. The smell of rotten flesh begins to fill my every breath. I gag, but I don't let go. Without warning, Ciara and I are lifted off the ground and slammed hard into the ceiling. My free fall to the cell floor makes me lose my grip. When I look up, Cormac's standing above me, smiling.

"Hello, sweetheart," he sneers just before his boot connects with my face.

SLOWLY, a sharp pain jolts through my body, and gradually my senses return. The agony intensifies as I take a mental assessment of my injuries. The copper taste of blood coats my mouth. I gently probe what feels like a nasty gash in the corner of my mouth. My eyes focus on the features of my cell in the dim light. A metal handle protrudes from a bucket next to me, and I can't help being amused that this is probably Cormac's version of mercy. The water looks fresh enough to drink, so I greedily quench my thirst and then use a little water to clean the dried blood from my face.

The sound of scratching in the pipe is getting closer today. I've planned this out in my head since my stomach started to growl yesterday. Getting into position, I prepare to kill whatever emerges from the pipe. I don't relish the idea of eating vermin, but who knows when I'll have the opportunity to eat again? I have to hang in there for a few more days at least. Holding a large piece of crumbled stone, I listen as the scratching gets closer to the opening.

Quickly picking up a second piece of stone, I decide to block the critter's exit, just in case I don't get it with my first blow. As I'm getting ready to slam this stone down on its head, a little nose pokes out the hole and snuffles. I freeze mid-swing as a familiar pair of oversized ears emerge from the pipe.

"Mojo? Who's a good boy? How did you get here?"

I drop to my knees, and he peppers me with kisses before wiggling out of my arms, clearly wanting to be free. He sits and stares at the door.

"What is it, Mojo? Is Q coming?"

He turns around, looks me dead in the eyes, yips quietly, then turns back around.

"Mojo, what am I supposed to do?"

He repeats the same process and backs his side up against my outstretched hand. This time I clue in and check the pockets of his jacket, pretty sure I'm on the right track because his little ears are twitching. My fingers close around an obsidian skeleton key. I jump to my feet and put my ear to the door. When I hear only silence, I slip my arm through the bars of the thick wooden door and feel each grain of wood until I locate the keyhole. It turns, the tumblers clank heavily, and the door swings open. Mojo must have been the scratching I heard, and this good boy somehow located and stole a key.

I lean into the hallway and check both directions. Seeing that it's clear, I turn back to Mojo for guidance.

"What now?"

Mojo takes off down the hallway. I follow him through a maze of damp halls, my heart beating harder with every step I take. The more cells we pass, the more dilapidated the building becomes. Crumbled stone and splintering wooden doors line the corridor as I struggle to keep up with Mojo in my weakened state.

Mojo slips under a half-collapsed door. I have to get on my hands and knees to follow him. The interior cell is filled with large, toppled stones. More importantly, the back wall lies in ruins, open to the elements, our gateway to freedom. "Lead the way, Mojo."

We wind our way through dense undergrowth until we are finally in sight of the shore. From this distance, I see crowds of fae and crouch in the bushes so that I can see what's happening. Dozens of children are being boarded onto small, peculiar-looking boats. Each appears to hold about twenty. In the center of each boat, there are four seats, two on each side, with pedals out in front of them that power a circular paddlewheel off the back. Cormac, Ciara, and Kira are nowhere to be seen.

"Fascinating isn't it, Love?" Shay whispers in my ear, appearing out of nowhere and scaring me half to death. This time, I don't care about being startled and throw my arms around him tightly. "What happened to your beautiful face?"

My face still aches from being punched and boot kicked. The coloring must be awful. I'm lucky I don't have a broken jaw. "It's a long story, but where did those boats come from?"

"Special cargo I had tucked away along with two dozen guards in hopes we'd find the missing."

"I overheard you saying something about that when I first met the cadre."

"Two days before reaching the Isle of Darkness, Riel, Gabe, Q, and I, along with a small contingent of guards, slipped off the ship under the cover of darkness. We took these skiffs a different route."

Have I been hallucinating or has he? "That's not possible. I saw you all at the helm."

"That was not me or my cadre, Love." His eyes twinkle with amusement.

"How?"

"We swapped out with body doubles."

"The unique items you asked Q to procure for you that same night. Of course."

"You are a clever girl, but I got the better of you this time!" he brags. "You didn't think my pampered, princeling ass could stand for five days straight with no sleep now did you?"

"Shay, you are brilliant." I start to laugh, but wince as my smile pulls the cut on my lip open. I spit fresh blood onto the ground.

"Who else is here with you?"

"It's just me. My sisters boarded the *Riptide* after I exchanged myself for their lives." I fill Shay in on everything that has happened since dropping anchor.

"What do you say, shall we get these children home?"

"Absolutely. But why are there only children?"

"There is a large arena-type room where the captives are being held that is guarded by Shadow Court soldiers and shadow beasts. Through one of the barred windows, we were able to make contact with them. Their parents pleaded for us to take the children small enough to fit through the bars. The innocence and potential of children are incredibly precious to us, Love. We know that conception can be a challenging process for many, and we believe this may be a way for the gods to help manage the balance of our world, preventing it from becoming overly popu-lated. Each child represents a glimmer of hope and future possi-bility, and the thought of denying them a chance at life weighs heavily on us all."

This is news to me. Yet something else my lack of education has kept from me."How many are in there?"

"Thousands. We were also informed that apparently these guards have become complacent over the last twenty years. So if we could get them enough weapons, they can fight their way to freedom from the inside. Any guards or shadow beasts that try to flee will run into us on the outside."

"And they look strong enough to fight after all these years of captivity?"

"Yes. One of the captive males told us that every solstice The Shadow King stands over the moonstone chanting. He has been using the forbidden magic, siphoning their powers and redirecting them to the curse repressing everyone's powers throughout Innisfallen. Unfortunately, we were also told that some often disappear from the captive group and never return."

Before I can respond to that, Gabe walks by me, holding what I can only assume is the moonstone. "How do we have the moonstone?"

"While Mojo was on a scouting mission, he located it by chance in a locked room and by chance discovered you. We had no idea you were here. Once you were freed, Mojo took Gabe and Q to retrieve it. The solstice is approaching. We can't let its power be used again."

"Won't someone notice that it's missing?"

"Not until the solstice. It's a risk we all agreed we needed to take."

"Hopefully on the way back, we'll catch up to the *Riptide* and my sisters," I muse. All I've wanted for four years was to see Willa, and I've been robbed of the opportunity yet again. At least this time, she knew I was willing to give up my own life to save her from a horrible fate.

"Sorry, Love, that's not the plan. The *Rapture* is waiting for us and we will not be sailing the same course as the *Riptide*. The plan is to rendezvous back at Port Kelsey. They're safe, Rea, you need to trust that."

I settle myself onto one of the pedal seats, eager to try the clever machine. It's entertaining for a little while, but after five hours, it's not so fascinating. Leg cramps throb in time with the damage to my jaw. Once we finally meet up with the *Rapture*, we get the children on board and the crew has hot stew and blankets waiting. It's a great relief when Shay and I finally sit down to eat.

Port Kelsey is four days' sailing from where we are, and the waiting is killing me. Willa and Emily will be there, safe and sound, I remind myself, but I worry anyway. Cormac said they would be followed. There's no way that a ship could have followed the *Riptide* without being spotted, but I also don't feel like it was a complete bluff. There's no way we could be that lucky.

CHAPTER 13

When we arrive at Port Kelsey, Shay is immediately informed that Nova, Hamon, my sisters, and a dozen guards left three days prior. The news shatters me, leaving me gasping for breath and feeling utterly heartbroken. It's a devastating blow. I know that the plan wouldn't have been changed without a good reason, and I worry that something might have gone awry.

I understand they need to get Willa and Emily back to the safety of the capital. They had no idea what was happening to me or if Shay's plan would work.

Every time I get close to Willa, she slips away from me. I know there are bigger concerns than my feelings, but I can't help wallowing in self-pity for the rest of the evening.

Shay and I make our way to Outpost Four while the cadre stays behind to set up base camp at the port, working to find out where all the children belong. The four inns opened their doors to the rescued children, and the whole town's helping. Bars and taverns even shut down to accommodate them. The hope that has spread with finding some of the missing loved ones alive is profound.

When we arrive at Outpost Four, I decide to take my food to

my room. After stuffing my face, I take a hot bath. It soothes my aching body, and I get out only after the water begins to go cold.

I ease into bed and get lost in the pages of a book, until I hear a sudden knock at my door. "Who is it?" I say from the bed. It's warm and I don't want to get up.

"It's Shay." He doesn't sound at all like himself.

I drag myself out of my comfortable bed and let Shay in. As soon as he enters, he picks up my book, peruses the cover, then raises an eyebrow and sits on the edge of the bed.

"A little light reading?"

I hop on the bed next to him. "I'm trying to learn about the gods and demigods." I pull a blanket over my legs.

"Tell me, Love, what have you learned so far?"

"There appear to be six demigods and six Shadow Demons."

"So, you can count. I was worried about that," he teases.

"Yes, I can count, read, and write." I punch him semi-gently in the shoulder and he smirks. "I never had a history lesson before, though."

"Were they not offered in your skills training?"

"Only to royal and high-born children. As far as anyone knew, I was the bastard child of a prostitute." I shrug this off. For once, I don't feel like getting into the social politics of the land. "I found lots of things to read, but nothing like this."

"Then let's see what more we can learn tonight." He fluffs a couple of pillows and leans back. I smack his booted feet off my bed and he laughs, removing his footwear and tossing it off the end of the bed.

We spend the next three hours talking and reading through the book when Shay stands and stretches. "I'm going to sleep on one of the chairs by the fire."

"The bed would be more comfortable," I offer.

"I'll be just fine over here."

"You, Nova, and I have been sleeping side by side for weeks."

"This is different, Rea."

"How so?"

"That is a bed. It's different from sleeping in a cave. It would be too intimate. Are you saying that's what you want?"

"Oh no, okay. I get it now. When we're back on the road?"

"I'm all yours."

"That's better. There's my cocky best friend." Did I say that out loud?

Shay turns and looks at me. He has a wide-open, carefree smile on his face, and it warms my heart. "I like the sound of that. I've never had a best friend other than my brother. My upbringing did not allow time for it."

"Funny we have that in common."

"Indeed, it is, Love. That's probably why we get along so easily."

"And right from the start, too. Some things are meant to be. I was wondering if you have anyone special in your life?"

"I do not."

"How is it that both you and Nova, princes no less, have remained unattached?"

"It's difficult being who we are. Not only does our work keep us from having social lives, but it also results in a lot of females and males only interested in us because of what we represent as princes and not who we are."

"That's kind of sad."

"We have an entire lifetime to find love. Now let's get some sleep. We both need it."

Blowing out my candle, I hope sleep will take me quickly.

SHOUTING WAKES ME. Jumping up, I reach for my boots and see Shay still has not moved from the chair by the fire.

"Shay, what are you doing, can't you hear that?"

"It's Nova."

"What?"

"It's Nova. He's been in my head for about an hour. He won't shut up. He's pissed. I told him we are safe."

"How's that possible? He was heading to the capital with my sist—"

The door bursts open and Nova stands there out of breath, a wild look in his eyes, his dark hair windblown into a beautiful mess. He's looking into me in that intense way that heats my body from the inside out, but there's anger in his intensity. I think he's not happy I jumped overboard.

"That was not part of the plan, Reagan."

He's so mad, no wonder he got here so quickly. It's impressive. I knew being pissed off would work. I'll keep that to myself, for now. "I didn't think, Nova. I jumped for my sisters."

"That's the problem—you don't think when it comes to your sisters. I understand why you did it, but I thought I'd lost you, and thinking about what could be happening to you consumed me . . . we had a plan. You're supposed to stick to the plan. That's what plans are for."

"Maybe I should've been a part of planning that plan." I'm standing my ground. If they wanted me to follow the rules, they should have told me about the plan.

"You were going to be informed once we made landfall. I've never been so torn up in my life."

"Informed? Excuse me, Crown Prince, but when the plan is concealed from me, you can't expect me not to make my own. They're my sisters."

"Reagan, promise me you won't do anything foolish like that again."

"I can't make a promise to you that I'm not certain I can keep. Especially if you're going to be scheming behind my back, keeping me in the dark on things that affect me."

A deep growl rumbles from his chest, but then he softens. "You're right. We should have kept you in the loop, and I don't blame you for being reckless." He smiles in spite of himself. "I wouldn't want you any other way."

"We," Shay speaks up. "We wouldn't want you any other way. Let's not forget I'm sitting right here."

"How are you here? I thought you were going to the capital with my sisters?"

"I only went as far as Outpost Three. From there Hamon and as many guards as he could muster will take them to the capital."

THE FOLLOWING MORNING, we board a ferry and sail down the west coast to a small port near the town of Ada Sound, where we'll then travel by horseback the rest of the way to Glendalough. From there it's a straight shot along the queens road into the capital.

Riel, Q, Gabe, and a few of Shay's guards will head to Outpost One with the moonstone. The boy's parents are heading there too. That was the note Shay handed off when I first met the carde.

Once on our horses, I start thinking about how Nova got my sisters to Outpost Three, then blew like a storm back to us. "Nova, I knew my idea of pissing you off would work."

He doesn't look happy about that. Shaking his head, he moves his horse closer to mine. As soon as I see his arm move toward me, I brace myself, but he's lightning fast. He shoves me off my horse, and I hit the ground with a thud. It's outrageous.

"What in the name of the Forgotten Gods was that for?"

"Which specific forgotten god exactly?" Shay quips.

"You," I point at Shay, "I will deal with later." Turning back to Nova I demand. "What was that for? You could've broken my damn neck! Are you that mad at me?"

"Reagan, now that you're pissed off, can you turn into a firestorm and bring us to the capital?"

"Or keep us warm at night?" Shay remarks teasingly. My blood pressure rises as I try to hold back my irritation.

They always know how to push my buttons. "I offered to keep you warm last night, Shay."

"Well, shit," Nova mocks me.

"Insufferable jerks, both of you."

"Rea, while I appreciated your offer last night," Shay grows serious, "it would have been too intimate alone on a bed with you. Besides you have enough of my scent on you as it is."

"What's that supposed to mean?"

"It appears, Love, that along with having no history lessons, you also never learned about, how should I say . . ."

"How about you just say it?"

"Okay, because you asked so nicely. You never learned about biology. Once males are fully mature at eighteen years, our primal instincts take over. We're able to not only detect certain things by scent when our body chemistry changes, but we also develop individual scent."

"What certain things can you smell?"

"Riel and your mother would be a good source of information for you."

"Shay, please tell me what it is. Quit being annoying and spit it out."

"We know you're a virgin."

"Oh, for the love of the Forgotten Gods, I wish I hadn't asked." Shay mercifully does not laugh at me. Another thought occurs to me. "What did you mean about your scent on me?"

"You should take my advice and speak with your mother."

"Why did the gods curse me with you for a friend? Tell me about your scent."

"Males can typically tell who females and males are with by the male's scent on them. And because Nova and I have been sleeping side by side with you, our scents are on your clothing."

"You have got to be kidding me."

"It's true, Rae."

"Wait, does that mean Hamon can smell you both on me?"

"Yes, because he is over eighteen. As I just said."

"Does he think I'm sleeping with both of you? Is that why Fin called me a whore?"

"Reagan, for the love of the Forgotten Gods," Shay says using my full name. "Have you been listening to nothing I've told you? Hamon can also detect that you're a virgin. As for that coward who abandoned you, he must not be of age."

I ask no more about it, hoping this conversation disappears into the shadows forever.

"Now that we have the moonstone, and the Winter Solstice is only a few weeks away, will we gather to restore our powers?" They exchange a look. "Don't do that. Don't talk behind my back. In front of me. Whatever. Because that's exactly what you're doing."

"Sorry. A force of habit, but you make a very good point," Nova remarks.

"Thank you."

"Once we reach Glendalough, we will escort your mother to meet with our parents," he tells me.

They share a quick glance and smiles that they try to hide.

"I saw that."

"Reagan, you seem to keep forgetting not only who our parents are, but also who your mother is. They're the King and Queens. They will be the ones who must decide how to proceed with the moonstone."

"I'm never going to fit in with court life. I wear pants, and I love stuffing my face with food. Princesses' waists look so tiny in those frilly dresses. I'll never squeeze into one."

"Shay and I both love that you're not afraid to eat and enjoy your food. Riel is like you. Most of the females in Shay's army are the same way."

"Worse," Shay adds, "Rea's face gets covered in food, brother."

"True, and we also find those formalities at court annoying, to say the least," Nova frowns.

"I can't bear to stand on ceremony," Shay complains.

"And I wish I had some food to stuff my face right now," I agree.

"And remember, Reagan, the three of us are also royalty," Nova reminds me.

I cringe at being reminded I'm royalty, but I'm so comfortable with them. I love how easy it's always been with them, right from the start. That makes me happy, yet at the same time, I can't escape the lingering thought about coming between them. It seems unfair. Who they both are and what they represent is too much to interfere with. I don't want to lose the friendships I have with them, although I also can't deny that I'm attracted to them. Both of them.

CHAPTER 14

Since I woke up, I've been restless and eager to ride hard, but doing so would be unfair to the horses. We are so far south of the mountains that I can see grass below the dusting of snow covering it. I wish I could smell it and feel it beneath my feet. The sky is not as foreboding here, but a gray haze mutes any hint of brightness. It's been four years since I have enjoyed the warmth of the sun on my face.

Entering through the gates of the city proper, I start thinking about riding hard again, right up to the castle steps. My heart thuds against my ribs at the thought of finally being able to see my sister.

"Easy, Rea." Shay pats my arm, startling me. "If you go charging in, the guards might think their queen is being attacked. Especially since their king has recently been murdered."

He has a point. The more we get to know each other, the more he can read my thoughts through my facial expressions—and I learn each day how much more annoying he can be.

"I'm nervous she won't be there."

"Trust your uncle, Reagan. We're in the city. Have faith and believe that they're in this city too," Nova chimes in, hoping to calm my anxiety. And, as always with him, it does.

"And unless Shadow Demons start raining from the sky, you have nothing to worry about right now."

The possibility of the unexpected is what worries me, but when one of Hamon's guards approaches us, bowing slightly, I have to hold back my smile.

"Captain Hamon sent me to retrieve you. One of his scouts spotted you about an hour ago. Please, follow me."

We dismount and follow him through a side door near the stables. The smell of hay and manure catches my attention, but not enough to keep me from noticing that Shay and Nova are communicating in their weird telepathic way.

"What are you two talking about?"

"We like Captain Hamon. Shay and I were wondering how long it would take for one of his guards to approach us and, having gotten to know him better, we agreed it would be once we entered the city walls."

"Why?"

"It's what we would do, Reagan."

As I twist and turn through the castle halls, the endless delay in seeing Willa makes my every breath ache. My chest is tight and constricted. We enter a dining room, one I've been in before, to find my mother, Willa, Hamon, and another young woman who I believe is Emily, bent over the table looking at a book. They're so engrossed, they don't even notice us entering.

"Willa," I whisper, the sound escaping me as a fragile plea. The moment my voice breaks the silence, everyone's eyes shift toward us.

"Reagan!" Willa gasps, and in that instant, a radiant smile blossoms on her face, lighting up the heaviness that has surrounded us for too long. We rush toward each other, my heart racing as we close the distance that felt hopeless for so long.

As I wrap my arms around her, the weight of all those years

crashes over me, and I struggle to catch my breath. My knees give way, and we tumble to the ground together, a mix of relief and joy momentarily overwhelming us. Tears spill down my cheeks, and I sob uncontrollably, each shuddering breath a release of the pain I've held inside. I cling to her, terrified that if I let go, she might vanish from my life again.

After nearly four and a half years of heartache and silence, I finally find the opportunity to speak the truth that's been buried deep within me. With a trembling voice, I say, "Willa, I never abandoned you."

"I never believed Mother when she told me you had left. I was afraid she'd done something horrible to you because I always knew you would come back if you could." She hiccups between sobs of her own. Those words make me cry harder. Willa rubs my back and reassures me. "Take deep breaths. I've missed and loved you every day, Rea."

My little sister is comforting me. "I love you, and I've missed you, too."

"It's over now. We're together." She lays her head on my shoulder, and I want to cling to this moment forever.

"Oh, my dear Willa." I gently wipe away her tears and take her face in my hands. "Help me up so I can take a good look at you. You have grown so much since the last time I saw you." Standing, I step back and hold her at arm's length, still seeing the little girl in the young woman before me.

"Rea, what in the name of the Forgotten Gods were you thinking when you jumped off that ship?"

"That I was going to rescue you, of course."

"I had a plan to get Emily and me to the boat. Cormac knew where you were hours before you arrived. He had small boats painted in spots of white, gray, and brown that camouflaged them from sight."

"Look at you, Willa. You're a fierce little fighter, like me. What did you say to me in the water? I couldn't hear you."

"That you're an idiot, but I love you." Laughter echoes throughout the room and I spot Emily walking toward us.

"Yep, that's her sister," I hear Shay remark over my shoulder. I ignore him, yet smile despite myself.

Emily crushes me in a hug. "Thank you. I have a lot to learn about bravery from both my little and big sisters."

"I'm only a couple of days older than you," I point out. "I have a lot I could learn from you, too."

"I'm a bit confused and can't remember," Shay says. "How are you all related again?"

"Willa and I are not sisters by blood," I begin. "Willa and Emily are half-sisters and share the same mother, Ciara. Emily and I are also half-sisters because we have the same father."

"We are sisters," Willa insists. "And always will be."

"Agreed." I smile at her and feel a lightness in my heart I could never have imagined.

"Reagan," my mother begins, "you will be pleased to know, my child, that your cousin, Fintan, has been a great help in your quest." The sound of his name causes me to cringe. I try my best to conceal my discomfort, but it's not easy. "He has been training as a scholar in the grand library and has uncovered important information that we need to discuss. The Winter Solstice is less than two weeks away."

Introductions are made between Shay and the girls, and then we recount the last two week's events, filling them in about finding the missing citizens and about the children that we brought back.

My mother gasps when we tell her that the moonstone has also been recovered.

"Nova,"—Hamon clears his throat to get everyone's attention —"when Ciara mentioned Nanaka, I remembered that she was a demigoddess and figured it might be a good idea to do a little more research on her." He slides the book they'd been reading across the table. "I saw this illustration, and it got me thinking more about the tip of your Staff. I think it might be an actual piece of the moon, from Alarick, like your histories tell. Fin found mention in this book on demigods and goddesses. It says the Sun Goddess Suvi gave her daughter, Nanaka, a Spear of great power, to provide balance." He turns the book so we can see the illustration. "That's the only mention of it anywhere he could find so far."

"That's different." I point at the picture of Nanaka. As I gaze at the image in front of me, my eyes fixate on the figure of Nanaka, whose powers possibly mirror my own. The image of Nanaka is holding a bronze Staff. The tip resembles flames and appears to be made of black and orange, flaming marble, which adds to its ominous appearance. I can't help but wonder about the significance of the Staff of Storms, Obsidian Sword, and Nanaka's weapon and what powers they might hold.

"You're right. It's called The Sun Spear," Hamon explains. "That's why we're theorizing that they're a matched set and that Nova's is the partner piece."

It's a beautiful bronze spear with an incredibly sharp-looking, fiery black-and-orange tip. A round orb that looks identical to the tip sits about six inches below it, surrounded in gold.

"Nothing was found during the searches of the temples on the outskirts of the city," Hamon continues, "and the temple on the Isle of the Crescent Moon was empty."

"If the temples are empty, where could it be? The boys and I should go to the temples. We might be able to feel something the guards weren't able to."

Hamon shakes his head. "We have a different location to target."

"What's that?" I ask.

"Fin also discovered an abandoned temple, The Pyramid of the Sun, which hasn't been used in over eighty years. It's on Phoenix Isle."

"I've never been there," my mother imparts.

"Where is it?" I inquire.

"It's a two-day journey," Hamon advises. "We have a ferry

waiting at the coast. Afterward, we will rendezvous with the Wolf King and Queen back at Outpost One." He looks at the boys. "A messenger arrived with a letter. They made it there safely."

"Hold on, hold on," I interrupt. "We've been traveling for weeks now, and we desperately need some hot food, clean clothes, and a little rest." My voice cracks with exhaustion. The weariness of the journey has taken its toll on all of us, and we are in dire need of some comfort and relief from the hardships of the road.

Willa and Emily come to my aid, while Hamon helps the boys. My mother tells us that hot food will be waiting when we return. I wash and change quickly.

The girls guide me toward a cozy dining room I hadn't seen on my last visit, and the aromas of freshly cooked stew and warm bread waft toward me. The boys are already seated and devouring their meals. The table centerpiece is adorned with large chocolate treats dusted with powdered sugar. My curiosity and hunger lead me to grab one of the treats and pop the entire thing into my mouth, savoring the velvety sweetness as I scoop out a generous portion of the hot stew. My enjoyment is interrupted by a *tsst* sound from my mother, indicating her disapproval of my manners.

"My goodness, Reagan, Willa was raised in the same home as you, yet she eats like a lady."

"I'm starving," I mumble around a mouthful of food, which seems to irritate her more. I swallow and wipe my mouth on a napkin. "Sorry, Mother." Then I scoop a large bite of stew into my mouth, as politely as I can. I notice the boys are smirking, and I want to smack them in their faces.

"You are a Princess, my child, and you must act like one if you are to marry one of the Wolf princes—"

I choke, sending chewed bits of food flying out of my mouth —right onto my mother's face. Everyone in the room freezes in shock as the queen gracefully picks up a napkin to wipe off the mess. Much to my embarrassment, food that I thought I had swallowed was still in my mouth. As my mother walks out of the room with a stew-covered face, my heart races with adrenaline.

"I will see you in the morning." She doesn't attempt to hide her distaste as she bids us farewell over her shoulder without looking back. The guards close the door behind her.

CHAPTER 15

With the burden of my fears surrounding Willa lifted, I am eager to talk to her about Emily and how they got by during their captivity together.

Willa tells me that, during this terrifying time for them both, she and Emily found comfort in each other's company. Willa shared the struggles of the low-born, which broke Emily's heart to hear. During two days without food, Willa's strength got Emily through until their next meal arrived.

Emily, a member of the royal court, has taken a generous step toward assisting the less privileged by requesting the royal staff to provide two hot meals per day in the main courtyard for the low-born of the court. In addition, free vendors have been set up with clothing and blankets for those in need. Fresh bakery items and hot drinks will also be available between mealtimes, all free of charge. The girls will be volunteering their time to help out every day. This is a significant effort to help improve the living conditions of those who previously had to live in the shadows.

In light of this, my mother suggested creating a list of essentials that her subjects require. I wanted to suggest that she should go out and do it herself, but since she is still grieving the loss of her husband, I bite my tongue. This is not the right time for that particular discussion.

Nova, Shay, Hamon, my mother, her Queen's guard, and I will travel to Phoenix Isle. The girls stay at the castle to assist Fin with research, which may lead to more helpful information. I refrain from telling my sisters about Fin. They may hear about his cowardice but not from me. Still, I haven't been able to forgive him. The memory of begging for his help in that cave still makes me sick to my stomach.

Leaving Willa at the castle is not as hard as I thought it would be because she's safe, and that's all I care about. The last thing I want is for her to be where the danger is. She is only sixteen, after all.

Traveling with my mother and her guards is much different from traveling with Nova and Shay. It gives me time to get to know her better, and honestly, I don't know if I'm ready for that. Before I met her, she was just the Queen—the one who helped keep the low-born like me in poverty—I hated her. I couldn't help it. She represents everything I resent about the world I have been born into. But then, I find out she and the King are my parents, and just after meeting them my father, the King, was murdered right before my eyes, her eyes, I felt sympathy for her. It was brief, almost fleeting, but it was there. That didn't change the rage in me, though.

Now, traveling with her, I'm starting to see her a bit differently. Yes, I have always known she was the Queen, but now I see her as a female, as mine and Emily's mother. She has been through a lot over the last twenty years under the glamor and curse, especially when she as a mother somehow knew Emily was not her flesh and blood, though she did not know why. It makes me reflect on the reasons I have hated her, and while those struggles are still there, I'm beginning to see her as a victim too.

Would she have been different, would she have made better choices, had there been no glamor? And more importantly, has she been a pawn in this game that she didn't know was being played?

Sometimes when we walk side by side, I struggle to see the Queen I once hated. I don't see a dictator full of authority, as I expected. She has weariness in her eyes, a sadness I did not anticipate. Is it all for the loss of her husband? Or is it for everything that has transpired? Maybe I have been looking at her all wrong. Perhaps she is not just a Queen who failed the low-born but a female who's carried the weight of her kingdom for too long.

Yet I can feel a change, a shift, but I'm not sure where it will take us. Maybe it'll lead to something better between us, or perhaps it won't. Either way, I know that the female I'm traveling with is starting to feel a little more like a... not quite a mother, but maybe a friend and I'm not sure if that's a good thing.

Once we reach Phoenix Isle, we can no longer continue on horseback. The abandoned area is covered in dense, thorny overgrowth, which would injure the horses.

As we set out on foot, Nova reminds me about the possible side effects of proximity to powerful artifacts. The nausea will be worth it if the Sun Spear is there.

We press forward in silence, feet crunching in the thick, sharp vegetation, each of us lost in our thoughts. What if it's true that the Sun Spear could turn the tide in our fight to free our missing loved ones and break the glamour for good? I pray to the gods that our efforts are not in vain.

"I'm willing to bet the temple is just beyond those trees," I announce, "because I'm feeling nauseous."

"Me too," the boys state in unison.

"Mother, what about you and Hamon? Are either of you feeling nauseous?"

"No, my child. That only happens to those new to power.

Ham and I were well over the age of eighteen when the glamour started."

Out of the corner of my eye, I see Ham rolling his eyes. "It's true."

I fight to suppress my smile.

As we finally clear the thick brush, a gigantic pyramid stands before us, towering above us like the trees. Its surface is adorned with ornate carvings that remind me of those on the staff and sword.

"It's beautiful," my mother breathes.

"Yes, it is. Why don't you use this anymore?"

"It's *we*, Reagan, and that's a good question."

"It's almost identical to the Pyramid of the Moon," Nova remarks.

"How so?" I ask.

"Ours is also a pyramid," he explains, "but ours has a moon rather than a sun on top."

The surrounding forest has almost claimed the lower half of the structure. My mother's guards take charge of clearing a path through the thick brush, creating an opening that allows us to access the stairs that lead to the pyramid's entrance. Then they cut a path around it.

Despite the overgrowth, we can't help but take a moment to appreciate the magnitude of the structure. As we walk around it, we marvel at the carvings and the sheer size of the massive blocks that had been used to create it.

"The runes are the only difference we can see," Shay observes.

"Three of its sides are solid, no access in," Hamon adds.

"The Pyramid of the Moon is the same, and it only has an open plateau at the top," Nova tells us. "No rooms or doors that we could find."

"I'm curious to see what's at the top," I state.

Finally, after taking one last moment to admire the ancient architecture, we begin our ascent up the stairs, eager to uncover the mysteries that await us. Each step of the gigantic staircase appears narrower than the last, making it quite a challenging climb. Finally, we reach the top.

The temple proper is wide open to the elements, and as we step inside, we are greeted with an awe-inspiring sight. The back altar wall is adorned with the magnificent Sun Spear, which is carefully nestled in a deep cavity that's been carved into the altars stone.

"It's here" I whisper.

"This is how we found The Staff of Storms," Nova tells us.

As we move closer, Nova cautions me to slow my steps. I heed his warning and walk slowly, taking in every detail of the Sun Spear.

The Sun Spear is truly a sight to behold. But what truly captures my attention is the fiery orb that sits below an incredibly sharp tip that completes the Spear's elegant design. It glows with an intense heat yet manages to maintain a delicate balance with the rest of the Spear. It is truly a work of art that deserves to be admired up close. The power thrumming off it courses through my veins. Warm vibrations begin flowing through my body in its presence, rather than shaking from chills with Nova's Staff.

"This, this belongs to me," I state. The heat that's radiating from the Spear is unreal. Yet nothing is holding the fiery orb that matches the tip in place. I point at the floating orb. "How is that possible?"

"I don't know. But it has the identical marking as the Staff and Obsidian Sword," Nova says.

As I take a final step forward, I am flanked by Nova and Shay, who follow closely behind. Above us, the sky begins to transform: thick, dark clouds gather and the atmosphere becomes heavy, charged with electrical energy that prickles along my skin.

"Maybe you should both wait down below," I suggest to my mother and Hamon.

They look as though they might argue but begin their descent back down the steep stairs.

I start to reach for the Staff, but something doesn't feel right. I hesitate and turn to the boys.

"Yes." Nova nods. "This seems too easy, like when we found the Staff."

"I agree," Shay replies, "but we need this. Your Staff breaks the glamour on anyone who holds it. I'm certain this will do the same."

"Take my hands," Nova requests. "If this is a trap, if I sense the slightest hint of danger, I'm going to get us out of here."

I take one of Nova's hands and Shay takes the other. "Ready?"

"Yes," they respond in unison.

As I wrap my free hand around the Sun Spear, a sudden surge of molten power and energy courses through my body, a sensation like an electric current running through my veins.

Despite the chaos around me, a sense of calm washes over me, as the power seems to make me momentarily invincible. When the swirling winds clear, I am standing alone. My hand grips the Spear, and my heart pounds as I try to make sense of what's happening. Suddenly, my knees give way, and I land hard on the hot stone floor.

The darkness that had been enveloping the plateau has cleared away along with the boys, and I can see again. But my relief is short-lived. As I try to rise, I'm suddenly engulfed in flames.

Crackling surrounds me, and the acrid smell of smoke fills my nostrils. Panic sets in, and I realize that I'm in serious trouble. All I can think about is how to get out of this inferno alive. The heaviness of the heat pushes me to the floor, and I'm swallowed by blessed unconsciousness.

～

"REAGAN, WAKE UP."

"What happened?" My voice is thick and barely audible.

Nova's worried expression changes to one of relief. "You passed out," he explains. "But you're going to be okay."

"But what caused me to pass out?"

"There was an explosion. I tried to protect you, but I couldn't shield you completely." He lifts me in his arms. "I have you now. Hold tight."

When I finally re-emerge from the disorienting darkness, I find myself behind my mother, Shay, and Hamon. Nova places me on my feet and then moves away from me as I try to make sense of the surreal experience.

"Mother," I manage to get out before I fall to my knees and vomit, hard. I guess that explains why Nova stepped away from me. Insufferable jerk.

"I take it you knew this would happen," I ask, then rinse my mouth from the canteen he hands me.

"Yes, we did, Love. No need to spoil all the mystery." Shay snorts with laughter.

"Is there anything I can do for you?" my mother offers.

"No, I'm fine." My words are more confident than my voice. "We have three weapons," I add. I collapse my Spear and strap it to my side.

"We do," Shay affirms, "and hardly any damage to the temple at all."

"Reagan," my mother says, "we must return to the ferry. We still need to collect the Wolf King and Queen before making our way to the Isle of the Crescent Moon in time for the solstice."

It takes us until nightfall to reach the port where the ferry is waiting to take us to Port Kennedy. Upon boarding the vessel, I immediately make my way below deck to seek some rest. My physical condition is shaky at best—I'm hot and sick to my stomach. I refuse to relinquish the Spear, though, in the hopes that the sickness I feel will pass faster if I keep the weapon nearby instead of exposing myself a little at a time. My mind is racing with an intensity that I've never experienced before. Despite feeling like garbage, I am comforted by the fact that the boys understand my condition. Nova, in particular, can relate to my experience since he too felt similar symptoms when he acquired the Staff, though his were rooted in cold rather than heat.

I close my eyes and take deep breaths, but the sound of someone approaching with a familiar swagger reaches me.

"What do you want, Shay?"

"Aren't you in a fine mood? If you don't want my help, I'll leave."

"No. Stay. I'm sorry. I do need to talk. I'm feeling a mix of emotions."

"Be honest, Love. What are you feeling inside? In your mind this time, not your body?"

Thinking on that for a moment, I answer honestly. "Like I'm bouncing back and forth between madness and joy."

"How does the madness affect you, Love?"

"Makes me wish I had this Sun Spear when Cormac took me. I could have killed him and his goons myself but was outnumbered. Or maybe I want revenge on those who have wronged me. Like Fin and Kyle for calling me a whore. I want them to know what it feels like to suffer. This darkness inside me, this hatred, has always been there. I've wanted to let go and lose control for a long time, but I was powerless. Now that I have my Spear—and make no mistake, this is *my* Spear—I'm not powerless anymore. I just need to learn how to control it."

Shay reaches his hand out toward my Sun Spear.

"What in the depth of the shadows do you think you are doing, Shay? This is mine!" I clutch the Spear and recoil from him.

"Let me have it for a moment, Rea. You need to catch your breath."

The back of my brain tells me he's making sense, that this rage is too much to bear all at once. My arm feels leaden as I lift it to hand over the Spear to Shay. The entire situation seems to be playing out in slow motion, and every movement feels deliberate and calculated. Despite my unease, I manage to hand it to him, but I can't shake the feeling that something is off. He carries the Spear across the cabin and sets it down—and my fury seems to dissipate.

"I'm sorry. I don't know what came over me," I sputter.

Shay walks back to me. "You will need to find a balance between the madness and joy, or the darkness will consume you."

"I don't know how."

"Neither do I. Yet one thing is certain, you cannot carry the Spear regularly. Nova got overwhelmed with the power of the Staff at first, too. Take it slow for now. Nova and I took turns carrying it at the beginning for his sake. I'm going to take it above deck to have a good look over it with the others. You should stay and sleep."

"I'm restless but am better now that the Spear isn't tucked against my side."

"Tell me, Love, what does the joy feel like?"

"I just want to make a positive impact on the world by helping the low-born."

"Focus on that and get some rest."

"Is that an order?" I can already feel myself drifting with the waves.

"It is."

As the boat approaches the dock, my heart starts racing with excitement. I can't wait to see Murphy and introduce him to my mother. She's been eagerly waiting to meet him too, and I can tell from the tone of her voice that she genuinely means that.

As the boat finally docks, I see Murphy standing on the pier, his arms outstretched in anticipation. I bounce on my toes as the gangplank is lowered. Finally, the thin bridge connects with the ground, and I rush toward Murphy, who embraces me in a warm hug. The feeling of his arms around me is like coming home after a long journey. "Murphy, I would like you to meet my mother, Avalyn. Queen Avalyn."

Murphy bows and then straightens before speaking. "It's an honor to meet you, your Majest—"

"Please, Lieutenant Murphy," my mother cuts him off. "I've already heard about your love for my daughter, and I can't thank you enough for taking care of her when I could not. I insist you call me Avalyn."

"Your Ma—"

"Avalyn," she corrects.

"Avalyn, I wish there was more I could have done."

"You have done more than any other person in her young life, and I would like you to start finding and training your replacement as soon as possible. I would like to offer you a new position within the palace."

I am just as surprised as Murphy by the offer. He will have a stable home at the palace, and I'll be able to see him all the time. Does that mean I'm considering living there too? I could be near my sisters and have the chance to get to know Emily and spend some much-needed time with Willa.

"Thank you, . . . Avalyn," Murphy grins, clearly stunned. "Call me Murphy." He leads us inside, where the Wolf King and Queen are waiting.

The boys definitely look like their father. He also has shoulder-length hair and bright blue eyes. Their build is similar, but Raiden has a leaner frame, and the boys are much more muscular and they are at least six inches taller.

Their mother, Talvi, is about the same height and weight as I am. She crushes each of them in a tight embrace. She has bright blue eyes and long dark hair that is parted and braided on both sides of her head. Braids seem to be a tradition in the Wolf Court, and I like it. The boys quickly update their parents on everything that has happened since Shay's last letter, and then King Raiden steps forward and speaks to me.

"When I received a letter from Shay, he spoke of an incredibly brave female who he and his brother cherish. It is my pleasure to meet you. Donovan, there was also mention in the letter of your powers changing, mutating, that you are possibly a Windwalker?"

"I could not recall the name of the power, but yes."

"Your great-grandfather was a Windwalker." Raiden nods approvingly. "He was able to become the very wind itself, bending time and space to his whim, teleporting himself over great distances. But he did not have the power of winter storms like you."

"I can carry two with me, a short distance, though I feel heavier with them, weighed down."

"I have never heard of my grandfather being able to bring another with him. This appears to be a new manifestation of our male bloodline." Nova's father proudly claps him on the back.

"The solstice is only days away. We must get to the isle and return the moonstone. The ferry is ready and waiting."

As I embark on my journey back to the Isle of the Crescent Moon, I find myself filled with a mix of apprehension and excitement at the prospect of finally being able to use my powers to their full potential.

We discuss our hope that this will finally break this wretched curse, or spell that has been repressing our powers for so long and allow all fae to fully harness our abilities—not just to help rescue those who are missing, but to live our lives as we were meant to.

CHAPTER 16

As we sail across the bay, Hamon reveals that he has already instructed Murphy to round up as many guards as possible as we are traveling with the Queens and the King. Murphy managed to gather around one hundred guards, and the Wolf King's Army has also provided an equivalent number of troops to join us on our journey. Gabe, Q, and Riel will be waiting for us at the Temple of the Rising Moon.

Upon discovering that Murphy had already appointed someone to take over his role, I was adamant that he should accompany us. Despite my eagerness, nobody raises any objections. Murphy was appointed as the captain of Emily and Willa's royal guard and will be heading to the capital after the solstice. This news was incredibly exciting, especially since Willa has now been granted the title of princess. I still find it hard to believe that I am a princess—and I am determined to never let anyone address me as such.

We finally arrive at the temple, just before the Solstice begins. Shay greets his cadre. The energy of the moonstone pulsates in my veins. The moonstone possesses immense power, and during the solstice, anyone within a ten-mile radius of it will have their powers restored. And that's exactly what we need right now. We've been weakened for far too long, and it's time for us to reclaim our strength.

As we step inside the temple, energy surges within me. We are here to take back what's rightfully ours, and nothing can stop us. We will not let anyone stand in our way, and we will do whatever it takes to restore our powers. With renewed determination, we head toward the dais, ready to claim our birthright. For safety reasons, we decide only me, the boys, our parents, Hamon, Murphy, and the cadre will enter the temple.

The walk to the center dais seems to stretch on for an eternity, each step heavier and heavier. Despite the weight, Gabe carries the moonstone with relative ease, as if it doesn't weigh over two hundred pounds. He approaches the obsidian basin and places the moonstone inside before stepping back to rejoin the others. I remember the three slots on each side that I thought were drawers with missing handles. The diameter looks the same as the tip of my spear . . .

"I have an idea!" I draw my Spear from its sheath and grip it firmly. A jolt of energy courses through my body as I attempt to fuse the Spear with the missing handle, but they don't quite fit. I take a deep breath and try again, determined to make it work.

"Now I have an idea," Shay says. "The runes on our weapons—the dots, dashes, and stars. They're swords, moons, and suns. Each side has one of the symbols. Let's try that order." He walks over to me and withdraws his Sword, sliding it right inside. "Perfect fit."

A clunk sounds from within the dais. Nova walks to the slot with the symbol of the moon, inserts his Staff, and another clunk sounds.

"We have no idea what will happen when I connect my Spear."

Even so, they're clearly designed to be used in this way. Excitement courses through me as I slide my Spear into the final opening, and a satisfying clunk echoes through the temple. The boys and I exchange a look, anticipation hanging in the air.

Suddenly, a surge of energy ripples through my core, signaling that something incredible is about to happen.

And it does, though it isn't what I expected. "My Sun Spear is getting hot," I tell the boys, "and my body is vibrating."

"My Sword is vibrating and becoming cold," Shay says.

"My Staff is getting cold, too."

My mouth starts watering and a wave of nausea washes over me. "I might be sick." I retch as if to prove my point.

"Reagan, drop it!"

I try to but my hands don't comply. I can no longer tell where my flesh ends and the metal begins, as if the two are melting together. "I can't! My hands are stuck to it."

"I'm stuck too, Love."

"Everyone out of the temple!" Nova shouts.

I can see my hands nearly glowing, turning red. And now my feet are stuck in place too. "I can't move."

"Nova, you're turning blue," Shay states.

Sweat drips down my face, and my back is on fire. I think I would collapse if the Spear wasn't holding me firmly in place. "I'm . . . weakening."

"Reagan, wings of flame are shooting out of your back," Nova tells me. "And something is off with your eyes. They look like a cat's eyes."

Feline eyes and flaming wings. Didn't I see that in a book recently?

"I might pass out," I groan weakly as dizziness slams into me like a physical blow. The world tilts and spins, and suddenly, the oppressive heat of my flaming wings feels too much to bear.

Then—Shay disappears.

"Shay!" I gasp, frantically searching the space where he was just standing, but the air is empty.

"Rea." His voice is faint and distorted as if echoing across a vast chasm.

"I can't see you." Panic tightens my chest, pressing the breath from my lungs. Everything is a blur of swirling reds and oranges as if the flames inside me have set the world on fire.

"Neither can I, brother." Nova's voice grows softer and more distant, and I feel a cold, crawling unease slithering through me.

"I'm still standing right here," Shay calls out, but his words are muffled like he's far beyond my reach.

Now, my heart is hammering. "We can't see you at all."

The temperature rises. My flames—my *own* flames—feel wrong. They're no longer empowering. They're devouring me. I don't know what's happening.

"I can see you both. Wait, Nova, I can't see you anymore." Shay's voice cracks.

"Me either, Nova. Can you still see me?" I can barely hear my own voice over the deafening rush of my pulse in my ears.

"No, Reagan, only flames of bright reds and oranges where you stood," Nova tells me, his words blending with the sizzling sound of burning air.

"My whole body is weakening. Shouldn't it be *strengthening?*" My breath catches in my throat. The acrid, bitter scent of smoke burns my nostrils, thick and suffocating. It coats the back of my throat, churning with bile, the taste metallic and foul. If I had strength, I believe I could breathe fire if I wanted to. It's there, flickering just beneath my skin, but it's *wrong*. My wings, my flames—none of it feels like mine anymore. This isn't what I expected.

The world around me spins, colors warping in a dizzying kaleidoscope. My vision goes hazy like my eyes are trying to adjust to some cruel, new reality. It's like I'm drowning in flames. I swallow back the molten bile rising in my throat, but it's too much.

"Reagan," Nova's voice comes again, but it's muffled like he's speaking from far away. "Open your eyes."

I force my eyes open, but the world is still chaotic. Briny sweat drips from my forehead, stinging my eyes, and I quickly shut them again, trying to hold on to the last shreds of clarity.

My chest is tight, my breath ragged. "Are you both still there?" I manage to croak out, my voice trembling.

"Yes," Shay says, though his voice has an echo to it, distant and hollow.

"You look like a shadow of yourself, brother," Nova adds, the words barely reaching me.

"Thanks, big brother. I feel like a shadow of myself right now." Shay's tone is still laced with his usual cocky humor, but it's strained, with the heaviness in the air.

I open my eyes again, forcing them to focus. The world clears just a little, but the nausea doesn't subside. Thank the forgotten gods for small miracles. I look at Shay, and the sight of him sends a shiver down my spine. He's not quite himself—not anymore. His form is translucent and smoky, a shadow of what he was, flickering in and out of existence, like he's become part of the air around us.

"He's being serious, Shay. We can see you now, though you're like a smoky shadow. I can see right through you." My voice cracks, panic creeping in.

"Am I still pretty?" Shay asks, his usual cocky grin still evident, even in his shadowy form.

I wheeze out a laugh, though it's hollow and strained. *If I couldn't still see his cocky face in the shadow form he now is, I think I might lose it.*

"My power is being pulled out of me," I whisper, staring at my hands, where the flames should be crackling bright and strong. Instead, they flicker weakly, like a candle about to be snuffed out. "Shouldn't it be flowing into me? Why isn't it flowing into me?"

"Reagan, look at me." Nova's voice snaps through the haze, sharp and clear, though it still sounds so far away.

I open my eyes again. And there he is, standing before me— but *not* standing in the way I'm used to. He looks as though he's made of snow; his form is pure white and untainted by flame or shadow. I almost don't recognize him.

The temple trembles beneath me. The ground shudders like it's alive, breathing beneath my feet. I lose my footing for a split second, my knees buckling as the air warps around me.

The edges of my vision pulse with heat, my wings crackling with power I can't control, and I feel the weight of the world pressing in, suffocating me. The sound of a low growl reverberates through the stone temple—distant, ominous.

I try to choke words out, but they barely reach my lips. "Something doesn't feel right."

The air thickens with a storm of shadow and flame, and the last thing I hear is the howls of pain from Shay and Nova, their voices twisted and distant, as though they're already being pulled away from me.

As I slowly regain consciousness, the acrid smell of smoke fills my nostrils, and a bitter taste of blood and ash fills my mouth. Blinking my eyes, I find myself surrounded by smoldering rubble. Heat emanates from the charred debris as I push myself up on all fours, trying to make sense of my surroundings. The dais is completely intact as if it is untouched by the chaos that surrounds it.

Reagan, Nova speaks softly, not sounding like himself at all.

When I turn around, I see a magnificent snow-white wolf with bright blue eyes and canines that look like daggers. As I try to stand up, something nudges me from behind, then it nudges my side.

I turn around and come face to face with an even larger, black wolf. Its striking blue eyes are the most beautiful I've ever seen, and they are familiar. *Shay. He's a massive wolf too, and gods help me if his wolf form doesn't have that same sexy smile.*

I knew you found me sexy, Love.

What is this?

We can teach you to switch it on and off, Reagan, Nova speaks in my mind, startling me.

"Why are you both in my head?"

You now appear to possess the ability to communicate telepathically with us. I can only assume it's part of the power of three, Nova surmises. *We will only enter your mind if it's an emergency, or if you welcome us in.* Then he snuggles his head against my shoulder.

"Thank you, Nova." I scratch him behind his ear. *Who's a good boy? I wonder if I can ride them like horses, they're big enough—* They startle me by laughing inside my head and howling out loud.

Oh gods, you heard that. How do I turn it off?

Their fits of laughter finally cut off in my head. Thank the gods. I used to think I wanted this ability. Not so much anymore. No one needs to hear what goes on inside my head.

We will teach you how to control it, Love. This should be interesting, to say the least. Then he winks at me, as a wolf. Incredible.

Suddenly remembering the chaos that happened, I look around for everyone else.

They're all on their feet. Cuts bleed through the torn fabric of their clothing. My mother is crying and smiling. Everything around us has been razed to the ground.

"Reagan, my daughter,"—my mother's voice sounds shaky, yet proud–"I do believe you have the demigoddess Nanaka's powers and you've come home to your rightful place, bringing the guardians of the Wolf Moon with you."

I try to speak, but first, I need to wipe the soot and blood from my lips. That's when I notice something strange. As I look at the faces before me, I see a mix of emotions: shock and awe, love and hope. Nova, a bright white wolf, stands on my right, while Shay, a midnight black wolf, stands on my left. They are my friends and loyal companions. I try to mimic their fierce expressions, aware of my own canine teeth now.

King Raiden steps forward and speaks before I do. "You three shall rise to fulfill the prophecy of the Power of Three." He walks up to me, placing a hand on my shoulder. "Reagan, you are the Sun, Nova the Moon, and Shay, The Darkness. And not only are you a shifter, like your grandfather and big brother,"—he proudly pets Shay's head–"you also have a new manifestation of the Windwalker powers, a Shadowwalker." I bet that's why he's always able to sneak up on me. Fascinating. "You will avenge The Phoenix King and your kingdoms. Your intertwined destinies are to destroy this Shadow King and bring peace back to our kingdoms before he has a chance to raise The Darkness."

The boys can't speak so I must say something. "I was just looking for my sister. Now I'm a princess, reborn in the likeness of a demigoddess, and fulfilling a prophecy to prevent The Darkness from rising? Well, shit."

MY PUPILS REMAIN VERTICAL SLITS, feline in nature, for a full five minutes before Shay says they're back to normal. Does that mean I could be a lioness like Nanaka?

"Rea, if I found out after all this time my powers couldn't do anything, I'd be a bit embarrassed, I'm just saying," Shay teases.

"Insufferable jerk. Go put some clothes on, for god's sake. Have you no shame?"

"No shame at all, Love."

No one else seems uncomfortable with Shay's nudity. His father's standing right next to him. Everyone else is not far away.

He's talking to his father, holding nothing but a ripped tunic over his crotch. His bare ass is exposed to everyone behind him. His chest faces me and it looks like it was carved from stone. I wonder if Nova looks like that too.

He does, Love.

You have got to be kidding me. I hear his laughter cut off in my head when out of nowhere, a pair of leather pants hits Shay in the face.

Turning to see where it came from, I see Nova, standing naked, canines exposed and looking all kinds of sexy. Unfortunately, his pack covers his crotch.

My gods, if those canines don't make him more sensual, more dangerous... My body starts responding to him immediately at the apex of my thighs. I wonder if he heard that exchange between Shay and me. I cock my eyebrow in question, and he nods yes. I take in my fill of Nova's toned, hard body. It's impossible, yet he seems bigger somehow. Looking my way back up, Nova is now breathing hard, chest heaving.

He looks into me in that intense way I love as his nostrils flare. He looks like he wants to eat me alive. A growl rumbles up from his chest and I take a step toward him. Before my foot lands, I'm consumed in darkness.

Rea, I've got you. Trust me, please, Shay urgently speaks into my mind.

Sight and sound leave me as I'm swallowed into a void of darkness. I can't seem to speak, but I trust he has a good reason. When my foot hits the ground, I'm on the hill above the temple, where I first looked down upon it.

"What's going on, Shay?"

"Do you want me to spare your feelings, or tell you like it is?"

"Tell me like it is."

"The surge of power kicked up our primal instincts that I told you about."

Now I might not want to know. But it's too late to back down. "Hit me with it, Shay."

"Nova scented your arousal and because of the power boost it hit him more intensely."

"You have got to be kidding me." I'm mortified.

"Again, I wish I was, Love."

"Meaning any male over the age of gods-damn eighteen could, too?" I wish I could disappear into the shadows.

"It barely reached my father and me—"

"Oh, my, gods. That's not helping, Shay."

"I'm doing the best I can to help you, Rea."

"Sorry, Shay. Please understand how incredibly awkward this is for me.

"It's okay. I needed to get you away quickly to spare you from everybody else knowing. My father was informing me that the first time getting your powers is difficult enough–he is struggling himself. Everyone is dealing with having their powers restored after all these years. The older males and females can feel the curse still repressing our powers, though they still have limited use. It appears only me, you, and Nova have full powers, though that is yet to be determined."

"Ciara said god-like powers."

"Whatever it is that the three of us now have within us, it also kicked our primal instincts into overdrive. Then add to that, Nova scented your arousal almost immediately. Our father is with him now. Remember, this is new for all of us."

"Can you please stop saying that word?"

"What word?"

"You know what word I'm talking about."

Arousal, he purrs into my mind seductively. *It's better than crotch.*

"You're insufferable."

"I'm trying to get your mind back on track. I know what it's like to be left on the outside, not having all the knowledge or information."

I know there's more behind that statement and I will remember to ask, but I have an embarrassing question first. "How long do we have to wait here?"

"Until you get your mind out of the gutter and remember every male in our party will scent the pheromones your body releases. Including me."

"For the love of the Forgotten Gods."

"Let's walk back, Love. It will give you more time to cool off."

We begin our way down the long hill. Once we reach the bottom, I stop Shay so I can share something with him.

"I'm glad it was you here with me. I've never been more comfortable with anyone in my life, and I'm realizing this is what having a real friend is like. Someone to have your back, someone looking out for you." I don't say any more because I might cry.

Shay doesn't speak either. He walks over and hugs me tightly, kissing the top of my head. Then whispers, "Hold tight, Love."

This time I'm aware of what's happening. It looks like I'm traveling within thick smoke made of shadows and darkness. As the temple gets closer, I spot Nova talking with his parents. He turns, looking directly at me within the darkness.

My feet no sooner hit the ground than I'm swept away in a beautiful wintery storm with snowflakes so large I can see the delicate intricacies of each one. It's breathtaking. They're swirling all around us in colors of blues, silver, and white. This is the first time I've ever enjoyed winter snow. It's fascinating. I love how he's able to create such beauty.

We land on the same hill above the temple that Shay and I were on.

Nova smiles at me and brushes a loose strand of my hair behind my ear. "I have a hold on myself now."

"I'm beginning to understand a little myself. Shay explained some of it to me."

"My father was starting to explain the different struggles we will face."

"Like what?" I see instant regret on his face.

"He had only begun when you and Shay arrived. Your mother was also looking for you."

If it was Shay, I would push for more, but for some reason, I know not to be pushy with Nova because it's awkward and embarrassing for both of us. I've had enough embarrassment today to last a lifetime. And I could use a good private conversation with my mother.

Nova extends his hand. "We should get back."

I take his hand in mine and he wraps me in his arms, kissing me on my head like Shay did before returning us to the temple in the same beautiful, snow-flaked winter storm. This time, though, there are extra snowflakes of emerald green, like my eyes. I'm feeling better already.

CHAPTER 17

We spent three full days camping at the ruins of the temple. Everyone's adjusting to having powers, however limited. It's honestly comforting to know that everybody else finds this as strange and difficult as I do. Maybe I was never as alone in the world as I'd once thought.

And how about the fact that mature males can scent things? I really wish I had known that from the start. If I ran the kingdom, I would make sure everybody had access to personal education, education of every kind, so nobody has to go through this kind of embarrassment.

I'm fully mature, and it's ridiculous that I don't know these things. I'm quite familiar with my own body, but the biology of males is something else. It's not like Murphy could have helped me with this...we couldn't have that kind of closeness in a military training facility. And the female teachers refused to teach me proper education because I was the daughter of a whore.

That wasn't my fault. However, it is their fault for how they treated me. Things need to change. The first step? Start educating myself while we plan and make ready to rescue the missing.

I'm alone at a campfire when my nose is flooded with the smell of freshly picked wintergreen leaves.

Nova, I speak into my mind.

Yes, Shay is with me. We wanted to know if you would like our company.

I now smell his peppermint. *Hi, Shay.*

Hello, Love. Would you mind if Nova and I suddenly appear in front of you? He chuckles.

Not at a— Before my words finish, they're standing in front of me. "That's a pretty cool trick you two share." I'm guessing one of the reasons they're here is to attempt to retrieve our weapons. When we first tried to remove our weapons, we all felt extremely sick, so we decided to wait a few days to adjust to the powers. I need to learn how to protect my thoughts, but for now, I have to trust they will respect my privacy. There are more important things to be done. "No sense dancing around the inevitable. Are you here because you want to try getting our weapons?"

"I've always said you're clever, Love."

Nova steps forward and takes my hand. Shay takes the other. Then we disappear into a beautiful snow-flaked storm of shadows and darkness.

I do envy their Windwalker abilities. We land about twenty-five feet from the dais. We need to figure out how to release whatever mechanisms have locked our weapons in place.

Currently, we are the only ones in the ruins of the temple. I'm grateful for that. Too many eyes have been on me and it makes me uncomfortable. We each try to remove our respective weapons, yet they're still stuck. Then I have an idea. "What if we try taking them out in the order we put them in?"

"That sounds like a brilliant idea," Nova responds. "After you, brother."

Shay places both hands on the hilt of his Sword. "Here we go."

"Nova, your turn," I tell him.

"Now you, Reagan."

"Anything?" I inquire hoping I don't sound desperate.

"No," they answer.

Systematically, I lift each of my fingers, making sure I'm not stuck, and fortunately, I'm not.

"What if we tried drawing up our powers," Shay suggests.

Pulling deep from within my core, an intense pounding begins. A surge of nausea washes over me and I begin to sweat. Suddenly, a single click sounds from within and I erupt into flames, my beautiful fiery wings springing open and free on my back.

Shay dissolves into shadow and Nova becomes a silhouette of snow. This time a surge of power envelops me. My muscles swell with strength and my elongated canines spring forth. "This was what I expected to feel the first time."

Unexpectedly, we fall backward, landing on our asses, our weapons having released at once. When I land with a thud on the floor, my Spear flies backward over my head, landing somewhere in the rubble.

Nova's already at my side offering his hand, taking it, I stand and brush myself off. "Anybody see where my Spear went?"

"It landed somewhere over there." Nova points.

Wings, I felt wings. I know I did. Could I possibly be able to fly? We look around for a few minutes before I finally spot it under a toppled column. Thank the Forgotten Gods.

"Wait a minute, don't move," Shay orders. "There's a piece missing from your Spear."

"For the love of the Forgotten Gods, the fiery orb that matches the tip is missing."

"Let's start searching the temple," Nova suggests. "It can't have gone far."

"I broke a weapon of the gods." Collapsing it, I strap it back at my side.

"We'll fix it, Reagan, don't worry. We should start with only the three of us searching, for now."

"I agree," Shay responds. "We don't need extra feet trampling around in here."

Hours of searching and no orb. Shay eventually has small groups come in and look. No one finds it. We even search the surrounding grounds.

I worry about how this will affect my powers. When I hold the Sun Spear, my canines, fiery form, and wings appear. Unfortunately, the moment I let go of it, they disappear. It's incredibly frustrating to not have control of my powers. Is this all because of the missing orb?

THE KING and queens decide we are going to travel to one of the Wolf Court outposts located north but between our Phoenix Court's Outposts Two and Three. It's called Wolf Crossing. It's their largest outpost and will easily accommodate us all. This is where we will make plans to rescue the missing. I'm eager for news about how things have been going at Port Kelsey and if the missing children's extended families have been located.

King Raiden and Shay are making plans to send a party to The Courtless when Riel approaches Shay with news of two Courtless spies caught in the woods.

Shay walks over to the two males sitting on the ground, hands bound behind them. "Why are you spying on us?"

"My name is Fergus, and this is my nephew Caden. We're not spies, though we are members of The Courtless. I was one of the few selected to be unglamoured when you were last here."

"Are you part of the council?"

"No, I am not."

"Why are you here?"

"I'm no spy," he announces again, loudly. "We didn't even know you were here. We were attempting to make our way to Port Kennedy before the council became aware of our absence."

"For what purpose?" Shay inquires.

"Now that my memories have been somewhat restored, I remember my parents were taken when I was only ten."

"Why do you say taken and not one among the missing?"

"I saw them taken. After being unglamoured during your visit, I spent weeks in a fog; however, I remember hearing when they were taken that they would be kept alive and not to fight. My parents didn't put up a fight because they already had me hiding in the woods. I tried speaking to the council . . . They want no part of it. They don't seem to care at all."

"That's the same feeling I got when we were there," I state. "I didn't like that they selected a handful of fae to be unglamoured." Taking the knife right out of Shay's belt, I release them from their bonds.

"Thank you. I didn't agree with that either. You were there to help. Who knows when we'd have seen you again."

"That's exactly what I was thinking." I like Fergus.

"What happened to the temple?"

"When we returned the moonstone, there was an accident," Shay admits.

"My nephew is twenty-five, and he was not chosen to be unglamoured despite what Sloane told you. Inexplicably, he and others started remembering things a few days ago," Fergus states.

I knew Sloane didn't unglamour everyone over the age of twenty.

"The glamour had to have been broken when we drew in the power of the solstice," King Raiden announces. There are many grunts of agreement.

Fergus looks at each of us standing here. "Did you all have your powers restored?

"We did. However, they still aren't at full strength," Shay informs him.

"I must find my parents. Can you help me?" Fergus pleads.

Shay fills him in with everything we know about the missing, then Fergus informs us that Sloane has complete control of The

Courtless. Anyone caught trying to leave has been imprisoned and their families are made to suffer as examples of what happens to traitors. After they're released, they fall back in line under pressure from Sloane and other council members.

Fergus and Caden shock us all by dropping to their knees, swearing fealty to The Wolf Moon Court. They want to be a part of this fight and I don't blame them. How many others feel the same way? Shay tells them that even without them having their power restored, the amount of courage it took to leave is worth one hundred males, and he would be proud to have them in the King's Army.

"I have an idea," I announce.

"Tell me, Rea," Shay requests.

"What if you send out riders throughout all the different villages and towns in the Kingdoms? See who's willing to join in this fight against the Shadow King and help rescue the missing. I'll bet there are a lot more like Fergus and Caden out there."

"That's a brilliant idea," Shay praises, and I smell a burst of peppermint so I prepare for him to enter my mind. *Haven't I always said you're a clever girl?* "Riel," Shay shouts aloud in his official Commander voice, "make it happen. Also, take the cadre and two units to advise the entire Courtless colony of what's transpired. Anyone wishing to leave will be welcomed."

Riel takes off and Hamon advises he will do the same for our kingdom. Murphy himself will be leading the unit of Phoenix guards, and I've never seen him so eager. I notice that he looks healthier somehow, too. Everyone does. Maybe it's the effects of finally having our powers restored. It is late in the day when the cadre returns with about one hundred and fifty members of The Courtless, and we decide to spend one more night before making our way to Wolf Crossing.

CHAPTER 18

The following morning everybody's up early, eager to go and I make my way to Murphy to say goodbye. But I stop in my tracks as I catch sight of my mother having a conversation with him. He's positioned near the horse's head, holding onto its reins while my mother grips the bridle and strokes the horse's head. Her body language seems informal and relaxed, rather than regal.

Giving them privacy, I decide to hang back for a moment. There will be no time for goodbyes once we reach port, as there will be chaos as we break into groups and board separate vessels. Half of the Phoenix and Wolf Moon guards will remain behind to protect the moonstone. We cannot let it fall into the wrong hands again. Shay will also have reinforcements and supplies sent over. As much as we want to practice with our new powers, it's six months until the next solstice. We need to conserve our strength for the rescue.

Wolf Crossing looks like a large village rather than a military outpost and there are children everywhere, which amazes me. Off in the distance, I notice rows of housing that must be for the soldiers and their families. Everybody looks happy here—children frolic about and it's clear that soldiers and workers are permitted to have their families living here with them.

"I'm going to rip their throats out with my teeth," someone threatens.

I turn my head to locate the origin of the voice, and my eyes catch sight of an incredibly gorgeous male— a striking winter fae— walking toward us. The way he walks, the aura he emanates, and the expression on his face send chills down my spine. This male could kill someone with just a glance. His hair is luscious and dark, intricately braided over the top of his head. The sides are shaved, revealing the smooth skin of his scalp. As he gets closer, I see his eyes are a piercing winter fae blue, and his jawline is sharp and chiseled.

His gait is similar to Shay's swagger, but there is something different about him. Shay's walk is confident, sensual, and alluring. However, this male's walk conveys a sense of violence and death, making him appear dangerous, and even frightening. As he approaches us, I can't help but think that he must be another member of the cadre.

His every step sends tremors through the ground. I cannot help but admire his beauty and wonder if I was born in the wrong kingdom. The males in the north are just as stunning as the females here. I am curious about what they eat or what they do to maintain such striking appearances. It's fascinating to see how different regions have their unique attributes and qualities.

As he takes the last few steps forward, his imposing demeanor suddenly softens, giving way to a warm and affectionate expression. He approaches Nova, wrapping his arms around him in an embrace so tight that it leaves him momentarily breathless. Then he turns toward Shay, his next target, and envelops him in a similar embrace, conveying a sense of deep affection and brotherhood toward both of them.

"Reagan, allow me to introduce you to Brody, a member of Shay's cadre and my most trusted friend."

Nova has a best friend. Why is this the first time I heard of this? I can see the similarities in them, particularly the intimi-dating way they both carry themselves.

"Why is this female covered in both of your vile scents?" He sniffs the air while looking me over. He's trying to get a read on me. His eyes do a quick survey of my body.

I brazenly return the favor before speaking. "It gets lonely on the road, Brody," I state, before walking away to join my mother and the others already heading inside.

"It's good to have you back, Commander." I hear Brody talking to Shay as I stride away. I also hear him advise Shay that everyone who was at Port Kelsey and both outposts are now here at Wolf Crossing and Outpost Three. A meeting is to be held in a half hour.

As I step into the meeting room, my gaze is immediately drawn toward the large, rectangular table that dominates the center of the space. The table is a sturdy piece of furniture, crafted from dark wood and polished to a high shine. It is surrounded by chairs and benches, each one neatly arranged and facing toward the table, as if waiting for a meeting to begin.

The room itself is relatively spacious, with plenty of open floor around the table. It is dimly lit, with a few small fae lamps set up on the walls, casting a soft glow across the room. The walls are made of rough-hewn stone blocks, much like the outposts that dot our territory. They are cool to the touch and give the room a slightly damp, earthy smell.

Apart from the table and chairs, the room is sparsely furnished. Against one wall, there is a single banner hanging from a hook. It is a beautiful shade of blue with crisp white trim and features a bold, stylized silhouette of a wolf howling at the full moon. The banner is a proud symbol of their Kingdom and a reminder of the strength and unity they share. Overall, the meeting room is a simple, unadorned space that serves its purpose well.

The rush of wintergreen assaults my senses. My signal that

Nova wants to talk. I nod slightly and then open my mind to him.

There's no formality at any of our outposts, only at the castle. You may sit wherever you wish.

Looking around, I spot Shay and smell peppermint.

Come sit by me, Love. I take the seat he's patting. *I noticed you looking around. The room is bare because it does not matter what hangs on one's walls. What matters is who sits within those walls.*

Nova sits next to Shay, and Brody sits next to Nova. Our parents, Hamon, members of the cadre, and about two dozen others file into the room, taking seats. I bump Shay under the table with my knee to let him know I want to talk.

How is it that Nova managed to make a best friend when you, as outgoing as you are, just did?

I was saving myself for you. He winks. *Tell me, Rea, what's your first impression of Brody?*

He seems more like Nova's brother than you do.

You would be surprised how little time Nova and I spent together growing up. Nova was fortunate to have Brody.

Is this what you were talking about, being on the outside? The look he gives me tells me exactly that. *Do you like Brody?*

Absolutely. He leads my cadre. I would trust him with my life. I'm certain you both will get along.

Shay, you're really my first true friend. I'm thankful we met. You're someone who's had my back from the moment we met, and I know you always will.

And I'm so much braver and better looking than your first friend, Fin.

You're an ass.

King Raiden's still talking with Queen Talvi and my mother, and I wonder if everyone else is waiting for one of them to speak when someone finally does. It's Shay, who I forgot has authority over the King when it comes to the army. Shay's in charge, and I realize the importance of him intentionally placing me on his right.

WE STAY UP LATE into the night, and when we finally make it to the boy's room, I am exhausted. The boys share an apartment in the outpost. There are two bedrooms, each having a private bathroom. I have my room with a private bathroom, which I assume was one of theirs as they are now sharing the other room.

I go over everything Shay said at the meeting in my mind. I'm not surprised at all that more arrived from The Courtless. I knew others would want to leave that phony place. I wonder how many will come now that the glamour has been broken. I can only imagine what will happen once the second regiment of guards shows up to recruit more. I wish I could see the look on Sloane's face.

Shay said this urgent situation requires the mobilization of all available vessels. The mission at hand is to rescue the missing, and any individual willing to lend a hand is welcome to join the effort. Riders had already been dispatched to all corners of our two kingdoms—from towns and villages to outposts and capital cities—to alert the populace of the looming threat posed by the shadow beasts. Those who choose to remain behind, however, will be directed to make their way to their respective capital cities, where they will be granted refuge and protection behind the fortified walls.

I was surprised to learn that the Wolf Court had constructed a tunnel through the mountains to enable faster travel. It's incredible how it takes only hours to cross the mountains instead days. I wonder why we haven't done this. Whatever the reason may be, it's fascinating and can make our lives easier and more efficient, and I can't wait to see it.

My mind wanders once again to thoughts of Willa and Emily. I can't help but worry about them. It's not just my close circle of loved ones that I'm concerned about either—I know that others throughout the kingdoms are worried about their friends and family. It's a difficult time for everyone. Despite my worries, I know that I need to stay focused and keep pressing forward.

CHAPTER 19

When I wake up, I'm starving. I bathe in the obsidian soaking tub then get dressed quickly, knowing food will be on the other side of the door. I don't know why I suddenly feel guilty for taking a few private moments for myself to relieve a little stress this morning. It's my body after all. Food will squelch that guilt right away. Shay is already seated at the table and more importantly, so is the food. I pour a glass of orange juice as I sit.

"Good morning, Love. I started my day off the very same way."

"What, with orange juice? This past year it's been hard to get to the outposts."

He's smiling like a wolf, nostrils flaring. Then he cocks an eyebrow.

"For the love of the Forgotten Gods, will nothing about my life be private?"

"I hope not, Love. It's so much fun."

Primal instincts. Primal annoyance is more like it. At least Nova will be respectful enough not to say anything. There are fresh fruits, cheeses, and lean sliced meats. As I pile food on my plate, Nova's finally joining us, and there's a knock at the door.

"I'm eating before I go anywhere," I state.

Nova opens the door and it's none other than Brody, his most trusted friend. A sudden peppermint breeze fills my senses, Shay indicating he wants to talk, so I open my mind to him.

What?

Brody and Nova will also notice as I did.

Don't make this worse. I will literally stab you with this cheese knife.

You're becoming so violent. It's normal, Rea. We are used to noticing these types of things.

Glaring at him, I swallow the mouthful of food, then wipe my face so I won't look like a slob. Shay, of course, tracks my move. Jerk.

Nova and Brody join us at the table.

Brody's nostrils flare, scenting the air. "Someone worked up a good appetite," he says by way of greeting.

Shay snorts out a laugh, failing to hold it in. Nova looks down trying to hide his smile while I sit here beet red in the face. Apparently, Brody is like Shay in that respect. Figures.

Grabbing a handful of grapes, I toss them in my mouth, then flip them both off. I turn back to Brody because he has yet to take his eyes off me.

"I'm very interested to get to know the female that stole my friends away." Without looking away from me, he adds, "Shay, you write such beautiful words in your letters."

"I didn't steal anything that wasn't already mine for the taking," I state.

Peppermint fills my senses again. Brody turns to Nova and they begin chatting about the glamour that has indeed been broken in both our kingdoms since the solstice was held.

What now, Shay?

You can be comfortable with him, I promise. If I had warned you ahead of time, would you have stayed seated? I shake my head no. *You're the female to lead the charge so others won't go through this without being aware. And look on the bright side, Love, at least you have three beautiful males to help you adjust.*

He's right. I know he's joking, but I get his point. I can handle this and I will lead that charge after we rescue the missing.

Shay, stay looking at me like this for another moment.

Based on your devious stare, I can't wait to hear what this is about.

I know these two excluded you from things when you were young, and I'm sure you've noticed they've stopped talking and are focused on us.

Indeed I have, Love. So, you figure it's my turn for a little payback.

Neither of us had a best friend or real childhood. We missed out on all kinds of incredibly immature things. I remind him.

Indeed. He smiles wider, letting his wolf show. I hold his gaze a little longer because it's so much more badass with the canines.

"So, tell me, Brody, what's so special about you that you're his friend"—I point at Nova—"and you lead this one's cadre." I switch to pointing at Shay.

"Blunt and direct. I like you already. Would you believe I'm royalty and was stuck with this one?" He points at Nova. "As his companion, no less."

Pausing, I observe him for a moment before responding. "Looks like things worked out pretty good for you."

He gives me a slight nod. His bright eyes remain fixed on mine, assessing me, studying me. "That they did, Reagan. They did indeed."

He is undoubtedly proud of who he is. Figures he's as beautiful as the boys. "I like you already too. Maybe it's because you smell like maple syrup and maybe that's because I'm hungry. Either way, please, call me Rea."

The three boys share a look between themselves, smiling in a way that makes my toes curl. What are they sharing with that look?

"So, tell me, Rea, how did a beautiful female like you wind up with these two?"

"Would you believe I'm also royalty and was swapped out a few days after my birth by my evil fake mother for my half-sister? Then, my evil fake mother dumped me in a training program where I was not welcome so I escaped and met these two."

His eyes still gaze into mine as he assesses me, again, no doubt wondering if what I said is true. He's gorgeous. Shay's right, things could be much worse for me.

"Looks like things worked out pretty good for you, too."

Blushing, I smile and roll with it. "That they did, Brody. That they did indeed."

Another knock sounds on the door. Nova and Shay exchange a quick glance and smile. Who could this be? Nova walks to the door, and when he opens it, someone hands him a bunch of wrapped packages. Shay and Brody start cleaning off the table, making room for whatever it is as Nova walks over and places the packages right in front of me.

"What's this?" I ask, excited.

"Most are from your mother," Shay informs me. "The rest are from Nova and me."

"This is all your mother's doing," Nova admits. "Murphy told her how you have no clothes, and that he gave you his wife's clothing."

Tears begin forming in my eyes. I've never received presents. A small part of me now wishes my mother could be here. A little thrill runs through me as I start with the package on top. It's new, knee-high, leather lace-up boots, in my size.

"Those are from me." Nova smiles.

"Thank you. They're wonderful." They're brand new and made for a female's foot. I've never had new boots, only hand-me-downs that never quite fit right. I hug them to my chest, unable to hold back the tears running down my face. I don't even care.

"Open this one next, Love." Shay hands me a slim box. I open it, eager to see what's inside, and, oh, my gods. It's a beautiful, hand-carved, obsidian dagger. The sharp blade looks to be at least six inches and it's double-edged.

"Thank you, Shay," I all but cry.

"Open this one next. It's from Riel," Shay tells me, handing me a light package. I struggle with untying the twine, until finally, I use my new dagger to cut it open. All types of little, colorful, silky, lacy items fall out. I pick up the black one and hold it up, turning beet red instantly. But I like what I'm seeing.

Quickly, I stuff them all back in the package, hoping to move on without any more talk about it. I start on the next one.

"It's all thick, warm, knee-high socks." I hold them up. "Thank you."

Nova pushes another package to me and this one's huge. "This is from your mother."

Opening it, I find all-new clothes, tops and bottoms, some even have soft fleece lining.

"I can't wait to wear these leggings," I tell them, laughing and crying a little.

"Riel also helped your mother with those," Nova reveals, "and with this one." He slides it across the table.

I tear it open to reveal leather pants and a coat. Standing up, I open the jacket, finding it's fur-lined and cut for a female's body. Shay slides another package across the table. I greedily grab it, ripping it open. Inside is a pair of new leather gloves, only different.

"The right glove has a built-in leather vambrace for wrist protection, like mine," Shay demonstrates by showing me his. I slip them on and oh my gods, they fit like a glove. Now that makes sense.

"Thank you, Shay."

"Even though we do not yet know each other, I have a gift," Brody tells me while unstrapping a dagger from his weapons belt. I had not yet noticed how many weapons it holds. "This is an Ancient Elven dagger from the world of Delunavir. My family has many, and I would like to give this one to you."

Looking down at the intricately-designed dagger Brody hands me, I am shocked by the his gift. The unique blend of silver and other metals make it stand out from any other weapon I have ever seen. The blade is so shiny that I can see my reflection in it. The hilt is adorned with delicate carvings, etched with words and symbols that I don't recognize. "Brody, I don't know how to accept this." I'm still mesmerized by the beauty of the dagger. "Thank you."

"Go try everything on, Reagan."

I scoop the gifts into my arms and make a run for the bedroom. If Riel helped pick the leather pants out, I hope they're fitted like hers. Another knock sounds on the door.

"Who is it?" I yell like I own the place.

"It's Riel."

"Come in! I need your help."

She opens the door and her eyes go right to me holding the new clothes. She smiles. She is also holding a package. I feel slightly dizzy—so many gifts all at once is overwhelming.

"You got your presents," she notices, following me into the bedroom without even a hello to the boys. I toss everything on the bed, when she hands me the package, and I rip it open as fast as I can.

"This will complete my outfit."

"Even though the pants are fur lined, I would definitely wear leggings under your leather pants."

"Will they both fit? They look so small."

"Oh yes, they definitely will." She twists around, showing me her back side.

I pick everything I'm going to wear, then slip into the bathing room to dress.

I ask her to braid my hair like the Wolf Queen's was when I first met her. She sits me, parts my hair in the middle, then weaves braids on each side, blending all my hair together. The ends of the braids fall to the middle of my back. This will be so much better than a ponytail.

When Riel is done, she pulls a small, charcoal stick from her jacket pocket, and lines my eyes with it. I'm amazed how it makes my eyes stand out. I grab the leather knee-high boots, slip them on and lace them up.

Turning slowly in the mirror, I get to get a good look at myself in fitted clothing. The leather pants conform to my full bottom perfectly. They sit just below my belly button, smooth against my almost-flat stomach, and hug my full hips perfectly.

"No more male clothing for me!" I assess myself in the mirror one last time.

Riel hands me her gift. It's a weapons belt. I secure it in place and strap my Spear on my right thigh, my obsidian dagger on my left thigh, and Brody's elven dagger to my waist in easy reach. "I need more weapons." I laugh.

"The boys are going to take one look at you and want to rip everything off."

"What's taking so long?" Shay shouts from the other room. "We have work to do."

Riel nods. I open the door and step out. The boys look at me and seem to freeze in place—all three of them.

Nova's holding another package. Without moving, he tosses the box to me and I rip it open. It's a solid Obsidian short sword. It's beautiful and I fasten it to my weapons belt immediately.

Riel grabs my arm, and when we walk out, Shay is the only one following. We're walking down the hall when Murphy rounds the corner, coming our way. I didn't know he was here. He doesn't look happy. I know that face, so I know I'm not going to like what he has to say at all.

"Murph, what are you doing here? I thought you were headed to the capital."

"I was until I received a letter at port. Reagan, listen to me, we need to talk for a minute and I need you to remain calm," he orders, in that Lieutenant tone of his that I am all too familiar with. Inwardly rolling my eyes, I follow him back to our rooms.

Quick introductions are made with Brody, Riel, and Murphy, and then we sit in the living area. Nova and Shay are seated on either side of me on the couch.

"Murph, why do I feel like I'm back in training, and you're about to scold me for something that was most likely not even my fault?"

"Reagan, I know how you are. I wanted to be the one to tell you that Kyle is here, and you need to hear me ou—"

"You have got to be kidding me," I cut him off, ready to spit fire.

"Who's Kyle?" Brody inquires.

"Kyle is the bully that made my life a living nightmare for years. He's the one that called me a whore and tormented me endlessly about my upbringing."

Thunder and lightning crack in the sky outside. Nova's eyes become winter storms and Shay's turn pitch black. Reaching out, I wrap my arms around theirs.

"Do not take off and do anything. Without me," I add, seething at the thought of Kyle being here.

Murphy shouts my name, but it's too late. We disappear into a violent winter storm of darkness that carries with it a promise of certain death.

The boys are tracking the scent that was on Murphy, and it leads us to the stables.

There, I speak mind-to-mind, pointing down while reaching for my belt and unstrapping my Spear. My canines and wings will show if I use its power. *Can you drop us fast and hard in front of him? I want to scare him.*

You are a devious one, Love, Shay purrs. *We'll follow your lead.*

Take us down, I order, gripping my Spear, feeling my elongated canines spring free. My powers fill me and I burst into flames. Wings unfurl from my back.

Hold tight, Shay commands.

Thunder cracks in the sky, and then we descend on a bolt of lightning, landing right in front of Kyle. He falls flat on his ass. Together we smile wide and viciously. He looks terrified as his nostrils flare, scenting the air.

Apparently, little Kyle has matured. I don't care if he knows

I'm still a virgin. All the better. What I do care about is that he can scent the boys all over me. Quickly I formulate a plan with them, then together, we sink down on our haunches. We glare at him for another moment. I can tell what Kyle's thinking just by looking at him. Shay reaches out, grabbing his ankle, while I help him out with the words he can't seem to speak.

"Yes, Kyle, what you're thinking is correct. Death has indeed come for you today."

We disappear into shadow and flame, Kyle screaming the entire time. We land hard on our feet, but Kyle is on his ass . . . again.

"I'm sorry I did not know who you were. No wait, that's all wrong—" Kyle wines.

"That makes it worse. Where does this hatred of me come from, Kyle? Even if my mother was a whore, I was a youth like you. Terrified. Even more so. At least you were prepared for the coming-of-age changes. How dare you?"

"I'm sorry. I wanted to look tough."

"Take a good look behind me, Kyle. That is what tough looks like. You are nothing but a vicious bully. And you should be ashamed of yourse—"

Nova disappears with Kyle, leaving Shay and me standing alone.

"He won't hurt him, will he?"

"Not very much, Love."

"That doesn't sound reassuring at all, Shay. Take me to them, please. I'm sure you two are communicating."

"As you wish, Love." He takes my hand and we disappear into storms of shadow and flame.

"I only wanted to scare him, make him think about things. I hope Nova won't hurt him."

"Nova's aware of that."

We land back at the stables. Kyle is face down in a pile of horse shit, Nova's foot planted on his back. Turning, I glare at

Nova. His look tells me that Kyle's lucky that's where he dropped him. Before I can say anything, the boys disappear.

"Insufferable jerks!" I shout. Strapping my Spear back at my side, I help Kyle to his feet.

After he washes off, we head inside to find someplace to talk. Without mincing words, I go for the jugular.

"You made me question my worth as a female. Imagine now, if, for the next four years, you had to deal with Nova and Shay tormenting you endlessly. How would you feel?"

"I don't even know how you did it. I was close to crying and begging for mercy. This is not who I want to be. I'm sorry, Reagan, I truly am. And whether you believe me or not, I know I deserved that. For what it's worth, you're the most beautiful female I've ever laid my eyes on. The stronger you became, the more jealous I became of your abilities. I volunteered multiple times to help Murphy find you when you went missing. I could see how devastated he was. I felt terrible about what I last said to you and thought it was my fault you left."

"Why were you still at Outpost Four?"

"I volunteered to stay behind and keep searching for you. Murphy granted my request. When he made that comment at Outpost Three about holding back anyone that's not mature enough, it hit me right then. I should have apologized before we left. I just missed you at Outpost Four when you came through."

Fin has not even said sorry and Kyle, Vile Kyle, drops a poetic apology on me. What in the depths of the shadows is going on?

"It's unfortunate we didn't get a chance to get to know each other better," I muse. He frowns in agreement. "What are your plans now that you're here? Are you going back to the capital?"

"No way, Rea." He hesitates for a second. "Is it okay if I call you Rea?"

"Yes, and I'll call you Kyle." A confused look crosses his face. "I called you 'Vile Kyle' behind your back."

"I deserved it. And no, I'm not going back. I need to be a part of this fight."

"Do you have family among the missing?"

"I don't, but I still want to fight. I need to be a part of this. It's what we trained for."

"Indeed, it is, Kyle. You should not expect Nova and Shay to be as forgiving as I am."

"Again, I deserve it," he admits.

"I also think it's wise to keep the 'most beautiful female' thing to yourself."

"They seem like the kind of males I want to be whenever I finally grow up."

Truth, honesty, and vulnerability from Kyle. Unbelievable.

"Kyle, you've already grown in leaps and bounds. Did you hear Fin abandoned me?"

"I heard all about it. Even what he called you. For what it's worth, I never would have abandoned you there."

"He has had two opportunities to apologize, and he hasn't. Anyway, I won't dump that on you. We should get going."

"I'm sorry, Rea. And I'm sorry Fin called you that. Somehow, I feel like it's my fault."

"We are each responsible for our actions and words."

Opening the door, we come face to face with Nova, Shay, and Brody who are smiling viciously, like the wolves they are. There's absolute darkness around them. This must look terrifying to Kyle. "Have you three been eavesdropping this whole time?" Shay reaches for me, taking my hand. "Insufferable jerks," I yell, as they whisk me away into a void of darkness.

We land back in the meeting room. I take my seat next to Shay on his right. Game on.

CHAPTER 20

S hay. Shay, I speak in my mind until he finally answers.

Yes, Love, what is it?

I don't have a peppermint leaf to stick up your nose. I don't know how else to get your attention. Would you like me to stab you instead? As you can see, I now possess many options on my weapons belt.

You're becoming more violent every day.

I am not. Is that your ancient advisor over there? I've never seen someone who looks so old.

Indeed, it is. His name is Sebastian, and no one truly knows how old he is. Or why after more than one life span, he chooses to stay here, rather than move on to the after realms, to live with the demigods.

What's his power?

Knowledge. "Sebastian," Shay speaks. "What information do you have to share with us?"

"It appears our primary objective is to prevent The Darkness from rising. Whatever this so-called Shadow King believes his goals to be, they're false. Sloane was correct when he told you the use of Forbidden magic is forbidden because no matter who wields it or for what purpose, the end result will release the Shadow Demons. They will lay waste to our world and make it possible for the Darkness to rise once again."

Hearing this confirmed is spine-chilling. Maybe I did not want to believe it the first time.

"Princess Reagan," Sebastian addresses me, and I cringe at the title, "you do have the power of the sun as King Raiden told you. However, the missing orb in your Spear is not an orb at all. And she will return to you when she's ready."

He's old; maybe he misspoke. "How can an orb that's not an orb return to me?"

He smiles widely. It's really, really creepy. His skin looks like meat left out to dry, his eyes have a milky cast to them, and his teeth show signs of decay. How many lifetimes has he been here? "The orb is the phoenix, and when she's ready, she will find you. This is only the third time in your kingdom's history that she has risen."

I'm playing it cool, nodding as he speaks. I'm trying not to think about having a phoenix or if I will be able to fly.

"What about the prophecy?" Shay asks.

"From what I have discovered about the prophecy of the power of three, you three are what are known as 'solstice siphons'."

"Meaning what, exactly?"

"It wouldn't matter if everyone was within ten miles of the moonstone, the three of you can, if you wish, take all the power for yourselves."

"That will never happen," Shay announces.

"I understand that, Commander; however, that does not change who you are, what you're capable of, and what you three now represent."

"And what exactly is that?" Shay inquires.

"I have discovered through my extensive research that it would allow the three of you to temporarily harness the power of the gods. No one in either kingdom will be happy that there are three among us who will have the power of the gods, no matter how temporary, with the ability to steal their powers twice a year. It could be very dangerous for you three, and precautions must be immediately taken."

"That will never happen," Shay reaffirms again.

"Again, I understand. I trust the gods have their reasons, especially at a time when shadows and darkness are again stirring. Shadow beasts have been awakened and a phoenix has risen from the ashes. Our kingdoms will not like that their powers can be so easily stolen, leaving them more vulnerable to an attack in these dangerous times. Again, we must prepare."

Shay rubs his brow. "You believe this could cause conflict?"

"Most certainly. Additionally, producing offspring is a danger to your lives if you and Nova were to have children with her," he reveals, pointing at me. "The powers those children could wield would be cataclysmic. However, if these children were raised properly—"

I cut Sabastian off right there. "No one will ever make that choice for me. Let me make that clear right now." I stare into his ancient, depthless eyes. He stares right back into mine.

"Think about the potential, Princess Reagan," he urges. "If you were to mate and breed with them both—"

The room descends into complete darkness. Thunder rolls and lightning cracks loudly in the sky outside. Connected mind-to-mind, we stand as one. Gripping my Spear, I burst into flames. My wings unfurl, lighting up the room.

"This conversation is over," I announce in no uncertain words, letting my canines show.

The boys growl loudly at my sides, canines also on display.

"I couldn't care less about what potential some prophecy predicts. Neither foretold fate nor anyone who believes they have authority will ever make those kinds of choices for me. I am not some livestock for breeding!" I glare into his ancient eyes. This time when he meets my gaze, I make sure he sees the depth of my power and the promise of a certain, sudden journey to the after realms if he persists with this discussion.

Resolve and a flash of disappointment wash over his face. I

don't care. The room lightens, the thunder stops, and I'm once again myself. We take our seats.

Shay begins his Commander's address again, without missing a beat. "There's no time to wait for reinforcements. We will take all available guards, along with anyone willing to join." Shay turns to his parents before continuing. "Mother and Father, you are to remain here or return home to Carrowmore, to be secured within the walls during active wartime."

"Your mother and I will both be remaining here," the king asserts.

Shay looks at my mother. She speaks before he does. "I will remain here. Hamon has complete authority of the Phoenix Queen's Guard."

"We only need one person running the show, Commander," Hamon replies. "I'm comfortable with that being you."

"Hamon, you're now my second-in-command. You will lead a company of two hundred made up from both the Wolf and Phoenix Courts down to Outpost Three. From there, you will travel south, staying on the east side of the mountains, cutting through so you will arrive at Outpost Four from the south, where you won't be expected."

"Understood, Commander," Hamon responds.

"My cadre and I will go directly through the tunnel with about four hundred, straight to our coastal outpost, clearing it and Port Kelsey. Hamon, after clearing your outpost you will rendezvous with us at Port Kelsey. From there we'll be boarding three ships to make our way to the Isle of Darkness. We leave in two days at daybreak. My mother has informed me there will be a proper send-off with dinner and celebrations."

A knock sounds on the door. It's a Wolf King's guard advising Sloane, from The Courtless, is outside demanding his subjects return with him, but they're refusing to leave. Shay sends the guard to retrieve Sloane.

"We'll take our leave," King Raiden imparts, standing.

Everyone follows, leaving behind me, Hamon, the boys, and the cadre.

"Rea, when he walks in, have fun and take the lead," Shay tells me.

I could kiss him for that. I hate Sloane. I quickly adapt to Shay's cocky arrogance. Pushing my chair back, I put my feet up on the table.

Nova growls his approval. The door opens, and Sloane walks in.

"What do you want, Sloane?" I'm not masking my disdain for him this time.

"I want the members of my court back. This is not our fight," he declares.

"They have loved ones among the missing," I reply as calmly as I can, like I don't have a care in the world. "This is everyone's fight."

"They are my subjects, and I will be taking them back. You have no authority over me."

"They are free, and they will remain here if that's what they choose. Your society is built on lies and you're a coward, Sloane." A surge of satisfaction that I was not anticipating courses through me. It's the darkness, where the madness lies, waiting to be unleashed.

"How dare you speak to me like that? You are nothing more than a child."

The room plunges into darkness once again. This time, we move only within Shay's shadows, emerging three feet in front of Sloane, before I burst into flames. Shay and Nova morph into huge black and white wolves and stand on either side of me.

"I would be very careful with your next words, Sloane, or they could be your last." I enjoy the look of fear on his face as I did with Ciara and think maybe Shay's right. I am becoming more violent. "They had to sneak away under the cover of darkness because you wouldn't let them leave. They have every right to search for their loved ones and roam where they wish. That's what free fae do. You are squatters on that sacred land and we do not recognize your authority."

"You cannot do this. We are peaceful. You are the monsters and will destroy us all! Everyone will hear of this, I tell you. Everyone!"

Shaking my head, I smile and chuckle. "Now why would you go and tell me that, Sloane? I'd be a fool to let you walk out of here now, don't you think? Brody, Hamon." I address them without looking away from Sloane. "Please send a delegation to The Courtless, that anyone is welcome here and homes will be provided for them. They do not have to fight. It's their choice." Hamon, Brody, and the cadre stand as one and walk out the door. "Boys, take this squatter to an uncomfortable cell."

The boys, my wolves, lean back on their haunches, hackles raised. They growl and snap viciously at Sloane. Razor-sharp canines drip with the promise of death. Together, they jump for Sloane in a coordinated attack by two wolves with the ability to communicate telepathically. As he screams, I smile wide, watching as they disappear into a storm of shadows.

THE NEXT TWO days move rather quickly. Everyone's helping in whatever capacity they can. At the dinner celebration, there is a lot of catching up and saying goodbyes, yet most of the conversations were about the missing and the shadow beasts. I keep thinking about that comment made by Cormac that Velius told us about. That the younger ones last longer. That still doesn't sit right.

Hamon's standing alone by an open brazier, and I head right over. It's about time we had a conversation about Jaelyn, though he speaks before I can.

"You're doing an amazing job handling yourself."

"Thank you, Uncle. I'm lucky I have you all to guide me."

"You're here to ask me about Jaelyn, aren't you?"

We're related. I can't fault him for being clever. "Of course I am. I want to make sure your head's in the right place. You know there's the potential she might not be alive. Not all of them will be."

"I'm completely aware of that, Rea, and my head is in the right place. Let's not forget, I'm not the one who jumped off a ship."

"You've got me there, Uncle. Still, it will be your feelings and emotions this time, your heart guiding you."

"I know. I will have you there to help me. All of you."

My mother, the boys, and a male I do not recognize join us. "Reagan, my child, this is Magnar, my advisor."

He does a quick, respectful once-over of me, before bowing slightly. "It's a pleasure to meet you at last, Princess."

"It's Reagan, or Rea, please. It's nice to meet you too." Princess. Ugh!

"Reagan, I can confirm that the fiery orb is the phoenix. Whatever shape shifting form you have, you will need the phoenix to complete that change. Given that you have canines when you hold your Sun Spear and feline vertical pupils, I'd say you're an apex predator, something similar to the Princes. You must not be afraid when she returns to you."

"Meaning what, exactly?" The look he's giving me is not reassuring at all.

"From everything I've read, she will return to you in a flaming ball of fire."

"Sounds pleasant." I smirk sarcastically, thinking it's going to be anything but.

"You will hear her song when she's coming."

"What kind of song?"

"Screaming. It will sound like screaming at first. Other than that, I could find nothing else. As Sebastian has already told you, this is only the third time in our kingdom's history that the phoenix has risen."

"So, I have a phoenix that will return to me... in a terrifying, screaming ball of flames."

"Plus," Shay offers, "you always have Nova and me to transport you within our wind."

Windwalking. I do envy their ability, although I keep that to myself. And most of the citizens don't even have their powers yet. I'm lucky.

My mother hugs me tightly. "You are wise beyond your young years, my child, and I am so very proud of you."

I know she will be safe here, as are Willa and Emily, back in Glendalough. "Magnar, what does a phoenix represent?" I inquire.

"Immortality, resurrection, and life after death."

What exactly does that mean for my future?

CHAPTER 21

As we reach the tunnel, I'm astonished by its immense size. It's truly incredible, and once again, I can't help but wonder why the Phoenix Court has never constructed a similar tunnel between Outposts Three and Four. The tunnel not only provides shelter but also offers faster travel through the mountains. This is yet another item to add to my list of necessary changes.

To get Shay's attention so we can talk privately, I try tapping him with my foot, but it goes terribly wrong. He stumbles and nearly falls over.

"What in the depths of the shadows are you doing, Reagan?" Shay shouts, using my full name. He's clearly irritated with me, and I don't blame him.

"I need to figure out a way to signal you when I need to talk," I tell him, looking as sorry as I can.

"And you thought tripping me was better than stabbing me?"

Nova looks at me, raising an eyebrow. I frown and shrug my shoulders like I haven't got a clue what he is talking about. Thankfully, Brody and Nova go back to their conversation. Then I smell peppermint.

Sorry, Shay. I didn't mean to trip you.

You're becoming more violent day by day, Love.

What are your thoughts about the phoenix?

I wish I knew, Princess. Maybe your mother's advisor will have more information when we return.

Do not call me that, Commander. What do you think Sebastian meant by mating with you both?

He's trying to hold his smile back, but he also knows I'm trying to understand, and they said they would help. *Nova and I have different powers; therefore, our children would have our powers combined with yours. The children might well be nearly as powerful as the gods, and they could create powerful bloodlines. The power continues to grow with each generation.*

Their lives would be in constant danger. They'd be hunted, wouldn't they?

Maybe, Rea. Yet, as you already so eloquently put it, we will not live our lives by some prophesied fate. Do not waste a moment of your happiness thinking about this. If you have a child, it would be the most protected child in our world. You are not for breeding like Sebastian implied. No females are. It's their choice.

The way Sebastian said it, it almost sounded as if it was normal to him. As if I would be the one doing something wrong if I didn't.

Sebastian is very old, and he comes from a different time. Remember I mentioned our primal instincts? Mating with the strongest is one of those instincts to preserve and strengthen our lines; nonetheless, we do not live in such archaic times as when Sebastian was once young.

Any other embarrassing things you might be able to let me know about?

He raises an elegant eyebrow. *"Excluding me, Nova, and Brody, how many other male scents have you noticed?*

I can't think of a single one. He's looking at me like he already knew this would be my response. As I'm opening my mouth to ask, Brody shouts ahead for Shay. He winks at me and then disappears into the shadows. Insufferable jerk.

Nova walks toward me and my mood improves immediately.

He is looking me over in a way that makes my toes curl. "I've been meaning to tell you that you look incredible in your new clothes." His eyes slowly travel up my legs to my backside, snug-tight in the new leather pants.

Suddenly Shay and Brody appear before us, scaring me half to death. "After we clear our coastal outpost and the port," Shay begins, "the four of us will slip away under the cover of night. We have a secret mission."

"What about Hamon? Why was I *again* not informed about the plan?"

"I didn't tell anybody except Brody, and now I'm informing you and Nova."

"This is the first I've heard of this myself, Reagan. Remember, Shay is in charge. I'm a member of his cadre and Brody leads it."

"At our abandoned outpost in the Northwest," Shay smirks, "we should be able to find a decent skiff to take across to the Isle of Darkness."

"And what happens if we get there and there isn't a so-called decent skiff?" I question, not masking my skepticism at all.

"Then I guess we'll see just how far Nova and I can windwalk."

"Meaning what, exactly?"

"We'll try using our powers to island-hop, Love."

"That's it? That's the whole plan for the four of us? Are you kidding me?"

Brody laughs "She doesn't sound like she trusts you two fools at all."

"Now would be a great time to fill me in on anything else I need to know," I insist, ready to breathe fire. "You told Hamon we'd be meeting him at Port Kelsey. I told him I would be there for him. I don't want him to worry about me."

"By nightfall, when Hamon's group stops for the evening, he will find a letter explaining what we're doing."

"If you had enough time to do all of that, then there was

enough time to let me know what was going on. I don't like being left out of the plans. Remember what happened last time?"

A low growl emanates from Nova's chest. When I turn and look at him, a glob of milky white goo drips on my face and shoulder. Before I can fully register the slimy coating and the stench that accompanies it, chaos erupts.

"Shadow beasts! Above us!" Brody shouts.

Dozens of them cling to the ceiling of the tunnel, writhing in a ghoulish mass. The first thing I notice is it's mouths with three rows of razor-sharp teeth big enough to take a head clean off in one bite. They're almost the size of a horse. As big as Nova and Shay, in wolf form.

The largest one, visibly wider than the others by at least three feet, opens its mouth. Two quick, high-pitched barks followed by three longer barks that sound more like screams echo through the tunnel. Are they communicating? Their hides, black as burned carcasses, blend into the darkness. The mass moves as one, as if tightening in after the barked orders. They are a living nightmare made of flesh. Gripping my Spear, I unfurl my wings and erupt in flames. The beasts immediately recoil, turning their eyes away from the bright light of my Spear and body.

Shrieking, they flee down the tunnel in the direction we're already heading. They're grouped so tightly together that they resemble a raging river violently flowing away from us. Racing after them, we quickly discover they're way too fast for us on foot. When I'm getting ready to voice that, Shay and Nova whisk Gabe and Riel away into storms of shadow.

Brody and I lead everyone else down the tunnel. Every pounding step I take makes me worry because I know we're close to the exit of the tunnel and it's nighttime. We don't want to lose sight of them.

As we round a bend, I spot Shay and Nova battling one beast and Riel and Gabe fighting the big one.

The impact hits me before I register what's happening. My Spear flies out of my hand and I land on my stomach, hard. Rolling onto my back I can't help the scream that comes out of me as I now find myself face to face with a shadow beast. My arms spring out on instinct alone, and I grip my fingers around its neck, holding it at bay. Its thick hide is hot to the touch. It snarls and snaps at me, dripping goo on my face.

Suddenly, my face is soaked in the creature's blood and it collapses on top of me. Heart pounding, I gag on the putrid, coppery taste. I can barely breathe from the dead weight crushing my chest. The constriction lifts, and I gasp a breath then quickly spit out the blood in my mouth over and over. I wipe the blood away from my eyes as Brody drives his sword into the beast's skull.

Scrambling to my feet, I scan the ceiling for more. "It came out of nowhere," I exclaim, maybe a little shaken. I need to keep myself together. This is no time to panic.

"You're okay," Brody tells me, helping me to my feet. "Take this."

I grab my Sun Spear and the light sends them reeling once again. The beasts climb the walls, screeching, fleeing from the bright light.

In that moment, I realize how much better my vision is when I hold my Spear.

The big one opens its jaw, and the scream that comes out of it reverberates through my body. Then it, too, takes off down the tunnel.

"Watch your back, Nova!" Brody shouts as another approaches Nova from behind and rears up on its hind legs.

The massive beast towers over Nova. But Nova thrusts his sword into the stomach of the beast, then steps out of the way of the claws that try to rip him to shreds.

"Nova, watch out!" I shout. Taking a few running steps, I launch my Spear. *Please let it connect.* It does. It lands right in the creature's open mouth and continues through the skull. When its body lands on the ground, it bursts into flames, leaving it a pile of ash. Interesting.

Shay walks over to the one that jumped me. Unstrapping his obsidian sword, he plunges it through the beast's skull. It too turns to ash. I retrieve my Spear and strap it to my belt. What in the depths of the shadows? I did not train for this.

"Q," Shay says, "send someone back to Wolf Crossing and get as many obsidian weapons as possible. Have them sent to Hamon's group, too. We will leave no bodies behind; we have no idea if they might reform." Shay walks toward me, grabbing mine and Brody's arms. "We need to kill them all, now."

We disappear into a void of darkness. Sight and sound leave me as Shay bends time and space to his whim. In the blink of an eye, we land outside the tunnel.

"Light this place up, would you, Rea?" Shay orders me like he hasn't got a care in the world. Nova rolls his eyes, having landed beside us a second later with Riel and Gabe.

Gripping my Spear, I bring daylight to the night, though I wish I hadn't. There are hundreds of them on the mountainside. Hamon will be outnumbered. They shriek at the light, but this time they remain in place. Outside the tunnel, my Spear's not as bright as it was inside.

Nova and Shay look at each other a little too long, and I know they're having a conversation without me. Before I have a chance to say a word, they disappear.

Keep that Spear held high, Shay orders in my mind. *I have a diabolical plan.* His sinister laughter echoes in my head as chills run up and down my spine.

I do as I'm ordered and hold my Spear high. Suddenly, about fifty shadow beasts disappear right in front of us. Howling is the only sound we hear until . . .

Boom, boom, boom! Three loud impacts hit the ground some distance away from us, one right after the other. *Boom, boom, boom!* They keep coming. It's Nova and Shay, dropping the shadow beasts from the sky. Diabolical is right; it's brilliant! They windwalk the beasts into the sky and then drop them to their deaths. They repeat the process a few more times, clearing them out incredibly fast.

"Anybody with obsidian weapons, turn them to ash," Shay orders.

Thank the Forgotten Gods the boys are Windwalkers because I don't know how else we would have cleared them out so quickly. My worry for Hamon and his group intensifies, but I stay focused. Twenty minutes later we regroup with the others at the mouth of the cave.

"We're only a few hours from our port," Shay says. "Nova, Brody, take up the rear. Rea, you will be up front with me. Light your Spear and keep it on." Gripping my Spear tight, I burst into flames immediately. "Gabe and Riel, left and right flanks. Have everyone with torches light them up."

Shay has us moving quickly and efficiently, and no one questions his orders. Except me. I have questions, but he speaks before I can.

"Rea, sometimes I have to make decisions, and I can't take the time to fill you in. I have to go with what I am trained for and how my instincts direct me."

"I understand, Shay. I do. Everything flows so smoothly when nobody questions your orders. When we're in situations like this, I will try to do the same as everyone else."

"Look at you, being all accommodating." He smirks. "However, I'm betting you have questions."

The look I give him conveys exactly that.

When we reach the coastal outpost, we find it thankfully empty of beasts. Shay instructs a company of fifty to stay behind. We continue on to Port Kelsey. It, too, is completely abandoned, except for Commander Velius. He's been tied to a stake in the center of town. He's bloodied and looks to be barely clinging to life.

An obsidian dagger protrudes from his chest. It looks like

the one that killed my father and it's probably the only thing keeping him alive. There are claw marks and what appear to be bite marks all over his battered body. Though he is alive, he smells of death. Rotten, foul. He was left for us as a message.

"My wounds are mortal," he breathes. "He knows you are coming for them."

"Commander, is there anything else you can tell us?" Shay cautiously probes.

"The spell that's repressing everyone's powers, it's bound to the Shadow King."

"So, if we kill him, we break the spell?"

"It's not that simple. If you just kill him, the spell goes on. The only way to destroy the spell is to kill the Shadow King the same way he gained his powers, through immolation. You must burn him." He starts coughing up blood. "Because you took the moonstone when you were last there, he will be leading many of the missing to the top of Mount Orpheus. He intends to sacrifice them to The Darkness to obtain more powers. You could push him into the volcano and let it destroy him along with the spell. My nephews were not among the children you rescued. Please help them."

Shay walks up to Velius, placing a hand on his shoulder. "Commander Velius, we will find your family. Is there anything I can do to help you?"

The commander looks into Shay's eyes. "Pull it out, please."

Before I've even registered what's happened, Shay pulls the dagger from Velius's chest, and he quickly passes on to the after realm. May the Gods forgive him.

Shay decides we will make our way to Outpost Four and clear it out for Hamon and his battalion, but when we arrive it's empty. He again leaves behind another company of fifty to await Hamon and to deliver a second letter to him.

Back at Port Kelsey, Shay lays a large map out on one of the tavern's tables. He explains we will make a three-point attack (four really, although only we four and the cadre know that). We can't take a chance of anyone else knowing in case one of them is captured. They might be desperate to make a deal with The Darkness for the sake of their loved ones. Who knows where Cormac is and who else might be working with him.

CHAPTER 22

Nova, Shay, Brody, and I have been sharing a room in a tavern at Port Kelsey. We have to stay for a few days to prepare. We busy ourselves with preparations and help load the ships for the voyage to and from Mount Orpheus. When the night finally comes, we board the *Riptide* and eventually make our way below deck. Then Shay windwalks us back to our tavern room where we will wait to leave on our secret mission.

Shay's second letter to Hamon was to advise him to board the *Rapture* as soon as they arrive at the port. He knows we won't be there, yet it still bothers me. I would have said more the last time I saw him.

Reaching out, we take hold of each other's hands. Nova and Shay will use their combined powers to get us a far from port as possible.

"Ready?" Shay asks.

Nodding, we disappear into a powerful winter storm of shadows.

Nova informs us that our current location is situated a little to the north of Shipwreck Cove, which used to be a port utilized by their northern outpost. However, due to the treacherous nature of the waters surrounding the cove, the port was deemed too risky for continued use. The numerous shipwrecks that can be spotted in the area serve as a testament to the dangers that lurk within these waters.

That was a huge step to take with the four of us and I can tell they both felt it. Especially after using their powers to take care of the shadow beasts.

"Let's get moving," Shay orders. "We should be able to slip up the coast unseen."

I'm finally putting my firepower to good use by using it to keep us warm at night. Although we don't have to deal with snow on the coast, we have to battle with the constant cold, wind, and rain. No one lives on the north side of the mountains north of Shipwreck Cove, as it's always rainy and chilly.

A few days into our trek, we stop for a break, and I take a seat on a dry rock. A delicious scent of maple fills my senses as Brody walks by, reminding me I'm hungry. Closing my eyes, I inhale deeply. "Umm, you smell so good Brody, you make me want pancakes."

No response. Absolute silence. I open my eyes to see the boys are frozen, eyes wide, staring at me. This can't be good.

"Remember me asking you a while back, Love, about how many different male scents you can smell?"

"Yes, I do. We were in the tunnels, and right now I can only think of the three of you. Wintergreen, peppermint, and maple. I'm starving and it's not helping."

"Just what are you hungry for, Rea?" Brody asks, looking sexier than I have ever seen him.

"What is it about me being able to smell your scents?"

Shay closes his eyes and takes a deep breath. "You can only smell males that you're attracted to, and not only that, only those males that would serve you best as potential mates."

An intense burning washes over my face. "You have got to be kidding me."

"Once again, Love, I wish I was. I urged you to speak with both your mother and Riel."

"You have to understand, that's incredibly weird."

"It's only weird to you, Love. And I bet you didn't know there is also a ritual where if we were to drink each other's blood, it would bind us together."

"What exactly does that entail?"

"If it were you and me, I would always be able to feel you and sense you. I could find you anywhere, and you could do the same with me. And more importantly, it would allow us to share power when the other is weak."

"I would have to drink your blood? Gross."

"That's how the bond would work. We drink each other's blood, consuming each other's energies and powers."

"Is it a mating ritual? Something you only do when you're in love?"

"No," Nova states. "It can be done with anyone."

"Have you ever done it before, with somebody else?"

"Shay and I started doing it as teenagers." This revelation surprises me. "We got quite drunk one night and decided to bond ourselves beyond what we already share as brothers and twins. Now it's part of our lives."

"How did you draw blood without fangs? I've read stories about creatures that survive on the blood of others."

"They are canines, not fangs, Reagan. We are not creatures of the night in the fiction books you read. It's not like that at all. We simply cut our wrists and fill our cups up some, then we drink it."

"Keep going, Nova," Shay chuckles. "You're doing well on your own, for once."

Nova rolls his eyes. "You could bond yourself to a potential mate or to someone you are deeply connected to."

"Meaning both you AND Shay?"

"I don't mean it sexually, Reagan. Merely so we would be able to find you."

"Wait a minute. You've been having conversations about sharing my blood and bonding yourselves to me . . . without including me?"

"Rea, we want to keep you safe. And remember, we already share this power of three. It makes sense to us. It will be your choice."

"For the love of the Forgotten Gods. What am I to do with you two? What about you, Brody? Don't you have someone? How would you feel about all this craziness if it was happening to you?"

"About all I have right now is the certainty that our world of Innisfallen is going to end, and I won't have a chance to start a life with someone if we can't stop what has already begun. If I were part of this power of three, I would want to bond myself to you."

"Remember, Love, this is only strange to you because of how you were raised."

"I understand your situation, Rea," Brody interjects. "Nova's filled me in about your upbringing and the lack of proper education. This is not the same thing Sebastian was talking about, mating with them to bear them both offspring. This would only be an exchange of blood and power."

This is so strange and frustrating. Yet, there is some logic to being able to share power and having the ability to help each other when one of us is weak. I like the sound of that, and though I won't admit it out loud, I do have a deep connection with them.

"It's something to think about, Reagan."

DAYS LATER, we finally reach the abandoned northern outpost of the Wolf Court. The place hardly resembles an outpost anymore. Only a single stone building remains standing amidst many piles of rubble. The air is thick with the smell of must and mold, and the overall atmosphere is quite eerie.

We make our way inside to see where we can set up for the night. It's too dark to try to cross the water, and it's definitely too dark to try "island hopping" as Shay called it. The only room with a usable fireplace looks like it used to be their meeting and dining hall. We get a fire going and set ourselves up right in front of it.

The boys rummage through their packs. Nova and Shay both have extra leathers in case they shift into wolf form. Then they pull the food tins from their packs. Fortunately, despite how much we've been eating, they're still loaded with dried meats, cheeses, and crackers that are more like little hard, bite-sized pieces of bread. I've never had them before, and they're delicious. Pulling the tins from my pack, I set them out. Mine has all the nuts and dried fruit, and I pop a handful in my mouth. Nova and Shay share a long look, and I have to speak up. "What are you two talking about? It's rude to leave Brody and me out of your conversation."

Brody grunts his agreement.

"We were deciding which one of us was going to tell you not to make any rash decisions this time," Nova admits.

"Insufferable jerks, the pair of you. My sisters are safe, so it looks like we can skip right over this topic."

"Your sisters are not the only ones you love and care for," Shay tells me. "We need to be prepared for what's possibly waiting for us. We might not all make it back."

"Why do you have to talk like this, Shay? We were having a perfectly fine meal. We are going in together and coming out together. None of you would leave me behind, and you gods-damn well better believe I won't be leaving any of you behind. That's the end of it."

∾

THE FOLLOWING MORNING, I'm awakened by Shay kicking my foot.

"Looks like it's going to be island-hopping for us today. On your feet," he tells me in his Commander's voice.

Why did I agree to follow orders? I have to listen to him now after my big statement at the cave. What I'd like to do is punch him in the face and then get a bit more sleep. Is Shay correct? Am I getting more violent?

"On your feet, Reagan," Shay orders.

No, I'm not getting more violent; he's getting more annoying. Once I'm all packed up and we're all ready to leave, I ask them to wait a minute. They freeze immediately, all eyes on me.

"I'm having second thoughts about island-hopping, and I want to talk about the power-sharing with the blood bond," I get out, knowing I'm already beet red. After what Shay said last night about not all of us making it back, now is the time. I'd regret it if I waited and something went wrong on our mission.

Nova steps closer. "With us having the power of three, the possibility of the powers we could exchange and share could help us greatly."

"I'm choosing to do this with you both."

"This should be interesting." Brody laughs.

"How will we do it?" I ask.

"Do it in two quick shots," Brody suggests. "Rea, you go first with Nova, then with Shay. Bite hard and drink quickly. We need to move out."

"What happened to putting it in cups?" I ask.

"There's not enough time for that and it's much stronger fresh from the vein," Brody replies. "You all have canines now."

"Are you sure, Reagan?" Nova questions.

Power sharing. Being able to find each other in emergencies, like when Cormac took me. So many positive reasons. "Yes," I affirm. Gripping my Spear, my canines lengthen, wings exploding out of my back as I erupt into flames.

Nova grips my arm, and I his. "Ready?"

"Ready."

I sink my teeth into Nova's wrist at the same time he does mine. A throbbing pain hits me first from his teeth. Then my senses explode with a dual sensation coursing through my body. The bundle of nerves at the apex of my thighs throbs to life in an instant. However, it's quickly overpowered by his taste, like warm wintergreen tea. I feel like I'm drinking power and happiness. It's like the joy I sometimes feel from my Spear. Memories of Willa laughing and giggling when she was a child fill my mind. Memories of Murphy and how much he cares for me. Wonderful memories of the friendships I have built with the boys. Nova tastes like joy and love.

"Switch," Brody orders.

Head still swimming with joy and laughter, I eagerly take Shay's wrist and drink deeply from him too, hardly noticing his canines puncturing my skin. Peppermint and darkness flow into my mouth, coursing down my throat with every mouthful. I taste loyalty, protection, and power. But mostly I taste anger. Memories of Fin calling me "whore" assault my mind. Then memories of me standing up to him, punching him over and over and how powerful it made me feel. Memories of Ciara and the way she beat me and stole my childhood from me come next. I can hear her in my head calling me useless and stupid. I want to show them all what I am now capable of. Would they dare to disrespect me? Absolute power and madness are what's flowing into me.

Before I know what's happened, Shay and Nova suddenly disappear into a winter storm of shadows. I'm left standing with Brody. A cold breeze washes over my face. Drifts of Nova's snow-fall are still swirling around us. It brings me back to the present. I lick the blood from my lips then take a deep breath, trying to process what we did, what we shared. I realize while Nova tastes like joy and love, Shay tastes like rage and love. Brody's maple scent fills my senses. He looks good enough to eat.

"Bravo. And stop looking at me like that, Rea. If you want

me, you can have me. But not when you're aroused by someone else."

I realize I do want him. My body vibrates with power and lust. I've never felt this way before and don't know how to hide it. Grabbing my pack, I notice Nova's and Shay's are gone. Brody grabs his pack and as we head outside, Nova speaks into my mind.

Are you okay, my Sunshine?

I'm feeling fine. What about you and Shay?

Equally, fine. No regrets here.

Or here. Where are you?

The docks.

We'll be right there. And, Nova, apparently Brody is a great male.

I hear him laugh in my head. *You should regret nothing, Reagan, and you should enjoy all the pleasures life has to offer.*

Maybe I'll hang back here with Brody? I'm half teasing, but only half.

Nova appears before me in a white squall. When the snow settles, he's on one knee with a drab-looking, mostly dead flower in his hand.

"I would be honored to be your first," he declares.

Laughing to myself, I stroll right by him, snatching the flower before I go. Adorable jerk. The sentiments are still there. Nova is every bit the joy and love he tastes like.

When I reach the docks, Shay's standing there looking all kinds of sexy. Why have I been denying my attraction to him? I freely take in my fill of him and when my eyes lock back on his, he winks at me.

"Such gorgeous green eyes," he utters.

I have not yet strapped my Spear to my weapons belt. "Nice face."

"Remember, Love, you always have choices."

"I'm aware of that."

"I felt your fire, Rea. Your burning anger and resentment and your longing for revenge."

Briefly I tell him what I sensed from him, keeping both Nova and the erotic sensation I experienced to myself. "When I was at Outpost Three, I used to dream of burning it to the ground. And the night before I escaped, I was certain that if I had gone to Outpost Four and they tried to keep me there, I would have razed that place to the ground."

"I understand your struggle, Rea. If we are honest with one another, then we can help each other."

"I like the sound of that Shay." I want to say more, but hear Nova and Brody approaching us.

"I can't believe we are about to do this," Brody expresses.

"Have I ever led you astray?" Shay inquires.

"As a matter of fact, many times."

"This time will be different," Shay imparts, holding out his hands.

We take hold of each other's hands, then windwalk away into storms of shadow and flame.

CHAPTER 23

Island hopping is going a little slower than we thought it would. Each time we land, we have to take the time to walk around and see which island we're going to windwalk to next so we don't drop ourselves into the frigid waters. On top of that, the rocky, mountainous islands are extremely difficult to navigate.

When Shay figures we're about halfway there, we're all so drained that he orders us to stop to rest for the night. Fortunately, the islands provide plenty of shelter, and we quickly find a cave to curl up inside for the night. Unfortunately, Shay tells me we are too close to the Shadow King to chance using my firepower for warmth.

We bed down, pressing tightly against each other, preparing for the long, cold night. I'm too spent to form words right now. The boys are too. We do our best to rest and, hopefully, sleep.

THE FOLLOWING MORNING, we start the process again, island to island. Once we can see the Isle of Darkness, we spot two of our ships already docked.

"They're already here," I point out. "We need to move."

"Easy, Rea, we have a plan and need to stick to it," Shay tells me in his Commander's tone of voice.

Trying to calm myself, I take a deep breath. When I open my eyes, the boys are looking at me, waiting for my reply.

"I'm ready."

"Draw up hard," Shay orders us. "I want to land on the coast of the isle this time. Rea, let's see those wings."

Gripping my Spear, I concentrate hard on every bit of power within me. I take deep breaths while I wait for Shay to give the final order. And when he does, we once again disappear.

The boys land waist-deep in water. Lucky me . . . I'm up to my chest. It figures. Breathing in this icy sea is practically impossible. Needles stab my chest as I pant like a dog and wade onto the rocky shore.

"Brody, Reagan, make your way to Gabe," he orders us, pointing toward the harbor. "See what you can do to help."

When we reach the harbor, Riel fills us in on the rescue that's well underway. Help is needed inside to get the rest of the missing out. The obsidian weapons and planned attack from inside and out made quick work of the shadow beasts. She also informs us Hamon's not here, and she suspects the second note Shay left for him had other orders because the *Rapture* has just arrived with three additional ships following behind.

Hearing a tiny growl, I turn and see Mojo standing behind Brody, trying to get his attention.

"Lead the way, Mojo," Brody tells him like he's a member of the cadre, which I suppose he is. We follow him into the same building where he helped me escape, passing by the same cell again. We eventually arrive at an enormous area, resembling an arena.

As I look around, it's hard not to be overwhelmed by the sheer number of fae crammed into this space. There are thousands of them, all with their stories, hopes, and fears. Despite the chaos, some of the stronger males and females have quickly emerged as leaders, taking charge and helping us organize and get everyone out safely.

But the scene is not without its horrors. Dead guards dressed in black are scattered around us, and innocent fae, too—a grim reminder of the violence that has taken place here. And scattered among them are the mangled corpses of dozens of shadow beasts, their twisted forms a testament to the dark magic that has been unleashed.

My ear catches a wailing sound I don't expect. Babies? Why are there babies here? Then I remember it's been twenty years some of them have been living here. This has been not only their prison, but also their home. Of course, some have found love, comfort, and protection with each other. With nothing preventative, babies would be bound to happen.

"Why didn't they send the babies with us the first time?" I think aloud.

"Parting with their young while still at the breast was something their mothers could not do," a female voice answers behind me.

A beautiful Wolf Moon fae with those bright blue eyes stands behind me. Her hair is in double braids, a hairstyle I've become acquainted with. I stand, transfixed.

"I'm sorry. I did not mean that negatively. I'm just surprised."

"We're grateful you've returned. Which way to shore?"

I look around, but Brody's nowhere to be seen. Mojo growls behind me. Perfect. "Mojo, lead these fae to safety."

And gods be damned, he does. And thank the Forgotten Gods, because a strange sensation begins coursing through my body . . . feelings that are not my own . . . fear, excitement, anxiety, and rage.

It's one of the boys, or maybe a combination of both. Things seem to be under control here so I sneak off to find Nova and Shay. They were heading up the volcano to the Shadow King. I can't windwalk like they do, so I have to get moving because something is very wrong.

As I exit the building, I find myself at the base of the volcano, eager to take the shortcut that leads up its steep incline. However, I quickly realize that holding my Spear makes the climb all the more difficult. Strapping it to my belt, I use my bare hands to grip the rough and crumbly volcanic rock beneath me. Sometimes, the loose ground gives way, and several times I slide backward, losing valuable time. I reach a point where the incline becomes too steep to handle, and I am forced to abandon the shortcut and switch to the winding road that leads up to the summit.

A swarm of fae comes running down the path in my direction just as I'm reaching a massive wide-open plateau—its outer edge hangs precariously over the sea below. It's a straight fall to the sea, so I quickly tuck against the wall.

"Keep running—ships are waiting for you in the harbor!" I shout.

A male stops in front of me. Eyes pleading. "Did the children make it last time?"

"Yes, we got them all back safely."

He takes off without another word. Once they all pass, I start running. Velius was right, the Shadow King was going to sacrifice them all to The Darkness.

As I turn a corner, I catch sight of Nova standing nearly thirty feet above me. Nova is locked in a fierce battle with who I believe to be the Shadow King. The latter carries a long obsidian Staff with three sharp tips. The sky above them is filled with the sound of thunder and lightning, making it difficult to keep track of the fight. Nova shields himself within his storms; however, the Shadow King appears to have storms himself. Storms of shadows and darkness, like Shay's. Where is Shay?

I push myself to the limit, sprinting up the last stretch of road, and I finally notice Shay—he's shifted into a wolf and blends into the darkness. With a mighty heave, the Shadow King launches his three-pronged Staff toward Shay. Despite Shay's attempt to dodge it, the Staff hits him in the chest. I stop in my tracks and watch him tumble twenty feet onto the path below. I hear and feel his painful impact.

Hold on, Shea. I'm coming, It takes every bit of strength I have not to cry to the gods, pleading with them not to take him.

Help Nova kill him, Rea.

I can't leave you like this.

You have to, Rea. Don't waste my death.

His voice lacks the cockiness I've come to expect and love about him. That scares me more than anything I've witnessed since I met him.

Don't talk like that. Please.

There's no response. I yank my Spear from my belt and my muscles explode with strength. I use the surge of power to drive my feet harder and harder into the terrain below. Above me, the Shadow King picks up Shay's Obsidian sword.

The Shadow King envelops the entire top of the volcano in darkness. I can't see Nova or his winter storms, let alone my steps in front of me. Holding my Spear up higher, I try to push the darkness back with each step I take.

Finally reaching the top, my flames quickly join Nova's storms, and we work in tandem, pushing the Shadow King closer and closer to the edge. We have to get him into the volcano. It's the only way to destroy the spell and free our powers.

The Shadow King's skull-like face is contorted into grotesque angles. It reminds me of Cormac's face but worse. He doesn't have a nose, only two gaping holes where the nose should be. His eyeless sockets seem to lock onto me, the empty, black holes, puckered at the edges, making me shudder involuntarily. How can he see? His skin looks as if it has been dried and shriveled from the sun. Every wrinkle and crevice on his face seems to deepen and accentuate the horror of his appearance.

Nova and I spread out wider and wider, until we're teetering on the edge of the crumbling precipice. The volcano's noxious fumes burn my eyes and nose and sweat drips over my entire body. We're losing ground.

Nova, we need Shay. It's the power of three for a reason. He can't be dead.

Don't think like that. We can do this together.

Nova formulates a new plan, and we set it in motion. We step away from the edge, then spread apart. We use the Shadow King as our focal point to form the three points of a triangle, making it more difficult for him to focus on us both at the same time. We push a surge of fire and ice through our weapons as hard as we can. Again and again, fire and ice pelt the Shadow King's face and finally he stumbles backward.

He blankets the mountain in darkness. I'm momentarily blinded. Then something connects with my face, hard, and I go down tasting blood and ash. My vision's blurry and my head is spinning so I'm not able to get to my feet. This is it. This is where I die. Shay is most likely dead, and Nova will be soon. The Shadow King is more powerful than we are.

Our mission has failed miserably and there's nowhere else to turn for help. Have the gods abandoned us? I'm left with the crushing weight of hopelessness and helplessness. The weight of the responsibility is too heavy for me to bear.

As I lay amidst the chaos, I can't help but feel overwhelmed by the magnitude of the situation. Nova and Shay had made a grave error by venturing out to face the enemy alone, leaving them with no backup. The weight of the world feels like it's on my shoulders, and I can't carry it all.

As a low-born, I grew up in the darkened alleys, subjected to abuse and constantly belittled. I was made to believe that I was worthless, that I would never amount to anything. But as I lie here, I realize that I have a choice to make. I could let everyone suffer in the darkness and revel in the knowledge that those who had wronged me would finally know true suffering. I could let the anger consume me and become someone who would let the world burn.

Or I could be the one to rise above it all and become someone who could bring light to the darkness, someone who could make a difference. I can be the person that Nova and Shay believe me to be, the person who is capable of anything.

The choice is mine to make and I know the right one. I take a deep breath, and with a newfound determination, I catch a glimpse of Nova in the darkness lying on his back, defenseless as the Shadow King prepares to strike him down. Desperately, Nova tries to hold him back, but the Shadow King is too powerful. My whole body aches as I struggle to stand up, but then my hand grasps something solid–it's Shay's Sword. Nova must have knocked it from the Shadow King's hand. A surge of rage and love courses through me, filling me with renewed energy. I leap up, feeling almost weightless, ready to fight with all my might. The blood in my veins pumps furiously, and I vow to never give up.

I will live to fight another day.

Once I'm back on my feet, I close in on the Shadow King, my steps quick and purposeful. He's standing on the edge of the precipice, and he doesn't even realize it because he is so focused on Nova. He also doesn't notice me until it's too late. I'm almost upon him now and, as he turns to face me, a look of shock crosses his disfigured, featureless face.

But I'm not afraid. I'm filled with a sense of purpose that I've never felt before. I raise Shay's Obsidian Sword high and bring it down with all my might into his chest.

It works. With a roar, he falls backward.

He grabs my shoulder, pulling me forward, my feet scraping uselessly as I scrabble to get a firm grip. He means to take me over the edge with him. No, he will never hurt anyone again, including me. I let go of Shay's Sword and it takes a piece of my heart with it. I punch him over and over in the face, but the blows are ineffective. An idea occurs to me. In one continuous motion, I swing my right leg backwards then bring it up, kicking him right in his crotch. When he buckles forward in pain, I drive my other knee into his face, feeling a satisfying crunch. Grabbing the hilt of Shay's Sword, I pull it from his chest. His eyeless sockets go wide in shock as my foot connects with his face, sending him over the edge into the molten lava below.

His screams fill my ears as he falls backward into the volcano. Nova approaches me, and we step closer to the edge to get a better look and watch as he descends into his torment and fate. More screams of anguish reach our ears as the lava begins to consume him.

I strap Shay's Sword to my belt as I step away from the crumbling edge. Spotting my Sun Spear, I secure that to my belt as well. "Is it over? Did we destroy the spell repressing our powers?"

The volcano starts to rumble, forcefully.

"We have to get Shay now, then I'll try to windwalk us away."

As we begin our way down I stop him, pointing toward the sky. "Nova, is that a Shadow Demon coming toward us? Gods, it's a ball of fire, like Shay said."

"The Shadow Demons would come out of the volcano."

I'm not convinced. Until I hear . . .

It's not screaming I hear—it's like a song. I feel the sound vibrating to my very bones. "It's my phoenix!!" Grabbing my Sun Spear, I extend my arm as high as I can and plant my feet in place, standing strong so she can return to the sphere, return to me.

She is much larger than what I had seen in the images with Nanaka. She is almost the same size as I am, not including her massive wingspan. As she approaches me, I can see her features more clearly, and I am mesmerized by her beauty. Her eyes are large, and they shine in shades of orange and black. To my surprise, her fiery form flies past me, leaving me in awe of her magnificence and feeling a bit annoyed and confused that she did not come to me.

"What in the depths of the shadows is she doing?"

She flies straight to Shay. Thank the gods. She removes the three-pronged staff from his chest then picks him up by the fur at the scruff of his neck with her massive talons and flies away toward the ships waiting below.

The mountain rumbles again, reminding us we need to get moving. Nova grabs my hand and we disappear into a winter storm, landing only forty feet below, on uneven ground.

"Your powers must be spent, Nova. Take both my hands, I will try to help power you. This is why we created a blood bond."

"You should conserve your energy. We have no idea what's coming next."

"Exactly, we have no idea, so take my hands now! Try to get us closer to the bottom. Don't take such a big step."

We hold hands and focus on our combined energies and powers, and this time when we disappear, we land more than halfway down the mountain. Incredible.

"One more step, Nova, that's it. Catch your breath. We can do this." He looks at me, gaunt and exhausted. "Together," I encourage. At least I hope it sounds that way.

We take one more step off the edge of the cliff. But my hands are suddenly empty. Nova disappears completely, leaving me free falling to my death. I scream so loud the gods might hear me. I watch the ground coming up to meet me—until something jerks me backward. I twist to look up and behind me. Fiery talons grip my shoulders. My phoenix came for me. We soar down toward a mortified-looking Nova.

It's not your fault— I start, but as we get closer, I notice she is not slowing down at all.

"Easy," I say to her, not knowing if she can understand me. She swings me backward and tosses me right into Nova. The two of us tumble in a heap of limbs on the ground. "You have got to be kidding me," I yell to the fiery bird.

She screams back, then disappears into a black hole that appears in the sky.

"Reagan, I'm so sorry. My power was spent." Nova squeezes me so tightly that the air leaves my lungs.

"It's okay. We are okay. Shay is not. We have to go now."

We run the rest of the way The last ship at the dock is the *Riptide*. Once our feet hit the deck, Riel starts shouting orders.

Surprisingly, Shay is sitting up, leaning against the rail at the helm. He's back in his fae form.

He has a blanket around his waist and is shamelessly naked otherwise. A female works her hands over a the third of three holes in his upper chest and shoulder, sealing it closed right before my eyes. The edges of his flesh pull together, sealing themselves closed. I have never seen a healer in action; it's fascinating.

He has a cocky smile for us, only I'm not buying it. Dropping to my knees I hug him tightly, on the uninjured side of his body, and start crying. He winces in pain.

"Sorry."

"I'm okay, Rea. Truly, I am. Your phoenix plunked me right in front of this healer."

Finally looking at her, I realize it's the female from the tunnels that told me about the babies. "Thank you for saving him," I say to her, still half-crying, wiping tears from my eyes.

"That's a pretty impressive trick you have with that phoenix," the female healer tells me.

"Honestly, it's the first time I've seen her," I admit.

"Shay was filling me in on everything that's been going on and who you all are," the healer informs me.

I spot Shay smiling like a wolf. He already has something else going on. He winks at me, then transforms before my eyes into Commander Shay.

"Nova, retrieve our dear captain immediately. We need to have a meeting now." Nova disappears into a cloud of snow and before the dusting has even cleared the deck, he's back with a disheveled and very pissed-off-looking Hamon.

"What is the depth of the shadows, Nova? You could have warned me you were going to do that," Hamon shouts trying to get his bearings. "What is so urgent?"

"Hamon!" Shay's healer scolds loudly. "What have I told you about using that kind of language?"

Hamon turns around to face her. His eyes go wide and the

color drains from his face. He takes one step toward her and then stumbles forward, falling to his knees. She takes the last two steps closing the distance, and he wraps his arms around her waist and begins sobbing.

The healer is Jaelyn. My aunt, Hamon's wife, and Fin's mother. Shay squeezes my arm. Nova wraps his arms around me, squeezing me tightly. He squishes against me, and I realize he's bleeding.

"Nova, you're injured." I start pulling his jacket off and discover he's covered in blood. "Jaelyn, please, help him. Sit down. Now!" I order, and he obeys.

Jaylen helps him remove his coat and tunic and has him lower his pants. There's a deep laceration that runs from his mid-rib to mid-thigh.

"Brother. My pain and blood loss must have masked your pain from me."

Why was I not able to feel this too, I cry in my mind, trying to hold it together.

You probably did not drink enough blood, Nova answers. *And maybe we did not take in enough of yours. It could also be from blood loss.*

Can I give you both some now? Will it help?

No! Shay orders. *You are too weak yourself. Not now. We have a Healer.*

Reaching out, I squeeze Shay's hand and leave it alone.

Jaylyn is alive. I'm not surprised at all. She's a born leader and a healer. Thank the gods for that because I could have lost both of my boys.

A loud explosion startles us all out of this brief moment of happiness. As we turn toward Mount Orpheus, another explosion sounds, and it's so loud that we feel the percussion from it. A massive fireball explodes out of the volcano high into the sky above.

"Shay, didn't you say something about Shadow Demons raining down from the sky?" Even as I say the words, I already knowing what I'm seeing.

"What goes up, must come down," he answers.

"Commander Velius also said something about Cormac working a separate agenda from the Shadow King," Nova reminds us.

We look on in horror as a total of six flaming balls blast into the sky. One for each Shadow Demon.

"We've been played," Nova announces. "By killing the Shadow King, we've unleashed an inferno upon Innisfallen."

CHAPTER 24

As a healer, Jaelyn can sense our energies, our powers. She says that she's never felt anything like us before. She tells me the three of us are interconnected, like puzzle pieces that fit together. Only something isn't quite right, like a piece is missing. She doesn't know what's missing, she can only tell that something is. We're all wondering the same thing: What's missing to make the final connection for the power of three?

Even though I don't like Sebastian's archaic beliefs of mating, we still need his knowledge on this issue. We have five months before the next solstice, and we have to regroup and get everyone ready to face Shadow Demons. Those who still have power will stay behind to protect the outposts at Port Kelsey.

The rest of us make for Wolf Crossing through the tunnel. Shay and Riel coordinate on the strategy. She will remain behind to run the companies on the West Coast. At some point, Cormac will have to make his way back for the Shadow Demons since they're useless to him if they're trapped on that island.

ONCE AGAIN, we're all gathered in the meeting room at Wolf Crossing, and I take my seat on Shay's right. Brody and Nova are to his left. Creepy Sebastian's here, but this time he's seated on a bench along the wall with Magnar.

King Raiden holds his hand up, silencing the room before he speaks. "I would like a report on the status of the next solstice gathering and a report on war preparations."

"First," Shay begins, "it has been confirmed that the spell repressing our powers has been broken. Those who received their powers at the last solstice are now able to use them fully. As for the solstice, the Temple of the Rising Moon needs to be repaired. In addition, and more importantly, for wartime strategic and logistical purposes, our current centralized location would serve best all-around as our base of operations."

"Excellent decision," King Raiden states.

"We need to remain fortified," Shay announces. "I have sent a company to retrieve the moonstone, and they will secure the entire temple grounds. I have ordered battalions up and down the east and west sides of the mountains and stationed companies on both entrances of the tunnel. I also have them at all coastal outposts in Ports Kelsey and Kennedy. Ships are staged along the western seaboard and they're making periodic sweeps throughout the islands watching for either Cormac's return or vessels which may be carrying the Shadow Demons."

"And what news of your powers?" King Raiden inquires. "Has anything changed? Any new developments?"

"Nothing new."

"Sebastian," the king says "have you discovered anything new about their connected powers in your research?"

"I have," he answers, then looks at the boys and me. "I would recommend that with the Shadow Demons back among us and the repression spell now broken, that the three of you use your solstice siphon ability to take the full solstice power for yourselves."

"Are you out of your mind?" Shay questions.

"You need to understand that Shadow Demons can raise the dead. The Army of Darkness, as they were once called, fought alongside the demons in the Great War long ago. We might learn more if you three take all the power."

"That will never happen," Nova and Shay echo in unison.

"Then let it be known on record that I tried to urge you all," Sebastian snips.

"We will not oppress our people and risk open war," Shay affirms. "The gatherings are for everyone, and it will remain that way."

King Raiden nods in agreement. "What of the ones not wanting to stay and fight?"

Of course, some will be afraid of Shadow Demons and want to flee. I'm afraid myself. When I have time, I need to sit down and do some more research on them. Wolf Crossing has a library, and that's where I need to go.

"They can either go to Glendalough or Carrowmore to be secured within the city walls. I was thinking anybody wishing to board ferries to the Isle of the Crescent Moon are welcome. They will be quite safe across the bay. We can set up a camp for them outside the temple."

"Make that a priority if you have not already done so. We need to avoid panic," King Raiden advises.

"Understood, Father."

THE FOLLOWING DAY, I head to the library and stop short just outside because I can hear Sebastian talking with the King. He's the last person I want to see, but I have no problem eaves-dropping.

"You must implore your sons to take the power during the solstice."

"You heard what Shay said, and I agree. We will not risk a revolt from the people."

"They've already been without power for twenty years."

"There's a difference; they weren't aware of what had happened to them. Now they are, and I will not ask a single fae to sacrifice their powers. Especially considering we already limited the number of fae present at the last solstice. Make no mistake Sebastian, the citizens are aware of it. We are not hiding that fact, and we will not make them wait any longer."

"Then what of mating both of your sons with the Phoenix Princess, breeding and strengthening your bloodline with hers? You need to make them see the potential for our future."

Gods, does he ever stop? I'd like to impale him with my Spear. Or crack him upside the head with it like I did to Ciara with Nova's Staff. That felt good.

"You heard how they feel about that, and I strongly advise you to stay out of it. That is none of your business, Sebastian. I hold none of them responsible if something happens to you if you continue to push your archaic beliefs and prophecies."

Okay, so I like King Raiden a lot. I can see where the boys get their sense of ethics.

"This is preposterous. Your ancestors knew to listen to my advice, my liege."

"My ancestors also knew when to pass on to the after realms. This conversation is over. I've had quite enough of you for one day."

At that, I slip back down the hall, hiding around the corner, only peeking around once the coast is clear. Once I'm sure they are gone, I head back to the library. I can't believe Sebastian had the nerve to push his mating ideas to the king behind our backs.

I've never been to a library, and I'm amazed at the sight before me. Row after row of book-lined shelves that seem to stretch on forever. I could spend a lifetime here reading every one of them. I have no idea how to find anything and just decide to start walking down the aisle I'm closest to, to see what I can find. At the end of the first aisle, I do indeed find something. It's the King, sitting alone in a chair, a stack of books at his side.

"Reagan, have a seat. Please join me. I caught sight of you ducking down the hall. Did you hear the entire conversation between Sebastian and me?"

There's no use denying it. "I did hear him talking to you about the boys and me taking the full power at the solstice... and also about the mating," I add, not being able to stop my eyes from rolling.

"Reagan, I'm with my sons on the mating topic. I had words with them the first time Sebastian spoke of it. I found it barbaric that he would even suggest something like that in any female's presence. Females are not for breeding. Mating has been and will always be a choice."

"I've let him get into my head."

"Look at it this way, child. The gods would not have made some of us prefer same-sex partners if we were intended only for breeding."

"What do you think about his suggestion to siphon the full power for ourselves?"

"My immediate response was and still is, it'll never happen. I will not deny that I can't help but wonder what would happen if you did, but that is a mental exercise, not a suggestion."

"I wonder, too."

"Are you here looking for information on Shadow Demons?"

"I am, but I have no idea how to use a library and search for the right books," I admit, surprisingly not embarrassed (for once) about my lack of formal education.

The king stands and offers his arm. "Then allow me the privilege of being your guide."

We link arms then I take my first guided tour of a library. It's amazing. Every aisle has different categories. There's an entire section on fiction, the only kind of books I had to read during training, but there's so much more here. The possibilities for learning are endless.

There are all kinds of educational books and there's even a

whole section on cartography and topography. I have no idea
what that is, yet I can't wait to explore more.

An hour later, King Raiden stops us suddenly in the middle
of an aisle. He takes my hand and kisses it softly. "Reagan, this is
where I leave you."

He said it in kind of a curious way, so I glance at the shelf on
my right, noticing I'm in the biology section. Glancing at the
shelf on my left, I realize why he left me here and left so
abruptly.

There are books on female and male anatomy. What a clever
little sneak he is. I enjoyed my time with him here today. He is
over two hundred years old, he and Talvi both, yet he looks the
same age as Nova and Shay. He told me this library is nothing
compared to the libraries in Carrowmore and Glendalough.
They have libraries ten times the size of this one.

Before leaving, I want to do a little research on *The Fea: a History
of Creation*. Placing the heavy tome before me, I trace my fingers
over the title before opening it. Three gods of creation built the
world of Innisfallen, which I had learned from a book Murphy left
in my room during training. But I did not know that when the Sun
and Moon gods no longer needed Orpheus and his power of
volcanic creation, they asked him to leave, as they had done when
they created the human world of Earth and the elven world of
Delunavir. He finally tired of being discarded and refused to with-
draw completely. He made the volcano known as Mount Orpheus
as his passage in and out of this world. In his solitude, he created his
children, the Shadow Demons, six of them, three males and three
females—creatures of dark power without anyone knowing. And
the Shadow Demons, demigods themselves, begat shadow beasts,
the very creatures now lurking in the corners of my thoughts.

The words on the pages replay in my mind like a haunting
melody. Three gods created the world of Innisfallen. It sounds so
absolute, so ancient. Then, the Sun and Moon gods discarded
Orpheus, casting him aside once the world was made.

I can almost picture it—Orpheus, standing alone, tired of being pushed away, creating a passage where he could come and go as he pleased.

I lean back in my chair, the weight of the story settling on my chest.

In the quiet of the library, I let the silence wash over me, trying to breathe in and out, but it feels impossible. I'm alone here, with only the pages of a book to keep me company, and yet, somehow, the weight of this ancient story makes me feel anything but alone.

After gathering all the books, I fill out a card at the front desk as King Raiden instructed me to do and stack them precariously so I can carry them back to my room. On my way, I spot Brody coming from the other direction.

"A little light reading?" he jokes.

"Just a bit."

He leans his arm against the door jamb. Bright blue hooded eyes look down at me. "Females that read are incredibly sexy."

I can't stop the blush that flashes over my face—and body. This flirting thing is so foreign to me. I try to think of a clever reply, but only manage to stutter out, "And why is that?"

"There are books on erotica. Most females I've seen reading them, let's just say they definitely have a leg up on the ones that haven't."

Now I don't know if he's flirting or trying to educate me. Either way, he looks gorgeous doing it. "Thanks for the advice. Mind getting the door?"

When we walk in, Shay and Nova are already seated at the table, so I quickly drop my books on the end table by the couch. I smell food.

"A little light reading—?" Shay starts, however, Brody cuts him off.

"I already used that line."

Shay flips him off then stands up and starts walking right

toward the books that I should have put in my bedroom. It's too late now, so I pivot on my feet and join Nova for dinner.

"Beef stew with rolls and sweet cinnamon butter," he tells me.

"I've never had cinnamon sweet butter, but I love cinnamon. It's one of my favorites." Picking up a roll, I spread some on while Nova scoops beef stew into a bowl for me.

Shay begins reading the titles off, one by one—insufferable jerk. "*The Female Anatomy and Understanding Your Body*, and *The Male Anatomy and Understanding Your Body*."

"Good luck understanding our bodies, Rea," Brody huffs. "We don't even understand them ourselves half the time. I'd stick with what I suggested."

"*The Fae: a History of Creation*. This one I should read. I don't remember much about it from my studies."

"That's because you were too busy making yourself pretty," Nova laughs.

"A romance novel. Why, Rea, I had no idea you were into reading romance."

"I didn't know I picked up a romance. But I'll be glad to read it. Fiction books were the only ones I could get my hands on during training. It's how I survived being alone, an outcast where I was not welcome. I knew every night when I went to lie down in bed, those characters in the stories were waiting for me. I could always count on them to brighten my darkest days," I express without shame.

"Thank you for sharing that. I've never looked at books that way before. Maybe I'll read this one myself."

Through the bond, I know he means it. "So much bad goes on in the world around us," I tell them. "Reading offers an escape. It has the power to take you to places you've never been or even heard of. Because some of them are crafted so beautifully you forget your troubles, if only for a while."

"It sounds like fictional literature is something we should include in education," Nova suggests.

"Think about how many fae, young and old, don't have access to books to help them through their dark times. The libraries should be open to all."

"And so they will be," Nova declares.

"You know, I also read tales of warriors who turned into wolves." Through the bond, I can tell that they're both interested in that. I'll have to remember to get them each something to read. When the Shadow Demons are destroyed, I would love to have a job working in a library.

WEEKS PASS with no reports of Shadow Demons or Cormac. More and more fae arrive every day, and temporary housing is constantly under construction. Shay has shipped many off to either Outpost Three or to one of the coastal outposts, depending on their skill set. He is also having the abandoned outpost in the north rebuilt, with regular patrols near the Isle of Darkness.

I've insisted better housing be provided for the cooking and cleaning staff. This place and all the others would fall apart without them. I, myself, have been dividing my time between building temporary housing and cleaning wherever and whenever I can. I've also taken up working in the library. I even read stories to the young once a week. If I could pick a dream job, it would be to work in a library.

CHAPTER 25

I need more blood. That's all there is to it.

As the Solstice approaches, we start having conversations about the blood-sharing bond. We want to be at full strength to take in as much power as we can. Now that the spell repressing everyone's powers has been broken, this will be the first time everyone present gets their full powers during the ritual. Will I be like Nanaka, a lioness with flaming wings?

"I don't understand why we can't just cut our wrists and fill cups as you and Shay always did in the past."

"As I've told you, Reagan, it's a stronger bond and shared strength if it's right from the source. Shay and I drink right from each other's wrists now that we have the canines to do it."

Does it have the same sensual effect on them?

"Nova and I are not attracted to one another, so it's not like that for us," he annoyingly answers my unspoken question. From his expression, it's obvious he can read my annoyance too. Perfect. It'll be fine. It's only a quick erotic rush, and then the power will follow.

Once we finish the three-way bite and blood fest, the boys leave to attend to their respective duties. I head for the library. I have research I've needed to do and have been putting it off for far too long. Hours go by, and the boys have still not returned. Brody eventually comes by to keep me company and have dinner.

I'm about to bite into a particularly crispy chicken leg when I begin to sense a mixed batch of emotions from the boys, the only one of which I can clearly identify is anxiety. One of them is scared, and I'm not even sure which of them is feeling it. I ask Brody if he would go see what's going on. He agrees on the condition that I go to bed and get some rest after I finish eating. He seems to be feeling empowered and makes it an order. He promises if something is going on with the Shadow Demons or anything else dangerous, he will come back for me immediately.

The following morning when I wake, I find that Shay and Nova have still not returned. Anxiety washes over me to the point of nausea. Something is going on. I'm about to wake Brody when Nova appears in the living room, walking right out of snow-flaked storms. The blood does help with powers, but he looks exhausted to the bone, like he has been up all night. Brody gets up without a word and walks out.

"What's going on? I felt so much from you and Shay last night."

"I'm sorry we worried you. Shay needed me and we had things to discuss between us."

Now with Nova standing before me, I can tell the feelings are all coming from Shay. It sets my teeth on edge. "Please, Nova, what's happened? Where is he?"

"He's fine."

"He is afraid. Right now he is scared and worried. What's going on?"

"Let's sit and talk—"

I have no patience for Nova's take-it-slow approach. I don't need a conversation. I need an answer. "Tell me, Nova. Please."

"Shay and I realized last night through our blood sharing that we are both in love with you." My jaw drops open. I was not expecting that. I can't come between them. I won't. "Whether we had suspected it before or were in denial, we are not sure."

"Okay. So why did Shay not come back?"

"He is ashamed of himself because he knows how much I love you. But he loves you too, Reagan, as much as I do, and has since we met you. Only he's kept it to himself because I'm going to be king. He wants to remove himself from the equation."

"I won't deny that I have feelings for you both." I've known for some time they both stir something in me. Do I love both of them? I might, gods help me. "But I'm not certain what I'm feeling. And for all Shay's talk about me always having a choice, he is removing himself from the equation? Literally taking that choice from me?"

The room explodes into a turbulent storm of shadows. When they clear, Shay is seated at the table. Feet up on top and hands clasped behind his head, looking annoyingly arrogant and sexy. The sudden change in him is palpable. No more sadness and shame. The boys must have kept their minds open to each other during our conversation. Then Shay quirks up that infuriating and cocky smile.

"Haven't I been telling you all along that you're in love with me?" Shay reminds me.

He has, from the very beginning, the insufferable jerk. "What in the name of the Forgotten Gods are we supposed to do now? I'm not sure what I want yet, but I do know that I won't come between you as brothers, especially because of what you both represent to your kingdom."

"It's not fair to make a decision based on what we represent to our kingdom," Shay counters. "You and I have had this conversation before. Because that's not allowing us a choice, either. We are what we are."

"Maybe I should get my own room, separate from you both. This is not something I want to focus on right now."

"No!" they all but shout in unison.

"I don't want things to become awkward with us sharing the same living space."

"This place is nothing to us," Nova admits. "This is where we work, it's a place to sleep. Our world of Innisfallen is under attack. We were brought together for a reason. For whatever this power of three is. We need you safe."

"I will stay." Through the bond that relaxes them.

"Thank you," Shay responds. "And remember, it's your heart we want you to figure out. We're not going to put any pressure on you to decide. You need time to experience life. There's no time limit on our love."

This is a situation I did not anticipate. How can I love them both and decide who to choose without hurting the other?

"Rea, do you remember I told you back when we first met about Nova pulling us both back on our respective paths?"

"Yes, I do."

"We were fourteen, getting ready to enter our skills training. The night before we left, we decided to bond ourselves, more than brothers, more than twins. After we finished, Nova felt and read my thoughts about the friendship he and Brody have shared since the age of five. And more importantly, how left out I felt. Since that night, it's been me and Nova against the world. Brody is now the one on the outside of our bond. We promised we would never let anyone separate us again. So believe us when we tell you we understand the implications of this situation. And no matter who you choose, the other will still be here for you both. Because now it's the three of us against the world, and nothing will ever come between us."

"The power of three," Nova adds.

THE MORNING of the Summer Solstice, a package arrives for me. Opening it, I discover it's a long silk gown in colors of reds, oranges, and black blended so beautifully that it looks like flames. The shoulder straps look a little thin, but I absolutely love it. The card attached to the box tells me it's a gift from my mother. It once belonged to my late grandmother who possessed phoenix fire and a fuller figure like mine. *Thanks, Mom.*

I quickly tuck it away in my wardrobe, not wanting the boys to see it yet. I decide to take a long relaxing bath before getting dressed for the evening. This will be my first time wearing a dress. The sound of the door opening and closing reaches me as I soak in the tub.

Nova yells that they will be getting ready and to take my time. Through the bond, I sense their excitement and anticipation as I'm sure they must sense mine.

After drying my hair the best I can and brushing it out, I decide to leave it down, pinning up the sides away from my face. After I outline my eyes in kohl, I carefully slip into my dress.

It hugs my full curves and shows off a little too much cleavage for my liking. Dividing my hair in the back, I pull it to the front, covering my décolletage perfectly. The dress hugs my body snugly around my hips and then hangs loosely in a long flowing pool of fire at my feet.

I chose my knee-high lace-up boots over the sandals that came with the dress. They will be warmer, and I'll be more comfortable this way. I grab my black cloak just in case, then do a final once-over in the mirror, silently thanking the gods that my youth and endless activity allow me to have this somewhat flat stomach to look so good in this dress.

Now that the curse has been broken, the winter storms have finally come to an end. The gentle chill of the last of spring in the air greets me, rather than the biting cold of winter. Summer has finally arrived, though perhaps a little behind schedule. The trees have finally begun to bud, and I can't wait to see them covered in leaves. It's been four long years of snow, but it's finally time for new life to emerge.

I wonder how different the ritual will feel, with the spell broken. Everyone has been so excited for tonight. There are already thousands packed into a ten-mile radius around the moonstone. Preparations have been underway for weeks.

The Solstice gathering is being held in a large valley north of Wolf Crossing. Word has come from all around about many being too afraid to travel because of the Shadow Demons. But that did not stop the thousands already present in the valley from both wanting and needing their powers restored.

As I step out of my room, ready to leave, I see the boys standing by the table. They take my breath away. Nova is wearing a dark blue tunic that matches the color of his eyes, but the fabric could never do justice to his eyes' beauty. On the other hand, Shay is wearing a blue and black tunic that blends so perfectly that it almost looks like his shadow storms are mixed with the blue of his eyes.

They are both wearing leather pants that show off their thick and muscular thighs, and they carry leather jackets draped over their arms. They have identical hairstyles, with thick braids going straight over the tops of their heads and then hanging down their backs. Additionally, two smaller braids fall from their temples, with cylindrical silver jewelry woven throughout. Upon closer inspection, I can see that the jewelry has runes carved into it.

"You both look amazing," I breathe.

They growl at my critique. Nova's holding something in his hand. It's a corsage made of fire lilies and it's beautiful. He slips it over my wrist, securing it in place.

"Reagan, you look like a goddess of fire."

My cheeks warm from the praise. "Thank you."

Shay takes my other hand, placing a kiss on top. "You look good enough to eat, Love."He winks.

My entire body flashes with heat. Mercifully, a knock sounds at the door, and Brody walks in. He stops in his tracks when he spots me.

"My gods, Reagan, you're stunning." He looks stunning himself in a solid blue tunic, similar to Shay's, but without the black. His pants and hair match the boys'. "Looks like things are still working out pretty good for us, wouldn't you say?"

"That I would, Brody. That I would, indeed."

Clasping each other's hands, we windwalk away into a wintery storm of shadows.

We land close to the moonstone, in an empty space where nobody has gathered. It appears that this area, probably a one-hundred-foot circumference around the stone, is for us, the center of the show. Figures. I suddenly feel self-conscious in this dress. Fae stretch as far as the eye can see, and on the other side of a rather large hill, there is another valley with another thousand gathered at least.

Sebastian's here, to our left, Shay speaks into my mind.

Averting my eyes from that direction, I spot my mother and Queen Talvi being escorted by King Raiden. My mother is wearing a dress identical to mine except for the colors. Hers is brown with wisps of gold, black, and white, and I realize it looks like the feathers of a falcon. It's perfect for her. She looks brighter and full of life today.

Queen Talvi is in a similar style dress of blue and white that compliments King Raiden's tunic.

"There are no crowns here tonight. This gathering is for everyone," Nova reminds me.

Looking closely at the king walking toward us, I can see the resemblance to Shay and Nova on his face. He walks proud and fierce like Nova, yet with that cocky smile on his face that's hard to miss, which is all Shay.

"Hello, my sons, Brody, Reagan," King Raiden joyfully greets us. "Reagan, you are a vision of beauty in that gown."

Smiling, I feel my face flush immediately.

"Father," they respond.

My mother hooks her arm in mine and we walk away with Queen Talvi. "Is something the matter, Reagan? You look a little uncomfortable."

"I'm a little nervous and feel a little awkward with so much of my skin showing."

"My child, there is nothing wrong with showing off your beautiful skin. Have you never worn a dress?" The look I give her tells her exactly that. "Put your cloak on if you would be more comfortable. I have hundreds of my mother's dresses. We will find something you will be more comfortable with next time."

"It's beautiful, Mother, I truly love it. I'll get used to it," I assure her. Thank the gods, she smiles and says no more about it.

"My sons cannot stop looking at you in that dress," Queen Talvi says. "Have you three shared a bonding celebration?"

"We did, a few days ago."

"Tell us everything," my mother eagerly demands.

I tell them about the blood sharing, both times.

Queen Talvi looks at me with kindness and understanding, before speaking. "The boys came to our room a few nights ago, ripping Raiden away suddenly, for hours." This is news to me.

There's confusion in my mother's gaze so I tell her they are in love with me, and that maybe I am in love with both of them, too.

"Reagan, my child. Understand it's not at all like Sebastian was implying. We understand you will have to choose. It's not something you need to focus on. If it happens, it will happen naturally."

"Thank you, Mother. You both look amazing this evening." I hope to change the subject.

"I spent twenty years knowing something was wrong," my mother reveals. "Even though I was glamoured, I somehow knew the child in my arms was not mine. I allowed my own life to fall by the wayside, living with depression for years. Your father and I haven't been intimate since you were conceived. I feel more like myself again now that you have come back to me, and I have something to tell you that might surprise you quite a bit."

Then a thought occurs to me from the last Solstice.

"Murphy," I guess.

"So maybe for my bright daughter, it won't be a surprise. I have gained the confidence to finally approach him. He needed time after finding out his wife was not among the rescued missing, and I needed time to grieve the loss of your father. Now neither of us has to be alone."

"I like the sound of that a lot, Mother. I do. Murphy has been like a father to me. Is he here?"

"No, we have been exchanging letters. He insisted on staying in Glendalough, to protect your sisters and our city." That's pride I'm hearing in her voice, and I'm happy for her. This will be good for both of them.

As the time to begin the Solstice ritual draws near, more and more fae have been filling in and there's now only about a twenty-five-foot circumference around the temporary altar holding the moonstone. The only ones standing within the center are Nova, Shay, Brody, the king and queens, and me. Everyone else stays back out of respect for us.

The collective power of everyone's combined energies hums like a vibration all over my body. A tingling sensation mixed with the fire in my core flares out along with the beat of my heart.

Shay and Nova take my hands. Through our shared bond, their power and love for me is tangible. It's Nova's joy and love, and Shay's rage and love.

Shouting from the crowd disrupts my euphoria. Scanning the crowd I seek out the source of distraction. The shouts become frantic and mix with screams. What in the depths of the shadows is going on? Suddenly, something splashes me in the face, and my eyes close automatically.

When I open them, Nova has an arrow through his neck.

CHAPTER 26

S hay explodes into storms of shadows, reemerging in wolf form. He stands over Nova and me, guarding us, howling at the Solstice moon. Screaming and chaos erupt around us. Nova collapses against me and I do my best to ease his fall. Shay's scanning the crowd, looking for whoever did this. Blood gushes from Nova's neck wound, spilling over me and filling me with rage.

"You can't have him! I won't let him go" I scream to the gods. "Shay, the power of three—we are solstice siphons. We have to take it all for ourselves to save him . . . now!"

Grabbing my Spear, I erupt into flames and spot my phoenix's fiery form soaring toward me. "I need you now. Please help me save him," I beg her.

As the energy of the Solstice begins to take hold, my phoenix soars toward me. She glows with an otherworldly radiance, and as she draws closer, I can see the intricate patterns of fire that flicker across her feathers. In a stunning display of power, she transforms into liquid fire and hurtles into my chest. Her power courses through my body, burning so intensely that sweat pours down my back as it pumps through my heart and veins, igniting every cell in my body.

Focus, Reagan! Shay screams into my mind. *It's starting.*

"Nova, please hang on until the Solstice is over," I beg him. "Please."

Connected through our bond, we feel Nova's heartbeat slowing to a dangerous rhythm and when his heart stops and his final breath leaves his body, I scream at the gods with everything I have. "Why? Why bring us all together only to take him away from us?"

The intense heat of the flames engulfs my body, and suddenly, I feel a jolt of energy coursing through me. At this moment, my transformation begins to take place. My arms turn into leathery talon-tipped wings, which emit a vibrant aura of blazing fire. My body rapidly expands and elongates, as a set of shimmering scales begins to envelop my entire being. My feet twist and curl, transforming into powerful, razor-sharp talons. I am a fiery dragon—a mighty creature straight out of the tales that I've read.

I tower over everyone.

Raising my head to the sky I roar my warning of death to come, not only to whoever took Nova from us but to anyone who thinks they can stand in my way.

Somebody bursts from the gathered crowd and runs toward us. I roar and Shay growls menacingly in warning. He stands there, hackles raised, while I struggle to maintain my balance in this massive form.

"I'm trying to save your brother, you fool," Jaelyn shouts. She punches Shay in his wolf face. He shakes his head, and in a quick burst of shadows, he's himself, standing on two feet, completely naked.

The sight of him snaps me out of my depths of despair and anger. There's a pull along my spine, and I know it's my phoenix trying to break free. In a flash of flames, I'm back in my fae form, also completely naked.

Jaelyn has one hand over Nova's heart and the other on his neck. The arrow has been removed. She has somehow managed to slow Nova's bleeding, but he's still losing too much. The guards form a wall around us.

"I have his heart going. Quick, give him your blood, both of you," Jaelyn orders.

Shay's beside me in a heartbeat, draping my cloak around my naked body. Flames from the corner of my eye draw my attention. It's my phoenix staggering away from us. She doesn't make it far before she collapses to the ground.

"Shay, do you have a knife to cut my wrist?"

He looks at me like I have lost my mind. He's utterly naked—of course he doesn't have a knife. He doesn't even have pants.

He grabs my wrist. "No, but I have these." He bites into me, hard and deep. He pulls my wrist to Nova's mouth, opening it with his other hand. "Drink, brother, please." Tears stream down Shay's face, as his anguish hammers through the blood bond.

Nova coughs. Flames again draw my attention away from Nova. It's my phoenix stumbling into a black hole she disappears into it, and it whispers closed behind her.

"Sit him up," Jaelyn orders.

Shay leans Nova against him, and he finally starts to take in my blood.

"Nova received little power from the Solstice," Jaelyn explains. "He will keep bleeding out until the wound closes. I'm also pretty certain that only you two had your powers restored."

"Only us?" Shay questions.

She nods.

We swore it would never happen, but we took the full power of the solstice for ourselves. I don't feel like a god. I'm beginning to feel dizzy, and I almost fall face-first on top of Nova. I've given him way more blood than I should have. Shay bites his wrist and places it to Nova's lips. This time Nova drinks immediately, though still mostly unconscious.

"We can't risk moving him tonight," Jaelyn advises.

"Then we won't," Shay states.

Jaelyn stops Shay from giving too much of himself when he starts to sway.

"Do not leave his side," Shay orders me. Then he disappears into storms of shadows.

He arrives a few moments later, partially dressed in unbuttoned leather pants. He has clothes for me and blankets and pillows for Nova. Shay holds up the blanket so I have privacy while I dress quickly. Shay drops to Nova's side, covering him with the blanket and placing the pillows under his knees. Jaelyn's hands cradle Nova's neck, to heal him and to keep his neck secured while Shay makes him more comfortable.

"Whoever has the bastard, bring him forward now," King Raiden demands.

It's Brody who comes forward, dragging Sebastian with him. I had completely forgotten about Brody in all the chaos. "If this was Sebastian's doing, I'll rip his throat out with my teeth," I promise.

King Raiden storms toward Brody and Sebastian, veins throbbing in his forehead. The king becomes more intimidating with every step he takes, and I see where Nova gets his menacing presence.

Shay grabs my hand, imploring me with his eyes to stay put. I'm unable to pull my arm from his vice-like grip. *I'm sorry, Love. But judgment is my father's place, not ours.*

"What is the meaning of this?" King Raiden demands. Brody drops a bow and a quiver of arrows at the King's feet. "Did you just try to kill Donovan? My son, your crown prince."

"I was not trying to kill him, my liege. I was trying to get them to take the Solstice power for themselves. It was for the greater good. Understand, Your Majesty, they needed the full power of the Solstice to complete the power of three. It's the only—"

The King cuts him off. "Donovan did not get any of the power from the solstice, you fool! None of us did. You ruined this for everyone and for what? Some gods-damned prophecy that means nothing to us? You had no idea if they'd even be capable of taking that much power."

"The next time it will work, Your Majesty. If only you would listen to me."

"There will be no next time for you, Sebastian."

In what almost appears to be coordinated movements, Brody twists, stepping away from Sebastian while the King draws his long sword from its sheath and, with one mighty swing, removes Sebastian's head. It rolls away and his headless body slumps to the ground, blood gushing from the stump, staining the ground crimson.

I can't hold back the vicious smile and intense satisfaction that creeps over me. I embrace the darkness, the madness. It's easier to endure than trying to consider a future without Nova in it.

"Shay," King Raiden speaks, "windwalk to Sebastian's rooms, collect everything you can. Station guards at his rooms. No one is allowed in."

"Understood," Shay responds as Brody reaches him. Then they disappear into the shadows.

We've been outside for hours when Jaelyn finally advises us it's okay to move Nova inside. We secure him to a flat board to protect and immobilize his neck in case the damage was more severe than Jaelyn was able to detect. Brody has one end of the makeshift stretcher, and King Raiden takes the other. When they stand with Nova secured in place, Shay steps between them, grabbing each of their arms, and then they disappear. He comes back a moment later for Jaelyn and me.

WEEKS HAVE DRAGGED BY, but Nova has yet to regain consciousness. Documents from Sebastian's room revealed information about the Priory of the Dragon and about two sarcophagi that have been buried within the pyramid of the moon and the sun. But it does not tell who lies within these sarcophagi or if they were sacrificed or died naturally.

I've been distracted, completely consumed with Nova's unchanging state. But in the back of my mind, I've been turning this information over and over. What did Sebastian know about me that I don't? It can't be a coincidence that I transformed into a dragon and he'd been reading about the Priory of the Dragon. What am I? Nanaka was a lioness. I had assumed I would take the same form.

I find solace in the dimly lit library. Sitting alone, searching for answers, I catch movement in the edge of my vision. Shay emerges from the shadows, and my heart skips a beat. His once-mischievous eyes are now red-rimmed and swollen from tears. I fear the worst for a moment, but I can feel Nova.

Shay smiles, reaches for my hand, and we disappear into a void of darkness, reemerging at the foot of the bed where Nova is sitting up, smiling at me. I ease onto the edge of the bed and lay my head on his chest, keeping the weight of my body off of him as I hug him gently. I'm afraid to breathe.

"I have been so worried about you," I choke out.

"Shay told me my recovery is thanks to Jaelyn, and apparently, you and Shay." Nova strokes my hair gently, soothing me.

Shay disappears, returning a moment later with a very upset-looking Jaelyn. Until she sees Nova.

She approaches the bed and hovers her hands over his neck and head, checking him over. "Tell me how you're feeling?"

"I'm honestly feeling a little claustrophobic at the moment," he half-jokes.

"Hush, you," Jaelyn tells him. "You've had us worried for weeks."

He drinks deeply from a glass of water that I hand him before Jaelyn grabs it from his hands.

"You need to start slowly, Nova. You have been consuming only their blood, so you need to take it slow. You've been lying here for eight weeks. I've done my best to keep your body active with daily exercises , but you are greatly weakened. You need to start moving today. Do you understand?"

"Understood," Nova replies.

Shay draws a bath for him. The hot water in the obsidian tub should help soothe his body. Shay and I leave him to relax and absorb what's happened. While two months have passed for the rest of us, to him it feels like it was only yesterday.

Shay and I discuss plans to make sure Nova exercises, and to make sure he does not overeat or drink. After eight long weeks of praying for this moment, I can barely believe it's real. This time has brought Shay and me closer to Jaelyn. She is a warrior at heart and never once gave up hope that help would come. She is now a member of Shay's cadre, though she will be stationed with Hamon, understandably.

A knock sounds at the door, startling me from my thoughts. At this time of day, it's most likely Harriet from the kitchen with dinner. She walks in carrying a large tray, and her seventeen-year-old son follows behind her with another. "I have broth for Nova, strict orders from Jaelyn. The rest is for the two of you. I also have two large pieces of chocolate cake," she whispers to us. "Don't tell Nova."

"Thank you," Shay smiles.

"They all live under the same roof now, Harriet, her son, and her husband Homer," I express. "She and her husband have lived separately for over ten years, serving in different homes. Her son had to move to the men's quarters at the age of fifteen. This is the first time they have lived together, as a family." Those who grow up privileged never stop to think about those who truly keep things running. Although I keep that thought to myself. No need to spoil Nova's recovery.

"We are indeed grateful to have our way of life and views challenged. It hurts me and my parents deeply to hear stories of people like Harriet and Homer," Shay frowns.

"I'm proud of the progress that's been made in both king-doms," I admit. "We must keep pushing forward and living our lives. Innisfallen will not stop because Shadow Demons walk among us. It will only stop if we give up."

"Haven't I always said you're clever?" Shay's brief smile darkens. "We have heard complaints about us taking all the power at the solstice gathering."

"Have you been reminding them it won't happen again? We panicked and tried to save Nova. And gave all the power to him so he wouldn't die. We didn't keep it and hoard it for ourselves. We are not walking gods."

"We have been telling them, Rea, I assure you. We do not want a revolt on our hands. However, the vast majority of the fae are not happy to have traveled so far during such dangerous times, only to leave without their powers restored."

"It's four months until the next solstice, Shay. That's a lot of time for an angry mob to form."

"We have been ensuring both kingdoms that we did not plan what happened. Many saw my father take Sebastian's head for almost killing Nova. We will not be anywhere near the moonstone during the next solstice. We have discovered from Sebastian's notes that we need to be within a ten-foot radius to siphon its full power."

"Did that seem to help calm their concerns?"

"Somewhat. What they don't know is that nobody will be aware of our whereabouts during the Solstice for our protection. As long as we are in a ten-mile radius of the moonstone we will have our powers replenished. We will camp away from the masses but still be within proximity to receive the power of the stone. But you, Nova, and I will remain out of sight during the Solstice. As you said, we will have the angry masses to deal with, and who knows how many others Sebastian may have had on his side?"

"Has anything else been discovered from his belongings in his rooms?"

"Everything of import has been handed over to Magnar, and he said one thing is clear. The Priory of the Dragon is a group of fanatics, religious zealots who believe in the prophecy."

"That does not sound promising at all." I take a bite of the chocolate cake to soothe the rash of bad news. "What are you planning for us on the Solstice, Shay?"

His eyes narrow, contemplating what he's going to say. "It's a surprise." Then he conveniently windwalks away into the shadows.

NOVA'S PROGRESS over the next month and a half is exceptional. Shay and I still give him blood once a week for strength, under Jaelyn's direction. She recently left Wolf Crossing and joined Hamon at Outpost Three. Nova has been taking up so much of her time, and I know she and Hamon are eager to be together after all these long years apart. She assures us Nova is out of the woods and that as long as he continues to improve the way he has over the last six weeks, he should be fully recovered in a few more. That's wonderful news for us all.

Nova has not made one single complaint and has stuck to the diet that Jaelyn set for him. Harriet's been a big help with that, preparing separate plates for him, although, when she catches Shay or me alone, she does sneak us some cookies. It's become kind of a special time for us.

He windwalks us away, and we eat our treats on a faraway hillside that overlooks Wolf Crossing. We've been sharing more stories of our lives from before we met. Part of me is attracted to his darkness, yet I love this relaxed, vulnerable side of him. When we're alone, he laughs freely and speaks openly.

Today, with Nova out of the woods and so much improved, we're more relaxed than we've been in ages. I love the way his eyes light up when I amuse him. I don't know how to describe it, but I feel lighter when he's happy. I want this feeling to last forever.

He wraps his arms around me to bring us back to our rooms, and I move without thinking. My hands wrap around the back of his head, lacing my fingers in his hair tightly as our lips connect. He opens to me without hesitation. His peppermint flavor nearly overwhelms me. I breathe him in as we exchange breath for breath while our tongues dance in a frenzy, craving more.

Through the bond, his love, respect, and concern for me are intense, but more than anything, his hunger ignites heat in every part of my body. My first kiss ends suddenly, and it was everything I dreamed it would be. I was so swept up in the moment, I did not even realize that we were in my bedroom until the shadows cleared.

Shay takes my hand in his and brushes his lips over my knuckles, then looks into me with those penetrating blue eyes. "Goodnight, Love." Then he takes a step back and windwalks away into the darkness, leaving me alone, breathless, a bit more confused, and incredibly turned on.

Well, shit.

CHAPTER 27

As we approach mid-fall, the deep green leaves of summer fade into reds, oranges, and yellow foliage that resembles my fire. The cool breeze has the leaves dancing along the ground, leaving a musky, sweet, and earthy scent in its wake. The temperature is just perfect—not too hot, nor too cold—making it an ideal season to enjoy nature's beauty. On my daily walks, I note that the grass still hasn't grown much here and wonder if it's the same in Glendalough.

Today we gather in the meeting room, and I'm eager for updates and progress reports.

Magnar raises his hand, then speaks. "Reagan, from what I have discovered in Sebastian's notes and my additional research, it would appear that the phoenix has not yet regained her full strength since rising, which might account for you not being able to maintain the dragon form with her."

King Raiden stands. "With the number of complaints about what took place during the last Solstice, the majority of the fae in both kingdoms have insisted the next Solstice gathering be held back on the Isle of the Crescent Moon, in the temple of the gods as it always has been. And so, it will be."

"I had to make a lot of adjustments, changing things around,"

Shay adds, "which is why Hamon's come up from Outpost Three to help coordinate. I have ordered all vessels on the eastern seaboard to meet at Port Kennedy to shuttle everyone across the bay."

The boys aren't happy with having to travel there during this time, especially because we will be traveling with the king and queens and now have their safety to worry about in addition to our own.

"When will we be leaving?" King Raiden asks.

"I insisted we arrive at least four days early to have time. Travis, our father's personal guard, wants to make sure security measures are in place. I've also sent a battalion ahead to set up our campsites. We leave at dawn."

When we arrive, I notice our site had been set up on the hill above the temple near the overlook where I saw it in person. It's the very hill where both Nova and Shay took me after our first Solstice together. Shay did that intentionally, I'm sure of it. We have not discussed the kiss.

Word has come that Murphy will be at the Solstice gathering with Willa and Emily. Despite the threat that looms over Innisfallen, Jaelyn assures us the mood is quite upbeat and everyone is excited.

Looks like changing the location back to the temple was the right decision. The grounds around the temple are set up the way I first saw them when I held the Staff. There's a beautiful city of tents surrounding the temple, and fae lights are strung everywhere, including inside the temple. Yet the temple itself remains empty. I wonder why?

Fae with psychokinetic powers were able to repair the temple, lifting the massive stone columns collectively with their minds. It looks as if it never collapsed. We arrive at the tent I will share with the boys, including Brody. It stands at least fifteen feet high in its center and the entire floor has thick, beautiful carpeting. An open brazier burns, heating the space. The center of the tent is designed to let the smoke escape through the top. As much as we might like to, we don't stay long as there's a lot to be done.

TWO DAYS LATER, we make our way to the tent that's been set up for us for our private Solstice party. There are five large couches and at least six comfortable chairs. The floor is also completely carpeted. It seems excessive to travel in so much luxury. I can't help thinking about the poor guards who had to lug this around and will eventually have to bring it back. I will be having words with Shay about this, soon.

Don't bother, Shay speaks into my mind,*"I windwalked it all here. I'm not a monster, Love,* he finishes with an adorable frown on his face.

I did not say anything.

It's written all over that beautiful, angry face of yours. Would you like a cookie?

Gods, my entire body betrays me, flushing instantly. He can read me like a book. I avert my eyes from his penetrating gaze.

"Reagan!" Willa shouts. As I turn toward her voice, she's already upon me, hugging me tightly as she has done every day since we arrived here. "Nova, Shay," she adds, addressing them and politely stepping away from me.

Already a perfect lady. While she, Emily, and I have spent a lot of time together over the last two days, she has yet to see the boys since our arrival. They smile saying their hellos. Through the bond and with the looks on their faces, I know what they're thinking. That Willa is a mini version of me, which she truly is, blood sister or not.

"Comport yourself properly like a lady, Willa," my mother scolds.

"Sorry, Mother," Willa responds, looking anything but.

"It's okay, my child. Please try to remember when we are in the company of others, especially males. You are still young. I have time to correct your bad habits, even though your sister Reagan is hopeless."

Before I have a chance to be offended, it hits me. My mother was true to her word: she has taken in Willa so completely that she calls her Mother. My heart swells so much with love.

"Willa has your intelligence, but unfortunately she also has your foul mouth," Mother tells me.

Willa and I share a knowing glance, our lips curling up in amusement as we attempt to suppress the laughter threatening to escape.

"And where is Emily and her raging hormones?" Mother asks. "She is nothing like you, Reagan, in that respect."

She is clearly not a fan of Emily's behavior. How bad could it be? How much trouble can she find within the castle and under the watch of guards? Or maybe she's getting into trouble with the guards. Maybe she and I should have a private conversation. "Would you like me to go look for her, Mother?"

"If she does not arrive soon, Murphy will go and find her."

No matter. I will find out what Emily has been up to later.

King Raiden and Queen Talvi enter with Travis. "Good wishes and Happy Solstice to all," Queen Talvi beams.

"Happy Solstice, Mother, Father," the boys respond in unison.

Everyone is dressed casually, as we will be remaining right here for the evening, or at least everyone thinks. The boys and I will be slipping away before it begins. It's their Solstice surprise for me, they call it. Hamon and Jaelyn join us shortly after the Wolf King and Queen.

The boys and I have been privately discussing sharing blood again tonight before the Solstice. Not nearly the amount we did last time, but due to Nova's injury we have not renewed the blood bond since the last Solstice. After spending a few hours celebrating with everyone, we make our way back to our tent. Shay and I didn't quite get a chance to feel how powerful we were last time, as we immediately gave Nova so much of our blood trying to save him.

Brody looks a little sad that he won't be joining the three of us at our special location. The boys notice it too, for which I am grateful.

"Brody," Shay begins in his Commander's voice, "please help Travis protect the king and queens for the evening." Shay's ordering him so he won't sit here alone through the Solstice.

"Understood," Brody replies, standing.

Nova walks over and hugs him tightly the way males do with that half-hug, half-back slap.

"Happy Solstice, brother." That seems to cheer him right up.

"Brody, my brother," Shay speaks, "I could not have done any of this without you. I know you and Nova have been close since childhood, but I need you to understand how much your friendship and loyalty mean to me." Then they hug that same way.

Walking to Brody, I extend my arms. "Happy Solstice, Brody."

After completing the blood bond, Nova and Shay windwalk us away into a beautiful, snow-flaked storm of shadows and darkness. We appear floating above the temple, about two hundred feet up. The temple and surrounding grounds with the fae lights shimmering softly look even more amazing from above. It looks like a sparkling wagon wheel. Nova's snowflakes are in deep shades of blue, while Shay's shadows surround us, keeping us concealed from sight.

As I gaze up at the sky, I'm struck by the sight of the full moon. It's a breathtaking moment, one that I have been waiting years to witness. The last time anyone saw a full moon was a long time ago, and the face of Aytac, our moon god, has been lost to us. But now, as I look up, there it is, smiling down upon us all.

In the presence of the moon, my body vibrates with energy. It is a moment of pure magic, something truly special. As the

Solstice begins, my body prepares for power, and I know that this is going to be a night that I will never forget.

Nova looks toward the sky. "Do you hear that?"

"Sounds like screaming," Shay expresses.

Oh, no. Not tonight. Please. But my entire body reacts to the sound, and I know.

"It's singing. It's her, my phoenix. If she comes to me now, we will be seen."

"Try to communicate with her," Nova advises.

Please, unless you have to come to me for the Solstice, don't let us be seen.

"It looks like she doesn't understand you, Love." She barrels straight toward us without slowing down. "We have to move or we will be seen," Shay shouts.

Our surroundings become engulfed in Shay's storms of shadows and her flames, trapping us in here with her, screaming so loudly that even the gods must be able to hear us. Suddenly, we erupt into a ball of fire and are thrown into a void of darkness. My body is propelled forward as if being pulled by a swift river, and all sense of sight and sound disappears. Amid this chaos, we cling to each other tightly, while my phoenix panics within the storm. The questions race through my mind: Where are we? Can everyone see us? Do they know it's us, or do they think something is wrong? And then, quite abruptly, we crash land. I roll over and over, sand pelting my face and my heart pounding with the fear of the unknown.

My head spins, trying to adjust from rapid motion into a swift stop. Then I vomit, hard. Pushing myself up off the damp beach, I get a good look around.

"My gods, we're back at Port Kennedy on the other side of the bay," I cry.

"We are too far away to have our powers replenished," Nova states.

Spinning around, I locate my phoenix. She's standing about twenty feet away, and gods, she's so beautiful and so huge. I'm pissed. I stroll right over to her, placing my hands on my hips. "Please take us back. We did not mean for you to get trapped with us. We were trying to move."

Large, ancient eyes of fire stare into mine. *Nix,* she breathes into my mind.

Her voice gives me chills so strong that I need a moment to catch my breath. "Nix? Is that your name?" She nods. "Nix, please take us back. We need the power of the Solstice, and we are too far away."

Did she shake her head no, or was she just shaking out her fiery head? I can't tell. Her massive wings spread out wide. They have to be ten feet long each. Springing at me, she grabs my shoulders in her talons and launches us into the sky. I can't stifle the scream as we fly so high that I can no longer make out anything below. She soars above the clouds.

"Nix, please. Where are you taking me? We need the boys!"

No response.

Well, shit.

CHAPTER 28

N ix keeps me in the air for over twenty minutes. I've repeatedly tried to communicate with her and the boys, but I can't reach anybody. I wonder if it's her powers blocking me, or if I'm too far away from them.

As we begin our descent from the clouds, the landscape below slowly comes into view. The magnificent temple and its surrounding grounds, shrouded in a soft mist, are visible in the distance. But my attention is drawn back to Nix, who is now hurtling toward the ground at an incredible speed. Her wings beat powerfully as she closes in on our tents.

Slow down. Please don't drop me into the tents, I plead.

Apparently, my phoenix has a wicked sense of humor because that's exactly what she does. Her talons release me above the larger gathering tent.

"You have got to be kidding me!" I scream to her fiery form flying away as I freefall about twenty-five feet to the tent below. Mercifully, the tent does help break my fall, but my weight partially collapses the tent as I bounce awkwardly along the sloped roof.

"Rea!" Brody shouts from within.

"It's me. I'm sorry. Give me a gods-damn minute, please. My

freaking phoenix dropped me on the tent," I shout to them, crawling my way to the edge, then rolling off ungracefully to the ground and landing in a heap. "Is everyone inside okay?" I call out.

"We're all fine in here," Brody responds. "Give us a minute to get the two center poles back up."

They have managed to fix the damage by the time I work my way to the front of the tent. "Where are the boys?"

"They're not here," Brody answers. "What in the depths of the shadows happened with your phoenix, Rea? And where are Nova and Shay?"

"Brody, you have canines," I sputter in shock.

"I'm aware of that, Rea. Focus. Where are Nova and Shay?"

"Give me a moment to try and communicate with them." *I'm back at the tent with everyone. Where are you?* No response.

King Raiden steps forward. "What's happened, Reagan? Because your sister Emily is also missing."

"What happened? Where is she?" I rub my hands over my eyes. I need to think for a moment. I quickly tell them what happened during my "Solstice Surprise" when my phoenix showed up.

"The princes are possibly on the coast trying to make their way back here," King Raiden tells Travis. "Have guards sent that way, immediately."

The tent explodes into a whiteout blizzard filled with darkness. I'm blown slightly off balance by its intensity. When the snow clears, Nova and Shay stand before us. Rage and relief are written all over their beautiful faces. I make my way right to them, hugging them tightly.

"It took us a while to windwalk back here," Nova states. "We don't have our full powers and we missed the Solstice."

"Me too," I inform them.

Shay walks forward, placing a hand on his father's shoulder. "Were everyone's powers restored?"

"They were."

"Thank the Forgotten Gods," Shay replies. "As long as those gathered here had their powers restored, I'm fine with waiting another six months."

My mother steps forward, holding a letter. "Emily has been taken, apparently as insurance that you three would not steal the power of the solstice. No one has located her yet."

The thought of someone acting against us directly enrages me, yet the letter left behind said she would be unharmed and returned to the temple once the Solstice was over. It also warned us that if anybody was seen trying to locate Emily, she would be killed and that it was in our best interest to let the Solstice finish.

Brody walks toward us, and I unstrap my Spear, the flames around me springing to life. The four of us take hands and then disappear into winter storms of shadow and flame. We land outside the temple. "Emily," I shout. "Can you track her by scent?"

"There's no fresh scent," Nova tells me. "Let's split up and search the grounds. If we find nothing in ten minutes, I can return to her tent for clothing for us."

"Sounds good," I reply. Brody is standing the closest to me. I grab his arm. "Let's go." We take off running around the temple in one direction, the boys, in the other. Nothing.

"I'll go back for some of her clothing," Nova advises then disappears.

Nova arrives a few moments later, looking a little uncomfortable.

"What," I demand, having no patience tonight. My sarcastic freaking phoenix spent it all.

"Emily is safe and unharmed. She is back at our gathering tent."

Collapsing my Spear I strap it back to my side. The look on his face tells me that, while she might be fine, something's going on. We take hands and windwalk back to camp.

We appear right in the center of the tent. My eyes zero

right in on Emily and while she is unharmed, her lips are swollen and rimmed in red. Like she's been making out fervently with somebody. I should know, having recently experienced it myself. Our mother looks angry as she steps forward to speak.

"She was released and instead of coming back here to ease our worry, found her so-called boyfriend, and only the Forgotten Gods know what they did."

This is the trouble Emily has been causing.

Is she still a virgin? I ask Shay and Nova.

The smiles that spread across their faces make me want to stab them both. And to make it worse, they won't even look at me.

I will injure you both, gravely.

Shay, you're correct. She is becoming more violent day by day. Nova smiles. *Yes, she is a virgin,* he finally confirms.

You are indeed becoming more violent. Confession, Love, it turns me on.

Gods, I need to get out of this tent now. Is Emily aware of our primal instincts? "Mother, have you already spoken with Emily?"

"I have, though I don't think she's heeding my words. Reagan, I implore you to talk some sense into her," my mother requests.

"Emily," I begin, "my tent, now!"

She follows me out. I don't say a word or look at her as we walk the two hundred feet to my tent. Once we enter, I turn around, looking her straight in the eyes, my smile stretching from ear to ear.

"Tell me everything. What's his name? How long have you been seeing him?"

She runs over, crushing me in a hug before we make our way to the couch to sit.

"His name is Kaiden, and he works with Murphy."

"How old is he? What does he look like?"

"He is twenty-four, not nearly as tall as Nova and Shay. He has ashy blond hair and olive-green eyes."

Okay, he's a Summer fae who has a good job. His age puts him just old enough that our paths did not cross in skills training, so I'm unfamiliar with him. Yet, if Murphy selected him for the royal guard, that's a good sign.

"Emily, what did they teach you in school about how female and male bodies work?"

"For the love of the Forgotten Gods, Rea," she rolls her eyes. "I know how not to get pregnant. Gods, I did not expect this from you."

"No, you misunderstand. I did not grow up with a proper education like you. I have only discovered this past year that males can . . ." I hesitate.

"Can smell when you're turned on," she finishes for me.

"Yes. It's incredibly awkward for me. And on top of that, I embarrassed myself by openly talking about male scents that I liked. I had no idea."

"Rea, it's nothing to be embarrassed about; it's all primal instincts. They teach us all of this in school."

"I'm aware of that, Emily, only as I just said I didn't get a proper education."

"Oh, you mean like at all." I nod in confirmation. "Big sister, it looks like I might be able to help you at last."

We begin sharing everything. Nova checks in a couple of times telepathically, and I tell him Emily and I are still talking and that I'll let them know when we're done. I also told him to go enjoy the Solstice celebration, because I want to stay right where I am, bonding with my sister for the first time.

We talk for hours until the sun comes up. Nonetheless, at the end of it (as much fun as we have had and as much bonding as we have done), I do need to step up as the big sister.

"Emily, you know you should have gone right back and informed Mother that you were safe."

"I know I should have. I honestly didn't think anybody knew

I was missing. The only thing they made me do was to sit with them. They said I would not be harmed and that they needed to make sure you three did not steal the power for yourselves. What were they even talking about?"

"I'll tell you later. Please continue."

"There must have been thousands of them, Rea, and they placed me right in the center. I never felt like I was in any danger. I could sense them more and more with every bit of power that entered my body. I'm a healer. Can you believe it? The Solstice revealed my abilities. When it was over, one of the males that took me apologized and said I was free to go."

"Why did you not go to our mother?"

"I made it almost to our tent, but I ran into Kaiden. He told me how beautiful I looked and then kissed me. I assumed no one even knew I was gone, because Kaiden would have told me if they were looking for me. I stayed and spent some time with him."

I mull over what she's saying, and it does make some sense. Why was Kaiden unaware she was missing given the desperate search? I'll have to speak to Murphy about that. He should have been informed.

"I understand your side, Emily. I do. You're fully matured, and you're allowed to have an active, adult life. However, if you're old enough to have an intimate relationship, then you're old enough to have continued to camp and let Mother or at least Murphy know you were okay."

"I'm sorry, Rea."

"You had Mother worried sick."

"You're right. I will go straight to her."

"Thank you."

I decide to go and find Willa because perhaps we need to have a similar conversation. She is old enough to hear about it. There are things she needs to know regarding males and females, given that she didn't have a proper education either.

I try to clear my mind, but one question keeps nagging at me: Why was Kaiden not aware that Emily was missing?

CHAPTER 29

W e're once again gathered in the meeting room at Wolfs Crossing to discuss further war preparations to combat the Shadow Demons. After the success at the Winter Solstice, we have thousands on our side. Trust has been restored, now that they no longer fear us stealing their powers.

"Brody, any word of Commander Velius's nephews and sister?" Nova inquires.

This perks me right up. I'm eager for news.

"Velius's nephews and sister were among the rescued. Word arrived today that they have already reached Glendalough and will be remaining there."

"Hamon," my mother speaks, "I want anyone returning to Glendalough who was among the missing put up in comfortable lodging."

"It will be done," Hamon replies.

"Travis, I want the same to happen in Carrowmore," King Raiden orders. "Get word to the capital immediately."

"Understood," Travis replies.

"Activity has been spotted on the Isle of Darkness," Shay reveals. "At least one Shadow Demon has been spotted by the harbor where there's now a ship that somehow managed to get past our patrols. I should have set up temporary outposts all along the coast. I'm working on that now."

Through the bond, I know that he blames himself. A knock sounds on the door.

"What is this?" Nova shouts. "This had better be gods-damn important enough to interrupt this meeting."

The door remains closed so Brody jumps up and opens it. "Can I help you?" The male standing before him looks a bit out of place and a whole lot of nervous right now.

"I'm Arthur. I want you to know that no one remains in any of the homes of The Courtless. It is completely abandoned and available for anyone needing lodging. It's across the bay and can provide safety and comfort."

Brody looks at Riel and she stands without question, leaving with Arthur. Ahh, The Courtless. It brings a smile to my face to think of Sloane rotting away in a windowless cell.

"We'll be relocating to Port Kelsey," Shay advises. "We leave tomorrow. I advise you all to use your time wisely." Then without a word, Shay grabs my hand and we disappear into the shadows along with Nova and Brody.

WHEN I WAKE up the following morning, I'm refreshed and starving (as usual), so I dress quickly. I hear Brody arrive, greeting the boys before I'm ready. There's a knock at the door and I'm hoping that's Harriet with breakfast. When I open my door, the scent of food reaches me immediately. But I am distracted by the black kohl masks painted from ear to ear on Brody, Nova, and Shay's eyes. "Wow."

"It's a Wolf Court thing," Brody informs me. "We are warriors heading off to battle."

"If I didn't know you, I would say it's quite intimidating." It also looks incredibly cool, and I want to do the same. I'll wait to see what Riel looks like. Nova and Shay both have their hair braided over the tops of their heads, the way Brody wears his every day.

After I stack enough pancakes and bacon on my plate to ensure I won't feel any hunger pangs before mid-day, I pour maple syrup over everything, and dig right in. "How was your evening, boys?"

"Not as restful as yours," Brody smirks. "More bacon?"

"You're becoming as annoying as they are," I declare.

"Hey, I'm an innocent bystander," Brody says. "Don't lump me in with those nitwits. But by all means, please remind me again how delicious I smell."

"Insufferable jerk. You're lucky I care about you."

"Why, Reagan, I didn't know you cared about–" Brody starts. "Sorry, Rea, I'm not even going to make a joke about that right now before heading off to battle Shadow Demons. I care about you, too."

"The four of us right here in this room," Shay begins, "this is what matters until we rejoin the others. We'll stick together this time. As Rea told us last time at our northern outpost, we're going in together and we will be coming out together. Understood?"

"Understood," Nova and Brody respond.

"Understood," I add.

"Brody, you're to order the cadre to do the same. They stick together, no matter what. They all go in, they all come out. Remind everyone."

"Understood," Brody answers.

Shay looks at me. "Rea, I need you to trust me as my cadre does. I need you to know that I can't always fill everyone in on my plans. Even Brody, who leads my cadre, doesn't always know every detail. In war times I need you to fall in line with the cadre and follow my lead without question. Can you do that this time?"

"Yes, I can. Without question, Shay. I trust you completely.

Though I make no promises as to what my facial expressions might look like."

"I can accept that," Shay replies.

"Do you guys think Nix intentionally kept us from the Solstice or needed to be with me during it?"

"Shay and I discussed this yesterday," Nova admits. "And we're not sure."

Shay stands and walks to the door. "I'll meet you outside. I have things to take care of."

"He's already planning something without us," Brody muses.

"Would you expect anything less from him, brother?" Nova adds.

"Not at all. At least his plans are brilliant. It would be nice to be included in them sometimes."

Despite my promise, not knowing drives me crazy. "Do either of you know what he might be planning?"

"With Shay, you never know. One truly never knows."

WE ARE silent as we ride our horses down the wet road toward the tunnel. Although none of us has mentioned it, the fact that Nova, Shay, and I did not have our powers replenished during the Solstice must be weighing heavily on everyone's minds.

I decide to wear a kohl mask like the boys and Riel and add braids on each side of my head, which is my preferred hairstyle now. Though the boys did not say anything, I could tell by their smiles that they liked my adopting the Wolf Court warrior style. It feels like I am finally fitting in with the cadre.

Once we arrive, we temporarily move into the Wolf Court's Port Kelsey Outpost. The three boys share one room, and I take the other. We have a small room connecting them with a table and four chairs, two couches, and a shared bathing room. It's very similar to Wolf Crossing. I'd sleep anywhere. Like Shay and Nova said to me before, it's a place to sleep.

Shay has battalions spread all along the west coast as far as the northwestern outpost. Word comes back that a single ship carrying a Shadow Demon has been spotted boarding a ship from the Isle of Darkness. We have a sizable armada that will be heading out to sea.

Shay informs us that heading them off at sea is the best option because now that the Shadow Demons are corporeal if they go into the sea, they will harden into volcanic rock. Unfortunately, they have incredible powers to combat ours. They are demigods, after all, the children of Orpheus. I can't help but wonder how powerful can one be if water can destroy them?

Just as the gangplank is being raised on the *Rapture,* word reaches me that my sister Willa has arrived with Murphy, and they're in the center of town.

"Wait," I shout to the crew lifting the plank as I run as fast as I can back to the center of town. She's standing with Murphy and a dozen guards.

"Willa!" I shout as I get closer. "What are you doing here?"

"Reagan, shouldn't you be on one of those boats?"

"Yes. Then someone said you were here. What in the depths of the shadows are you doing here?" I don't need this added stress and anxiety.

"I came with Murphy on a quick supply run. We were heading back to the tunnels—"

A bolt of lightning almost knocks me off my feet as Shay now stands before me looking anything but pleased.

Without a word, he extends his hand and I take it without question, realizing my mistake. I put my sister above everyone on our ship . . . again. We disappear into storms of shadows, landing hard in the captain's quarters. The wood beneath my feet groans with the sudden impact of our combined weight.

"I thought we discussed this, Rea."

"When I heard Willa was here I feared she was going to be boarding one of the ships," I try to explain.

"That does not matter. You were given orders and you disobeyed them by abandoning your post and crew!"

"I didn't think. I reacted."

"How am I supposed to trust you out there? How are my cadre or my other soldiers going to trust you if I can't?" Anything I say will sound like an excuse now. "I had to send Nova and Brody out to look for you. You have delayed our departure."

"I'm sorry, Shay."

"I don't want to hear your apologies, Reagan. I want you to fall in line with everybody else. Stop being so selfish and do the job that you were ordered to do."

For once, I finally know the right thing to say. "Understood."

"Get up on deck and watch for Brody. When he returns, you are to follow his orders." Without another word, Shay steps away into a swirling void of darkness.

I've never seen him more upset or disappointed with me. The ship is finally getting underway as I make my way to the deck. Selfish. That word punches me in the gut over and over with every step I take. How could I have been so stupid? "Rea?" Brody speaks, surprising me with his approach. "We have a cache of weapons below deck that we need to check over. Let's go," he orders. He doesn't even make eye contact with me.

"Understood." I follow him below deck. My stomach is sick with shame. If I focus on what I've done wrong, that will distract me from what needs to be done right now. But it's so hard because everyone on board knows that I'm the cause of the delay in our departure.

We make our way toward the back of the ship and of course, I forget what it's called. I won't be asking that question anytime soon. I'll wait till somebody shouts it again. Brody still won't meet my eyes. He's pissed at me. Nova must be, too.

"Have a seat," Brody orders.

Obediently, I sit. "I'm sorry Bro—"

"Don't," he cuts me off. "This is all new for you, and I understand. We all make mistakes. The past five years of your life have been focused on trying to get back home and take care of your sister. We were raised as warriors, raised in a military setting. Your single-minded concern your entire life has been for the safety of your sister. I understand. Shay does too, but you have to follow orders and think before you react."

"I'm doing the best I can, Brody." It begins snowing below deck, indicating Nova's arrival.

"It's not the end of the world yet," Brody imparts, pulling me to my feet. He hugs me quickly before putting his hands on my shoulders and stepping back. He knocks a finger under my chin, lifting my face to look at him. "I'm here whenever you need someone to talk to. But you need to get it together. Understood?"

"Understood. Thank you, Brody."

"There's somebody who thinks they're hiding in the shadows waiting to speak with you," he chuckles.

"I believe you are correct."

"When you're ready, make your way back on deck. Then come find me, immediately."

"Understood."

Nova steps from the shadows, walking right to me, and pulls me into an embrace.

"Through our bond, I felt your shame and anger. Let it go. Brody's right, don't hold this against Shay. You are part of his cadre, he is our Commander. Orders need to be followed. He still cares for you and loves you."

"I've disappointed him and let everyone else down."

"Mistakes happen. Refocus. We will get through this as always—together."

Through the bond, his joy brightens my mood. He always has a way of doing that. Nova's body jerks intensely, then we disappear in a burst of winter storms, reappearing on the deck above.

The sea before us is in absolute chaos. The majority of the armada is in flames, destroyed, and sinking in the waters.

As I stand in the center of the ship, my eyes fall upon something that leaves me awestruck. It is a creature unlike anything I have ever seen before, but I recognize it from the books in the library. The Shadow Demon towers at a height of at least eleven feet. Its imposing form is adorned with two enormous horns that jut out from its head, and its entire body is completely black.

However, as it moves, I notice something strange—cracks resembling lava peeking through stone appear on its surface, adding a surreal and eerie element to the already haunting sight. I can't help the shiver that runs down my spine as I gaze upon it. *Oh my gods.* "It has wings."

"They're not able to use their wings in their corporeal form," Nova assures me.

It's terrifying and as I'm turning to say something to Nova, the Shadow Demon launches a massive ball of fire toward our ship.

"Abandon ship!" Shay orders.

Before I know what's happened, I'm swallowed by darkness. I suddenly find myself plummeting toward the icy waters of the turbulent sea below.

Well, shit.

CHAPTER 30

As soon as my body hits the icy water, a jolt runs through my limbs, causing me to tense up involuntarily. My heart starts racing as I kick vigorously, trying to propel myself up to the surface. The water is freezing, and my muscles are already starting to ache from the cold, but I must keep kicking.

Finally, after what feels like an eternity, I break through the water's surface and gasp for air, my lungs burning from the lack of oxygen. I blink to clear my eyes and look around. The sea is filled with hundreds of fae, frantically swimming toward the closest island to them. It's quite far, and the waves are high, making it difficult to see where we're going. Every time I take a breath, a wave hits me in the face, causing me to choke.

Despite my best efforts over the last twenty minutes, I'm getting weaker and weaker. My arms and legs are heavy from the cold and the effort of swimming, and my body's starting to give out. At this rate, I don't think I'll be able to make it to the island. Suddenly, something grabs me. Before I have a chance to panic, I am plucked from the icy waters with at least six others. Then I'm once again free-falling along with everyone else to the shore below. We crash-land together in a pile of bodies. At least we are out of the water.

Turning to face the open sea, I spot hundreds and hundreds out there struggling for their lives.

Had I not run after Willa, could we have helped avoid this tragedy? Am I to blame for this?

"Rea!" someone shouts.

It's Brody. Dozens of others plunge into the shore before me. It appears Nova or Shay left me here with Brody and the others as they headed out to use their windwalker powers to rescue as many as possible.

"Everyone start gathering wood and let's get some fires started, now," Brody orders.

Brody stands alone, looking out over the churning sea, now littered with the remnants of ships. The screams for help still assault our ears. It's overwhelming being stuck on shore, unable to help.

"We completely underestimated the power of the Shadow Demons," Brody utters. "Just one of them almost took out our entire armada. You do not leave my sight on this island, Rea."

"Understood."

For hours we wait on the shore of our small island, our sanctuary. We haven't seen the boys at all. We catch flashes of Nova's winter storms as he plucks as many as he can from the sea. It's hard to see Shay's storms because they're always cloaked in shadows that blend in with the smoke and the fading light.

A swift, dark cloud begins moving toward us, then Shay appears on the shore in front of us face down in the water. He's barely able to lift himself. Brody and I run into the water after him, pulling him to shore and placing him by the fire.

After removing his soaking wet clothes, we wrap him in whatever clothing is dry and available. His body is frozen to the touch.

"I'm going to give you my blood, Shay," I say, knowing he needs it because he looks terrible.

"No, Rea, you did not get your powers replenished either. Save it for yourself," Shay urges.

"I've been sitting here for hours. This is the whole reason for the bond so I'm going to help you whether you allow it or not."

"Fine, only a little bit. Nova will need some too, I'm sure," he concedes through chattering teeth while his body shakes violently. I extend my wrist to him, and he takes it without complaint. When he finishes, I curl up in front of him, my back to him, and he wraps his arm around me. Brody climbs behind him, doing the same.

"Don't get any ideas, brother," Shay jokes with Brody.

"After all these years of trying to get you to share my bed, it looks like I finally have you where I want you," Brody says, chuckling.

"Rea, any chance you have your Sun Spear nearby?"

"Yes, sorry, I should have thought of that myself." Heat begins radiating from my body the moment I take the Spear in hand. After about ten minutes, Shay stops shaking.

WE WAKE with Nova kneeling over us. "Brother, are you okay?"

"Yes, I'm fine at the moment," Shay replies. "How did the rest of the rescue go?"

"Over three hundred unaccounted for. Fortunately, a few ships survived the attack. They're searching for survivors now."

Shay gets up and retrieves his leathers, dressing quickly. "You should have come back for me sooner."

"And you should not have taken as many as you did each time," Nova counters.

"I'm their Commander. It's my responsibility to rescue them."

"You can't rescue them if you're dead. You almost killed your-self out there."

"Yet here I stand."

Nova looks at me. "Were you injured?"

"No. What about you? Do you need anything?"

"Just some rest."

"Rea, I want you to stay here and keep an eye on Nova while he sleeps. Brody and I will do a sweep around our little island and get a head count."

I turn around and find Nova is already changed and out cold, so I decide to gather more wood and keep our fire burning until we're rescued.

THOUSANDS of us are spread out among the small mountainous islands, waiting for any available boats to come to our aid. Shay insists that everybody else be taken back to Port Kelsey before us, and on the third day, our ship finally arrives.

Once on board, we huddle together the best we can. We have two blankets between the four of us and there's fresh water, cheese and crackers, and some dried fruit. At this moment, it's the most delicious thing I've ever had. Unfortunately, news has come that over two hundred and fifty were lost at sea. But we also receive word that the black ship carrying the shadow demon was sunk.

When we reach Port Kelsey, wagons wait to cart us around. The boys and I head back to the Wolf Court's Outpost and then make our way to our rooms, barely taking the time to eat some chicken stew before we climb into our respective beds to get some sleep.

Too soon Nova wakes me, telling me I have to get up and eat something and that we will be having a brief meeting during breakfast before we leave. Reluctantly, I drag myself out of bed, making a quick stop in the shared bathing room before joining the others at the table. The word "selfish" still rattles around my head, leaving a sick feeling in the pit of my stomach.

Oatmeal and waffles are on the table and that perks me up a

bit. We eat in comfortable silence, taking in the food, juice, and water our bodies need.

"We're going to need to regroup with everyone once we finish," Shay announces.

"Understood," Nova and Brody respond.

"Rea," Shay begins. He's speaking in his Commander tone of voice, but it's laced with weariness. "Had you not delayed us at the docks the morning we left with your foolishness of running off to your sister, we would have been in the center of that ambush. Nova and I would not have been able to save as many as we did. So do not, Reagan, for one minute, waste a second of your thoughts wondering if you are in any way responsible for that surprise attack. Am I making myself perfectly clear?"

"Yes," I respond. The weight of guilt that lifts at his words was heavier than I realized. Only with it's cessation do I recognize how much I was hurting.

Once again he was able to tell what was on my mind. We finish breakfast in silence and then make our way to the stables. It's only a fifteen-minute walk to the port, but it's difficult for Shay to walk. Brody has noticed too, and we make eye contact. Brody's nod conveys that we need to keep an eye on Shay.

As we dismount near the docks, Riel approaches us. "We have a female prisoner, Gabe's escorting her off the ship now." Gabe comes toward us and I can't believe my eyes. Kira. What a complete turn of misfortune for her. This brings on feelings of joy and madness that spring from my vengeance, and I allow the flower of revenge to blossom within me. "She was hiding among stranded crews on one of the islands, disguising herself as one of us. Nobody knew her, and she was acting suspiciously from the start. The crew already had her tied up when we rescued them."

"That's my fake big sister Kira. The last time I saw her, she punched me in the face."

"Riel, go cut Gabe off. Don't let him come our way right now. Bring Kira directly to the cells at our outpost," Shay orders.

"Understood," she responds.

"Everybody's focus today is to be on the injured and sleeping arrangements," Shay tells us. "We will regroup this evening for a meeting."

"Understood," we reply.

"Rea, you're with me," Brody states.

Without question or even looking back, I follow him.

As the sun begins to set, we finally make our way back to the comfort of our rooms. The day has been long and arduous, but we are grateful for the tireless efforts of the many skilled healers who tended to the wounded both on the islands and here.

After arranging for lookouts, Nova and Shay have been discussing war preparations.

How can they be planning to go back out there, especially when Shay's powers are completely spent and I'm sure Nova's are not far behind? After a quick dinner, Shay informs us he wants to have a private conversation with us.

"Riders have been sent to notify the families of the deceased." Shay frowns.

"Brother, I know you wanted to do it. But it's wartime so you made the right call."

"Riel's crew took out the black ship carrying the Shadow Demon, and she confirmed it did go into the sea. That leaves only five demons."

"If the Shadow Demon is retrieved from the water, would he come back to life?" I ask.

"Absolutely," Shay answers. "They are demigods. I believe that one was a test, to see what we are capable of."

Brody stands and begins pacing. "How are we going to kill them if they make landfall?"

"Our weapons are not strong enough. Only Nova's Staff and Rea's Spear are. I would have to be standing on them for my Sword to be of any use. We need an obsidian Trident."

"I thought you said you didn't have any obsidian weapons long enough?" I ask.

"You're correct. However, the trident the Shadow King stabbed me with is long enough and it's made of solid obsidian."

"That's still on the Isle of Darkness at the top of Mount Orpheus," I remind them.

"Do you think we will have to return to the temple on the Isle of the Crescent Moon with it?" Nova inquires.

"I do, brother. Below the tines, there is a four-inch section with a free-spinning cylinder embedded into it. It's called a cryp-tex. It has ancient runes carved into it like the Sun Spear, the Staff of Storms, and my Obsidian Sword. And something was inside."

Brody stops pacing and looks at Shay. "What do you think the trident is?"

"I'm certain it's the third weapon of the gods. If Orpheus created his children in secret, it's possible he created a weapon for himself. The Sword's design and the fact that we needed it at the temple tells us it's an important artifact as well."

"What are we going to do now?" I have to hear it from him to believe it.

"Securing the trident is crucial, so we must return to the Isle of Darkness to retrieve it," Shay informs us with a hint of urgency in his voice.

"Well, shit."

CHAPTER 31

The following morning I'm informed that Brody and I will be going to Outpost Four to check in with Hamon and Jaelyn, and Nova and Shay will head to the north-western outpost, checking in on the sites in between. They want to ensure that there hasn't been any Shadow Demon activity we aren't aware of. After our trip to Outpost Four, Brody and I and the rest of the cadre will rendezvous with the boys at their northwestern position.

Shay attempts to mount his horse but falls off and lands on his back with a thud. Brody grips my hand, silently urging me to stay still and quiet.

"This is ridiculous, Shay. I'm enacting my authority over you due to your physical state." Nova declares. "Brody, you're now with me. Shay, you're with Reagan and that's the end of it. You are in no condition to travel like this."

While Nova helps Shay back to his feet, Brody leans in and whispers to me.

"Keep an eye on him and try to give him more blood. You know he won't want to, so you must persuade him. I'm worried about him. I've never seen him this physically weakened before, ever."

"Understood," I respond.

Brody mounts Shay's horse, and then he and Nova head north.

"Shall we make our way to the cells? I'm interested in meeting your sister."

He's embarrassed by his fall and trying to act like his usual cocky self. I play along and mirror his demeanor, even though I don't quite feel it myself today. I don't want him to feel ashamed of his physical weakness, and if this helps distract from that, it's the least I can do.

"I would love to introduce you to my fake, evil sister. Please, lead the way."

As I link my arm through his for support, peppermint fills my senses so I open my mind to him.

Thank you for offering me your arm.

Always. You know I will support you in whatever way you need me to.

The lower-level cells are cold, even colder than where I was dumped after Kira punched me in the face. My mood changes immediately. I feel that violent side of me taking over. Shay opens the next door, another set of descending stairs awaits us, and we work our way down to another level. The stairs are slippery with damp moss, and it smells musty. Lovely. I hope Kira's enjoying her stay.

Ready to go have some fun?

I am. I love this vengeful side of Shay and what it brings out in me.

Shay opens a final door, and we walk into a small hallway with six cells, three on each side.

She's in the last one on the left.

Walking up to the cell, I get a good look inside. She has blankets and a cot, and I'm not pleased about her having these comforts at all. Someone has clearly been feeding her, while during my incarceration, I was ready to eat whatever crawled out of the wall. Thank goodness it was Mojo.

She looks up and I speak. "What an unfortunate turn of events for you, big 'sister.'"

She has the nerve to glare at me. "I won't be here long," she declares confidently.

I smile harder. "What makes you say that? Do you have another ship coming for you? We will send that one and anyone onboard to the bottom of the sea just like the one you were on."

"I have someone who will come for me." She smirks.

"Nobody's coming for you, Kira, but you are correct about one thing. You won't be here long. Not long at all."

I turn away from her cell and she shouts for us to come back. Shay slams each door behind us as loudly as he can as we begin our ascent.

That's it? Shay raises his brow as we exit the cells. *I was expecting more from you. I have to admit I'm a little disappointed.*

I wanted to go in the cell and get a little payback. But I'm just not feeling like myself with all that's happened.

Say no more. He wraps his arm through mine. *We can support each other today.*

That sounds like a fantastic idea.

We head back to the stables to find that we have a wagon outfitted to take us to Outpost Four. I'm excited to see Hamon and Jaelyn and find out how everything's been going with them. I'm grateful they both survived the ambush at sea.

We make a brief stop in town before heading to Outpost Four. Shay wants to check on things here first since Brody had been tasked to do this before he and Shay swapped missions.

We arrive at Outpost Four a few hours before dinner, and both Hamon and Jaelyn are still attending to their official duties. We make our way to the kitchen, looking for something light to eat. After a snack, Shay decides to take a nap by a fire. I make my way to the library to do more research on Shadow Demons.

When word comes that Hamon and Jaelyn have finished their work for the day, I grab my books and join them in

Hamon's private dining room. When I arrive, they are already chatting with Shay.

"Fancy set up, Commander Hamon." I formally greet him with his new title, bowing slightly.

"It's a pleasure and honor to have you join us tonight, Princess Reagan," he replies, bowing slightly at the waist.

"It's almost annoying how much their sense of humor is alike," I overhear Jaelyn telling Shay.

"I find it interesting she allows the princess title when it suits her," Shay muses.

"At least they're both funny," Jaelyn retorts. "Some of the time, anyway."

"I smell roasted chicken and vegetables." I peek under the lids of the dinner dishes.

Hamon shakes his head. "Reagan, have you no manners at all?"

"As you've clearly established, Uncle, I am the Princess. Princesses set their manners."

Everyone joins me, and we fill our plates in comfortable silence. Once we're all seated, Shay speaks up.

"Jaelyn, would you be free tomorrow to visit Rea's fake sister, our new prisoner, with us?"

"I would be. I can meet you there around lunchtime?"

"Sounds perfect." Shay nods.

"Is this prisoner already injured, or will they be once we get there?" she inquires.

"Maybe a little of both."

"Understood," she replies.

"See how easy that was?" Shay teases.

The look I give him tells him I couldn't care less.

"Rea, are you still having problems with following orders?"

"Not at all, Uncle," I say, lying right through my teeth.

"Fin is coming for a visit," he tells me.

"Here? To this outpost by the sea? Where there's danger?" I don't mask my surprise or disdain at all.

"Yes, he's coming by way of the southern road."

"Is the entire Queen's Guard escorting him here, Uncle? Is he aware that danger still lurks in the shadows? That actual Shadow Demons now walk among us?"

"I wish you would give him a chance, Rea."

"He has not once apologized for abandoning me to die. He took the gods-damn food with him," I remind him bluntly. "If taking the food wasn't an indication he wasn't coming back for me, then I don't know what was. And he called me a whore."

The sound of breaking glass has us turning in Shay's direction. Blood drips from his hand, which he is currently wrapping in his napkin. Jaelyn takes his hand in hers.

"I was not aware he had yet to apologize. I'm sorry for bringing it up." Hamon shrugs.

"You have to understand what that was like for me. I thought he was my friend."

"I can only imagine, Rea. Again, I'm sorry. I was not aware. He told me he was going to speak to you when you were last in the capital. Evidently, he did not."

"He definitely did not, Uncle."

"I will be having words with my son when I finally see him tomorrow night," Jaelyn says.

"You have not seen him yet?" I'm honestly surprised.

"I requested many times for him to come visit me. There is work to be done, and I am needed. I was stolen twenty years ago and I never stopped fighting to survive so I could make it home to him and his father. I begged him to attend the last Solstice, but he refused to come."

"What a fool," I spit. "Not only because he hasn't seen you since he was born, but he also could have received powers that could have helped him. Sorry."

"Don't be, Rea. Everyone is responsible for their choices in life. He will have to choose how to proceed with the choices he has made. His father was too soft on him. Now that I'm back, those days are over."

Her eyes lock on mine. Trauma and determination stare back at me and I'm certain she sees the same in mine. We are females who have been facing nightmares, confronting battles, and choosing not to run away. This is why I have such a strong connection with her. We are very similar in spirit.

After dinner, we move to the couches near the fire. The conversation flows much better now that we've gotten the discussion of Fin out of the way. It's been a lovely evening, yet, as things always do, it eventually comes to an end.

"I'll walk you to your room," Jaelyn offers, linking her arm through mine. We walk out the door ahead of Hamon and Shay.

"We don't have enough space for you to have separate rooms, but the one you're sharing is sizable. There are two beds. Although maybe you won't need them." Jaelyn smirks.

"You are a wicked fae."

"Maybe this will help you choose. You can thank me later."

"I'm not thinking about any of that until after this war is over."

"He's not too weak to lay there for you."

"For the love of the Forgotten Gods."

"Be gentle with him."

"I will stab you, Jaelyn."

"I can heal myself, Reagan."

"Then I suppose we have reached an impasse."

"I suppose we have."

As Hamon and Shay catch up to us, my uncle takes his wife's hand and they turn left while Shay and I continue straight down the hall to our shared room. I'm going to wait until tomorrow morning to offer Shay my blood. There are other things about my powers that I would like to learn and tonight would be a perfect time.

Once we are situated in our room, I place a stack of books on the table and then head into the bathing room. After changing into my fleece leggings and top, I tie my hair up in a quick pony-tail in preparation for a night of studying. I'm hoping the books

I found can teach me more about the Shadow Demons and that Shay will help me learn more about my powers. Shay is seated at the table with a stack of papers before him.

"Remember last time we were here? I was reading about the shadow beasts."

"I do," he replies without looking up. "What do you have on the agenda for this evening?"

"I was hoping you would teach me how to get your attention the way you and Nova get mine with your scents."

"I can't teach you that, Rea. I wish I could. Nova and I send our scent to you on the wind that we can control."

"Is there no other way then?"

"I don't know. Your powers are different from ours. What were you and Jaelyn talking about in the hall? Because I assure you, you have my full attention right now, Love."

"What in the depths of the shadows? Oh gods! Of course, you can tell I'm aroused."

"Funny how things work that way sometimes, isn't it?"

"You're such an ass. You could always read my face, even if I was not . . . you know."

"Aroused in your crotch," he laughs making fun of me.

We burst out laughing. It's a good, hard, long belly laugh. Tears fall from our eyes.

"Why do you use the word 'crotch'?" Shay laughs. "I have to know. I've heard you use it so often."

"On top of the lack of education, that was the only word I ever heard for that part of the body. Males were always swearing, saying they blew out the crotch of their pants."

"That makes perfect sense," he wipes tears from his eyes. "Thank you for sharing that with me."

"I'm here to entertain."

"I also heard what Brody said to you before he left."

"That was a quick change of topic. And?"

"I agree that it is a good idea for me to take in your blood."

"Thank the Forgotten Gods. I thought I was going to have to fight you on this."

"I have a different idea of what I would like to do though."

"Different how?"

"I want you to first take some of my blood."

"No way. You are too weak to lose any."

"Reagan, for the love of the Forgotten Gods, would you let me finish what I have to say before you go off half-cocked like you always do."

"Fair enough."

"Once you take in my blood, I will then take that same amount back, plus what I planned on taking. It should refresh my blood and rejuvenate me. I've never felt this weak. And, I can no longer feel you through the bond. I want to feel you. I need to."

My entire body responds to those words. I know he means to feel me in his blood. But something tells me he meant it another way. And a part of me needs to be able to feel him too.

"Understood," I respond, noticing his nostrils flare.

Well, shit.

CHAPTER 32

Late the following morning, we make our way back to Port Kelsey. Even without needing the bond, I can see Shay is doing better, and I'm glad nothing happened between us last night. I'm still trying to figure out what I want—with either of them.

And maybe the bond affects me more than I thought because I can't shake the feeling that there's a piece of me missing when Nova's not here. So why did I kiss Shay when I was uncertain? Am I sending mixed signals?

He appears to be somewhat back to his cocky, playful self and I'm ready to play along. Kira is waiting, after all, and it's my time for some payback. We need all the information we can get from her.

"I would like to check in at the port with Riel and see how everything is going," Shay announces.

"Understood, Commander."

While he does not look at me, a smile spreads across his face. Pulling back on the reins, he stops us. "You make me want to be a better male, yet at the same time you bring out this dark side of me."

He's opening up to me, being vulnerable. "It's the same for me."

"I know, Love. You're in my blood now. However . . ."

"What is it? Are you worried I won't like that side of you? You don't frighten me, if that's what you're worried about."

"It's not, Love, it's—"

"Was the second bed necessary?" Jaelyn muses, sliding up behind us on horseback.

"Good morning, Jaelyn," I grumble, a bit irritated and wanting to know what Shay was about to reveal.

"Morning? It's lunchtime, and I'm starving." She smirks.

"I knew I liked you for a reason. I'm starving too," I tell her.

"Both of you are always starving," Shay says. "That word loses its meaning when you females throw it around like that."

"No one asked you," Jaelyn jokes.

"Can we make our way to Port Kelsey now, ladies?"

"Not if you and Rea need some more alone time."

"Jaelyn, for the love of the Forgotten Gods," I utter.

"What?" She's trying to look innocent.

"We have work to do, ladies. Shall we?" Shay snaps the reins and gets us moving.

WHEN WE REACH the center of town, Riel approaches, informing Shay that word has come from Nova. He and Brody's arrival will be a bit delayed at the northwestern outpost. They've teamed up with a larger group heading north and are stopping to help repair weather damage at the different temporary outposts on their way.

"Riel, make preparations for us to leave first thing in the morning," Shay orders.

"Understood," she responds.

Shay looks at Jaelyn and then at me. Jaelyn is like us, filled with anger and darkness after twenty years of captivity. "Let's go interrogate our prisoner." Shay smiles wickedly.

Jaelyn and I link arms with Shay and make the long, cold descent into the lower level of the dungeon.

"Back to see me so soon, sister?" Kira brazenly mutters as we enter the cell.

"Your day of reckoning has finally arrived," I reply.

"Are you going to kill me now?"

She's trying to be brave, but fear is written all over her face. It feeds that dark part of me.

"Now where would the fun be in that, sister? I have brought you a gift."

"And what would that be?" she scoffs.

"A healer."

Her eyes flare in fear.

Are you sure you're ready for this, Love? Shay speaks into my mind, and I nod.

Without saying a word, I close the cell door, trapping Kira in here with us.

Baby, I was born for this.

"She's all yours. Do your worst," he encourages.

Kira presses herself tightly into the corner.

"Where do you think you are going to go, sister? Into the stones? There is no pleasant way out of this for you. You can press as tightly as you'd like into that corner; it won't save you. Nothing will."

Unstrapping my Sun Spear from my belt, I close my fingers around the shaft and feel the heat spread through my limbs. Flames erupt and engulf my body. Canines and wings burst free. She's never seen who I truly am before, and she looks terrified. Inhaling deeply, I smell her fear and smile widely, letting my canines show.

"Rea, I was only doing what Ciara told me to do," Kira whimpers.

"We found a male named Cormac, injured and desperate for

help," Shay lies. It's all part of the game. "He was very willing to give us the answers we wanted."

"He informed us last night that you are the Shadow King's daughter," I lie. "So don't try playing sweet and innocent with us."

Kira's eyes widen, knowing part of what we said is true. How much will she reveal?

I keep going with my story. "Cormac said he works for your father. Gibbs is what he called him. Said the crazy bastard actually killed his wife and burned her body years ago on the Isle of the Crescent Moon. Claimed it was a hunting accident. He said you and Ciara are following the Shadow King's orders, and that he tried to contain you, but that you're insane."

"Don't forget, he also told us that her father ripped his ears right from his head to gain power," Shay adds.

Nice touch, I speak into his mind. A low growl emanates from his chest.

"Cormac is our brother, and he's a liar. I told Ciara he couldn't be trusted. He was not following our father's orders at all."

"He's been very cooperative, and it looks like he's been a victim here. He's going to be transported back to the Isle of the Crescent Moon where he will be healed and allowed to live out the rest of his life comfortably. You, however, are going to suffer a fate much worse. Because I've seen your and Ciara's brutal cruelty my entire life, so I know what you're capable of. That poor injured male upstairs is just a pawn in your game."

"No, please. It's not me. I'm not the one doing this!"

"We will be back in a couple of days, or maybe a couple of weeks," Shay taunts, "to transport you to face your fate in Glendalough. You will stand trial for treason for your part in killing the Phoenix King."

"And, Kira, I will be the one taking your head," I inform her. "Get ready, because it's Shay and I who will be transporting you to the capital, and I plan on making it a long, slow, and painful journey."

We walk to the door, unlock it, and then leave without another word. Her cries reach us before Shay slams the first door shut.

"I almost thought she was going to crack and tell us everything," Shay snorts. "A couple of weeks rotting in that cell should make her quite ready to talk to us when we return from The Isle of Darkness."

"Now why did you have to go and bring that up?" I frown.

"Sorry, Love. We are leaving in the morning."

"If we're finished here," Jaelyn speaks up, "I'd like to return to Outpost Four to get ready to see my son for the first time since his birth."

I hug her tightly. "Yes, please go. Thank you for coming."

"I would like word sent as soon as you all arrive back safely from the Isle," she requests.

"Absolutely. I will come and see you myself."

"Shay, drink blood at least two more times before you begin the mission. And for the love of the Forgotten Gods, take care of yourself," she orders him.

"Understood," he responds.

We head back to our room and dinner is already waiting for us. We eat in comfortable silence. After that I make my way to the couch.

Shay walks over and joins me. "Are you ready for what's to come?"

"Are you talking about Kira or the trident?"

"I need that trident, Love. WE need that trident."

"There will be five Shadow Demons on the Isle and you are almost out of power. Nova and I barely have any. It feels like a suicide mission." I finally admit it.

"There is something about it. When it pierced me, I felt the power you and Nova describe with your Spear and Staff. I know it will power me back up the same way your artifacts did for you. We need to take it to the temple."

"We can't be sure of that, and there is still the little matter of getting to it. You know, on the Isle that now has eleven-foot-tall Shadow Demons living on it. And what happens if it's not at the top? Have you thought about that?"

"Details."

"Seriously, Shay, this is going to be extremely dangerous."

"We will take care of each other out there. My cadre will be there and I trust them all with my life."

"Maybe I need a good night's sleep. I can look at it with fresh eyes in the morning."

"Sleep is exactly what we both need. Off to bed, you. We will be up early."

THE FOLLOWING MORNING, we begin the trip north. This time we are taking enclosed wagons full of supplies for the outposts along the way. Halfway between Shipwreck Cove and the northern outpost, we stop at one of the temporary outposts for the night.

"Shay, do you hear scratching?"

"That's Mojo."

Excited, I jump right up and let him in. "Hi, Mojo!" He runs right to Shay. "What, no love for me, Mojo?"

Shay reaches into one of Mojo's vest pockets and pulls a note from within. "Mojo, go give Rea a little love, but not too much. Understood?"

Mojo nods his little head and then runs over to me, jumping up on my lap and then into my arms.

"See how even Mojo can respond with 'Understood'?" Shay teases.

"There's my Mojo kisses. Who's a good boy?" He freezes for

a moment with his front paws on my chest, looking me in the eyes. "He has such intelligent eyes."

"Mojo, come," Shay orders. "He is incredibly intelligent. Let me show you how truly amazing he is." He slips a coin into one of Mojo's pockets. "Mojo, take this coin to Reagan. Once she has it in her hand, twirl around three times in her lap, kiss her cheeks once on each side, then leave through the hidden hatch."

"There is no way he is going to remember all that."

"Mojo, now."

Mojo jumps from Shay's lap, completing the entire task. Then he jumps to the floor, grabs hold of a tiny rope I had not noticed, opens a trap door, and leaves.

"You were saying?" Shay laughs.

"That was incredible. Please bring him back. I wanted to snuggle him and sleep with him."

Shay smirks at me.

"For the love of the Forgotten Gods, Shay, tell me what I'm missing."

"Q can link his mind with Mojo. He is the reason Mojo can follow orders from everyone."

I start thinking about all my interactions with Mojo. "Was it Q who came into my cell when I was looking for the key in Mojo's pocket?"

"It was."

"He must have thought I was an idiot."

"He thought you were adorable."

"I'm sure." I roll my eyes. "Wait, what about the last time I was holding Mojo, giving him kisses."

"That was all Mojo. When you don't see Q and Mojo together, he is sharing Mojo's body and mind."

"That's kind of incredible."

"I told you before, Love, my cadre is made up of what I consider to be unique fae."

"Indeed you did, and indeed they are. Gabe is a mountain. Is there more to him than that?"

"He is an unusually large male and also unusually strong. And don't even ask the question that is already forming in your mind."

"I was not going to ask anything."

"That's a downright lie. You're wondering how big everything is on Gabe. I can see it written all over your inquisitive face."

"Okay, so I was wondering. Haven't you?"

"Of course. We all have at one time or another. But no one would ever ask him."

"Does he have anyone special in his life?"

"Gabriel has many special females in his life. I almost asked Riel one morning because she and Gabe not only share a female lover, but the three of them also shared an intimate night a couple of years ago."

"Curious, because when she was braiding my hair she told me about the females she has at every port of call, yet not a word about Gabe."

"Can you promise me something, Rea? When you do ask her about Gabe—because I know you will—let me know, would you?"

I'm not going to argue that because I was thinking that very thing. "What are Gabe's powers?"

"Strength and endurance, even more than you might expect for someone his size. His family has a long line of enormous males both in height and girth. Their stories tell of one male who was eight-and-a-half feet tall."

"What about Riel? What are her powers?"

"Riel is the purest form of a shape-shifter. That is, she can become anyone or anything she chooses."

"And what of Brody?"

"We do not yet know. While his canines appeared during the solstice, he has yet to take the time to research his family history."

"I can't wait to find out what he is."

"Me either. He'll figure it out when he's ready."

"Come on. He's not only in your cadre, but he also leads it. He must be especially unique. Or exceptionally powerful."

"He is not afraid of anything. He's fiercely loyal, to a fault, and he has an extremely heightened sense of smell and hearing and can track anything or anyone."

"Well, that seems handy." I yawn and stretch, and as much as I enjoy Shay's company, I'm too tired to keep talking.

Shay sees my exhaustion, and I can tell he's no better off. "Let's get some sleep. We will finally be rejoining Nova and Brody tomorrow."

ONCE WE ARRIVE at the northern outpost, we see Brody poised outside to greet us. They have done a great job with the rebuilding. It's a lot more than I expected considering what this place looked like the last time I was here.

"Miss me?" Brody teases.

"Like a bad rash."

"Nova's in our room," he tells me, then gives me directions to locate it.

Heading inside, I go straight to our room, only having to ask for directions once. The moment I open the door, Nova's standing there facing me, and his joy and love instantly fill me through the bond. It overtakes my fears, my doubts, and most of all, my darkness. Running without thinking, I wrap my arms around him, squeezing tightly.

"I've missed you, my sunshine," he tells me.

"I've missed you, too. We have not really had a chance to talk."

"We will once this mission is over. We will have time to regroup and reconnect."

"I'm worried about this plan. Shay is still weak, whether he'll admit it or not."

"He will have us to help him. Please don't worry." It's so

strange how Nova makes me feel compared to Shay. In my heart, I'm once again conflicted. "We can do this together. We are the power of three. We need that third weapon of the gods."

"The power of three," I scoff. "That is such a stupid name."

"I agree. Maybe we will discover a name more befitting in Sebastian's documents . Or maybe we can make up our own."

"You seem quite confident."

"I'm always more confident when I'm with you."

Chills erupt all over my body. "It's the same for me when I'm with you."

"Let's join the others. We still have much to do."

The sound of thundering hooves reaches us as soon as we leave the sleeping quarters. We rush out to the courtyard to see what's going on.

"On guard!" Shay orders.

Six riders approach the gate flying a Wolf Court banner.

"That's Travis," Nova states.

"So it is," Shay replies.

The boys' anxiety and fear almost overwhelm me. Travis is shouting something, but with the sound of the horses we can't make it out.

When his words finally reach us with the unforeseen, life-altering news, the words still take time to sink in. King Raiden has been gravely injured by none other than Cormac himself. The injured king is being transferred to the capital City of Carrowmore. Furthermore, Nova must return to the capital immediately—to be crowned King.

CHAPTER 33

Complete and utter chaos ensue as the boys struggle to comprehend and adapt to the information Travis delivered. Shay and Nova are both torn between wanting to be with their father and continuing the mission to the Isle of Darkness.

Shay's and Nova's anguish is so intense, it buckles my knees.

It's not my place to step in with my opinion or advice. Travis, Brody, and Riel are already trying to help them.

Nova shifts in direction, heading my way. His expression is unreadable. He takes my hand and leads me down a hall, eventually stopping at an alcove. Cupping my face with his hand, he caresses my cheeks with his coarse thumbs. He inhales deeply before speaking.

"I must return home. Please watch after my brother and yourself."

"I will. Brody too."

His piercing gaze turns gentle, and then he leans in and kisses me softly on the lips. When I open my eyes, my favorite Nova smile spreads across his face.

"Reagan, you will always be the sun that chases away my shadows."

Hearing those words, my heart swells with joy and love, and I immediately respond. "And you will always be the moon that brightens my darkness."

He leans forward, and my heart beats faster. His wintergreen scent mixes with a musky scent that I've never noticed before. He kisses me deeply. As soon as his lips touch mine, all my thoughts disappear. I'm carried away in a sensual and emotional tempest that rivals one of his winter storms. Nova kisses me passionately, and hope for the future burns through every beat of my heart.

As CROWN PRINCE, Nova is currently the acting King, whether he's wearing the crown or not.

Travis calls for an emergency meeting. "Nova and Shay. I have delivered the news and instructions I was sent to. However, if your father was awake, he would want you to proceed with your mission. He would tell you that the fate of the citizens is in your hands. I'm suggesting that you proceed with your mission and get that trident. Then meet me back at the capital where you"— he points to Nova—"will be crowned King, and you and I will visit Cormac." He points at Shay.

Nova and Shay make eye contact, clearly communicating with each other. Then they answer as one.

"Understood."

Travis walks over to Nova and Shay and hugs them tightly. He whispers something to them, but I'm unable to make out the words. Then the boys, including Brody, walk back outside to see Travis off.

Once they return, Shay holds up his hand, silencing the room.

"I know this is going to be incredibly difficult for everybody. Our King is on all of our minds. Let's use this additional emotional burden to fuel our resolve as we head out to retrieve that trident. We will do this for our King, and we will save our kingdoms from the filth Orpheus has allowed to infect our beloved world of Innisfallen. The gods created this world for us, not for them. We will not allow our world to fall into his dark, twisted hands." He stops and seems somehow to make eye contact with everyone present. "For King Raiden!"

"For King Raiden!" we echo.

Nova, Shay, Brody and I will take one skiff, and Riel, Gabe, and Q with Mojo will take another. Shay doesn't want to risk one of the larger ships being spotted. The *Riptide* will set out two days behind us. I inspect the skiff as we approach the docks. It's one of the small paddle boats we used to rescue the missing children.

Brody and Nova take the two seats in the rear, and Shay and I sit in the front. Our gear has been secured to the remaining two seats.

As the hours pass, we pedal with all our might, driven by our emotions of anger and sadness. The cold, salty sea relentlessly splashes against us, soaking our clothes and chilling us to the bone. We may be bundled in winter gear, but our main defense against the frigid sea wind is the constant movement of our legs, which keeps us warm and prevents us from succumbing to the cold. However, as we venture farther into the sea, the waves grow increasingly violent, and I feel my strength beginning to wane. Suddenly, our ears are assaulted by a frantic cry for help coming from behind us, causing my heart to skip a beat.

"Their skiff has broken apart," Nova shouts.

"Stop pedaling!" Shay orders. "Pick up the oars and dig hard on the right!"

It takes longer than I would have thought to turn this thing around.

"Help Mojo!" Q screams.

Poor little Mojo. He is so tiny, I almost don't see him. But I spot him paddling furiously, struggling to stay on top of the enormous waves. We push ourselves as hard as we can in their direction.

"Rea, get Mojo," Shay orders.

Climbing out of my seat, I lean over the bow. Wave after wave hits the wreckage of the cadre's boat. We make course corrections in response but keep getting tossed away from them. I extend my arm as far as I can but still fear I won't be able to reach Mojo as he paddles frantically in the water. Another wave hits us all, pushing us farther away from the rest of our crew.

Come on . . . almost there.

A little head bobs on a wave. I reach out even farther, afraid I'll topple in with him. Instead, he manages to swim forward enough that the next wave rolls him into my arms.

"I've got him," I shout, then quickly tuck his frozen body into my jacket.

Q grabs hold of the side of the skiff as we maneuver alongside him. Thank the gods. Gabe's just ahead.

"Grab hold!" Shay shouts to him.

Gabe has to swim hard to his left, or we will pass him and lose him in the choppy seas. Nova reaches out with a paddle. Gabe barely grabs it. Unfortunately, another wave hits us, and Nova is pulled overboard by Gabe's weight.

"Rea, get in the middle seat," Brody orders.

"Dig hard on the left," Shay commands.

Again it takes forever to turn around.

"There!" Shay yells.

Suddenly, Nova and Gabe's massive bodies are lifted out of the water. On top of a creature I must be hallucinating.

"What is that?" I've read about sea monsters, but I thought they were myths. And yet, no matter how many times I blink to clear my vision, I still see a scaly hide and Nova and Gabe seated astride its massive back.

"Hard on the right," Shay orders. "Follow her! It's Riel."

I think I'm in shock. "Riel can shape-shift into a sea monster?"

"Focus, Rea," Brody orders. "Dig hard."

"Land!" Shay points.

I gaze out at the vast expanse of the ocean, and my eyes fall upon a small island. Thank the gods. I've been so preoccupied with the fact that Riel possesses the ability to morph into a sea creature that I had completely missed it. After a tense twenty minutes, we finally reach the safety of the shore.

Riel, now completely naked, winks at me. Unbelievable. Apparently, we have a lot to talk about, but our priority is setting up camp for the night. Once we have a fire going to ensure that no one suffers ill effects from the frigid waters, Shay gets down to planning our next steps.

"Riel," he says, "you are to remain here and await the *Riptide*."

"I will not sit here doing nothing," she replies.

"You will do as you are ordered," Shay responds.

"Like Nova is following orders to return to Carrowmore?" she counters.

She does have him there and she knows it. It's written all over Shay's face.

"What did you have in mind, cousin?"

"That I leave with Mojo to get the *Riptide* immediately and rendezvous with you near the Isle of Darkness."

Shay thinks this over. Is he crazy? Why would she leave with Mojo in those violent seas?

"If Mojo and Q allow it, then so will I," Shay concedes.

Clearly, I'm missing something, but for once, I keep my mouth shut.

"Mojo and I will most definitely allow it," Q responds. "Mojo said he would leave me for Reagan if I tried to stop him."

"Really?" I beam. "I knew he loved me."

"Seriously, Reagan," Brody snaps. "Get your head in the game, for god's sake. Priorities."

My cheeks burn, but I hold my tongue and turn my attention to Riel. "You can shift into a sea monster?"

"You will not like what I tell you," she responds.

"You won't like it at all, Rea," Shay chuckles. "But I can't wait to see your face when she does."

Riel walks closer to me, not fully clothed.

"I'm only able to shift into what's right in front of me. What I can physically touch," Riel tells me.

Oh gods, that creature was out there. It could have swallowed little Mojo, whole. I literally have no words.

WE'RE up before the sun. Riel and Mojo are long gone, and I wonder why she took him. We say our goodbyes to Q and Gabe, who will wait on the island for Riel and the *Riptide*.

With the Isle of Darkness now in sight along the horizon, a storm hits. This is all we need. Our wooden skiff cracks, straining against the onslaught of waves and our combined weight. What if that sea monster is still out there? Would it follow us? Hunt us as food? We pedal as hard as we can manage to close the distance to shore.

Two hundred yards from landfall we pass a tiny island but decide to keep going.

"If we get separated," Shay shouts over the sound of the turbulent sea, "we are to meet on that island."

No sooner do we pass it than a massive wave takes us out. Dumped into the salty water, I start swimming with the waves, trying to get myself to the rocky beach. It feels like for every twenty feet of progress I make, I'm pulled back another ten. Fighting the current is wearing me out.

"Reagan, grab the back of my jacket and hold onto my back," Brody commands.

For once, I'm glad to follow orders. I'm exhausted. Amazingly, even with me on his back, Brody manages to swim powerfully through the choppy waves and gets us to shore.

Brody leaves me about twenty feet from shore and then

swims back out for the boys. He ferries Shay back the same way he did with me, then repeats the process for Nova.

"Brody, I think your power might be related to water, because I have never seen anyone swim like that before."

"I've always been a strong swimmer." He drags Shay's weakened body through the water and onto the beach.

Shay looks like a rag doll. He's not even trying to help Brody. I've never seen him so helpless.

"We will be spending the night here then making the climb in the morning," Nova advises as Brody drags Shay's limp form onshore.

"Shay, you look like a dead body. You are taking blood right now from Nova and me," I demand. "Don't even argue with me." The scent of wintergreen fills my nose.

Thank you, Reagan. This will all be over soon.

He always says that. When, exactly, is "soon"?

THE FOLLOWING MORNING, we begin the climb up the shortcut but don't make it very far before realizing that we will have to spend another night resting. Shay is already spent and Nova is now looking a little sickly himself. When we reach the wide-open plateau, we decide it is a good place to sleep. We are almost there. We curl up tightly for one more night.

The moment we wake, we have Shay take a little more of our blood. Then we begin the final climb to the last place we saw the trident. This quest seems endless. I'm so tired, I long for rest, but I can clearly see the spot where Shay fell and almost died. It's not much farther from here.

I know I'm in the area Shay fell. "It should be around here."

"Here, I have it," Shay announces.

The moment his hand connects with that obsidian trident, a shock passes through my entire body like lightning. I close my eyes, taking in this new sense of completion.

But I'm not the only one who sensed this shift. When I open my eyes, a Shadow Demon is standing in front of Shay.

"Look out!" Nova shouts.

"Run!" Shay screams.

I have never heard him sound terrified, and his fear courses through my blood, through the bond. Nova and Shay are about ten feet behind me as we run down the winding road. Brody is about five feet ahead of us. The downhill momentum allows me to move incredibly fast, but the loose rocks leave me scrabbling for solid footing. My weakened muscles strain to keep me from stumbling.

The open plateau appears, but unfortunately so does a second Shadow Demon. It blocks our path.

Brody stops in his tracks, but my momentum takes me past him before I can stop. Nova and Shay skid to a halt behind us.

"Ouch! What in the Forgotten Gods was—" Brody starts, yet Shay cuts him off.

"Brody, take Rea and jump, Nova and I will be right behind you!"

"Behind you, Shay!" I scream, as another Shadow Demon appears. Swinging the trident fast and hard, he slices a deep gash in its leg. Lava flows from it rather than blood, and the scream the demon emits pierces my eardrums.

Brody grabs my arm, dragging me toward the cliff's edge. "Don't look down!"

He pulls me over with him , but I twist in the air, looking back. The Shadow Demons are blocking the boys' escape. It's the last thing I witness as I begin my free fall to the icy waters below.

The wind greets me with unbelievable force as I try to keep my body from tilting face down. My eyes take in the view before me. The vast ocean and endless islands. I spot the one we are to meet at if we get separated. Then I make the mistake of looking down. Crashing waves beat against the jagged rocks, spraying mist that obscures exactly where we are headed and I begin to panic.

Making eye contact with Brody, I can tell that something's wrong with him. His eyes are crimson red. Before my eyes, he explodes into a horror-filled mass of thick skin, muscles, claws, razor-sharp teeth, and a strip of shaggy fur that runs from the top of his head to the tip of his tail.

"What in the depths of the shadows are you?" I shout because he's extraordinarily frightening. It's not like the boys in wolf form. Is this still Brody? He loops his tongue out of the side of his mouth, maybe trying to look less scary, yet it's even more horrific and it makes me scream. Then he rolls those creepy red eyes.

Preparing for impact, I take a deep breath. I know when my body hits that freezing water it's going to lock up painfully. Closing my eyes, I hope I don't land on a rock.

Plunging into the water feels like razor blades slicing my flesh. My chest seizes up, and I have to force myself not to suck water into my lungs. Kicking as hard as I can for the surface, I break free. I spot the beast that is Brody through the choppy waves fifteen feet away, still looking like the personification of a nightmare. I'm trusting that he's still himself on the inside, and I swim for him, then we head for the island we planned to meet on if we got separated.

Halfway there, fatigue begins to overtake me, I'm freezing, and I have no choice but to hold on to Brody's neck and allow him to swim me in. Once we reach shore, Brody starts shaking water from himself like a dog would, then appears to be vibrating. In a quick flash, he's lying naked and prone on the shore.

"Brody, are you okay?"

It takes a moment, yet with my help, he gets back up on both feet. Then I notice his arm is cut, bleeding heavily. I rip a strip of fabric from my shirt and wrap it the best I can.

Once I'm satisfied Brody will be okay, we look for the boys.

They're still on the cliff. Storm clouds build in the sky above them. Thunder rumbles and lightning streaks across the sky.

"Did the trident restore Shay's powers?" I don't know what else could explain that jolt of electricity that shot through me.

"I might be some type of black dog," Brody states, ignoring my question.

I tear my eyes away from Shay and Nova and focus on my naked friend for a moment. "Why did the change happen at that moment? Why would free falling cause your powers to manifest? It makes no sense, Brody."

"Why does it not make sense?"

"What in the depths of the shadows would a horrifying dog's body do to help you fall to your potential death?"

"It got us to shore quickly enough," he defends. "Shay did something to me with that trident. I felt it."

"Did something how? Injured you or powered you up?"

Thunder booms loudly as Shay slams the Trident into the ground and the mountain around them explodes into darkness. Lightning strikes the plateau repeatedly.

"Not power like I got during the Solstice. It felt different, malevolent. Then it was gone. I'm not sure if that is what transformed me into a black dog or not. I didn't pay attention during my family history lessons."

"Your family history didn't interest you?"

"Not then, because I didn't know it would ever affect me."

Brody and I are startled by a roar that almost stops my heart. We both freeze, waiting to see what is happening. As the darkness clears, we can see cracks of lava coming from the demons. It's hard to see anything clearly until a swift-moving breeze blows away the smoke and ash, revealing a clearer view of the distant scene.

"No!" I need to get back up there and help. Why did they tell Brody to take me away from the fight? We're supposed to stick together.

A Shadow Demon dangles Nova upside-down by his legs and turns toward the sound of my screams of protest.

The demon looks down at Nova, then back to me before releasing another thunderous roar. Then it throws Nova high into the sky. He disappears into the clouds, leaving Shay alone with two Shadow Demons.

BOOM! The plateau is enveloped in darkness.

"There's fire within the darkness." I point. "Where is Nova? Did you see him land?"

My questions remain unanswered as I try to make sense of what's happening. The fire has reached the edge of the cliff, and I see the Shadow Demon falling backward off it. To my surprise, Shay is standing on top of the demon with the trident stuck in its chest. He pulls the trident free and takes two running steps across its body before leaping from its head. Shay disappears into the sky, in a reverse lightning strike that streaks across the sky. A blast of heat and electricity knocks me off my feet. The last thing I remember before I black out is searching for a glimpse of Nova and Shay. But I don't see either of them.

WITH EVERY BREATH, my body rocks back and forth. The sound of waves slapping against a ship finally coax me back to consciousness. Memories ebb and flow before I can bring myself to open my eyes. The boys, the Shadow Demons, Brody's crimson eyes. Is Nova on board? How much power did Shay get from that trident? And more importantly, why was I unconscious? Fear for my boys shakes me awake. I find the stairs and stumble toward the light coming from the open hatch above me. Once I'm above deck, the scent of the briny sea fills my nose, as the cool mist hits my face.

"Reagan," Nova yells from across the deck.

Not believing my eyes, I collapse to the deck, crying as sobs of relief wrack my body.

Brody reaches me first. "We are all here, Rea. Deep breaths. We're safe; it's over."

I wipe the tears off my cheeks and notice Shay approaching, looking healthy and strong. Power radiates from him, rippling the air with every step he takes closer to me.

I look at the long three-pronged obsidian trident that's as tall as he is. "You have it."

"You doubted our abilities, Love?"

"What is that at the top?" I ask. There's a four-inch cylinder embedded below the center tine, similar to where my phoenix once sat as an orb on my Spear.

"It's the cryptex I told you about, and there might be a key inside."

"To what?"

"That is what we need to figure out, Love. This trident is also a key. The three holes in the basin below where the moonstone sits, are for this."

"The markings on the cryptex are also on the pyramid of the moon and sun," Nova adds. "So those will be our next three destinations after we return to Carrowmore to see our father."

"Shay, how much power did you get?" He no longer looks weakened.

Before he can respond, I hear my phoenix's song and look skyward. I spot Nix heading toward the ship. No. She is dive-bombing us.

"Nix, what is it?"

Help is needed, she speaks into my mind.

"Where is help needed?" I speak out loud so all can hear.

The sky becomes so bright around her that we need to turn away, shielding our eyes. Talons grip my shoulders, ripping me from the deck. Pressure begins building in my body as time and space bend around me. Then I'm absorbed into a void of darkness. No sound, no sight, only the intensifying pressure.

I can't speak, I can't move. My body burns so intensely I might combust. As light begins to enter the void, I notice I'm floating in a pool of liquid fire. It's at once amazing and calming. One by one my senses return.

Nix, what is going on?

Help them, she tells me as we emerge from the darkness heading straight toward Outpost Four.

Our union is now complete, and we have become one entity. Our wings, talons, teeth, and claws have merged to form a fearsome, fiery dragon. We are now a magnificent being possessing the power and strength of each individual part. Our combined abilities make us a force to be reckoned with.

As I soar high above the outpost, I spot a group of ominous shadow beasts emerging from the depths of the sea. Their dark silhouettes are unmistakable against the vibrant blue waters. Without a moment's hesitation, I tuck my fiery wings close to my body and dive toward them, determined to protect the outpost and its inhabitants.

As I draw closer, I can see that the situation is even more dire than I had feared. Outside the walls of the outpost, Hamon, Jaelyn, and the brave guards of the Phoenix Queen are engaged in a fierce battle against a group of black-hooded combatants. They seem to be completely unaware of the looming threat that is headed straight for them.

I know that I must act quickly if I am to save them all. With a burst of speed, I close the distance between myself and the shadow beasts, ready to engage them in battle and turn the tide of this conflict.

I dive, extending my talons, and grab two struggling beasts, one in each claw, snatching up a third tightly between my jaws. I try to maintain my balance and forward momentum as I fly straight up, but the combined weight of the creatures is pulling me off course. Desperately, I search for a safe place to drop them, but with their frantic movements and my struggle to stay airborne, I find myself tilting too far to one side. Everything turns upside down as we fall, my wings flapping furiously as I try to regain control and prevent a disastrous crash. But it's too late. We crash through the roof of the outpost.

I right myself and get back on my hind legs using the claws at the tips of my wings and scanning the area for any signs of danger. The beasts lurking around me are massive and ferocious, with razor-sharp teeth and claws that could rip someone apart in seconds. I know I have to act fast.

Without hesitation, I lunge toward them, tearing off their front legs with my powerful jaws. They try to fight back, but I am too quick, too large and, too strong for them. In a matter of seconds, they lay dying at my feet.

I don't have time to rest. There are more beasts out there, and I need to take them down. I leap back into the sky, scanning the horizon. Spotting a group of beasts in the distance, I fly toward them with lightning speed.

I am relentless, attacking them with all my might, dropping them into the outpost with the others until every last beast bleeds before me, some dead, some dying.

Breathe, Nix urges me.

I roar my fury, releasing purifying flames of vengeance upon them all. They shriek and scream but to no avail. They are unable to escape my inferno.

You have done well, Princess of the Sun, Nix praises.

There is a tension along my spine, and I feel as though I'm being ripped in two. I fall to the ground landing on my stomach as Nix's fiery form breaks free of my body. The next thing I know I'm kneeling in the courtyard of Outpost Four, fully fae and fully nude. The acrid smell of rubble and burning flesh fills my nose.

"Reagan!" Jaelyn shouts.

I look toward her voice, and she's running to me, holding out a cloak. She wraps it around my body and then leads me away from the smoldering remains of the shadow beasts and the outpost that's been razed to the ground.

Funny, I remember I once said I would do that. As Shay would say, it's interesting how things work out. As if my thoughts could conjure him from the air, thunder rumbles in the sky then lightning strikes the ground twenty feet in front of us. When the smoke clears, Shay, Nova, and Brody stand before us.

"Looks like we missed all the fun," Shay grunts by way of greeting. Fun looks like it's the last thing on his mind. He looks angry, and power radiates from him.

"What took you guys so long?" I grumble.

"We searched Port Kelsey and our outpost first," Shay replies. "Hamon, casualty report."

"I haven't got a full count yet," he frowns. "I'll update you as I learn more. These were my guards." I hear the anguish in his voice, despite his strong front.

"Understood," Shay responds. "I'm sorry we couldn't be here sooner."

"Reagan, we must return to the capital. Our father."

"Yes, of course. Jaelyn, will you be okay here?"

"My cadre is almost here," Shay informs her.

"Yes, we will be fine. Go to your father."

"Take hands now," Shay orders Brody, Nova, and me. We ascend into the sky in a reverse lightning strike, then we shatter across the sky.

In the void of darkness that I'm growing accustomed to, I can't help but steal a glance at Shay. The look on his face makes me wonder just how powerful he is now. No sooner do I finish the thought he turns and looks at me with a preternatural grace that I've never seen him display. He knew I was thinking about him. He knew I was looking at him.

Twin black orbs hold mine captive. Depthless and haunting, yet inviting. Danger lurks beneath his skin, and to be honest, I kind of like it. Shay's darkness has always called to mine. Flames flash over those obsidian eyes as he winks at me.

In the blink of an eye, we're on the other side of the world—having crossed from the western coast of Innisfallen in an instant—and landed in the Northeast, in the heart of the Kingdom of the Wolf Moon's capital city of Carrowmore. That was an unbelievable distance to windwalk, and he did it alone, carrying the three of us. Apparently, he's gained more power than I can even begin to comprehend.

Well, shit.

Acknowledgments

My heartfelt thanks go first to my friend and mentor, **William Bernhardt**. Your *Red Sneaker Writers* book series changed my life—and so did your guidance, encouragement, and belief in me. Having you as a mentor and a friend has been one of the greatest gifts on this journey.

To my brilliant editor and dear friend, **Lara Bernhardt**— thank you for making this novel shine. You had your work cut out for you with my neurodivergent, dyslexic self, and you approached it with grace, patience, and incredible skill. I am endlessly grateful for your insight and dedication.

To my beta readers—**Akshata Shirodker**, **Carmen of Red Ink Book Reviews**, **Susy Smith**, **Alex Little, and J.B. Cain** —thank you for your time, thoughtful feedback, and support. Your insights helped shape this story into its best form.

Thank you to **100Covers** and the brilliant designer behind my book cover. Your artwork captured the soul of the story in a single, unforgettable image. I'm truly honored to have your vision represent my words.

A huge thank you to **Abbie Rigley** with All About the Maps for creating my beautiful hand-drawn map. Your talent brought my world to life!

ABOUT THE AUTHOR

 Jenny Simard LaBranche is an award-winning author of supernatural, fantasy, horror, and paranormal thrillers. A former IT Specialist and retired Firefighter/EMT, her path to becoming a full-time writer has been anything but ordinary. Despite a lifelong struggle with dyslexia, Jenny held onto her dream of writing fiction. In 2021, she left the IT field for good and became a writer, finally embracing her passion. Her debut novel has already earned two literary awards and marked the beginning of an exciting new chapter in her creative journey.

Jenny has been married to Paul LaBranche for 27 years, and together they share their home with their adorable chihuahua, Mojo. When she's not conjuring chilling tales and fantastical worlds, she enjoys the outdoors, spending time with family and friends, and getting lost in a great book.

www.ingramcontent.com/pod-product-compliance
Lightning Source LLC
Chambersburg PA
CBHW031201020726
47499CB00002B/438